Praise for

ECHELON

"A honeypot for the hi-tech conspiracy theory crowd. . . . Makes deft use of technological issues and developments."
—*Kirkus Reviews*

"A tasty little thriller about a conspiracy really worthy of the twenty-first century."　　　　　—*Booklist*

"A nightmare of paranoia and high-tech intrigue."
—*Library Journal*

"A classic thriller . . . retrofitted through the dark scanners of the science fictional gaze."　　　　—*Matrix*

"[Presents] an eerily plausible future."　　　—SFFWorld.com

"A terrifying glimpse into the future. Jam-packed with intrigue, terror and suspense. Conviser is a writer to watch."
—ALLAN FOLSOM, author of *The Day After Tomorrow*

"This fast-paced info-tech thriller takes your breath away, both with the speed at which events unfold, and the sheer imagination of the author . . . Ryan Laing is the twenty-first-century James Bond."　　　—FREDERICK P. HITZ,
former inspector general of the CIA and author of
The Great Game: The Myth and Reality of Espionage

ALSO BY JOSH CONVISER

Echelon

EMPYRE

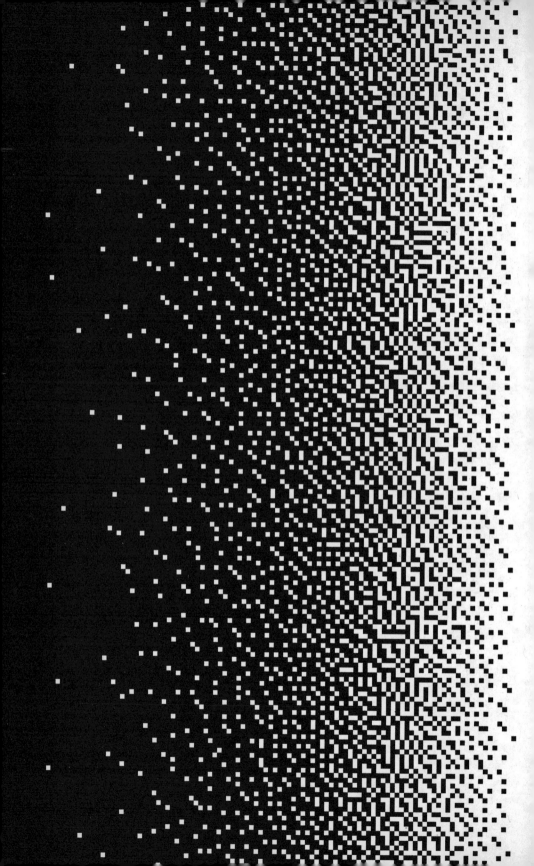

EMPYRE

Josh Conviser

BALLANTINE BOOKS

NEW YORK

A Del Rey Trade Paperback Original

Published in the United States by Del Rey Books, an imprint of The Random House Publishing Group, a division of Random House, Inc., New York.

DEL REY is a registered trademark and the Del Rey colophon is a trademark of Random House, Inc.

Library of Congress Cataloging-in-Publication Data

Conviser, Josh.
Empyre / Josh Conviser.
p.   cm.
ISBN 978-0-345-48503-8
1. Intelligence officers—Fiction.   2. United States.
Central Intelligence Agency—Fiction.   I. Title.
PS3603.O564E67 2007
813'.6—dc22   2007021518

Printed in the United States of America

www.delreybooks.com

9 8 7 6 5 4 3 2 1

Text design by David Goldstein

For Babs, I love you

PROLOGUE

Zachary Taylor.

I am Zachary Taylor.

The words tumbled through his mind but could not find purchase. They rang both foreign and familiar, as if from a childhood language that time had stripped away.

I am Zachary Taylor.

He couldn't lock a definition to the words. The loves and hates, mistakes and accomplishments, that went into that name had blurred, a roadside mural lost to the whipping rush of traffic.

The man squinted into the high mountain glare, waiting. He spent a lot of time waiting—for the perfect shot, the clean kill. In those small eternities, he toyed with memories of his life before. There had been a childhood, a father he loved, a lover he abandoned—and a kid of his own. But all that was gone now, wiped to a distant flicker. Gazing back into that life, *his life*, he felt like a voyeur.

He had a new life now. A new existence, circling a different star. Now he ran on clean assurance. No doubt. No confusion.

And yet the memories caught his attention like scratches on an old film reel. He shook them away. Just glitches in the system.

I am Zachary Taylor. The words calmed him. Like a Zen koan, they stilled his thoughts and allowed him to wait. It was almost time.

The city of Lhasa sprawled through the valley below him. What was once a Shangri-la nestled under Himalayan peaks had faltered with time and the demands of progress. Gone was the exotic mystery that had enshrined the city. In its place, Lhasa had become a center of trade and finance, a haven for hackers and hard-core city men. Amid the vaulting peaks, Lhasa sprawled dark.

Taylor gazed down from the roof of an eighty-story tower. The boxy vertical farm dwarfed most of Lhasa. Its dark carbon frame, cut at angles by huge sheets of plexi to reveal the thick vegetation within, had become one of the city's trademarks. The tower was crucial to Lhasa's prosperity, offering a consistent food supply despite the harsh climate and political strife that plagued the region. It had allowed Lhasa to thrive. And it would now be the setting for Tibet's ruin.

The slow whack-thump of wind turbines gave rhythm to the teeming masses below. Over Taylor, giant blades sliced through deep blue sky, powering the farm.

I . . . am . . . Zachary Taylor. The words had the pathetic humor of a bad joke told by a drunk. The Zachary Taylor of his memories would have shrunk from the act he was about to perform. No, he was not Taylor. He was a stranger—even to himself.

Pulling a scope to his eye, he sighted in on the procession forming at the main gate of the Potala Palace. Built in 1645, the palace crowned Marpo Ri, the Red Mountain, and marked the center of Lhasa Valley. Its inward-canted walls, rising up to rows of windows, had once been the most formidable structure in the area. Seen from above, those sloping walls became a pedestal, a building designed to cradle the city's beating heart. For centuries that cradle had lain bare. No longer.

"Zach Taylor," the man whispered to himself. He rolled the words in his mouth like marbles.

Taylor rubbed his hands together to fight off the Tibetan chill. His fingertips itched, an aftereffect of the print-removal operation. Part of the price. He lived with that itch and woke every morning to a face he did not recognize. So much knife work in the last years. So many faces, all fading to blank.

The man shrugged off the discomfort as he watched the procession advance through the smog-strangled streets below.

It was time.

Taylor turned and walked back to the rooftop's main vent, next to which another man stood rigid. Chinese, thin, graying hair. He had the deep-sagged eyes of a man who worked long hours. The terror in those eyes contrasted with his body's stiff immobility. Taylor ran his hand up the man's cheek and dug the neuro-block from his temple.

It popped free and the man crumpled into a prolonged seizure. As the racking spasms eased, he propped himself on an arm, breathing in stuttering gasps. Finally, he looked up, doe-scared. "Please," he stammered in throaty Chinese. "Just let me go. I won't do it. I can't."

Taylor responded with a brittle smile. His face felt different after all the operations, removed—like a mask to be manipulated. He replied in English. "You have no choice, Cheng."

"No choice," the man whimpered, his fear thick and twitchy.

"In minutes, it will all be over," Taylor said. While he tried to infuse his words with hope, they hit Cheng with cold finality.

Desperation drove up through Cheng's terror, supplying a final beat of resistance. Taylor watched the emotion crimp the man's features. So many times, he had witnessed that rush.

Cheng rose on wobbling legs and locked eyes with him. Zachary Taylor might have cared about this man's plight, but the stranger he had become felt nothing. He stared back with cruel indifference.

Cheng held under his gaze, fighting surrender. "Kill me. It does not matter. I will not—"

Taylor cut him off. "You don't want to say no to me." He stepped close. "Saying no comes with a heavy price—one that others will be forced to pay."

Taylor's hand shot forward and Cheng flinched. The hand stopped short of Cheng's cheek and opened. In it, a com-link chirped.

Taylor flipped the link to active. Through the device came a scream so full of pain that it made Cheng stagger.

"Zhen?" he croaked, recognition amplifying his horror. "Zhen!"

The screams settled into hulking sobs, then a cracked voice. "Father?"

"Yes," Cheng sputtered, "it's me! Please, are you okay?!"

Another wild shriek. Then slushy breathing.

Cheng looked at Taylor, a silent plea that found no purchase. Taylor shook his head and motioned to the link.

Zhen spoke. "Mother is here. She's bleeding. There's a knife in her . . . in her eye. And there is so much blood." The girl's voice skipped along the ragged edge of shock.

Cheng surged forward on a tidal rush of fury, hands raised to strike. Taylor slipped away from the fumbling attack and countered with a carefully placed knee to Cheng's stomach. He needed to get Cheng's attention but couldn't risk incapacitating him or leaving visible marks. The blow sent the smaller man sprawling across the rooftop.

Cheng scuttled into a crouch, gasping. Rage burning hot, his eyes flashed with crazed ferocity. His hand closed on a frayed scrap of hard carbon lying beside him.

Cheng lunged forward, threatening Taylor with the razor edge of the construction material. Taylor held perfectly still. "You took everything!" Cheng choked out.

"No, Cheng. Not yet."

On cue, another scream ripped through the com-link, an inhuman shriek, like metal on dry ice.

Cheng's eyes bulged. "No! Stop!"

The scream faded. "Father," the girl struggled for words. "I'm . . . I can't see Mother anymore."

Cheng whimpered, the carbon shard trembling with his sobs.

"I can't see!" the girl wailed. Her crying ebbed to a low moan.

"Zhen? Zhen!" Cheng cried.

The voice returned—devoid of fight, welling up from black horror. "I'm sorry, Father."

"No . . . *No!*" Cheng raged. He pulled his gaze from the link and held on Taylor. "You are a monster." Venom laced his words.

Taylor only nodded, watching with dispassionate curiosity as the man before him succumbed. They always broke. Taylor's will ran too cold to crack.

"Okay," Cheng said. "I'll do it. Whatever you want."

Taylor held up the com-link. "Say good-bye."

Cheng forced cold air into his lungs. "It's okay, Zhen. You will be okay now. No more pain."

"No more pain," the girl mumbled.

"I love you, Zhen."

"Love you," the girl whispered back.

Taylor killed the link.

Cheng stared at the shard in his hand. "You'll kill her." His words misted into the cold air.

Taylor said nothing.

"You'll kill me," Cheng said.

Taylor stepped forward and Cheng instinctively raised the shard to his throat. Taylor did not flinch. "You're already dead, Cheng. Nothing will change that. But you can save her."

Cheng pushed forward, the makeshift blade drawing a thin line of blood across Taylor's neck.

"It's an amazing world we live in," Taylor said. "So many possibilities. A world where Zhen's eyes can be regenerated. Where her memory can be wiped. She can live out her life without ever knowing what happened to her—and to her mother." Taylor's voice fell to a whisper, just audible over the wind turbines. "A world where we can keep your daughter fully alert, feeling the pain of each cut, each extraction, until she is nothing—"

"Enough!" Cheng screamed. The shard fell from Taylor's throat and clattered across the rooftop.

Cheng's head dropped in slow surrender. "Enough," he whispered again.

As they descended into the grow-room's lush vegetation, the Himalayan chill faded to a distant memory. Banana palms rose over stubby pineapple plants. Thick, leafless papaya trunks jutted from their tanks, heavy with fruit. The syrupy air coated Taylor's lungs. Despite the humidity, an electric buzz ran through the milling audience.

A harried group of politicians and party officials approached Taylor and Cheng. Taylor slipped into the foliage before he could be noticed.

An aide's hand fell on Cheng's shoulder, causing him to jump. "Sir! So sorry for disturbing you, but we really must go."

"Oh, yes. I, uh . . ."

A thickset man cut between Cheng and the aide. Cheng recognized him immediately and bowed.

The man flashed a plastic smile, his forehead sweat-slick. "Cheng, I know how you hate this, but we really must insist. It's not often that a simple engineer gets an audience with such a dignitary."

The politician didn't allow Cheng to reply. Instead, he threw a meaty arm around the thin man's shoulder and led him away.

"Come on. We'll get you back to your precious grow-tanks soon enough."

Before fading into the masses, Cheng threw a glance over his shoulder. Taylor stepped from the foliage and nodded. Then Cheng was swallowed up. Taylor turned and disappeared into the vegetation.

I am Zachary Taylor.

I am . . .

He was gone before the killing began.

The mingling politicians and patrons, bloggers and businessmen, went silent as the man entered the grow-room. An expectant energy buzzed; history was being made. The Dalai Lama had returned to Tibet.

The nineteenth reincarnation of Avalokiteśvara, the bodhisattva of compassion, walked with his entourage, dressed in the traditional orange robes of a Buddhist monk. His diminutive size did nothing to diminish the aura he exuded. As he strode through the foliage, every eye in the vast room tracked his progress. After centuries of exile, the religious leader of the Tibetan people had returned to his land.

The man stepped up to the stage, an orange swatch in a swarm of gray-suited party officials. The corpulent Chinese politician, his suit now drenched with sweat, stepped to the podium. His face puckered with nervous tension as sound amps and hover cams focused in. In an era of violence and conflict, this moment held promise far beyond Tibet's borders. The eyes of the world were locked on this room.

"As the representative of the People's Republic of China, it is my sincere pleasure to welcome His Holiness, the Dalai Lama, home." The words came out tinny and forced, but with enough hope to draw applause from the crowd.

The politician scanned his prepared speech, savoring his moment in the spotlight. Looking up, he realized that His Holiness had stepped to the lectern. All eyes shifted to him. The party man reluctantly stepped from his position. The monk smiled and bowed.

The Dalai Lama stood silent for a long moment, hands clasped in thanksgiving. When he spoke, his voice ran low and rhythmic, like rocks tumbling down a riverbed. "For centuries, my people have walked the Middle Way, praying for this moment—this reconciliation. Now, here I stand. I am home."

Applause engulfed the grow-room.

The Dalai Lama bowed again and continued. "Today, we plant the seed of peace in ground that has seen so much blood. May that seed sprout and hold strong in our rocky soil. May the next years be the water that will nourish a new era of harmony."

More applause filtered through the humidity. The Dalai Lama's smile faltered. His eyes drew back from the future he saw so clearly.

His voice lowered to a wave roll. "We open our eyes to a new day. But, looking forward, we must not forget the nightmares of our past. For Tibetans, I speak of exile and hardship, of centuries spent longing for our homeland. But I also speak to the world as a whole. I speak of the black dream that held us all. I speak of Echelon."

The word settled over the crowd, stilling the excitement.

"Yes," he said, nodding. "We must acknowledge that nightmare in order to move forward. For a century, the future was not ours to decide. Echelon decided for us. Echelon controlled us. Echelon maintained order. It did so without our knowledge. Without our consent."

The audience hung on His Holiness's words. "Five years ago, the nightmare ended. The manipulator died. And only then did we see that we were, each of us, pawns in a game that was not of our design. The manipulator's footprints had trampled our history—a history that we can no longer truly call our own. Left without a past, we have fallen on each other. Violence has ripped our world apart—mistrust and fear have become our constant companions. The manipulator's demise has caused such suffering."

The Dalai Lama continued with renewed vigor. "But it is that very nightmare that makes this dawn so beautiful. Peace without freedom means nothing. It is hollow comfort. This is a day we have long struggled to reach. From hatred and fear, blood and war, we now turn toward peace."

The Dalai Lama stepped from the podium, his actions tracked by hover cams and the expectant crowd. He approached a peaty grow-tank that was surrounded by engineers. Cheng stood foremost among them. In his hands was a small box, exquisitely inlaid with gold.

Settling to one knee, the Dalai Lama continued. "My hope, my prayer, is that our efforts here will mature as this seed does, spreading the message of peace beyond our small country and across the globe."

Cheng hesitated, hands trembling. Then he broke the box's seal to reveal a single seed. The Dalai Lama reached in and took it.

He held the seed between his clasped palms for a moment of prayer before continuing. "Today, we have chosen peace, knowing the ravages of war. Today we take our first steps into a future of our own design. Today . . ."

The Dalai Lama's voice trailed off as he opened his eyes and caught the look on Cheng's face. For a moment, he was not the Dalai Lama; he was merely a man—and he was scared. The image held for a single instant— the holy man kneeling before his executioner.

Then the transformation began.

The Dalai Lama buckled, wracked by a thick cough. He brought his fingers to his lips. They came away bloody. His face clenched in hot pain. He stared into the engineer's eyes, confused.

"I am sorry," Cheng whispered, even as his own lungs filled with fluid.

The Dalai Lama's features glazed, his consciousness lost to the pain. He slumped forward, tipping into the dirt. His hand opened on impact, revealing blistered skin. The seed fell onto black soil, watered by his own blood.

For a moment, there was silence.

Then a thunderclap of panic cracked the crowd's shock. Confusion boiled. Some tried to help the fallen holy man. Others fled. The pathogen spared no one.

Cheng did not run. He knew there was no escape.

In minutes, only the dull hum of hover cams broke the silence.

They transmitted their gory images to the world.

PART I

Chip, chip, thunk.

His axes biting into clean ice, Ryan Laing tried to recall the events that had led him here—clinging to a granite fang under Antarctica's cold sun. Surely there were better ways to start the day. So why was this the only place he felt comfortable? Climbing ice and rock in a barren land. Alone.

The past lapped over Ryan, his own mixing with that of Antarctica's extreme topography. Tension and release played out here in the slow thrust and ebb of granite and ice. And it played on a grand scale.

Chip, chip, thunk.

His axes cut into the vertical.

Antarctica was dreamed in myth long before its actual discovery. Aristotle and Ptolemy predicted a great unknown Southland as a counterweight to the landmasses of the North. To Ryan, that felt about right. To be here was to cling to the world's keel.

Queen Maud Land lay between the trailing tip of the Stancomb-Wills Glacier and the encroaching thrust of the Shinnan Glacier. Its twenty-five million square kilometers were claimed by Norway, but this was a place beyond claiming. There were no permanent residents here—no indigenous populations. Here, man was a tourist. That suited Ryan just fine.

Most of Queen Maud Land lay encrusted in thick ice. Thousands of kilometers of frozen desert. And then, like something out of a fairy tale, granite spires sprouted from the white and vaulted into the sky. Once these spires had stood bare but, with the climate change, there was now enough moisture and heat shift to generate ice sheets on their lower flanks. The ice rose like a wolf's gum, locking each massive tooth into the snow.

It was here that Ryan climbed: It was here that he tried to escape his past. And the world he had created.

Chip, chip, thunk.

Shards sparked down on him with each swing. He lost himself to the smooth beat of his axes crunching ice, finding purchase, taking his weight. Churning thoughts stilled with the slow burn of exertion. His arms ached with the strain, fingers curled tight around the handles, wrists chafed by the axes' leashes.

Heat suffused him, wiping away the last of his morning sludge. A glance through his legs at the gaping space below offered the familiar adrenaline rush that beat the shit out of any cup of coffee. Ice descended below him, then flattened into an unending white plane. Each exhalation puffed a soft cloud into the air, forcing life into the landscape. Everything else stood angled sharp and dead still.

An unyielding rage had driven Ryan to this farthest end of the earth. Every morning, he woke consumed by it. This morning, like the one before, and the one before that, he had pushed it away, refusing to acknowledge that rotten space within him. Instead he closed it off, boxed it down and let it settle into a sour, acid rumble deep in his gut.

It hadn't always been like this. For a time, there was hope. There was a future. There was a woman. Sarah Peters had filled that black space within him.

Chip, chip, thunk.

Like the ice shearing under each swing of his axes, Sarah had helped him discard the shell that a lifetime within Echelon had generated.

Two pillars had supported Ryan Laing's existence: Echelon, and the woman who helped him destroy it. They had done it for the right reasons. But that didn't matter anymore.

Even now, years later, Ryan found it hard to fathom the scope of his decision. The hubris of it. He had altered the course of history. He had destroyed the quiet conspiracy that ordered the world. Chaos followed hard and fast. With it came regret.

Ryan tried to forget the world he had ended—the century of peace that Echelon had generated. But the longing wouldn't release him. He craved the security of that time with an addict's frantic need.

For a century, all information had flowed through Echelon's spigot. Through subtle manipulation of that data yield, Echelon had quieted those ideas that were deemed too dangerous or unsettling, thus maintaining a peaceful, if numb, status quo. Echelon was the benevolent and unseen dictator, smoothing out the fits and starts of humanity's progress. Echelon made life easy.

And Ryan had been a believer. He'd been the goddamned poster child. As an operative within its clandestine ranks, he had thought Echelon infallible. His faith had been pure. For the cause he had done things, questionable things; there was blood on his hands that would never wash away. But always there had been the pure faith that he did right. That Christopher Turing, Echelon's director and the closest thing Laing had to a father, would never lead him astray.

Losing that faith had cracked Ryan clean through. He had been dragged, kicking and screaming, to recognize Echelon's fatal flaw—that, sooner or later, absolute power corrupts absolutely.

A conspiracy had risen within Echelon. Sniffing it out, and knowing the ramifications of such an organization's turning from the greater good, he had no choice. Ryan couldn't allow Echelon to fall into the wrong hands. So he dragged it all down. In the process, he had been forced to kill Christopher Turing and, with him, a century of peace.

The incursion had nearly killed him. Maybe it should have. Crashing the Echelon system had also crashed the technology that kept Ryan alive. What had begun as nanotechnology in the twentieth century found its zenith in Ryan Laing. Within him, another intelligence had been implanted. A collective, artificial intelligence that healed him, jacked his perception and strength and linked him to the world's data flow. Ryan had a drone army coursing through his body. Or was it their body? At this point, the line between man and machine had blurred.

When Echelon fell, the code that ran Laing's drones crumbled with it. Their collective consciousness fractured to a billion microscopic intruders chewing through him. Ryan should have let them complete their meal.

But Sarah had pleaded with him to fight. And he had loved her enough to try. Ryan had offered the dictionary of his own being for the drones to adopt. Symbioses evaporated. No longer did he need to interface with them. He became the swarm and they him. Man and machine were one.

Just one more reason to live beyond the hand of man. He couldn't rightfully call himself human anymore.

Chip, chip, THUNK.

Lost in the past, Ryan's concentration faltered. He missed hard ice, the axe sinking into flake. It exploded into shards, one of which lanced Ryan's cheek. The pain threw him off balance. Laing scrambled, the talons of his crampons losing purchase. At the same moment, the ice gripping his left axe exploded under the added weight. Ryan fell.

Adrenaline flooded him. Time petrified. His world ratcheted down to a single flailing swing with his right axe. It slammed into the hard ice, scraped down its surface, then bit, jolting Ryan to a stop. The axe's eagle beak had caught on a slight imperfection. He hung, his continued existence pinioned on that ripple in the ice sheet.

Every muscle in his body demanded action, but he fought off the gulping need to scramble for purchase. Deep breaths forced patience. The slightest jerk would kick his axe off the knob. In an excruciatingly slow dance, Ryan moved his left axe up to match the right. He rested the axe's point on another imperfection. He softly kicked his crampons into the ice, reassured by the resounding thunk of their purchase. He stood up and swung his axes into the ice.

Chip, chip, thunk.

Safe—or safer—Ryan's vision opened out, released from the fall's ratcheting perspective. Blood ran down his cheek, pooling in the hollow of his collarbone. The flow didn't last long. Within his blood, gray drones swarmed. Ryan sensed their coordinated tug. The gash on his cheek knitted down to a sliver of cold pink flesh.

Then, nothing.

Not even a blemish. With drone augmentation, his body healed so quickly that he found it difficult to keep his past in solid state. He had no scars to ground his experiences.

Christopher Turing had once grounded him. But he was dead. Then, it was Sarah who had linked him to his past, and offered him a future. He'd fucked that up too, or maybe she had. It didn't matter. With her gone, it all faded to a dull wash. Past, present, and future meshed into a blur that left him numb. So he climbed, trying each day to lose himself in the vertical.

He shook away the last of his high and looked up to the pitch ahead. Ice for another twenty meters, then smooth granite. Larger than the walls of Yosemite, this fang and its brothers offered a new mecca for the world's climbers. Three colors dominated: white snow and ice, blue sky, and black granite. The simplified palette settled Ryan.

Maybe that's why he had come to this end of the earth, because it was so different from Tasmania's saturated green. Ryan wished he could wipe his memories of that place and the time he had spent there with Sarah.

After Echelon fell, she had found them an isolated prefab deep within Tasmania's rain forest. Suspended over gnarled Huon pines, the house floated on a sea of green. A single stanchion rising from the forest floor was all that connected the structure to the ground. When the wind blew, the house swayed to the tempo of the ancient trees below.

"You need time to recalibrate," she had said, her words cold and analytical even as her hand, brushing his forearm, offered warm heat.

Chip, chip, THUNK.

Ice. Rock. The shock of blue sky. Laing slammed his axe home with more force than necessary, the hard act only amping the recall of her skin on his. Even Antarctica couldn't wipe the memory of her.

He had tried to recover. Really. For her. For a future that should have been bright. Echelon was gone. Humanity had its freedom. He had Sarah. He was a hero, right? He deserved a happily ever after.

She had shielded him from the truth for as long as she could. Looking back, he thanked her for that time—that moment of hope. But it didn't last. Even as she pleaded with him to stay present, his curiosity boiled.

"Ryan, please." Standing on the prefab's balcony, watching night consume the forest below, she had begged him. "Leave it be. You've done enough. You've seen enough."

He remembered the way her hair floated on the gentle breeze. The soft smell of her rising over the forest's rich funk.

"Sarah, it's fine. I'm fine," he had said with unaccustomed optimism.

Sarah looked at him as if mourning something not quite lost. Ryan didn't see it at the time—the regret in that look.

Above him, stars had pierced the dusk. In the space between, Ryan felt the flow's tug. He eased his mind into a neutral state—the place between man and machine. Sarah's pleading fell away.

Drone input blossomed. The rain forest faded to background. The flow rezzed in from its cardinal points, wrapping him in virtual. It ran over him, a cascade of data. He plunged in.

Data jacks and node points rose before him, a virtual representation of the flickering weave of connections that linked humanity together. He sank deep.

And here his hope faded. In a blink, his future went gray. He saw what he had wrought.

He had expected a time of panic and fear as Echelon's invisible hand released its grip. Freedom after so many years of tyranny was not easy to digest. Russia's confused rush to capitalism in the twentieth had showed the world what a difficult pill freedom could be.

Ryan had expected chaos. What he saw, writ large, was his fuckup. A mistake that changed everything.

His incursion had succeeded in destroying Echelon, but failed to erase it completely. Ryan had killed the beast, but left its corpse for the world to see. Echelon's existence had come to light. Every man, woman, child, corporation, and country saw that they had been played.

Rage gripped the world. Fear. Distrust. Suddenly, nothing of the last century could be relied on. Within the flow, Ryan watched the disintegration of the European Union, old grudges rising from Echelon's ashes. Nations, conglomerates, and demagogues rose and fell in tumultuous succession. No control, no shape, just a brutal hunt for equilibrium. The strong held fast. The weak bent under the onslaught.

Standing on that balcony in Tasmania, Ryan had shivered in spite of the heat. A creak in the flooring as Sarah shifted to him. She touched his arm, soft, like the wind's rush. So full of regret.

The air smelled different with her presence. She charged the atmosphere. Her breasts, soft and demanding, ground into the small of his back. She wrapped her arms around him.

"It will be okay," she whispered in his ear.

Ryan closed his eyes, refusing the comfort of her presence. She tugged at him but he didn't budge. Couldn't. So she melted into him, pouring honey soft over his rigid frame.

"Please. You need sleep, Ryan."

"What have I done?" The words echoed through him, unrelenting.

"Only what was necessary," she replied.

He stepped away from her.

She forced him to turn, hard eyes locking his. He sensed her determination to connect. But he couldn't. Not now. Not with guilt draping over him like a cloak.

"Don't do it," she said. "Not after all we've been through." The cool analysis in Sarah's voice lowered to fragile fear. "Don't push me away."

Ryan did not move.

Abandoning words, she pulled him close, her lips finding his. Drones swarmed into her, active in her while she remained physically connected to Ryan. Through them, Ryan and Sarah shared each other's sensations. Her need forced his. Ryan felt Sarah's longing as if it were his own. She needed to know him—demanded complete connection. He buckled under that will. Their kiss became an exploration. He submitted, his emotions, fears and desire spilling into her. She pushed further. Too much. Too close.

—*Please.*

He thought the word and it rose in her mind through their drone link. She relented, grudgingly, breaking their kiss.

—*I will share this with you, Ryan.*

Ryan shook his head.

"I will," she said aloud.

He watched her for a long moment. The dark curve of her eyebrow, the tight-lipped determination. Sarah's skin glowed in the starlight. He reached for her, then stopped himself. She took his hand before he could pull back, drawing it to her cheek. The softness of her skin felt distant— barely registered through the wind tunnel he had become.

She pushed closer, backing him up against the balcony's railing. Sensations mingled. The cold metal digging into his back. The slick heat of her mouth. She pulled away from their kiss and buried her head in his chest.

She slipped lower, forcing his desire. Her mouth, lips, and tongue stirring him. She rose up, brown hair flying wild, her eyes green and deep.

His rough desire amped with the dance of light over her figure. He pushed it away, turning from her and gazing into the night.

"Sarah . . ." His words drained into the warm air.

Before he could put his hands on the railing, Sarah jammed her knee into the back of his, throwing an arm around his chest and sending him crashing to the floor. His breath blew out.

She attacked him with animal ferocity, straddling him and sinking down in a single thrust. Her eyes dared him to pull away. He didn't. Slow friction between them. This wasn't lovemaking. She fucked him, forcing connection.

Under her, Ryan melted into a pounding mesh of pain and pleasure, love and confusion. It drove him and, for a time, filled the darkness. But it wasn't enough.

Chip, chip, thunk.

That was gone now. Sarah was gone. Tasmania's green replaced by Antarctic white. Ryan climbed, trying to push out the past. He was here to forget.

The ice gave way to raw granite. It rose up over his head in a single thrust that seemed to puncture the sky itself. He began dry tooling his way up the face, using his crampons and ice axes in lieu of fingers and toes. The granite ran smooth, with only minuscule fissures for Ryan to insert the tip of an axe, or a single point of his crampons.

He lost himself to the climb. The ache of muscle and flow of movement filled him as Sarah once had. This was better. Permanent. For this, he needed no one. Solitude, amplified by the environment's stark beauty.

In this way hours passed, as they had yesterday and the day before. An unending stream of concentration and adrenaline that washed him clean.

Ryan reached a small alcove in the rock, just under the summit. Off in the distance, black mountains rose from the ice. On opposing ends of the horizon, the sun and moon buoyed each other, balanced for a precious, freezing instant. Standing at their fulcrum, Laing glimpsed peace. He turned away.

The summit hung over him, meters away. He gazed up at it, but today, like yesterday and the day before, he turned back. There was a rhythm to this life. To climb those last steps would break the dance, and that he could not do.

The chill tunneled into him as he began to down climb. He accepted it, reveled in it. He had driven everything away, failed at everything except this. He could live forever in this cold limbo.

He could live without memory.

Without Turing and Echelon.

He could live without Sarah.

Happily ever after.

2

One more time. Once more and it will be enough.

Expectation made the image before her tolerable. The mirror reflected Sarah Peters perfectly and not at all. Brown hair. High cheekbones and skin flushed from the shower's heat. Her sharp nose conjured a patrician elegance. The delicate contour of her chin settled her face, consolidating her strong features.

Others called her beautiful, but the mirror said differently. Objectivity frayed under the lash of Sarah's scrutiny. She gazed into those green eyes and felt betrayed. Tendons in her neck twitched. She wanted so badly to look away, to avoid the inevitable, but the cycle would not release her. As on every other morning, her pupils drew her in. In those black wells, she didn't see strength. She didn't see beauty. She saw only emptiness, a dull lack that defined her. Nausea suffused her and still she couldn't turn away. The reflection wrenched her down to that core place she so loathed—a clear view right into the sewer of her soul.

Once more and it will go. After this, I won't see it.

She pulled free from the mirror's glare, the itch of her internal body armor offering distraction. The hex-woven carbon nanotubing tattooed into her flesh was weeks old. Sarah was still getting used to the idea of being impenetrable. She drew a finger down her neck, across the hollow of her clavicle and over her chest. No loss of feeling. Her fingernail's slide drew goose bumps.

She dug in, gouging the skin over a rib. A droplet of blood formed under her fingernail and slid down her stomach. Sarah pressed harder, but her flesh refused to yield further. The body tattoo held firm. The cut hurt, but not quite enough.

Sarah pulled back and powered on.

She wasn't supposed to. Not yet, anyway. The body tat and neural augments were still settling. But she couldn't help herself. The possibility of release was too tempting. She brought her internal diagnostic online.

For a moment, integration held firm. She reveled in the tech-meshed high, jacking her serotonin levels to wash away the emptiness. The buzz inundated her, gave her focus, clarity, consistency. The black faded under a sparkling white capability.

Then the glitch hit. Every day, same thing. Interface eroded into digital backwash and emotional loss. She slumped back into herself—into the old Sarah. After such a tantalizing fantasy, reality was a bitter pill. But soon, the interface would hold. Today's augment would finish her evolution.

One more operation. One more time.

The thought pulled her from the mirror. She toweled the last of the water from her skin, reentered the master bedroom, shrugged into a loose cut dress and worked her hair into a black *khimar.* The head scarf made her slightly claustrophobic, but after so many trips to the United Arab Emirates, she had grown used to it.

She descended the marble staircase to the living room of her suite, her toes sinking into thick purple carpeting. The room's cream-thick opulence bordered on stifling. Luxury defined Dubai—the center for all things material. Sarah flipped a switch and the floor-to-ceiling windows transluced to reveal desert and ocean. She stepped to the slanted plexi and gazed into the distance.

Her hotel, the Burj al Arab, jutted into the Persian Gulf on a slender, man-made spit of land. Over three hundred meters tall, the building's Teflon-coated fiberglass shell appeared to billow like an old dhow's sail. Below her, the gritted desert and sparkling scrapers of Dubai City melted into a gray sea.

She tried to push into a future only hours away—when her implants would run clean. The possibility of relief flooded her, a twitchy neurotic need. She felt that eye turning inward again, unsatiated by the interplay of desert and water. Sarah shrugged it off, setting the window back to opaque.

To distract herself, she kicked into the flow. Laser tracking embedded throughout the suite locked on her eye and hand movements, allowing her to guide the data stream rezzing on the vid-screen before her. The rush of data that formed the world's interchange flushed out before her. Sarah used the eye track to sift through a backwash of spam and clutter to the flow points she hit every morning. Mostly news blogs. Sarah tracked as many as she could, trying to draw truth from a thousand opinions.

A news alert drew Sarah from her data skim. She pulled up her favorite blog, cutting away advertising tendrils to skim the raw feed. The words rose before her, eliciting an eerie sense of déjà vu.

Lhasa, Tibet.
Dalai Lama assassinated by a Chinese national with links to conservative paramilitary organizations . . .
Uprisings of minority populations throughout China . . .
Chilled relations with India . . .
New peace between the superpowers lies stillborn . . .

Sarah's mouth went cotton dry. She slurped at her coffee. It didn't help. Flipping out of raw blog, she watched clips of protests raging through India and within China's own borders. The events playing out felt staged. And she'd written the screenplay. She had run this exact event progression.

A tingle rose in her gut. Was it guilt? No. She pushed it away. She was just an analyst. She wrote reports—found links in the random, and threw out what-ifs. That was it.

No one was better at event projection than Sarah Peters. She found the linchpins around which history turned. It was her gift, her skill. Now, it was all she had left.

After Echelon, she had tried to walk away from the whole thing. She and Ryan had done their part. She was ready to let others worry about the big picture shit. But Ryan had slipped away. She had pleaded with him to stay with her. To love her. Not in words, she was too proud for that, but with every fiber of her being. He had refused.

So she had left him to his slow rot and pushed into the new world they had created. She told herself that her skills would help ease the tensions that Echelon's revelation had sparked. Truth was, she didn't know what else to do.

So she went private, working event cascades for the highest bidder. As a contractor, she had done jobs for Brazil's Agência Brasileira de Inteligência, Japan's Cabinet Intelligence Research Office, and France's Directorate-General of External Security. For each of these institutions she had run complex modeling ops, forecasting possible futures based on the patterns she pulled.

Basically, she was a fortune teller. But her combination of gut instinct, pattern recognition, and masterful data mining allowed her a veracity rate that Nostradamus couldn't touch.

Two years ago, Sarah had been pulled off the market by an organization she knew only as EMPYRE. She had done a cursory check before accepting the offer. EMPYRE had roots in the United States. She suspected it was a well funded think tank, possibly even a shell for part of the American intelligence infrastructure. But what she had really cared about was the pay. She'd developed a habit—a need really—and it cost a lot. With EMPYRE's money, she began modifying her body.

Now, she stared at the clips coming out of Asia. Sarah had run this event cascade for EMPYRE three months ago. She had forecast that the Dalai Lama's return to Tibet from his exile in India had a high probability of shifting the balance of power. Peace between China and India would have resulted in a decline in American hegemony. American political and economic power would have slipped had China and India overcome their long-standing animosities.

The Dalai Lama's assassination shifted events down a new track. It would cause just enough anger to keep the conflict simmering. But India wouldn't retaliate. Though the religion had been born within its borders, India was not a Buddhist country. Escalation held little political promise.

And then there was the added benefit, to the United States, of increased domestic tension within the middle kingdom. With China fighting its own, the Shanghai Stock Exchange would take a hit. All this would bolster the United States' position.

That she had drilled out how critical the Dalai Lama's return was to the balance of power only meant she'd done her job well. No way a simple report had anything to do with the assassination. She refused to believe it. If EMPYRE was something other than what she had thought, something darker, she would have to give up the paycheck allowing her to complete her transformation.

An arc of adrenaline punched through her. She pushed the thought-line away and killed the flow link. She'd honed her mind to see patterns in the chum of life. Sometimes that need to lock pattern drew ghosts.

And some things were too horrible to consider.

In the dead screen Sarah caught her translucent reflection and tickling need urged her to action. She downed the last of her coffee and headed for the door.

Two businessmen spilled into the hall from the room across the corridor. As the door to their suite closed, Sarah spotted the dregs of what had clearly been an all-nighter. Women lay draped over couches. Men drank in corners, shades drawn.

The two before her looked far worse for wear, suits rumpled, ties hanging loose.

"Fuck, Rob, I don't think I can function."

"Hey, we gotta close this thing. Work hard, play hard. We got the play out of our system."

The businessman's gray features cracked into a brittle smile. "True."

"So let's get the work done."

There was a reckless consumption underlying Dubai that these two captured, a drive to push the limits, to suck up every indulgence before the world's turmoil caught up to them.

The businessman nodded. "Okay. Just hate playing hardball with Si-Tech when I'm oversexed, underslept, and—"

Reaching the elevator, the two noticed Sarah's presence behind them and clammed up. She nodded and they both looked at the floor. In the ride down, the two quietly transformed. On floor twenty-seven, they looked trashed. On reaching the upper lobby, they had pulled themselves together, straightened out their rumples and drawn their ties flush. Exiting the elevator, they melted into the faceless throng. Sarah followed suit.

Rooms within rooms, lives hidden, realities secreted away. That was the nature of Dubai, and the reason it had become so prosperous. In Dubai, exterior was everything. Morality and modesty were just shells to be worn and discarded when the public eye blinked. Sarah felt comfortable here.

She followed the suits into the lobby. Over her, the atrium vaulted into a billowing sail of curved white. She descended the escalator, which cut through cascading water features. The falling water offered an undertone to the mix of languages pervading the lobby.

From the cold luxury of the Burj al Arab, Sarah stepped into the Middle Eastern sun. The land's carnal heat blasted her. She sidestepped into a waiting Rolls-Royce, the driver shutting out the sauna with a satisfying thunk of the car door.

"Where can I take you, ma'am?" he asked as he settled into the driver's seat.

"Dubai Mall, please."

The Rolls's engine produced a throaty hum as it slid past the other limos and out onto the road connecting the hotel to the mainland. Reclaimed from the Persian Gulf, the land under the hotel was only big enough for the scraper itself. Behind her, the structure ballooned out over the Gulf and hung ephemeral in the desert air, a dream made solid.

Sarah settled into the rich leather, trying not to fidget. This life, this opulence, didn't suit her. She had come a long way since her days in Scotland, living in a reclaimed industrial zone in New Inverness. Nights spent raging in her punk band. Days spent in Echelon's employ, honing the world's future to a razor's edge.

She longed for it sometimes, the power that she had possessed under Echelon's aegis, the simple mandate to forge order from chaos—to keep humanity on track. But that was gone. Now it was every man for himself.

She shook off her musing and watched Dubai City slide by. Looming before her stood the Burj Dubai, the massive scraper at city center. It shot into the sky in fits and starts, rising from a massive base and spindling down to a needle spike.

The limo veered into the sparkling white entrance of the largest mall in the world. A rippling structure butting up against the scraper, the Dubai Mall swelled through the city, swallowing up most of its downtown. Pulling to a stop under the waved roof jutting out from the structure, the driver rushed to the door and Sarah allowed him to lead her into the mall. The cool rush of air conditioning sent a shiver through her.

"I'll be fine from here, thank you."

"As you say," the driver replied with a nod.

Sarah let the mall's size and sizzle pervade her. Plexi sheets overhead allowed an unobstructed view of the scraper. And around her, a rambling city of shops sprawled for kilometers. The new Hong Kong, Dubai was a city built on money. You came here to make it or spend it. There was little else. Its initial boom had been fueled by an oasis of oil. Now, with petroleum's ebb, the United Arab Emirates had shifted its focus to technology and trade.

Sarah strolled through the mall, losing herself in the unending array of stores. Amidst the glossed goods and services, Sarah's fellow shoppers struck her as utterly bland, clasped tight and conservative. But behind the scenes, in every hotel room and opulent boutique, the most outrageous tastes in human consumption were indulged to the limit, and beyond. Dubai was a town of secret lives, where the more you spent, the less attention you drew.

Sarah negotiated the maze alongside gilded women clutching their shopping bags like lifelines. The desperation in those eyes startled her. Was there something of herself in those looks? No. No, she wasn't here for hedonistic indulgence or to blur a harsh reality with opulence. She needed this.

Sarah made her way through the throngs and entered a zone built to look like an Italian piazza. She could just make out the *Adhan*, the Islamic call to prayer, running discordant to this staged set. A haunting, rhythmic expression, it broke through the mall's sterility. Sarah's heels clicked over the faux cobblestones in time with the call.

She stopped at a frosted glass door, the word *Harry* running down its length. From the mall's bustling glitz, she entered an atmosphere that ran to the slow cadence of a different era.

Hot light gave way to the rich woods and deep banquettes of Harry's Bar. A favorite of Ernest Hemingway back in the twentieth, it had once been the defining watering hole of Venice, Italy. As the city sank, its pieces were sold to the highest bidder. Harry's Bar was transported—down to the last chair and tumbler—to Dubai.

The place made Sarah uncomfortable. Its verisimilitude was total—even down to the rich, musty smell and ancient Italian bartender. But any aura that Harry's Bar once possessed had been sapped dry. It had become a theme park where, for the right price, you could stare back into the past and ogle. Sarah settled into a booth and the barman approached.

"Something to drink while you wait?" The man's soft wrinkles matched the ambience to perfection. Sarah found it hard to believe that the old man ever left the establishment for Dubai's glare.

"Hello, Claudio. Bellini, please."

The barman bowed and went to get her drink. When it came, Sarah drank it down in great gulps, the fruity liquored froth taming that urge to turn her gaze within—to think about the pattern growing around her. Tibet was not her fault.

"Another, ma'am?"

"Oh, no thanks. Probably shouldn't have had that. It's still morning. You'll think I'm a lush."

Claudio smiled, warm and congenial. "At Harry's, another drink is always the order of the day. Besides, they're running late." He put a slight inflection on the word *they*, as if he were drawing her into a private intrigue.

Sarah smiled back. "Well, then. Why not?"

Sarah let the alcohol do its work. She snatched glances at the silhouettes surrounding her. In the low light, they hunkered over their drinks, talking in conspiratorial whispers. This was a place for lovers.

The thought dredged up an image of Ryan Laing. She thought she saw him in the silhouetted face of a man sitting at the bar. Had he come for her? Sarah's heart skipped a beat. The man felt her gaze and turned. His features found the light, resolving into those of a stranger. She looked away, embarrassed.

Suddenly, she hated Ryan. Hated herself for obsessing over him. She tried to restrain the urge and couldn't. She accessed his flow point and linked to him.

—*How's my explorer?*

She hoped her derision pounded down the link loud and clear.

—*Sarah?*

The word formed in her mind, its pattern familiar, which only heightened her anger.

—*Bumblefuck treating you well?*

—*No complaints.*

—*There was a time when explorers were the courageous ones. You've bucked a long trend.*

She hated the ensuing silence. It made her want to be cruel—as it always had.

—*I'm going under today. Finishing the augment.*

Another long silence.

—*Don't do this, Sarah. Please.*

—*What do you care? I'm always the one pestering you. You haven't linked to me in years.*

—*You asked me not to.*

—*You really don't know a fucking thing, do you?*

—*I've proved that well enough.*

Anger boiled in Sarah. She shouldn't be doing this. What was the point in dredging up old feelings?

—*Good-bye, Ryan.*

—*No. Please, think about what you're doing. I know what I'm talking about here.*

—*So arrogant.*

—*Some things can't be undone, Sarah.*

—*You're right.*

She cut the link, relishing his hurt and ashamed of herself for craving it. It was better this way. She needed his pain and her anger. Sarah refused to miss him.

The Bellini came just in time.

3

"Go fuck yourself." Frank Savakis wasn't a screamer. The words came out dead cold.

They had the desired effect on the man sitting before him. The man's eyes bulged, his capillary-tracked cheeks flushing hot.

Sure, those three words would probably end Frank's career. The CIA might foster a relaxed, school-tie chumminess, but underneath that shell of congeniality, the chain of command stood inviolate. You didn't tell Andrew Dillon, deputy director for intelligence, to fuck himself and come to work the next day. For Frank, it was worth it to watch the shit-ant squirm.

Seconds earlier, Frank had barged into the DDI's office belching a torrent of expletives. He had been angry on getting orders to leave Tibet and return to Langley. Touching down in D.C., he was running on pure rage. By the time he reached Dillon's front office, there was no stopping him. Hannah Beck, Dillon's assistant and one of the most feared gatekeepers in the Company, didn't slow him down.

"I'm sorry, sir," she had sputtered to Dillon as she trailed Frank into the office. "He just blasted by."

That was when Frank uttered his career-ender.

Now, he held Dillon's gaze—and his full attention. With effort, Dillon's face relaxed. The spark faded from his eyes.

"It's okay, Hannah. Frank was expected."

"But he's not on your appointment—"

"You can go," Dillon cut her off. "We'll be fine."

Hannah turned, throwing Frank a quick nod and whispering, "Be nice," as she closed the door behind her. Dillon didn't notice the interchange.

"Been a long time, Frank. Prague was what, fifteen years ago?" He pushed from his desk and leaned back in his chair, not offering his hand. Frank wouldn't have taken it.

Dressed in a dark blue suit, shirt starched crisp, Dillon was the model Company man. Manicured fingernails, perfect hair. Couldn't have been further from the rumpled suit that hung limp over Frank's boxer frame, or the stubble that darkened his mutt features. Frank was gratified to see that age had shriveled the skin under Andrew's eyes. The DDI's face had settled into the dispassionate mask that found every spook eventually.

"Time hasn't been good to you," Frank said.

Andrew's laughter didn't quite reach his eyes. "The great game has taken its toll."

"It's no game. Not to me. Never fuckin' was."

"Yes. You made that very clear all those years ago," Andrew replied.

"You remember Prague so well, you should know that my instincts are fucking bankable." Frank spat the words with machine-gun force. "So why would you engineer my extraction from Tibet? You have no right. You're not even NCS," he said with obvious disdain. Among the National Clandestine Service—the part of the CIA that did the hands-on work of spying, and within which Frank had made his career—there was a general disregard for the planners who sat back and analyzed while the dirty work was done by others. To Frank's eye, Dillon typified just that kind of arm-chair espionage.

"Out of curiosity, how did you know that I was the one who had you pulled from Tibet?" Dillon asked.

"Are you kidding? You may rule the roost, but I know each and every chicken in this place. Nothing goes on here I don't know about."

"Always out in the cold, aren't you? Always working your sources."

"That's right," Frank said. "So why bring me in? I was so close and you pull me before I can fire my guns."

"Ah yes, your mythical Phoenix. I saw your report."

"No myth," Frank growled. "Read the report again."

Andrew laughed. "Not necessary. You're barking up the wrong tree. Not one single analyst, agent, or asset has put skin and bones to your bogey-man. Phoenix is exactly that: yours. He's a figment of your imagination."

"Your desk jockeys don't see it and it doesn't exist, huh? Phoenix is real enough. My contacts are chirping the name, and they're scared. We're talking about a well-coordinated, highly efficient organization with seri-ous reach. And it's got teeth. I've got Phoenix pegged for the EMP attack in Berlin—"

Andrew cut him off. "Which was claimed by the New Revolutionary Cells—a leftist terrorist group that picked up as Echelon disintegrated."

"The assassination of President Gloria Sanchez in Mexico," Frank blasted back.

"A contract killing paid for by rivals."

"And now—Tibet."

"Which we've attributed to a right-wing paramilitary group in China."

"Bull-" Frank let the word draw out, "-shit."

"Frank—"

"I was fucking *there*, Andrew. Explain that away. I tracked the action to Tibet. Now we got a dead guru and shit all over the fan."

"The Dalai Lama is slightly more than a guru," Andrew replied. He gazed at Frank for a long moment, then switched gears. "Okay—give me a name. One name linked to Phoenix."

Frank looked away.

"I pulled you because I couldn't have a rogue officer spinning fantasies."

"Go. Fuck. Yourself."

Andrew rose from his desk with slow deliberation. Frank readied for a physical confrontation, almost longed for it, but Dillon walked right past him.

At the door, Andrew turned. "You coming?"

"You know I won't drop this."

"I know you, Frank. I know you're a pit bull. Your jaws lock down and you never—ever—release. But with your mouth so full, I also know you don't see beyond the kill. There's a wider world out there."

Frank took a breath, trying to calm down. His words came out slow and measured. Almost a plea. "Damn it, Andrew. This threat is real. I don't have any names but Phoenix is real. Only a matter of time before the U.S. learns that the hard way."

Andrew shook his head. "Long time ago, you showed me around Prague. Showed me a thing or two. Now it's my turn."

Dillon turned on his heels. Frank couldn't think of anything to do but follow.

Frank Savakis thought he knew every inch of the Langley sprawl. Dillon proved him wrong. The CIA had grown over the years in haphazard fits of necessity. New buildings jumbled over their predecessors, creating labyrinthine passages pocked with unmarked doors. In the newer buildings, you punched an end point into a monitor and—if you were cleared for access—the biocrete walls guided you through the maze with electric luminescence. But here in the CIA's bowels, the ball of string ran out.

They dropped into the belly of the Original Headquarters Building. A less-than-poetic title, but the Company wasn't much on novelty. As they descended, Langley's trademark sterility gave way to the slow rot of age and disuse. Frank caught the flicker of a spider moving across the wall. Dust puffed into the dead air with each footfall.

Lost in the gray, Frank's mind wandered to the last time he'd walked with Dillon. Prague was a lifetime ago. And it was yesterday. Both were young, both eager to make a name for themselves in the CIA. Andrew's connections had lofted him to station chief. Frank started at the bottom.

They had been strolling down the Charles Bridge, scuffing timeworn cobblestones under the statues of saints that ran the bridge's length. Street vendors lined both balustrades, hawking to the tourists. Frank took particular glee in scowling at them. He hated this part of the city, ancient and fairytale pretty.

"It's magnificent," Andrew had said.

"Huh?"

"Prague Castle, Frank." Andrew pointed up at the majestic structure on the hill before them. Old Prague had been left alone over the centuries. Modern development ringed the ancient city, slender spikes rising high over this old world playground. The circling scrapers made Frank feel exposed.

"Fuck the castle, Dillon. We got shit to do. You goin' to drag me through the whole tourist trek?"

"I might," Andrew had said with a smile.

Frank had liked Andrew then, in spite of their differences. They were developing an Odd Couple chemistry that made Frank think they'd get some shit done.

Grudgingly, Frank had pulled his eyes up to the castle. Nice enough. Nothing special.

He knocked into Andrew, who had stopped dead. In front of them, a young man, maybe twenty, rosy cheeked and bright eyed, had pulled a small pistol from his pocket. In that crucial instant, Dillon froze.

Frank charged.

He lunged forward and crashed into the boy, smothering the gun with his torso. The discharge barely made a sound. Frank remembered the hard thump of impact—like he'd been hit by a sledgehammer. Ribs cracked. His body armor caught the bullet before it pierced flesh. Frank didn't let the impact slow him. He wrenched the gun from the boy, twisting the arm until he heard a sharp, satisfying crack.

Frank yanked the kid's head into his shoulder, muffling the scream. He wedged the would-be assassin against the bridge's stone rail.

"Dillon! You okay?" Frank asked.

Andrew stood stunned, unable to break out of his shock.

"Andrew!?"

"Yes. Yeah—I'm okay, Frank."

"Still think this castle shit is pretty?"

"Who is he?" Dillon found his breath. He brought a trembling hand to his temple, swiping at a bead of sweat. It was November.

Frank turned his attention to the boy. "He's a New Commie. You can see it in that idealistic rosy-cheeked stupidity. Real question is where his little coven is hiding out and how they knew we'd be here. What do ya say, pal? Interested in playing?" Frank sucker-punched the assassin in the groin.

A crowd had begun to form around the three men. Color returned to Dillon's face, even as the boy blanched.

"Frank," Andrew said, glancing around him. "We have to turn him over to the Czechs. We don't have the authority to interrogate him."

Frank turned on Andrew while keeping his body pressed against the assassin. "Come again?"

Dillon's poise had returned. Frank could see the wheels spinning and knew Andrew was about to piss him off.

"Frank, we have to turn him over. The Czechs have a hard-on for these bastards. It'll up our position here. And . . ." he motioned to the crowd around them ". . . too many eyes on us."

"Are you kidding me?! This fucker almost shot you—and he broke my damn ribs!" Frank's fury swelled to bursting.

"I know, Frank. Doesn't change a thing. No room for revenge in this game."

At that, the boy's eyes lit up—reprieve seeming likely. Frank saw it. Mistake. He held himself in check, for the moment.

"Okay. Your call, Dillon."

Andrew nodded.

"Go back to the office," Frank continued. "I'll drop this fucker off."

"No, I'll come . . ."

Frank cut him off. "Listen, when it comes to keeping you safe, I'm top dog. Two broken ribs gives me that right. Get back to the office, make your calls. You'll get the credit. I'll deliver the package."

Andrew wanted to argue but, looking into Frank's cold determination, decided against it. He stuffed his hands into his jacket pockets and slipped through the crowd. Frank snatched up the boy's broken arm and led him in the opposite direction.

He caught the boy's broadening smile and whispered to him. "Might not be a place for revenge in his game, but I play on a different field. You and I are going to have a long fuckin' chat."

He wrenched the arm, bringing tears to the boy's eyes. They headed for the dark alleys that Frank liked so much. Several hours later, Frank dumped what was left of the kid at the Czech Security Information Service. He filed a report, outlining an attempted escape during which Frank had been forced to strike the assassin—repeatedly. Several days later, the police found seven members of the New Communist Party dead in a ratty apartment. Someone had reported the smell.

For Frank, the ledger was set straight and the street knew not to fuck with the Americans. He figured his afternoon of wet work had saved a bunch of lives. Andrew saw it differently. After that day, the careers of the two men had diverged.

Now, years later, Frank played by the same rules, and, with Echelon out of the picture, the rest of the world was catching up. Deep in the Company's bowels, he rounded a corner and passed through a massive metal door. A quick inspection revealed that it had been installed recently.

Dillon's pristine elegance ran discordant to the room's ragged age. He took in his surroundings as if noticing them for the first time. "Unlike the Czech Republic, the CIA builds right over its history. Lots of history made in this room. This section is from the twentieth. Been out of use for some time. The whole suite is a giant vault. Shut the door and we have total privacy."

"We?"

Dillon touched the key screen and the metal door slid closed, bolts screwing into the frame. Andrew led Frank though a series of cubicles and into a conference room.

As he entered, the color drained from Frank's features. Men and women sat around a long table. He stared at each face with unabashed shock.

"Welcome to EMPYRE," Andrew said.

4

"They are ready for you, ma'am," the barman said.

A bolt of adrenaline coursed through Sarah. She swallowed the last of her Bellini and slid out of the booth.

One more time. Then I'll be right.

The drink's fruity tang lingered as the barman led Sarah to an unmarked door in the darkest corner of the bar. She waited a moment, savoring the potent possibility of release.

One more time and it will go.

Sarah waved her hand over the door lock and it slid open. She entered a different world. World on world jammed together here—all linked by money and desire. In Dubai's celled-out society, tech ran flood fast, unhindered by rules and mores. Next-gen body augmentation found a happy home here.

Sarah found comfort in the clinic's jet-black design. The room's gentle curves and arced seating offered the promise of infinite oblivion. She slumped into a lounge and lost herself in the monochrome.

A hulking figure entered the room. The skintight sterile suit did little to improve his appearance. Despite his weight, his soft gait and delicate movements revealed an innate grace.

"Welcome," he said in a lilting English accent.

"Judson." Sarah stood and shook his hand. His light grip belied his substantial bulk. The man's fat defined him. In an age of easy transformation, the choice threw Sarah. "You're looking—"

"Prosperous?" Judson replied with a hearty smile and a slap to the belly. "Life is good."

"Seems so," Sarah responded, her own smile forming up to match his.

"Didn't think I'd see you back so soon," the man said as he led her into his inner sanctum. The waiting room fed into a curved hallway.

"I . . . I need to finish it out."

"Of course you do. But the timing. The tattoo needs time to settle—and the implants in your cortex must mesh completely before I engage them."

"Jud, I know the risks."

The man grunted, jowls folding into each other like flowing magma.

"With a normal skin job, I wouldn't bat an eye. But we're installing some shit here. You flip with this much 'ware, and you'll become a very dangerous person."

Sarah glared at him, cold and hard. She stepped to a monitor embedded in the door and keyed in the money link. Digitized instructions flashed through the flow and deposited a hefty chunk into the clinic's account. Judson's eyes bulged.

"That's a lot of zeroes," Sarah said. "Lot of easy living. Or, if you really think I'm not ready, I could cancel the trans." Her finger wavered over the monitor.

Judson's arm shot out, snatching Sarah's fingers. "Ah, no!" He loosened his grip immediately, cupping her small hand in his immense mitts. "It is my professional opinion that you are fully prepared for the job. Sometimes caution gets the better of me," he said with a smile once again creasing his pulpy cheeks.

Sarah nodded and confirmed the transaction. As she did, the door slid open. Judson entered first and settled in front of his flow port. Sarah stepped in and held.

The thought that all this might not work gripped her. The possibility of leaving in the same condition as she now entered filled her with a leaden dread.

Finally, Judson pulled her from cycling anxiety. "Come on, you know the drill," he said. He turned back to his pre-op work before she could reply.

No, this will be it. After this, I . . . I won't be so . . . alone.

Sarah touched a door in the wall and it slid open. She undressed in a quick rush. There were no mirrors here. Thank God. The room's sterile chill pocked her arms with goose bumps as she emerged. She shivered, settling into the operating table. The foam drew her in, wrapping around her in a full body hug. Then a slight tickle as Judson introduced a microbicyte swarm to eat the contaminants off her skin. He didn't approach until the sterilization was complete.

"You really want to go through with this? Last chance," he said.

"I want full control of my augments, including the tattoo."

"Full color, broad spectrum?"

"Yes."

"That's a ton of bandwidth."

Sarah shot him an ice-sharp glare.

Judson waved it away in a placating gesture. "Okay, okay. It's your body," he said. "What do I know?" He tapped instructions into the foam and it began to envelop Sarah's head.

"Wait," she sputtered.

The hulking man tapped on the pad and the foam regained viscosity, pushing Sarah's head back to the surface.

"I want the hawkeye as well."

"Are you kidding me? Your noodle will have enough to deal with just acclimatizing to the tat. Don't push your luck."

"I'm touched you care."

Judson loomed over Sarah, forcing eye contact. "You've had more 'ware installed than anyone I know—and I know a lot of knife jockeys. An internal flow-link coupled with a neurointegrated mathematics processing unit. Sensory enhancement and endocrine system control. Pain vaccination. And then the tat. Just activating those systems will flood you with information. Input overload is serious, you know. Those stories about brain fry aren't wives' tales."

"I can handle it," Sarah shot back.

"You gunning for cyborg of the year?"

Sarah held quiet, head just visible above the foam. "The hawkeye," she said.

Judson shook his head and left her field of vision. He returned with a round metallic object, held it over Sarah's head and tapped the shell. It split in half, flipping open to reveal two linked hemispheres which resembled nothing more than a giant set of eyes.

"This little beauty has full sensory perception, high bandwidth, quantum encryption, and a range of fifty klicks. When not in use, the hawkeye recharges using the host's body heat." As he spoke, slender wings inflated over the eyes. Once full, the thing lifted off Judson's hand and floated around the room.

"I want it."

Judson just shrugged, snagging the hawkeye out of the air. "You got the dough, I'll do the work. But no refunds if you wig."

Sarah smiled and closed her eyes. The foam encased her. As the anesthesia kicked in, she floated off and Judson got to work.

Her consciousness frayed at the edges, then burned like paper over a flame. She sank into darkness, coveting this final moment of expectation.

Once more and I'll be whole.

CENTRAL INTELLIGENCE AGENCY, LANGLEY, VIRGINIA

"Welcome to EMPYRE," Dillon said, his tone reverential.

Frank tried to process the words as he registered the room's occupants. He knew each face—but not from the back alleys and third world cesspools where he plied his trade. These were famous men and women. People who shouldn't be in the Company's basement. Sam Hansen, secretary of homeland security, sat at the table's head. To his right, Barbara Cox flicked a pen around her finger. What the hell was the head of the NSA doing here? Lieutenant General Mike Stanton from the Defense Intelligence Agency and Richard Humphrey from the State Department filled out the seats.

"You're all here for me?" Frank asked.

"As I said, you were expected," Andrew replied.

"Guess I'm not getting fired."

"Take a seat, Frank," Dillon said.

Frank quickly recovered from his surprise. His shell of cynicism locked back down. "So, what's the game here? Some kind of interagency initiative?" Frank turned to Andrew as he settled in. "I'm not a team player, Dillon."

"No initiative here," Hansen said in a deep baritone. The voice didn't match his slight frame. "EMPYRE stands outside the normal chain of command. Here, we operate beyond the mandate of our agencies. Or, more accurately, we combine our respective abilities to further broad ends."

"Broad ends covers a lot," Frank said.

"It certainly does," Hansen replied.

"We're the secret within the secret," Andrew said.

"So what do you want from me?" Frank asked.

"That remains to be seen," Stanton barked. He leaned forward, the panel of medals on his chest catching the light. EMPYRE's members shared a brief conspiratorial look.

Frank didn't catch the move until it was too late. The leather of his seat cushion melted under him, seeping over his legs and solidifying instantly, locking him to the chair. Frank raged at himself, trying to jerk free, but the material only cinched tighter, constricting his thighs. Finally, he settled down, drew in a breath and relaxed into the constraint. He looked up to see that Andrew had pulled a needle gun from his jacket.

"Not really your style, Dillon," Frank said contemptuously.

"Things change," Andrew whispered.

"The fuck could I have done that you'd want me dead?"

"You uncovered our dirty little secret," Barbara Cox said, her pen never stopping its twirl over her thumb.

"Not so little," Humphrey snorted.

Realization swept over Savakis, freezing out his anger. He stared into the middle distance, trying to digest it. "Phoenix." It was all he could say, and it came out in a whisper.

"I told them you wouldn't quit, Frank," Dillon said.

"You knew? All along?" Frank sputtered.

"Of course we knew," Cox said. "Phoenix is our asset."

"We are the fire from which Phoenix was reborn." Hansen's baritone rumbled through the boardroom.

Frank's shock settled into a slow acid churn. "Phoenix is no god. He's a fuckin' terrorist."

Barbara's pen stopped mid-spin. "I told you he wouldn't see it," she said to Dillon. "Let's end this and get back to work." She motioned toward the needle gun in Andrew's hand.

Dillon turned from her and focused on Frank. "Big picture," he said.

"The fuck kind of game you playing? Where's the big picture in waxing a Mexican president?"

"That one death paved the way for sweeping reform in Mexico—and the ascension of a new leader intent on keeping his northern neighbors happy."

"The pulse attack in Germany? Thousands died when the city grid shut down," Frank shot back.

"A pinprick that burst the German economy," Dillon replied. "The terror it sparked fueled a run on the Frankfurt Stock Exchange and pushed the country into a recession."

Richard Humphrey pushed in. "With Germany struggling, American interests in the European theater jumped a notch."

"And Tibet?"

"Low-level conflict between China and India is in our best interest," Stanton said. "EMPYRE solves problems the politicians don't have the stomach to handle. We're a necessary evil. Necessary to further American interests."

"I find all this hard to believe," Frank said, turning to Dillon, "considering the source."

"Fair enough, Frank," Dillon said. "From a man like you, we probably deserve that. But times have changed."

"Echelon is gone." Hansen let the words hang in the air.

"We're picking up the pieces," Humphrey said, his high-toned voice adamant. "There's no all-seeing eye anymore. To achieve our ends, we found a new path."

"We looked into the past to find techniques that would shift the game with minimum financial, political, and military exposure," Dillon said.

"Terrorism?" Savakis whispered, unbelieving.

"Let's call it 'targeted destabilization,'" Stanton responded.

"Call it what you fuckin' like," Frank shot back. "Doesn't change the body count."

"EMPYRE's strikes are surgical," Humphrey said. "Researched extensively, planned down to the wire."

"Who's choosing the targets?"

"The best," Hansen replied.

"The fuck does that mean?"

"It means we borrowed from our predecessor," Andrew said.

Dillon looked around the room, getting nods from the other members. He waved to a wall screen. A surveillance image of a brown-haired woman rezzed out. "Sarah Peters. She was a data rat for Echelon. Especially capable at pattern recognition."

"And now she's here?"

Hansen shook his head. "She started working freelance a couple years ago. Taking any gig that paid. We saw her talent and bought her out. Exclusive contract."

"And she just up and told you she was Echelon?"

Barbara smirked. "Yes. It was the only piece of information she gave us free of charge—as she was the one who destroyed Echelon in the first place."

"No shit."

"Sarah and another operative named Ryan Laing took Echelon offline and zeroed out the tech that made the system possible."

Frank chuckled at that.

"Something funny?" Barbara snapped.

"My kind of people," Frank said. His hands inched toward Dillon's weapon. In the heat of conversation, the move went unnoticed. "But why would she tell you?"

"EMPYRE had locked on to Laing," Dillon said. "He took down Echelon using some kind of artificial intelligence. We found markers in the flow that pointed to him, and led us to believe he was a threat."

"Peters found out," Humphrey continued. "She told us about her past—about Laing's past. In exchange, we pulled his termination order."

"We couldn't risk losing Peters," Hansen said. "Her analysis is too good to disrupt. It makes our—endeavors—possible."

"You're saying we have two people to thank for the Echelon crash?" Frank asked. No one responded. His laughter bounced off the concrete walls. "I fuckin' love it."

His casual laugh softened the mood in the room. Dillon took his eyes off Frank, and Frank pounced. His right arm snapped out, grabbed the needle gun and yanked it free. Andrew fell back stunned, disarmed before he could react.

"Interview's over," Frank said, his legs still pinned into the chair.

Silence gripped the room.

"I told you he was our man," Dillon said. In slow succession, each member of EMPYRE nodded. Andrew's hand slipped over the table. Frank trained the gun on him, ready to fire. Dillon touched a key and Frank's restraints loosened. He hopped out of the chair, backed into a corner of the room and considered his options.

"You've got the job," Dillon said.

"I'm not your man, Dillon. You know that."

Andrew stood, arms raised. "We need muscle—a street fighter."

"For what?"

"For purposes we'll discuss with you when it suits us," Cox replied.

Frank panned over the faces in the room for a long moment. "It's Phoenix," he said. "You don't trust him."

"Phoenix is well tethered," Cox said.

"More bullshit . . ." Frank wanted to push further, but Dillon stepped in, drawing his attention.

"Okay, Frank," Dillon said. "No bullshit. Phoenix is ours. EMPYRE created him. Or re-created him maybe. And EMPYRE is a terrorist organization. We use terrorism like a surgeon's scalpel, advancing American hegemony with every cut. Power through the targeted application of fear. That satisfy your bullshit meter?" Andrew let the words settle.

"And you came up with this?" Frank stared at Dillon. "You put these people together, convinced them to bloody their lily-white hands? You found men who would kill innocents for you?"

Andrew could not hold Savakis's gaze.

"There was another—" Cox stuttered into the silence.

Before she could finish, Dillon regained his composure and pushed back in. "Look around you, Frank. Echelon is gone. It's every man for himself—every nation stands alone. And I'll be goddamned if the United States doesn't come out on top. You really give a shit where EMPYRE comes from—or do you want in on the fight?"

Frank studied the soft faces before him. Under their cold analysis, under their game play, the fear rippling through them was palpable.

In the Echelon century, the CIA, along with the other organizations represented at this table, had become mere societies populated by the scions of wealth—one step up from Skull and Bones or the Bohemian Club. With Echelon, the tangled web of human need always smoothed out, leaving the people before him to do a tad of spying and take long lunches.

That was the world Frank had barged into all those years ago. He had never submitted to the Company's country club sterility. His hands started dirty and stayed that way. Frank Savakis had left a trail of smudged fingerprints on everything he touched.

He gazed at the people before him. He should be horrified, he knew that. But all he felt was a cold vindication for a lifetime of hard decisions, of doing what had to be done. Finally, Frank could play by the rules he'd grown up with. That lure was too strong to ignore.

"Okay," Frank said, lowering the gun.

Around the room, the tension eased.

"That's good, Frank. That's very good—" Dillon began.

"Because we have a problem," Humphrey chirped.

"Our data rat is out of sorts," Andrew said.

"Peters."

"She's slipping, Mr. Savakis. Her analyses are growing erratic. We've run psych profiles and we're . . ." Cox hunted for the right word, ". . . concerned."

"You think she might do to you what she did to Echelon."

"We think she's borderline," Cox replied. "But, in the end, she's just an analyst."

"It's the other we're concerned about," Hansen said. "He's the wild card we need to deal with before we can ascertain Peters's continued viability."

"Continued viability," Frank parroted with a laugh. "Just cut to the chase. You want Ryan Laing."

"On a platter," Andrew Dillon said.

"Alive if possible," Cox interjected. "His AI could be very helpful to us."

"So set Phoenix after him," Frank said.

"Phoenix is a valuable asset we don't want involved in this," Dillon said, shaking his head. "Laing is very dangerous and, Frank, you are—"

"Expendable?" Frank shot in.

A long second passed before Dillon continued. "I was going to say that you are the best. But, yes, you're also expendable."

5

Consciousness returned grudgingly. The anesthesia's lingering effects weighed Sarah down. Her limbs were lead heavy. After long moments of concentration she found the will to crack her lids. But the darkness refused to submit. Black enveloped her—she couldn't break free. Her tongue stuck to the roof of her mouth, chalk dry. She tried to move an arm and found she couldn't. She tried the other—nothing.

A hot surge of adrenaline whipped her up to the brink of hysteria. The operation had gone wrong! Jud had fucked up the implant and severed her spinal cord. Endorphins pumped through Sarah in stabbing beats as claustrophobia settled in. She tried to scream, but couldn't open her mouth.

Was it minutes she spent in that panic? Hours? Hard to tell. Finally, her body began to tire. Tension eased and she forced herself to calm. She extended her consciousness, willing herself to acknowledge each piece of data available to her. She clenched and flexed. Her muscles worked. Unless this was some sort of phantom limb deal. She pushed that thought away.

A tickle in her nose pulled her out of the fear. She worked her nose around, realizing there was something hard running up both nostrils. She breathed deeply—pulling in cold, sterilized air. Breathing tubes! She wasn't paralyzed, but locked in the surgical foam. The realization swept over her in a gushing flood of relief.

She worked her arm against the foam, managing some movement. She stretched and scratched. After an eternity, her index finger poked free to the operating room's cool air. She then tried to move her torso and made some progress, but it would take hours to work free.

Where was Jud? Why had he abandoned her? She let her strained muscles relax, and took deep breaths. At the moment of complete relaxation, she felt it.

A neural tingle. Must be a glitch in her system—maybe from the drugs. Then it came again—flickering sensory input. Not from her own eyes or ears, but from others that rezzed cleaner. The hawkeye! Judson had installed the link successfully.

Sarah relaxed further, letting her consciousness abandon her physical being and refocus through this other. In a jarring vision snap, the operating room resolved before her—a translucent image hanging in the black of her own internal perception. She saw the room, and her own body encased in foam. Surgical instruments lay on a tray at her side, bloody.

Sound! At first scratchy and distant, then evolving to pure tone. The clarity startled her. It was Judson's voice. And it didn't sound good.

"Please!" he squealed in obvious terror. "I did what you asked. It's all installed. The trigger's operational. She's your fucking weapon now."

Sarah couldn't figure out how to shift the hawkeye's view. Judson stumbled into the frame, crashing backward into the tray of surgical instruments. The instruments flew everywhere, clattering to the floor. A scalpel sliced the finger Sarah had managed to work free of the foam. She barely felt it, lost in the hawkeye's feed. Judson sprawled out next to the body encased in foam.

My body encased in foam, Sarah reminded herself.

Jud's eyes teared. "No!" he yelped. "Please, you don't have to do this. I did everything you asked!"

Sarah watched the feed, unable to believe that the event was occurring right next to her. A man stepped into the frame. He moved with cold grace, looming over the fallen giant. Judson tried to skitter away, but the man raised his right foot and kicked him in the nose with practiced assurance. A sharp crack as the man's heel crushed Jud's nasal bone. Blood spurted, engulfing his lips and neck. Sarah watched his eyes dance with fear, then settle into dull shock.

The man stooped down. He wore a dark suit that blended with the color of the walls. His left hand reached out, touching Judson's cheek. The giant quivered. Sarah watched the man cock his right hand. She tried to scream a warning, but nothing came. The man's hand shot forward in a spear punch, crushing Jud's larynx with a hollow pop.

The giant choked out surprise, then terror, then nothing. His eyes glassed over. Sarah watched. She felt her own death looming in that slim figure now standing to look down on her. He pecked at the pad and the foam around her softened.

Through her fear, her pumping heart, her nausea, she scratched for a plan—for something that would save her. The gash in her finger stung—and her heart leaped. She wrenched her fingers loose and gripped the scalpel. A chill ran through her as the surgical foam drained away.

The man stood over her. Sarah kept her eyes closed. She continued to watch through the hawkeye, not sure what would happen when her vision meshed with the machine's.

Black suit. Medium height, medium build, a face so easily forgotten that she couldn't find a distinguishing feature to center on. She locked on the man's smile—cold and cruel.

He leaned over her, his breath hot on her face. "Sarah Peters," he said.

Her fear almost stalled her out. No! She wouldn't die here—not now. Not without a fight. She gripped the scalpel and, with the man's face almost on hers, she struck. The blade found the man's neck. Blood gushed.

Sarah opened her eyes to the bloodbath. After seeing through the hawkeye, her own vision felt like a pointillist painting. She coughed on the man's blood and tried to push him away. He caught the side of the operating table and pulled her down with him.

They crashed to the floor, Sarah's legs still locked in the foam. She lay crushed into him, face to face. Eyes wide with shock, he stared at her. Blood frothed from his mouth. Sarah tried to pull away and couldn't.

"Not necessary," the man gurgled. "Not to hurt . . . you."

"Who are you?!" she screamed, terrified and jacked on adrenaline.

The man's eyes rolled back. The blood geyser ebbed to a steady flow. He went pale white.

"Nobody. I'm nobody." With that he faded. Sarah lay on top of him, gasping for breath.

Zachary Taylor watched from a dark banquette as Sarah emerged from the clinic and pushed through the bar. She was holding up well. She didn't run—didn't panic. Instead, she walked slowly, not marking herself. Only the eyes gave her away. She slipped through the bar quickly so no one could get a real look. When she had gone, Taylor pulled a secure com-link from his pocket.

A voice crackled over the link, tone shifted from the encryptionware. "Phoenix."

"She's in play with your package on board," Taylor whispered. "Peters is now patient zero."

"Excellent. Cancel the supplier's contract."

"Done. Peters killed him." The dead man was a soldier—like Taylor. One day, Taylor's own life would be canceled with the same callous precision—but that was the nature of the game. No escape now.

"Did she learn anything?" the voice crackled.

"The man had no information to give."

"See to the rest."

Taylor clicked off. He rose and headed for the exit as he made another call.

"Language?" the voice on the link asked.

"English," Taylor responded.

"We cannot lock your signal. Please state the location and nature of your emergency."

"I'm at the clinic behind Harry's in the mall."

"Nature of the emergency?"

"Two men have just been killed." Taylor's voice rose on a wave of panic befitting one who had just seen his first murder—an event too far back in his past to be retrieved. "It's—it's terrible. You need to get someone over here! I saw her do it!"

"Who?"

"Some skin junkie. They worked her and she just flipped. Lost her mind and killed them. She came after me, but I got away."

"Do you know her?"

"No—well, a little. Oh God, it's terrible."

"Sir, please."

"Right. Don't know her name—but she's staying at the Burj al Arab."

"Please stay where you are, sir. Officers are approaching the scene."

"Yeah, okay. Right." Taylor killed transmission.

Within seconds, the bar erupted in a cacophony of incoming com-links, the patrons receiving a barrage of voice and data messages. Inside info had gone mass market in Dubai and no one wanted to be caught up in a murder investigation. Taylor slipped into the flood of patrons racing for the exit.

He was long gone when the investigators appeared.

6

Finding Ryan Laing had been a real bitch.

Frank had hunted men before, but he'd done it civilized—through cities and scrapers, down alleys and into dark places. Nothing like this shit. An hour here and even the memory of darkness vanished. Freezing light beat down. The glacier spread before him, a vast wasteland. In the distance, he could just make out the jagged black fangs of granite that Ryan Laing called home. Bat-shit crazy, all this outdoor crap, as far as Frank was concerned. His jungle lay far from here.

Even the trip had been a bitch. Going low profile made life tricky. Frank had wanted to drop into Antarctica gun-heavy. He'd been told in no uncertain terms that EMPYRE didn't operate like that. A mass op required the sharing of information, and that EMPYRE did not do.

While Frank understood, he hated the delay going solo necessitated. Laing gave him a bad feeling—like he was in for a serious brawl. Frank couldn't pin the extent of the rogue operator's tech, but if it was hard enough to take out Echelon, it was hard enough to be a real pain in the ass. A head-on fight would probably end badly.

So Savakis had gone undercover, blending into the odd crew of climbers milling around Santiago, Chile, conning and bribing their way to Antarctica. He didn't like them. They were a tight clique, totally shut-in. Beyond their obsession, they saw little. He felt their need, though, raw and strong. That distant stare, the longing. A junkie's stare. He watched their awkward haggling to get transportation.

Frank acted like the outsider that he was. The climbers didn't accept him. They wouldn't, he suspected, until they saw him on the rock. But they did let him tag along. Getting to the continent proved interesting.

With a couple climbers, he found a pilot willing to make the flight—for a fee. That the pilot and his plane were Southern Air Transport gave Frank a good laugh.

Southern Air Transport was the longest-running front in the Company's history. In the mid-twentieth, it was part of Air America, the CIA-controlled airline. At one time, Air America was the biggest airline in the world, shuttling supplies, running guns—whatever the CIA deemed necessary. Over the years, Air America had dwindled. Now the Agency hired out—contracting with private military firms for their combat needs.

Made deniability easier. Still, Southern Air Transport remained in operation. The flyboys were only too willing to dump a payload of climbers into the wasteland.

What did surprise Frank was the ancient plane they used. The whale lumbered onto the runway in Santiago and Frank thought they were fucking with him. No such luck.

Halfway into the fifteen-hour flight, they reached the point of no return. No matter what, they needed to land on the frozen continent to refuel.

The touchdown—wheels on blue ice—rattled Frank's fillings. The plane slipped down the makeshift runway and finally skidded to a halt. Frank couldn't have been happier to get out of that fucker.

And then Antarctica hit him like a ton of bricks.

White on blue, and blinding sun. Stark, sparkling clarity. No particles to fuzz the view. Vertigo hit Frank. He'd never imagined a place so . . . big. As the climbers packed their sleds for the ski into Queen Maud Land's peaks, Frank prepped his Sidewinder.

Named after the desert snakes of the Mojave, the Sidewinder was next-gen all-weather transportation. Frank had brought the best; there was no room for a fuck-up this far from civilization. The Sidewinder's seat and engine case sat atop a slender tread that ran perpendicular to the vehicle's forward motion. Getting comfortable in the saddle, Frank engaged the engine. As it hummed to life, the machine threw coils of its tread forward, moving over the ice in long, J-shaped strides. This distinctive, slithering lope offered increased traction. The Sidewinder's wide weight distribution also diminished Frank's chances of plummeting down a crevasse.

He accelerated toward the saw-tooth ridges in the distance, black spikes drilled into the white. As he gained speed, freezing wind lashed him.

Fuckin' deranged, he thought, *living in this wasteland.*

No wonder EMPYRE hadn't been able to find Laing. Who would believe the man who changed the world would hang here? Frank still wasn't sure he'd located the bastard, but his nose told him the track was good.

EMPYRE had run down all the hard leads and come up empty. So Frank went tangential. He caught his marks by their vices. Every man had one. As far as Frank was concerned, vice defined the human condition. Some fucked. Some slapped derm patches. Some liked to watch. Sarah Peters had mentioned that Laing was a rock climber. Not very juicy, but Frank figured that was a good place to start.

In the backwater atoll of hard-core mountaineers, Frank had found mention of a man with an elusive past who ticked off previously unclimbed mountains in a blistering succession.

Now, Frank just had to find the fucker and get off the ice in one piece.

DUBAI CITY, UNITED ARAB EMIRATES

Sarah couldn't hold it all in her head. It was too much, too fast. Her ordered existence had careened into a wall of violence and disintegrated. She knew only to run—to flee. But what had happened? Had she killed the man in the clinic? Even within the flighty pump of fear, guilt washed over her. She pushed it away. No time.

She couldn't return to the hotel. Too easy to track her there. No, she needed to hunker down somewhere quiet and hack her way out of this mess. She just needed time. Her body ached. It felt like Jud had implanted a cuckoo clock in her head.

Oh, God, Judson. Dead.

Sarah pushed through the mall, trying to hold her cool. She could handle this. Maybe she wasn't a field operative like Ryan, but she'd been in tougher spots than this. Just a mellow ride out of the city, a few hours in the flow and she'd work her way out. No problem.

Then life got a lot worse. Sarah usually ignored the pop-up holo ads that peppered public facilities. Everyone did. They were just part of the clutter in a world polluted with product placement. Get pegged and the ad tracker would throw up holo on holo trying to pull you into a store, buy a gadget, eat at Joe's, whatever. Usually, Sarah pushed through them, oblivious. But not today.

Today, she stopped short. The ad before her, an impossibly lithe woman cooing over a bottle of perfume, flickered out. When it snapped back in, Sarah stared at her own image. She spun around—every holo in the mall showed the same image. Her thousand faces floated in full three as the holos emitted the beep-beep-beep of an emergency override.

A voice rose up through the holo's mouth—her mouth. "This is an emergency cut-in. Have you seen me? I am wanted in connection with a police matter. If you spot me, do not attempt to detain. Please contact the authorities immediately."

Sarah watched her own mouth speak the words, repeating them in language after language. It made her skin crawl. In the Emirates, crime was unheard of. For a cut-in to be authorized, the situation had to be dire. Sarah drew her head down, sneaking furtive peeks at those around her. Mistake. Hands pulled com-links from pockets.

She broke into a run. Another mistake. Three security men flashed in, skittering around the Chanel gallery. Fast-response shock troops. The UAE maintained absolute safety with a hard-core no-tolerance policy. Any lawbreaking and the shock troops came in. Run and they shot to kill. Breathe wrong and they shot to kill.

Equipped with mechanized exoskeletons, their blocky armor didn't slow them. Instead, the troops saw Sarah and kicked into high, loping gaits. Impossibly high, the exoskeletons augmenting their strides. They rocketed down the mall's corridor, gaining on Sarah.

She pushed harder, knowing it was hopeless. But fear kept her moving. Fright sparked flight. She whipped around the corner, only to see another team coming at her. Sarah ducked left, timing the move perfectly. The troops behind her crashed into those oncoming. The resulting mangle left the men scrambling and gave Sarah a crucial lead.

She sprinted hard, whipping into a long, narrow hallway. The high-rez sign over her advertised a water park.

"Shit!" She cursed herself, pulling up short. But there was nowhere to go. A trooper sprinted down the corridor, closing fast. Sarah whirled and ran. She slipped through the entrance, the ticket taker yelling at her. Behind her, the trooper blasted through the barrier. Sarah saw her chance and took it. She whirled left, pushing her way to the waterslide.

The slide curved and twisted the full ten stories down to a massive pool. Sarah cut through the line of people, shoving up to the front. Any anger from the bathers around her dissipated on seeing the trooper. Everyone pulled back to let him pass.

Reaching the slide, Sarah dove in headfirst. Immediately, acceleration took hold. The trooper behind her dove in as well. Spinning wildly, Sarah could see that he was gaining. Fear pumped white hot.

The trooper pulled his Glock 60. He struggled for aim, the bulky gun plinking off the slide's shell. He fired wild shots, the explosions sending shock waves through the tight space. Above her, the slide exploded, the bullet missing her by centimeters. She caught a jagged view of white-blue sky before rocketing past. While her tat might block a bullet's puncture, the force of its impact could well be enough to kill her. A direct hit would certainly end any chance of escape.

The trooper stopped firing wild. Instead, he concentrated on steadying himself. He slowed his spin, managing to get his feet facing down. He steadied his gun between his legs and waited for a clean shot.

Sarah lengthened into a dive position, trying to eke out every extra bit of speed. Lying with her back to the floor and facing backward, she could see the trooper nearing, his gun leveling. Through the flashing rush of speed, she thought she could make out his finger tensing around the trigger.

The next moments meshed into a single stomach-flipping wrack. Just as the gun discharged, the bottom fell from Sarah's world. The slide had shifted to near vertical. Sarah plunged—speed warping her vision—the bullet flying high.

The trooper followed her down. The acceleration caught him off guard as well—which saved Sarah's life. He lost the gun in his struggle to find center. Three stories—fast fall. And the trooper gained, his hard skin armor offering little friction.

The trooper crashed into her. They melded into a tangle of arms and legs, one struggling for purchase, the other for escape. Speed allowed neither.

And then it was over. The slide spat them out several meters over the pool. Locked together, they crashed down, Sarah taking a good bit of the impact on her side. Water ate their speed even as the two continued to struggle—and sink.

The trooper's weight dragged him down. He pulled Sarah with him. She fought against him in the white froth. The trooper managed to pull a blade from his thigh holster. He slashed Sarah's throat, the cut drawing a gush of blood. Sarah's vision clouded. The pain shocked her into gulping a mouthful of water. She threw a hand over the cut, probing wildly. The body tat had held, the knife only puncturing the epidermis. Desperate, she squirmed to get free, but couldn't break from the trooper's grasp.

Unable to swim with the weight of his suit, the trooper took Sarah down. Her body arched and jerked in a spasmodic need for air. The trooper hit bottom. Getting his feet under him, he pushed up with all the force his exoskeleton-jacked legs would offer.

The rebound almost snapped Sarah's neck. Even the trooper had misjudged the force of his push. He catapulted out of the water with Sarah wrapped in his arms. High in the air, Sarah just caught the screams of the bathers surrounding them. Then they fell. The whirling spiral ripped Sarah from the trooper's grasp. The two crashed back into the water, but this time, she was free.

She watched with dazed wonder as the trooper sank. He sprang off the bottom again, gunning for Sarah. She thrashed and the trooper missed a clean grab. Instead, his shoulder plate hit her in a sidelong impact that ripped any remaining air from her lungs. The trooper continued his arc. He sailed into the air and out of the massive pool, landing in a heap amid sunbathing tourists.

The blow stunned Sarah into cold shock. She sank, even as the flow of blood from her throat eased. Darkness edged in, reality dimming around her. *No!* This wasn't how she'd go. Not her—not without a fight. Every fiber of her being railed against the darkness reaching out for her. Maybe it was the internal thrust of energy, maybe just the implant finishing its post-op reboot, but she found herself able to flow-jump.

She had no address, no lock point—only one place she knew—one place the flow's tide would take her. The one place she had promised never to return to. Ryan's flow-link and the blue water enveloping her meshed. She thrashed through both and screamed into the void.

—*Ryan!*

QUEEN MAUD LAND, ANTARCTICA

The razor line of blue sky extended across the horizon, cut only by the jagged fangs of granite before him. Ryan Laing sat on a jutting pinnacle of rock, suspended out over the overhanging face he'd just climbed. Above him, the summit ridge loomed. Shaped by ravenous winds, dry snow had formed into impossible fins, wild flights of fancy made real.

Laing gazed out, lost in the view. He'd lived vertical for days, unwilling to slip back into the world below. One more night on the rock, then he'd resupply.

Lost in this world, his dreams found weight, imagination augmenting reality. Ancient Norse myths cycled through his fantasies. He dreamed, eyes open, of Fenris, the wolf that would usher in the end of the world. Laing sat on the wolf god's fang, its flank sealed under the ice. With the slip of its chain, the wolf's mouth would snap shut and it would rise—drawing the world to the end times. To Ragnarok.

A speck of movement pulled Ryan from his dream. Below him, in the valley of white. People coming. He looked away. This was better—living cool and free. Living liminal.

Then, the iced peace within him splintered. Laing's mind exploded—a white-hot flash that sent him reeling. He tried to comprehend the pure, raw magnitude of the incursion. He tried to push it away. The drones within him bristled and stilled, bristled and stilled. A single word rose and crashed through him.

—*Ryan!*

As quickly as it came, the transmission degraded to white static. Laing slumped to his side, gasping. The scene around him regained resolution.

—*Sarah?*

No reply.

It was her. Had to be, but something was wrong with her tone—there was less hate in it, and more fear. He slipped into the flow and tried to reengage the link, but it fizzled—as if signal jammed. Worry caught him up, and maybe guilt. As if he didn't have enough already. Responsibility for Sarah's slide into body mod weighed heavily on Ryan. Maybe she would have found another means to turtle out the world. But she had chosen to follow his path.

He probed the link further, but it was stone dead.

—*Fuck you, Sarah.*

He knew she wasn't receiving, but the anger gripped him. He was done with the guilt, the responsibility. Done with her. So he was a coward. So what? He'd earned the right. If she wanted to sever their link permanently, fine with him.

—*Fuck you*, he thought into the void.

DUBAI CITY, UNITED ARAB EMIRATES

Taylor watched Sarah's flight from a distance. He saw her plummet into the pool, struggle with the trooper and break free. Determined woman. His analysis of her held true.

The voice on his link cut into the scene. "She attempted to link with our target. The jamming bug held."

Taylor smiled. "She's on her own."

The voice went rich with pleasure, then slid back to monotone. "As is Laing, wherever he is. Don't let Peters drown. She's only good to us on the run."

"I have the situation in hand," he whispered back.

Taylor felt tension flooding the link. His own life rested in the balance. If Sarah died here, his life was that much ash in the wind. Taylor savored the sensation—life or death on a roll of the dice.

He gazed down into the pool and waited.

Sarah blazed white hot in the flow-link, craving the connection. And she had felt it, felt him. A far-off comfort. Then nothing. Had Ryan cut the link somehow? Had the augment bugged it? She pushed hard and regained the signal for an instant. She caught a single transmission,

—*Fuck you, Sarah.*

The link faded, then died. She wanted to scream, to cry. Why had she thought Ryan would help her? Or even care? She didn't live in that kind of world. Not anymore.

She sank to the pool's bottom, its smooth contour cupping her body. She wanted only to inhale. Then something flicked across her face, tingling soft. Her perception spiraled down and yet the sensation remained. Far off, the sensation clicked. It was a stream of bubbles. Air bubbles!

Energy surged within her. Groping, vision dwindling, she found one of the small holes from which the bubbles escaped. She exhaled dead air and lip-locked a hole. Air—oxygen! Her lungs burned with it. She exhaled before the added buoyancy could pull her away and took another drag.

Focus ratcheting back, she saw that she lay on a blanket of air holes. The bubbles rising around her broke the water's surface tension, easing the waterslide's landing.

She relished the moment, living breath to breath, knowing her reprieve would be short-lived.

Above her, Sarah caught the blurred thrash of feet and arms—swimmers being ushered out. She had one shot. She grabbed another gulp of air and took it.

In a flurry she pulled free of her clothes and swam with everything in her. From the slice in her side, she unholstered the hawkeye. It came free with a fleshy release. She prayed it would work. Sure enough, it unfolded and pushed through the water at her side.

She needed to blend—to meld with the mob leaving the pool. Her underwear would pass for a bathing suit, but she needed more. The implant throbbed, her mind already pushed to fracture by the hawkeye's extra stim. No choice. She hoped Judson had installed the full package.

Sarah surfaced among the throng. She swam with them. As she did, she initiated the body mesh. The neural implant opened pathways in her mind, linking her to the tat. Sarah stared at the slick flesh of the man next to her. She wrapped her mind around the color, letting it flush through her. She could only hope it worked. Judging from the man's reaction, it did. His eyes flashed wide. Then they reached the pool's edge and were separated.

Sarah pulled herself out, struggling. The enhanced arm of a trooper grabbed her. Sarah knew it was over. But the trooper looked her right in the eye and pushed her away, retuning his attention to the pool. Her transformation had worked, the shift in skin pigmentation enough to confuse her pursuers—for now. Sarah stumbled back, meshing into the jumble of terrified bathers.

She moved with the confusion. For the first time, she took in her surroundings. Above her loomed the slide in which she had descended. The pool area was shielded from the Arabian heat by a thin transparent film, pressurized to puff into the open space. Lounges were sprinkled around the meandering pool. Cabanas ringed the structure.

Sarah slipped into a yellow tented cabana. The maxed crush outside gave way to the interior's sumptuous luxury. A thick, white sheeted bed pocked with pillows nearly filled the space. The imprint of bodies still held on the bed's temperfoam. The occupants had been pulled from their tryst by the action outside.

Clothes lay splashed across the room, ripped off in the heat of passion. Sarah found a stretch form corset, soft silk underwear, long leather boots. She grabbed the boots and stuffed her feet into them, lacing them up to her thighs. Then she found it—the conservative dress that had cloaked the woman. She grabbed it and jumped to the mirror. Only then did she get a real look at the person she had become.

Standing before her was a woman in thigh-high boots and white underwear. But instead of the pallor that contrasted with her emerald green eyes, her flesh was deep black. The tat was working! Sarah stepped closer, examining her face. She augmented the pigment around her eyes and pulled some from her cheeks. While her underlying bone structure stayed constant, the alteration to her coloring shifted her appearance substantially. She gazed at a stranger's reflection.

Slipping into the long dress, she cinched it high on her neck, making sure it covered the gash. Blood still seeped from the wound. With a head scarf thrown over her hair, her own parents wouldn't recognize her.

Sarah stepped from the cabana and was immediately caught up in the mayhem. Hopefully, the disguise would hold. It had to.

Taylor tracked her departure. He exited before Sarah—only then realizing that her disguise would not get her through the cordon of troopers. Sarah's pursuers had pulled her bioprint from the hotel's records. They quietly scanned each person on exiting.

Sarah passed the trooper with quick assured steps—a rich woman who wouldn't be put out for anything. The trooper gazed transfixed at her stunning physique, just hinted at under the flow of her dress. Only after she passed did his eyes drop to the readout. He had a second to register. Then, the micron-thin shaft of Taylor's blade pierced the man's neck between the second and third vertebrae. The strike was an assassin's favorite. Instant death with almost no blood.

The trooper fell into Taylor's arms, eyes staring at him in wide shock, then fear, then nothing. Taylor calmly set the man down and walked away. In the confusion, the trooper wouldn't be noticed. At least not immediately. Taylor let a smile play across his lips. His work was done. His lifeline would continue to spool out for another day, another week.

I am Zachary Taylor, he thought, the mantra chilling his satisfaction. Any emotion pulled focus, and that he couldn't allow.

He faded into the city and tracked Sarah's flight.

7

Sarah stared into the froth churned up by the boat's prop, her emotions equally chaotic. Even as she skimmed across the Gulf, she knew her freedom neared an end. She settled back on the thick cushions and tried to chill. This wasn't happening. Couldn't be happening. The barge sliced through the water in a clean streak, its propulsion system releasing only a soft hum.

She let the movement settle her, trying to neutralize the terror of the past hours. Her flight from the mall had taken Sarah into the searing heat that crisped Dubai. Stepping onto the wide street, she had slowed her pace, trying not to mark herself.

She had walked, lost in fear and revolving plans of action. Hours slipped away. Finally, the resonating call to prayer wrested her from her inner turmoil. The call rose up in a lyric chant that grounded the city in its past.

Acting on impulse, Sarah followed her fellow pedestrians to the spindling minarets of the Jumeirah Mosque. What better place to find refuge? The mosque retained the dignified cadence of age—a reminder of another time.

A woman flanked Sarah. Dressed conservatively, she rushed for the mosque—one more commitment in her busy day.

As she walked, she spoke into a com-link with a crisp English accent. "Yes, yes, buy at twelve thousand euros. Buy and hold. I'll be back in a few minutes." She listened to the reply and broke into a smile. "Yes, Steve, Allah calls. I'm holding on to my immortal soul, and if that means losing a point or two to the market, it's a sacrifice I'm willing to make." The caller responded again, but the woman cut off the conversation. "Bye, Steve . . ."

She flipped the link, setting it to vibrate and clipping it to the outside of her purse. Sarah decided this was her chance. She let the streaming crowd push her into the woman, bumping her softly.

"Please forgive me," Sarah said in Urdu, and stumbled away before the woman could get a real look at her. The com-link now in Sarah's hand, she pulled out of the crowd and melted into the winding garden behind the mosque. There, she removed her veil and sidled up to a tour group of Westerners who were admiring the architecture.

She pulled the link and locked the site she never thought she'd need.

"Code," the voice said.

Sarah drew the link close and whispered a progression of prime numbers. Silence on the other end, then a series of clicks and scrambles as the encryption package came online.

"Sarah? Thank God! We've got you popping all over our stat reports here." Andrew Dillon's voice crackled.

"I'm in it here. Someone's after me—people died."

"We know."

"I'll bet you do. No one could have found me without your data. There's a leak on your end—and it's going to get me dead!"

A long silence over the link. "You may be right, Sarah. You're too careful to be tracked. With that in mind, I have to ask—"

"What?"

"Why are you calling?"

"Because I don't know what the hell I'm doing! And I don't have anyone else."

"Okay, Sarah. I'm bringing you in. EMPYRE has you covered. But it's going to cost."

Sarah's head slumped. She remembered to move her feet and stay with the tour group. "I know that. There's no alternative."

"Now, get to Tierra del Fuego and I'll bring you in."

"Tierra del . . . what the hell are you talking about? That's a world away."

"In Dubai, the world's smaller than you'd think."

With that, the link went dead, leaving Sarah to the tour guide's dull drone.

It hadn't taken her long to realize the meaning. High among Dubai's list of outrageous developments was a series of man-made islands built into the Gulf, each shaped like a country or continent. The rich and famous could buy up slices of the globe and barricade themselves in opulence.

Sarah had managed to get to The World's harbor without being spotted. She hopped the barge and now skimmed through canals between the islands, watching mega mansions slip by.

The freshly activated implant sent an itching nag through her mind. She tried to shut out the augmented stim stream, but found it difficult to hold focus. Now fully operational, Sarah was linked both to the flow and to her internal neural and cognitive enhancements.

Sarah itched to flow-jump, to run the data streams where she was most comfortable. There, she could manipulate reality to suit her whim. She could lift up reality's face and gaze at the logical, if tangled, web of coding underneath. But that was an itch she couldn't scratch; her pursuers might have piggybacked a flow-tracker onto her system upgrade.

Questions ripped through her, ones to which she wasn't sure she wanted answers. *How much tinkering have they done to me? How deep did they go?* The raw horror of violation threatened to overwhelm her.

To distract herself, she gazed down at her hand. Initializing the tat, she flexed that new muscle, shifting the color of her fingers to suit her mood.

Sarah looked away, stuffing her hand under her armpit. It was all too much. The barge wound down the coast of South America, finally rounding Cape Horn and pulling into Tierra del Fuego—and refuge.

CENTRAL INTELLIGENCE AGENCY, LANGLEY, VIRGINIA

Andrew Dillon burst into EMPYRE's situation room, heady with expectation. Meeting Sarah Peters, talking with her face to face, maybe he could unlock the mystery that was Echelon. But even if that was not to be, holding a person of such capabilities was a huge boon. Despite her psychological instability, the woman's knack for sniffing out patterns of cause and effect was extraordinary. In fact, now that she was here and under his thumb, her vulnerability would itself become an asset. Dillon would use it to draw her into EMPYRE's fold. And once Savakis took Laing out of the picture, Sarah would be truly alone and even more easily manipulated.

He entered the conference room to see the rest of EMPYRE already seated. He preferred to arrive last. Sarah sat by herself at one end of the table, hunched and small. The fiery will that had kept her from them in the past was gone. She looked hollowed, the fight in her slumbering under a heavy blanket of fear and isolation.

She gazed up at him and he was immediately struck by her eyes. A mesmerizing blue-green. They set off a flow of line and form that made it hard not to stare. Her beauty was striking.

"Sarah, we're so glad you're safe."

Sara glared back at him. "Not sure if I should thank you or blame you for all this."

"Let me assure you, everyone in this room has your best interests at heart."

Sarah nodded and gazed at her fellow occupants. "I assumed EMPYRE was U.S.-based. Just didn't think it would be this prestigious."

Sam Hansen chuckled at that. "We all appreciate your amazing contributions."

"And now that you have me in the flesh, I'm sure you'll be thrilled to let me go."

Silence in the room.

Sarah nodded, turning back to Andrew. "So, the attack, everything, was a mechanism for getting me under your thumb?"

Dillon held her gaze. There was still fight left in her. He pushed back in his chair and shook his head. "Sarah, I won't lie to you. We considered it. While we didn't know your exact whereabouts, we could have hacked it out."

"But," Barbara Cox cut in, "there was a good chance you would have caught the trace and disappeared."

Sarah stayed on Dillon. He felt her boring into him.

"The truth, Sarah, is that we couldn't risk losing you—even to ensure your—" Andrew hunted for the right word, "—cooperation."

Sarah continued to hold his gaze. Finally, she nodded and looked away. Andrew let himself exhale. Now she was his—theirs. He foresaw hours of conversation, the trickle of information flowing between them slowly building to a torrent that would change everything.

"So, I'm free to go—once you sort out this mess?" Sarah asked.

"No. We'd like you to be our guest. We've used your information, Sarah. I think we've used it well. But we were never able to give you the full parameters of our strategy."

"Nor our capabilities to so implement," General Stanton interjected.

"But now, thanks to the vicissitudes of fate, you have me here and can do with me what you will."

"Consider yourself an honored guest, Sarah. While your physical freedom may be restricted, the thing you love most—your true world—will be yours to roam," Hansen said.

"You see, we want you to stay of your own volition," Dillon said. "We want you to help us. We'll give you the big picture and make you a true member of EMPYRE."

Dillon watched Sarah's expression shift. He saw struggle in those perfect green eyes. He saw the fire. Then they went cold blank.

Confusion filled Andrew. He had seen that look before—on the man upon whose shoulders EMPYRE was built. A man he had manipulated for years. They were the fish-dull eyes of a psychopath. Dillon had played such men throughout his career. All it took was finding that fulcrum and shoving. But that wasn't Sarah. She didn't fit the profile.

Andrew watched Sarah's green eyes dull out. He sensed danger, adrenaline flooding him. But by then it was too late.

Sarah Peters exhaled and life as Andrew Dillon knew it was over. Alarms pierced the silence.

Inside Sarah, something kinked. Her thoughts, her perception—all snapped shut, screen dark. Reality melted into a pool of impressions. The internal processes of her body slushed around her, foreign and out of control. Horror filled what scraps of consciousness she retained.

"What the hell is that?!" Barbara shrieked over the needle-sharp alarm.

Andrew flipped his handheld and read the alarm. "Bioagent," he said in dull confusion. Then, looking up at Sarah, comprehension hardened his gaze. "Oh my God. No, no, *no!*" The first was confusion, the second horror, the third pure rage.

As Sarah watched, the skin on Dillon's forearms went papery, then bubbled red. He coughed blue-black blood.

Through wheezing hacks, Stanton forced out a single word: "How?"

Dillon held on Sarah, his skin pocking into a ghoulish mask. "You? Why . . ."

Shock and horror warred within Sarah. She watched the people around her fall to wracking pain. Words slipped from her mouth, her voice a desiccated husk. "It's not me."

But what else could it be? She waited for the coughing to reach her, almost longed for the sickness to set in. But she felt fine.

Dillon's eyes bulged, then bled, spasmodic hemorrhaging throwing him back in his chair. The others shared Sarah's horror—until they too succumbed. Gurgling, wrenched cries gave their transformation a sound track. Sarah stood stock-still, unable to grasp the death show playing out before her.

She locked on Sam Hansen. He alone didn't scream. Instead fury flooded him, his suffering masked by rage. He held position, muscles locked tight. In a spasmodic jab, Hansen freed a needle gun from his jacket. The mere touch of the fabric shredded his hand, flesh peeled from muscle in black sheets. Sarah could not move—could only watch in horrified fascination. Even as his flesh liquefied, Hansen gripped the gun. He sighted, eyes filled with blood—a cataract of red. He fired.

Sarah couldn't pull herself from the red eyes. Needles whizzed past. She heard them bore into the wall behind her. With a final flicker of perception, Hansen saw he had failed. Then, his head and neck went into convulsive spasms. The convulsions shot through the rest of his body, torquing him into a rigid arch. The pain arcing through him burst out in a primal scream. But on expelling the air, he sputtered, unable to draw breath. Asphyxiation set in.

Hansen gulped and jerked, eyes wide. In a final act, he pushed the gun under his chin. The wracked spasm in his cheeks eased—relief was near. He fired. Needle pierced skull and ended his torment. His head blew forward, hitting the desk with a mushy crack.

Sarah couldn't hold time. It surged past her in waves. She stumbled to her feet, unsure of her next move—of anything. How could life continue after such carnage? Had she caused it? She checked her hands, then ripped her sleeves up to reveal—nothing. No pustules, no lesions. She was fine—totally fine. Her lungs still felt pulpy, but that was it.

She forced herself to look around the room. Everyone had followed Hansen's symptoms, though at varying rates. The process had taken longer in some than others. Coughing, bleeding, then a pause before the convulsions set in. Cox's back had snapped under the pressure of her spasms. Finally, each had gone still. Dead still. Eyes wide open. Body rigid.

Through her terror, Sarah's pattern recog wouldn't shut off. Something was off pattern—a single fact in this death play that didn't fit.

The same symptoms for everyone—except Dillon!

Dillon had not gone into convulsions. With shuffling wariness, she neared the grotesque form that had been Andrew Dillon. Sarah's urge to run was almost overwhelming, but she needed to know. She stooped over him, reaching out instinctively to place a hand on his cheek, but not daring to touch him. Fear battled pity for dominance. She inched closer. The smell of death overwhelmed her.

As she neared his face, willing herself to touch him, Andrew's eyes flew open. He jerked away from her, sprawling onto the floor. Sarah bolted back—shock scared. On the floor, Dillon drew air in crackling rasps.

He had fallen to his side, facing away from Sarah with his head crushed into the carpeting. The idea of touching him revolted her. But she couldn't leave him like this.

"Andrew . . ." she whispered. "Please. I didn't know." The words sounded hollow and ridiculous as she extended a shivering hand, gripped his shoulder and pulled.

Dillon's bulk rolled heavily, his ravaged face flopping over to meet her gaze. Through the blood and gore, she could barely recognize him. She saw his hate, though, glossy and clear.

It was only then that she noticed the gun he had pulled from his jacket. The mere act of hefting it sent him into a coughing fit. Blood erupted from his lips and trickled down his cheek.

His eyes didn't waver. He pointed the muzzle at Sarah's chest. No way he could miss. Sarah froze, kneeling over the dying man, the gun between them. Whether or not her tat trapped the bullet, the force of impact would cause massive trauma.

"Please, Andrew . . ." She tried to show in her eyes what she couldn't say.

Dillon's only response was a clenching of the jaw, a steadying of the gun.

"Traitor," he gurgled.

No doubt now. He would fire. He would kill her. She held still, staring down at him. The hammer rocked back, nearing its apex. A dull submission filled her. She almost longed for the bullet.

The shot echoed through the room, filling Sarah's consciousness.

The tension in her arm brought her back to reality. She refocused to see her hand, grasping Dillon's wrist, wrenching his gun arm down and away from her. She followed the line of the barrel to Dillon's bloody pant leg. He continued to stare at her, pain clouding his eyes.

Sarah scuttled back, shocked at what she had done, at what she was willing to do to stay alive. She pulled up to her feet, wrenching herself from the death around her. Time whipped and slowed as she backed away and staggered through the halls.

Removed and distant, her feet pounded over the dusty carpeting, up through the old building and into the wide hall that centered the Original Headquarters Building.

The hall was thick with people. Life! She breathed a sigh of relief—having suspected that the plague had hit and she'd be the only one standing. She approached a security guard, grabbing his shoulder. He turned to her.

"I need help," she managed.

"Hey, where's your badge?"

He took her arm, suddenly suspicious. Those passing by gave them a wide berth.

"I . . . I don't know. People are dead. Please!"

"Ma'am, stay right where . . ." His words were lost to the piercing wail of the Agency's alarm system. The rest of his breath came out in a grating cry. Then it began—the transformation—the black death. Sarah pulled back, scanning wildly. Through the hall, people fell, succumbing.

She was doing this! Somehow spreading this plague while she remained untouched. The enormity of it spread over her.

She stumbled over a corpse and scrambled free of the gore, slipping in the blood. Finally, she found her feet and sprinted—hard—with everything in her. Behind her, a trail of death ran all the way down to EMPYRE itself.

PART 2

PART 2

8

"Fucking bitch," Frank mumbled through clenched teeth. The words expanded into the air, then dropped in a cloud of condensation.

Bristling fury rose off Savakis as he gazed up the vast wall of granite. In the dull glow of Antarctic night, he could just make out the man moving up the rock, a thousand meters overhead. Frank stamped his feet and watched, letting his anger boil through the insistent chill.

He had his issues with Andrew Dillon and the rest of the EMPYRE. But, at the end of the day, those men and women were his men and women—his team. No one got away with this shit—no one.

He kicked free of his brooding and looked back into the link in his hand. On it, images of the carnage at the CIA whirred past. Frank fixed on a grainy feed of Dillon, face wracked and sallow. Somehow, he had managed to cling to life, but his prospects were bleak. The med-techs didn't expect him to regain consciousness.

Poor fucker, Frank thought. He forced himself to study each and every detail coming through the feed, sharpening his anger to a razor's edge.

Frank scrolled through the rest of the transmission. The woman had left a wake of death in her path. Everyone involved with EMPYRE—dead or dying. A string of deaths rising up out of the CIA's guts and into the light. She had walked right out the front gate, thwarting the CIA's countermeasures by the sheer audacity of her act.

Then, at the gates, the slaughter stopped. Once outside the Company's grounds, her trail had gone cold. While the true facts of the massacre were being withheld from the public, Peters was now the focus of the largest clandestine manhunt in U.S. history. So far, she had eluded capture.

The full weight of the attack beat down on Savakis as he terminated the link. EMPYRE was his now. With Dillon pounding on death's door, Frank was the only person who knew what all those VIPs had been doing in the CIA's basement.

Peters's attack simplified Frank's plans. No longer was there nagging doubt as to EMPYRE's means. EMPYRE was dead. Peters had killed it.

Eye for a fuckin' eye, Frank thought.

Retribution was his to reap, and he savored the raw clarity of purpose. Ryan Laing seemed like a good enough place to start. Frank looked up at the man—letting his anger draw him to action. He could dispense with all this covert shit and just go.

Revenge made life simple.

Sharp angles. Clean lines. The hard glare of black, blue, and white. Antarctica's spartan geometry soothed Laing. He dry-tooled over the granite. He eased out into the void, placing the single fang of his left crampon on a knob. He twisted on it, slowly shifting his weight. The knob groaned, but held. Laing longed to disappear into the movement and grace, the adrenaline and awe.

But each time he neared a state of oblivion, tension jolted him from peace. Sarah's transmission haunted him. Hanging over the white, suspended on needle point, Sarah's image refused to fade.

Something of her had touched him and no amount of hate would shake it. He ground down, placing an axe into a slim vertical fissure and cranking it into a jam that would hold his weight. It was nothing to worry about. Sarah was fine. Fucked up, but fine.

Ryan let it go. He moved farther out onto the face, concentration calming him. Worry faded. He slipped into the movement with greedy expectation. But before he could lose himself in the climb, a sound pulled Laing from his peace.

A crackle of electricity, the sharp tang of an active coil field. A man moved up the wall below Ryan. The coil pack generated a huge charge that magnetized the granite, drawing the man up the rock in spurts. Laing watched the man approach, mesmerized. He had a stocky frame—not that of a climber. Out of place. His build, his tech, everything. A bursting drive to bolt flashed over Ryan; his exposure was total. He smothered the urge, settled into a comfortable position and waited.

The man rose in swooping, surreal surges. Pulling even with Ryan, he retracted his helmet's mirrored face plate. The scowling face of Frank Savakis emerged.

"Where is she?" Frank growled. He ripped a plastic needle gun from his jacket. Anything with metal in it would draw to the coil. Ryan felt his axes and crampons shimmy, pulled by the magnetic field.

"Where the fuck is she?" Frank asked again, wind ripping his words into a gentle hush.

Words croaked up from Laing's gut, his voice cracking from disuse. "You want something from me?"

Frank drew closer. "I want information."

Ryan gazed with dull confusion at the man's anger. It seemed from another place, another world—discordant with this reality.

"I've left it," Ryan said. "I'm out of the game."

"You may be hanging out here with the crazies, but you're still in play, Mr. Ryan fuckin' Laing, destroyer of Echelon."

Shock flooded Laing, and his concentration wavered. His left axe jittered with the magnetic pull. It popped free from the crack and skittered over the rock. The leash kept it from falling down the face, but the shift in balance threatened to pull Ryan off the cliff.

"Okay," Frank said. "Now I got your attention. I know you. I know your past. I even know the sob story that brought you here to this," Frank waved his hand holding the weapon, "this stupid fuckin' death wish."

Ryan tried to calm himself. "Just leave me be."

"Sorry."

The two stared at each other over the void.

"I was tasked with retrieving your AI. And I was kinda looking forward to cutting it out of ya," Frank said.

Ryan shook his head. The man knew everything. He pushed for a path forward, deciding on honesty as a first course of action. "The drones in me are coded to my DNA. They'll be useless to you. I'll give you a sample."

"Oh, you'll give me more than that. In the time it took me to get here, plans changed."

"I'm telling you—"

Frank cut Ryan off. "Sarah Peters changed 'em."

A blast of chilled fury shot through Ryan. His eyes hardened. "Sarah tasked you with finding me?"

Now it was Frank's turn to chuckle. "Not quite. Sarah Peters worked for my associates. Two days ago, she offed 'em—all of 'em—plus a good fifty others."

Ryan slumped into the wall, a chill seeping through his protective layers and burrowing into his chest.

"No." It was all he could manage.

"So, plans have changed. Sarah Peters is a dead woman. Anything she loved or cared about—dead. She plays tough. I'm tougher."

"Sarah?" Ryan stammered, unable to wrap his mind around the man's words.

Frank nodded back. "Now, you and me gonna take a nice slow descent and have a little chat about your girlfriend's whereabouts."

Ryan's right foot popped free. Even as he scrambled, his world blurred to murky confusion.

Not Sarah. Not possible.

Standing on the wall's face, Ryan let the drones work, accessing the flow, boring into it. Firewalls did little to slow him. Within the CIA's system, he linked the man before him to a dossier.

"You're CIA," Ryan said.

Frank nodded. "That's good tech you got. Now, hold on tight. Got a little show planned for you."

Before Ryan could react, the CIA's system had sucked him deep into its core. He was helpless against the surge, like a swimmer caught in a riptide.

Ryan had time to register that this man had expected Ryan's incursion—planned for it even. That horrifying fact was forgotten as the system dumped him over a vid file. It blossomed around him and Laing watched Sarah walk down the hall with death following.

The drones within him latched on to Sarah's familiar pattern and searched. Ryan's mind flooded with the updates, analyses, and alerts—the chatter of her manhunt. Image on image. The woman he loved—had loved—hunted. A murderer.

No! He raged against it. *Oh God, no.*

But there it was. And he had let this happen. Sarah had called out for him and he had pushed her away.

The carefully crafted armor Laing had erected now liquefied under the barrage of images. The emotions he'd tried so hard to block came flooding back and the sharp geometry of his created world cracked with the weight. He couldn't hold it—couldn't process it all.

The images overwhelmed him.

Frank watched Laing crumble and part of him thrilled at the sight. But something about Ryan's reaction felt wrong. The calculating part of him, the part that allowed him to see what others couldn't, that part told him that Laing was as shocked by Sarah's act as anyone.

"You didn't know," Frank said, the hard edge of his fury dulled.

Ryan's eyes . . . They swam in confusion and something Frank didn't think a man like this would be capable of—fear. Pure, raw fear.

Laing's arms jittered. He sensed the loss of balance too late. His right axe came free of the crack with a grating screech. Ryan flailed, trying to right himself. In that moment between holding and falling, he caught Frank's eyes, which had filled with shock.

Then life became acceleration and blur.

Even as he gained speed, Laing raged against the inevitable. Sarah had needed him. She had no one else. And he had pushed her away—again.

Failed her—again. Axes dangling from their leashes, Ryan scraped his hands over the granite. His gloves sheared away—his fingers grinding down to broken, bloody nubs in an instant. Gray drones coated the rock. He didn't slow.

Through the acceleration and pain, Ryan caught movement. The man above him—the killer—descended in giant loping arcs. He flicker-fired the coil field, positioning himself straight down. Finally, he shut the field down completely and drew into a tight dive. He threw the gun into the wind. That move cracked through Ryan's shock. The man was coming for him. Trying to save him.

Laing arched out, opening to the fall. He positioned himself facing up so he could track the man above him. The friction of his body slapping against the cold air slowed Ryan, even as the man above accelerated. Ryan cringed into the approaching crunch, knowing they neared the end. He knew it in the gaping rush of his fall. He knew it in the man's eyes.

No! Can't let this happen. No!

He saw the man slap at his coil field—giving up. But Ryan wouldn't yield. He threw his right arm toward the slowing figure. A spindling vine of drones arced from his mangled hand and shot toward the man. The man's eyes bulged wide.

The vine spindled up and wrapped the man's torso. Ryan willed contraction, and the drones pulled Laing into Frank's chest. Ryan gripped hard, wrapping himself around Frank. The coil field sputtered, unable to hold the added weight.

Ryan and the man tumbled over each other. As Laing tipped over, he saw white ice approaching. Deceleration ripped at him, but it wouldn't be enough. At the last moment, he flipped himself over, armoring the man against impact. Any moment . . .

But instead of the bone crush he'd been expecting, Ryan felt only a slight impact, then dark acceleration.

Crevasse! His mind stumbled over the word, even as they punched through the snow bridge covering the deep fissure in the Antarctic ice shelf. Light faded to a sliver.

Then Laing got the deceleration slap he'd been expecting. His head slammed into ice and perception faded to zero.

Frank struggled out of Laing's grasp. His stomach settled to a dull ache, recovering from the adrenaline shock of the fall. He flexed his muscles, surprised to find himself in working order. A teary spike of pain on inhale informed him of a badly broken nose. He welcomed the sensation—any sensation. It beat the fuck out of the alternative.

Savakis took in his surroundings. They had come to rest on a snow ledge about twenty meters into a crevasse. The eerie silence of the ice fissure spooked Frank. He realized just how far he was from his element.

He flipped himself over to check on Laing. The bulky man lay on his back, arms splayed out. Frank watched in amazement as drones coated Ryan's hands in a protective gray. He sensed that fingers, fresh and pink, would soon emerge from the cocoon. The sight so captivated him that it took a moment to notice several other facts. The first being that Laing had an ice axe skewering him.

The second realization was more troubling. They were not alone.

9

A gut-wrenching tug dragged Laing back to consciousness. He cut through a bleary haze to see Frank sitting next to him, holding a gory ice axe in his gloved hand. Even as he rezzed in, Ryan sensed the drones putting him back together. The crevasse hung in cold shadow, not black, not quite twilight.

A spine tingle. Laing felt other eyes on him. He turned his head and stared into giant brown irises. Ratcheting back, he saw teeth, large and edged, lips bared. Death-gray skin stretched over a face that wasn't human. Laing skittered back, almost knocking Frank off their shared ledge.

"Hey! Hey, there. It's dead," Frank said.

Laing stared at Frank, trying to comprehend. Then he turned and looked again.

"It's a fuckin' seal," Frank went on. "Hope we fare better than he did."

With the word floating through his mind, the image before Ryan finally settled into a recognized form.

"Welcome back to the land of the living," Frank said, rubbing the axe along the ice wall to free it of gore, then implanting it in the ledge between them. "You're a hard man to kill."

"Harder than most," Laing croaked. He looked again at the seal.

"Must have fallen in like us," Frank said.

"We're a long way from the ocean."

"Okay, it's a mystery," Frank said in exasperation. "Call *National Geographic.* Just do it after you get me the fuck out of here."

Ryan reached out to touch the seal. His fingers ached, joints stiff and pulsing with growing pains. "It could be thousands of years old."

"Nah, it would rot."

Laing turned on Frank. "Nothing rots here. Stop moving here and you freeze true."

"Again, a good reason to get the fuck out."

Ryan paused for a long second, going over the events that had led him here. "You saved me," he said finally.

"Let's call it even. You took the brunt of the fall."

"I thought you wanted me dead."

"Laing, I'd like nothing better than to fry you up with a little seal blubber."

Ryan pushed down an urge to shove the man off the ledge. "But?" he asked.

"But I read people pretty good. Got a few years in the field. You didn't know about Sarah Peters. I surprised you right off the rock."

"She didn't do it," Laing said. It sounded stupid—even to him.

"Oh, come on. This ain't a place for bullshit. You know she did."

"There must be a reason."

"Laing, I don't give a fuck. I want her. And you're going to help."

Laing stretched, starting to feel better. "Not likely."

"Oh, you will. Right now, you and I have the same goal. Find Sarah Peters."

"I'm not going—"

"You'll go," Frank cut in.

Laing held silent, lost within his inner struggle.

Frank pushed the deal. "You'll go because you can't bear to see Sarah die. And she will die. With the Company on her ass, it's just a matter of time. Got to catch her before she goes viral again and takes out a city."

"If you find her, you'll kill her."

"Probably," Frank replied. "But you got some time to sway my resolve. Until then, we need each other."

Ryan turned to the seal's dead stare. What had led it to this dark place? And how different was he? Ryan's decay had only been more active. The animal was lost. Maybe he could be revived.

Maybe it was time.

Sarah. She needed him. He wouldn't abandon her. Not again. If she had flipped, and Ryan knew it was possible, he needed to get to her first.

He turned back to Frank. The drones had done their work. He reached out with pink fingers to shake Frank's gloved hand.

"Okay. But hurt Sarah and our relationship ends."

Frank smiled thin. "One way or another."

IO

Sarah ran. Her body ached, her mind reeled. She had killed them—all of them. The time after her escape from the CIA had been a blur of motion and shock. She ran. She hid. She moved without direction, hitching a string of unmanned long haulers that kept her far from human contact.

The last hauler dropped her in Alexandria, Virginia. Night ran blood dark over the Washington, D.C., suburb, a jumbled mesh of old world brick buildings and next-gen housing complexes battling for space.

Sarah passed through, trying not to disturb the night. She stumbled past restaurants and shops catering to the commuters who made Alexandria home. The plexi of a pizza place had been switched to passive entertainment for the lonely wanderers who had missed dinner.

The screen flipped to news. Sarah stared at an image of Sam Hansen. Words flashed as the screen flipped through the other faces of EMPYRE.

Tragedy at Sea.
Sam Hansen, Secretary of Homeland Security, along with Barbara Cox of the NSA, Richard Humphrey of the State Department and Lieutenant General Mike Stanton from the Defense Intelligence Agency have died en route to a summit with their European counterparts.

The image faded to a shot of wreckage spread over rough oceans.

Reports sketchy, but it appears that a mechanical glitch in the plane's pressurization system caused the crash.

Sarah knew she should keep moving but couldn't pull herself away. She waited for information on the CIA bioattack, letting the news do a full cycle. Nothing. The total lack of disclosure frightened her more than anything. If the CIA was lidding this thing, that meant Sarah could never see the light of day. There would be no due process for her.

"Oh, God." The words fell limp, trailing to a stunned whisper. She stood frozen, staring though news of the latest football scores to a place where this was all a bad dream.

The net closing in on her would be quiet and very deadly. Desperation engulfed her. She was heavy with it. Welling tears fuzzed her vision, so it took her a moment to realize that the news feed had vanished. Her own image now cut through the passive feed. She staggered back.

"Stop!" A low booming voice coming from the screen. "Sarah Peters, you are wanted for questioning. Do not move."

The voice echoed through the night. Sarah knew that a good amount of research had gone into massaging the tone and timbre of that voice to maximize its effect. She pushed through the desire to submit.

Stupid! she railed at herself. The shop had a tagger. Had she just passed by, it wouldn't have had time to collect her facial features, but she'd stopped and the tagger had plenty of time to run its scan. Her pursuers had piggybacked on the consumer identification interchange, catching the facial features that the tat could not hide.

Sarah fled, the booming voice suddenly squelched by the scream of high-powered coil bikes approaching. Her feet pounded, and Sarah's mind reeled. Maybe she should turn herself in—let them quarantine her. The thought of more death sickened her.

She wanted to stop. To scream. To end all this. One more block of freedom. Then she'd let them take her. She ran to bursting.

The retrieval team followed, sirens piercing the night. Sarah dug the hawkeye from its holster and hurled it into the air. Wings inflated and it soared. Coming online, Sarah saw herself and her pursuers in its flying gaze. She adapted to the new input—but not quickly enough.

Coming around the corner of Washington and King streets, she slammed into a young man getting into his car. She fell backward and scuttled away, terrified that she had infected another. But looking up at his face, she didn't see the blistering pustules. She saw only his hand, reaching down.

"Hey, there. Slow down, will ya. Here, let me help you up," he said.

Sarah took his hand. On her feet, she stared at him, shocked dumb. Finally, a silly glee filled her. The man was okay! She wasn't contagious. In that moment, she knew she would not turn herself in.

"You okay? Looks like you seen a ghost."

The man tried to pull his hand away. Sarah saw the hawkeye's view of the net closing around her and knew what she had to do. She stepped from the man, whipping his hand around and wrenching him to the ground. The man yelped in pain. Sarah pulled his finger around and let the car's scanner find his print. It hummed to life. She left the man whimpering, jumped in and squealed around the corner just as the coil bikes approached.

Sarah gave the retrieval team a moment to scan the car before stomping on the accelerator. The car lurched forward, whipping into the darkness. She used the oncoming traffic, throwing off a wake of squealing cars—obstacles for her pursuers to negotiate.

It would give her *just* enough time. She wrenched the car into a tight arc and slammed on the brakes.

"Input," she said.

"Go ahead," the car responded in a cool tech-tinny voice.

"Directions to Florida," Sarah said as she opened the car door.

"Plotted and ready. Door is ajar," the car replied.

"Ignore door. Engage auto-drive."

"Engaged. Have a pleasant drive."

The car clicked into action, moving forward, gaining speed. Sarah watched her pursuers through the hawkeye. Seconds before the bikes rounded the corner, she hurled herself from the car, managing to close the door with a twisting shove before she hit pavement. She tried to roll off the momentum, but succeeded only in scraping up her hands and back.

She stumbled into an alley as the coil bikes rounded and accelerated after the car. Her deception would work for minutes at the most before the car's 'ware was overridden.

Sarah spun, desperate. She longed to continue her flight. But something in her, the place unaffected by the disaster her life had become, ran cold calculations. Flight narrowed her decision matrix. She calmed her desire and worked out a plan.

The hawkeye soared high. Sarah moved with it, both guiding and following, running dual inputs. The unfinished tower before her would suit her purposes—for the moment.

A spindling double helix, the tower pushed up into the night sky, then frayed into carbon ridges at its apex, where work continued. Entering the construction zone wasn't difficult. Only cursory security protected the site, blocking the average looter or junkie. Sarah had more subtle means at her disposal. She used the hawkeye's augmented perception to stay clear of the motion sensors. Once found, the building's central node was a quick hack. She drew the hawkeye back to her and entered the woven scraper.

The building smelled new-car new. Spindling fibers of carbon made up the entire structure, giving it a black, organic creepiness. Super-long fibers ran the full height of the building, forming a helix-flexed skeleton. Its structural integrity was all tension—each piece of the building pulling on the next. That torquing hold filtered into Sarah's consciousness. She felt spring-loaded, ready to burst.

This being a full mechy build, only machines broke the carbon-muffled silence. Sarah entered the upward spiral that wrapped the building's interior. As she walked, heels clicking on hard carbon, she gazed up through the fiber mesh and into the vastness over her, watching the two behemoth robots work the build. A spider bot spun carbon threads at the scraper's peak, followed by a braider that wrapped those threads into the structural weave.

Sarah pulled herself from the robotic rhythm, hunting for a place to settle. She veered off the central spiral and pushed into a premolded office. The entire room, including the desk and shelving, was made out of the same weave as the building itself.

As the door slid shut, a desire to wither to nothing and disappear filled her. She refused the urge, revolted at her weakness.

I won't do it. I can't.

And yet she was under the desk in seconds, knees pulled to her chest, the scratching work of the bots her only company. She dropped her head onto her knees and let herself sink.

Dull indecision lulled Sarah into a torpor. The wake of carnage she had left behind haunted her—each face, starting with Andrew Dillon and meshing into a collage of pain and shock. So many eyes, blood-red, staring at her.

Sarah slammed her eyes shut—desperate to still the horror. She balled up tighter. Exhaustion pushed down on her, but she didn't dare sleep. The possibility that those faces would consume her dreams drove her into a waking trance. The mere thought of sleep drew bile.

So she stared into the carbon weaving, losing herself in the single braid that made the building. She had some time. Alexandria's very proximity to Langley offered a measure of security. Few would suspect that the terrorist who wreaked havoc within the Company's hallowed walls would hole up so close to the scene. They'd expect her to run—to panic.

They got the panic right.

The faces, the gore, meshed into a low pain, which then resolved into something else, something familiar. She felt the pull. That tug. The need to go back under the knife. It all hurt too much.

Once more. Just one more time, and this too will fade.

The mantra formed a rhythmic percussion in Sarah's mind.

One more session. Only one . . .

Yet even this couldn't stem the tide of images that flickered past and would not submit. Finally, she let them come, allowed them to consume her. The tears came with them. She cried into the building's silence and the anguish eased—if only slightly. As she relaxed, a realization struck her. She ran over the news feeds she had seen. And there it was. Or, more accurately, there it wasn't.

One member of EMPYRE hadn't been mentioned. That could only mean one thing: Andrew Dillon was still alive.

II

Reentry was a bitch.

Antarctica's razor-edged reality melted under the flickering static of civ life. Laing clung to the clarity he'd spent so long erecting, even as it crumbled around him. He was home; culture shock engulfed him.

Glancing at his travel companion, Ryan saw that even Frank looked shell-shocked by the pulsing rush of the East Coast Transit Corridor. Laing worked air through his lungs as Frank plunged into the traffic stream. The trip had been a blur. It almost felt like a magician's trick. He looked down at his hands, remembering the feel of cold granite and trying to resolve a world in which Antarctica and this frothing splash of speed-frenzied commuters could coexist.

Frank weaved through the traffic, nudging the line between aggressive and reckless. Laing white-knuckled the armrest and watched the people in their cars as they flashed by. Each had that resolute blur to his vision— cruise control all the way through. Opening himself up to the flow stream, Laing peeked in at their distractions.

Added to the visual cacophony that most saw, Ryan could make out the viscous data soup that poured over everything. With effort he could cut it away, but the pure mass of input was tough to handle.

When the drones had first come online, their interface with his own mind had been just that—an exchange between separate entities. When Echelon crashed and the drones lost their operating code, they dragged Ryan down into a well of digital gibberish. He had nearly lost himself in that black place. But, endlessly malleable, the swarming AI had shifted to operate within the parameters of his own genetic code. In that transformation, the duality melted. Man and machine became one. This synthesis contained parts of both entities, but was also something new, an amalgamation stronger than its parts. As Ryan adjusted, his consciousness continued to evolve.

Now, Laing breathed deeper as the car accelerated around a tripledecked cargo hauler. He blocked out Frank's driving and plunged into the flow. Hard reality shifted into digital representation. Around him, each car, each hauler, even the people in them and the buildings surrounding them melted and re-formed into the flow representation of the information each housed and broadcast.

Beyond flesh and bone, plaz and biocrete, the city was information: teeming, tumbling arcs of code, built and destroyed, digested and regurgitated. Ryan ran that net, a spider crawling the web underlying reality.

Buildings erupted in pulsing data bursts. Banks and brands, ads and promotions—everyone looking to draw in the flow rider. Ryan pulled up out of his geosynch and scanned the blogs for mention of Sarah. Nothing on the nodal points.

Most of the stories focused on the United States' market rebound. The hostilities in Asia had propped up the dollar and the Dow. The trade deficit with both China and India had dipped, as each gorged on America's greatest export—weaponry. The incident in Tibet had dragged India and China back into the military posturing that had consumed them for centuries. Something in the clean perfection of the assassination irked Laing. He let it go—didn't concern him.

He zoomed out, cascading through the flow, running sticky for data on Sarah. His web caught no trace of her. He tried again to hack out the corruption in her flow point and reach her directly, but it wouldn't go. He'd been cut off.

Pulling out, Ryan felt Frank's eyes on him.

"You been lost awhile. What are you doin' in there?" .

"Checking the flow. No pickup on Sarah."

Frank nodded and gazed back out at the road. "Figured that. The Company's still running quiet on the threat."

"Threat?"

"Yeah—threat. The fuck you think? Sarah Peters is loose and, however you wanna play it, she's got a pathogen in her that's super-nasty."

Ryan shook his head. "You don't know." He gazed out at the flashing scenery as Frank made his way into the Clinton Tunnel. The car went to full auto as they entered. Darkness was total; no need for lights when no one was driving. Ryan stared into the black. "She'll reach out. She will."

Frank snorted. "Anyone jacked enough to rip through Langley like it was cheesecake won't bob up in the flow for us to pick off." Catching Laing's glare, Frank quickly corrected himself. "Or retrieve, as the case may be."

"Well, she isn't in Manhattan. That I guarantee."

With surge barriers wrapping Manhattan like a condom and hard security control on the tunnels, the city would be a tricky place to enter for someone on the run.

"Limited egress," Ryan continued. "Coming here would back her into a corner. Not a move she'd make."

"We're not here for Sarah."

Ryan hated this—not being in control. The clean ice simplicity of his recent past melted away. Confusion, chaos, and the gritty glint it produced in him reemerged. He held Frank's eye as the tunnel flushed them into Manhattan.

"We're here for the one that got away," Frank said.

"Sorry—"

"Andrew Dillon."

"He's dead."

"Not that lucky," Frank replied. Ryan held his cold stare and Frank continued. "Dillon had some genetic modification done several days ago. He had been tagged for rheumatoid arthritis. Somehow, the fix to that autoimmune disorder fought off the pathogen, or at least slowed it down."

"You mean the pathogen Sarah carried—"

"Sarah delivered," Frank shot back.

Laing shook off his annoyance. "It was coded? Targeted to specific people?"

"We're not sure. Other than Dillon, everyone in EMPYRE is dead. And everyone she infected on leaving the building is dead. One hundred percent kill rate. Officially, Peters released anthrax . . ." Frank trailed into a silence that implied much more.

"And—as usual—the official line has little to do with the truth."

"As fucking usual," Frank agreed. "Whatever Peters is actually hosting is fast acting. When triggered, it strikes hard—anyone in her radius goes down. But it's also short-lived. The pathogen burns out quick."

"And somehow Dillon survived."

"Not in any way he's happy about."

A grinding spasm worked its way down the nape of Laing's neck and into the meat of his back. Frank hit Broadway and barged into traffic heading south. The move didn't help Laing's tension any. He shifted, trying to ease the kink. Around and above, scrapers misted into the muggy air. Claustrophobia settled on him in thick waves.

Sarah, what the fuck are you into?

12

Andrew Dillon drifted through a sea of carnal impulses, lost in a waking dream. Desire and gratification sloshed over him in a pulsing flux. In their grip, he could almost forget.

In life, there were distractions, pieces of the puzzle that refused to move. Not here. Here, fantasy became real. Here, he indulged.

A shot of pain rifled through him. He swallowed it down. That pain was from another place—a wracked body that was no longer his own. That wasn't here.

A distant memory rose to fill his reality. A trip to Maui National Park when he was a boy. The class had hopped out for a day of "nature." Dillon hated it. As the others milled around, eating their lunch, Dillon wandered off. He pushed deep into the jungle, trying for high ground—a place where he could find perspective.

But the thick green hemmed him in, flipped his senses. In minutes, he was lost. After an hour of wandering, fear overcame his embarrassment and he screamed for help. Nothing. He yelled himself blue, crying thick tears of shame. Then, just as he thought all was lost, he recognized a stream from the hike in. Dillon followed it through the dense foliage. He found the trail. Relief flooded him as he reentered camp but, for days after, he could not wash away the shame—the knowledge that he had been so helpless.

In memory, the trail led him back to camp. But here, in this nether world, he pushed shame away, turning from the memory.

The foliage closed in around him, ratcheting down to darkness. When the iris reopened, the green was gone, the trail replaced by a hallway crammed with books—a Babel that was his to explore.

Dillon floated down an aisle and pulled a book from the shelf. *The book.* Doing so opened a secret door, leading to yet another hall of books. He pulled another, opened another door, his access unfettered. Book on book, room on room, until at last he stood at the center of Babel itself, at the core.

Standing in that place, contentment filled him. The point of clean perspective. He knew this was all simulation—a world constructed by integrating his memories with software designed to calm him. All so that his body could heal. But even if it was fake, there was no reason not to indulge in the mirage. Here, all doors were open to him. There was nothing he could not know. Here, he could relax.

And then, reality tugged. Helplessness washed over him. He was back in the jungle. Lost.

Fantasy slow-faded. Andrew opened his eyes. Over him stood Frank Savakis.

Frank stared down at Dillon, trying not to let his revulsion show. Andrew lay flat, suspended millimeters over a mag bed. It made him appear weightless, ethereal. Dillon's eyes scratched open. Red ringed his dull brown irises. A rivulet of fluid drained from one eye, forming a piss yellow tear. It grew slowly, finally overcoming surface tension to drip down his pocked cheek.

"Fuck me." The words escaped Frank's lips before he could rein himself in. He almost regretted them.

The words grounded Dillon in reality. His papery lips shrank to a thin line frown—a face set to weather the gale force of his pain.

Andrew resolved Frank's looming form, his disgust evident. Dillon bridled under the scrutiny. This man was a cog in *his* machine. More than most, Frank had needed to be convinced of his place—forced into Dillon's perspective. Now, that carefully created reality had crumbled. He saw it in Frank's cold pity.

Andrew pulled himself up. The magnetized platform beneath him shifted with his movement, taking its shape from his own. It curled under him as he drew into a seated position.

Once settled, Dillon engaged the gyroscopic balancing system. The wheels under the bed arched up and went to vertical. It raised Andrew to roughly the height of a man—an unbroken, whole man. Dillon's mouth stayed set, his eyes boring into Frank's, daring him to say more.

Before the test of will resolved, Dillon noticed a man in the corner. His grimace broke.

"You found him," he croaked. His vocal cords vibrated under a viscous coating of phlegm, sinking his normally high-toned voice into a deep gurgle.

"Dillon, Ryan Laing." Frank stepped aside and motioned Laing forward.

Andrew leaned toward Ryan, the balance shift rolling him forward on the gyros. He closed in on Laing, who held still in the corner. Andrew's vision blurred in and out. With a herculean effort, he raised his hand.

Laing watched the gangrenous appendage come toward him with a combination of horror and fascination.

"Nice handiwork, wouldn't you say?" Dillon forced the words through cracked lips. "I'm starting to think someone doesn't like me."

Andrew's arm held firm. Ryan stepped in, the stink of dead flesh snuffing out the apartment's lavender-scented sterility.

Ryan's fingers curled around the hand. Dillon's pressure surprised him. He saw in the man's twisted grimace just how much effort the act required.

"Not worried about transmission?" Dillon asked, releasing Laing and sliding out of Ryan's space.

"I've got a hefty immune system."

"So I've heard."

A white swarm invaded the room to Ryan's left. He made out four faces within the sea of coveralls. One of the med-techs approached, slamming a vial into the mag bed. The fluid filtered through the bed, gapped the distance to Andrew's flesh and entered through the pussing fissures in his dermis.

"Sir! No flesh contact. Any contamination makes our job harder."

Andrew smiled stiffly, keeping his eyes on Laing. "You see what I have to deal with."

"Please," another med said, this one a pear-round woman with a shock of white hair.

"I know, I know," Dillon broke in. "It's for my own good. Have to maintain that genetic integrity." He looked himself over. "There might be a battle or two left in me—but the war is lost."

"Sir, our stats show marked improvement."

"We just need time to decode the retrovirus—"

"Okay—I get the picture. Point made. Laing—you'll have to restrain yourself from now on."

The glint in Dillon's eye disarmed Ryan. He cracked a smile.

"Come!" Dillon croaked. "We'll talk on the patio."

He shifted forward and the gyros fought to catch up. The meds chased after him in a flurry of worry. Ryan caught Frank's eye.

"He's a good man, Laing."

Laing nodded and followed the scent of slow rot.

80 South Street reminded New Yorkers that their city had a past. Designated a historical landmark, it stood under vaulting scrapers that couldn't quite manage to overwhelm it. Designed by Santiago Calatrava, its block and ladder design had become an intrinsic piece of the New York skyline—even if that skyline now dwarfed the building.

The building contained ten separate domiciles, each a massive plexi

cube cantilevered in an alternating pattern off a central support. Stabiliz-
ing spires ran up either side of the building. The building resembled a set
of blocks stacked by a child who didn't yet know that gravity negated such
fantasies. The tension of form captured a moment in architecture. It had
stood the test of time.

Andrew Dillon lived in the penthouse. His life had evolved in a smooth
progression to this pinnacle. He grew up an only child to Ellen and Oscar
Dillon. Andrew had moved effortlessly through the dance of schools and
societies that made up the bedrock of his parents' life. Each piece locked
into the last—a succession of clubs and cliques leading him to the ulti-
mate secret society, the CIA.

Dillon loved that world, the gritty thrill of secret knowledge, the back-
stage manipulation—the rush of shifting the world to his whim. As
deputy director for intelligence, he assumed the control that was his right
and used his power well. All the pieces fit.

He wheeled through the massive living room, Ryan and Frank following behind. What had been perfect white—the chairs and carpet, the
sofas and wall hangings—had now been smudged by the dull gray of med
gear. Dillon couldn't abide hospital life. He refused to let others—civs—
see him like this. And he had the means to force the issue.

In the far corner, med-techs huddled over the rotating display of Dillon's genome. It spiraled before them, a three-dimensional holo of that
which defined—and now destroyed—him. Somewhere in that genetic
mass, Sarah's retrovirus had injected its code, which was now slowly, brutally killing him. The meds reached into the rez, pulled code from it, altered it and slammed their manipulations home, trying to engineer a way
out of the slow death creeping through their patient. They looked up at
Dillon as he passed, but only as another distraction pulling them from
their hack.

"Progress?" Dillon barked.

"Slow," one med responded. They all looked the same to Dillon. "The
mutation rate has really slowed us down. The coding's genius. Getting at
it means hacking into your most basic operational directives, both physical and psychological."

"You're digging into my mind?"

The med-tech shifted away from Dillon and centered himself on the
code. "The debugging may be worse for you than the virus."

"What could be worse than this?"

The med-tech didn't reply. He turned back to the rez, dug his hands
into the holo and resumed work. Dillon tried a shake of the head. The
move drew belting waves of pain.

"We can give you something to edge that out," another med said quietly.

"No."

"Only other option is to go back into the sim."

"Not quite yet." Dillon pushed forward, bobbing toward a plexi shield that opened onto the patio. He motioned to Frank, who touched the release. The shield slid open.

"Sir," the head coat sputtered, "the contaminants out there . . ."

Dillon wheeled around on the tech, gazing down with his pus-red eyes. The tech turned back to his holo. Dillon whipped back to Frank and Laing.

"Join me," he said as he slipped out.

Laing followed Dillon into the heavy air. Before them, the East River cut a lazy meander into Manhattan's flank. Laing stepped to the plexi railing—the only thing marking the building's edge—and stared out.

"Inspiring, isn't it?" Dillon asked.

Laing found it difficult to respond. He could never live with such a view. "It's claustrophobic," he said quietly. "Especially from this height."

At just over three hundred meters, 80 South Street was an ant staring up at a mountain. Before them, slicing down the river's length, the Wall vaulted into the sky. Its soft undulations mimicked that of the water running below. The Wall ringed Manhattan, cutting it from storm surges that had ravaged Long Island and New Jersey.

The Wall's translucent biocrete allowed Laing to see the differential in waterline on the other side. He felt the water's mass crushing in on the city, longing to pour into this little enclave and expend its potential.

Dillon wheeled to Laing's side. Even with the mingling city smells, the man's rot ran.

"It won't hold," Laing said.

"It has for decades. The Wall allows New York to survive. To thrive."

Laing just shook his head. He looked up at the scrapers ringing them. He felt small—hemmed in. Finally, he turned away from the view and sat with Frank by a long narrow pool that ran the length of the structure. Dillon wheeled over, his bevy of med-techs hovering around him.

"I've come for Sarah," Ryan said.

A grating cackle erupted from Dillon. Nothing resembling mirth. "You have?"

"Andrew—" Frank tried to calm Dillon.

"I think you've come to admire her handiwork."

"No. She didn't do this—she couldn't."

"You're here, Laing, to explain the why," Dillon said.

"I haven't seen Sarah in years."

"But you're so damn sure of her innocence."

"I know her. I worked with her."

"We know," Dillon forced out. "She told us about Echelon. About you."

"She . . . ?" Laing couldn't believe it.

"Oh yes. To have pissed such a prize away," Dillon continued. "Shocking."

Laing couldn't hold back. "Always the planners, the manipulators, who think they have the right to play God."

"Right?" Dillon sputtered, the word drawing a trickle of bile which spilled down his chin. "We have the obligation! Without us, what would happen? Look around you, Laing. Look at this fine city. Without the Wall we'd be underwater. Humanity needs surgeons to slice away the gangrene. You dulled the most perfect blade, Mr. Laing. Now, we're left with coarser methods to reach our ends."

"And Sarah helped you cut?"

"She decided where to slice. Others did the surgery. But you know that, don't you?"

"I know that Sarah is in trouble. I know you put her there."

"I put her there?" Andrew barked, his frustration boiling up. "Look at me! Look at the work she did! I want her, Laing. Do you get what she ruined? The game she cut short?"

Laing turned to Frank, who also seemed surprised by Dillon's rage. "What am I doing here?" Ryan asked.

Suddenly his field instincts, so long in hibernation, bristled. He sensed the strike coming but not in time to thwart it. In an excruciating instant the blade cut his spinal cord—cleanly inserted between the vertebrae at the base of his neck. Before paralysis, Ryan had managed to swivel just enough to see one of the techs holding the instrument. Pain lanced him, then dissipated to nothing.

He couldn't move.

Frank lurched out of his chair, unprepared for the attack. "The fuck?!" he sputtered.

Even as he went to Laing, Frank felt the tip of the tech's blade at his own neck. He froze.

"That's not a move I'd recommend, Frank," Dillon said.

Very slowly, Frank sat back down, the blade never leaving his skin. "What game are you playing, Dillon?"

"That's not really your concern. You can sit and watch, or join Laing. But your spine won't regenerate."

Frank eased back and kept quiet—letting the scene play as he struggled to submerge his rage.

Both men turned their attention to Laing. Andrew noticed Ryan's finger twitching manically. He wheeled forward, took the blade from the tech and held it to Laing's cheek.

"The reports don't do you justice, Ryan. A full cord break and already the drones have you wiggling your fingers. Unfortunately, you won't be operational in time to help yourself."

Laing formed the word on his lips, unable to draw the breath to expel it. *Why?*

Andrew's blood-caked lips extended into what had once been a grin and now made him look like a sentient jack-o'-lantern. He flicked the blade, slicing into Laing's cheek and gritting over bone. The gray-black ooze slipped out, stanched blood flow and retreated as quickly, sealing the cut and zipping Laing's face back to whole.

"You're linked to Sarah."

Ryan's eyes swam. He mouthed words but Andrew cut off even that.

"We know you are. Now—I want her. You're going to make that happen."

Ryan found his voice, drawing huge breaths as his respiration rebooted. "It's . . . the connection fried."

Andrew drew back, shocked at Laing's recuperation. "You are a specimen, Mr. Laing. I'll give you that."

"Jesus, Dillon," Frank said.

Dillon's slow stare stifled further dissent. He turned back to his target.

"I . . . can't," Laing gasped out.

The crease of Dillon's mouth only widened. He took a vacuum-sealed gel pack from the med. With the blade, he cut a hole in the packaging and a slow, transparent ooze slipped free.

"Why don't you try? Call it my last request." Andrew swiped the blade through the slick glop. He raised it to Laing's face, brushing it liberally over Ryan's lips.

A sharp tingle broke through the other sensations warring within Ryan for attention. He closed his mouth, trying to eject the gel. Before he could, the med bent over him and traced the gel's path with a light stick, triggering the reaction.

Frank watched in horror as Ryan's lips stitched together to become one continuous piece of flesh.

"Bonding shells, Ryan. Something I've become intimate with over the last few days. Silica beads covered in gold. When exposed to infrared, the material fuses flesh to flesh. These men have used it to hold me together. I'm enlightening them as to its other possibilities."

Laing's eyes teared over, fear gripping him.

"Link to Peters. Tell me where she is and this all ends."

Laing shook his head, attempting to rid himself of the shells.

"No?" Andrew asked, his tone darkening. "Maybe you require deeper concentration. Let's remove some distractions."

In a slow swipe, Dillon ran the blade over Ryan's left eyelid. The med aimed the light stick and fired. The lid sealed instantly.

"Dillon, that's enough," Frank said. "This man came willingly. The fuck is wrong with you?"

"The fuck you think?" Andrew replied, running a hand down his ghoulish form. He enunciated the expletive with the precision of a man unused to cursing. "Life jumped up and bit me in the ass. You were right all along. Hard times require hard acts. I'm sorry you had to do what I couldn't all those years ago in Prague. But you seem to have gone soft. A message must be sent. This is my medium."

He turned back to Laing. "Is my message getting through? Any ambiguity that needs clearing up?"

Laing's hands thrashed wildly, sensation returning. The drones did their work with unvarying efficiency. With his single good eye, Laing watched Andrew dip the blade into the gel.

"Ryan, you are the perfect subject. Your limits run so much higher than most. By the time we finish, you'll beg me to kill you—to end the suffering. The last days have given me a crash course in the subject. I will make you suffer. I will find Sarah Peters—and I will make her suffer. No one outplays me. This is my game. My . . . game . . . ," he reiterated.

"It's no fuckin' game," Frank said.

Submerged in rage, Dillon couldn't hear. The med-tech stood behind Laing, watching with the same cool eyes that had gazed into Dillon's genome. Two equal puzzles, nothing more.

Andrew drew the blade up to Laing's open eye. Glassy terror shone there. Dillon raised bloody digits to Laing's face and fumbled the eyelid closed. He slopped gel over it. The med bent, shining the infrared ray into the seam. Lids fused instantly.

Frank gazed down at the two men before him, not sure which specimen was more hideous. Ryan Laing's mouth and eyes had become mere creases in meaty flesh.

"Let's begin," Dillon croaked.

13

This is a bad move. It's impulsive. Stupid.

The thought pecked at Sarah Peters with woodpecker persistence. To maximize her chance of survival it was time to get as far from Langley and Dillon as possible. There was safety in that plan, but no resolution.

She couldn't live with a willful fall into oblivion. Sarah had to know who had done this to her—and why. Right now, Andrew Dillon was her only lead. The one member of EMPYRE who had survived. Was he behind the carnage? Was this a consolidation of EMPYRE's power? No mention had been made of EMPYRE's existence in the flow. Even in death, EMPYRE was running deep.

But Andrew Dillon had survived the outbreak and Sarah had to know why. Hunting him down had not been hard. Entering Manhattan undetected was the trick. Sarah had remembered something Laing had told her a lifetime ago. Hide in plain sight.

To do that, she linked up with an acquaintance of hers from the punk scene. Long ago, Sarah had played bass in the mega-punk band Agamemnon's Mitten. While that certainly didn't make her a star, the band did have a following—mostly due to the fact that the rest of the members had been murdered during the Echelon debacle. As the sole survivor, she had a little clout in the scene.

At least Matt Black thought so. Sarah wasn't sure if that was his real name or just a tag and wasn't about to ask. He went by Black. She called him Black.

They met in a swamped Hoboken warehouse where Black squatted when the waters were low enough. Around her, the building shook to controlled pulsing beats, creating a stomping, crashing rhythm. Black worked the mix, operating the resonance generators that transformed the warehouse into a giant speaker system.

Over the slamming sounds, she yelled out her need to get into the city.

Black looked up from his mix table and took her in. He shut down the system and the building creaked to silence. "Fuck's wid the civ gear?" Black asked. Black's clothes matched his name. Layers of tight-fitting poly, ripped and shredded. His hair flopped over his face in thick dreads. Black's crew crowded around him—all in similar dress.

Best to deal hard with these guys. They pounced on weakness. "This shit?" she asked, fingering her rumpled slacks and blouse. "Needed it to get here."

"You're hot," Black said, his tone icy. His crew went fidgety, scanning outside the warehouse for cops. With post-Echelon violence still ripping American cities apart, the punks were high on the authorities' shit list. They rarely caused more than light mayhem, but bucking the system in this day and age brought with it a lot of attention.

Sarah considered her response. "Smokin'," she said finally.

Black stared at her for a long second. Then he broke into a huge grin, revealing the rotted teeth that were his trademark. "Woulda been disappointed if you wasn't!" His crew relaxed at that.

"You in luck," Black continued. "We're island bound. Playin' a gig in Harlem."

Black was part of the new urban sound. No instruments involved. Instead, they used resonance generators to vibrate buildings at varying frequencies. It was a loud, blistering sound that often climaxed with an impromptu demolition. Sarah had seen a show in Paris. Lots of rage. The gigs ended when the cops arrived. Usually didn't take long.

"Take me," Sarah said.

Black nodded. "We got ways into da city. We get you in. Only one thing . . ." he paused, clocking Sarah. "You need kit. No civs in my crew."

Sarah ripped off her blouse without hesitation and threw it at a gawking skin-and-bones groupie. Black laughed, eyes twinkling. "Set her up," he said.

In minutes, she had punk gear like the rest. It was good cover. The hair-over-the-face do would mask her from electronic recog systems. And her pursuers certainly wouldn't expect her to be wrapped up with a crew so bent on drawing attention.

Black and his entourage entered the city through an abandoned Port Authority Trans-Hudson tunnel, once used for subways. It was hours of slogging through moist darkness. Hours of fear that the tunnel wouldn't hold. With each passing meter, the groans and creaks got louder.

"Dying to play the PATH," Black said. He waved at their surroundings. "These all just cast iron tubes on da river bottom. Make a cool racket."

"You play here—you die here," Sarah replied.

She caught Black's gap-toothed grin. He was fucking with her. "Yeah, dat did occur. Maybe I do it remote like. But then I got no means to get island bound."

Sarah slogged on, not sure whether she should breathe though her mouth to kill the stink, or take the hit and filter out the particulates with her nose. It was a long walk. She hoped Dillon would be worth it.

NEW YORK CITY

They didn't bother incapacitating him. They didn't need to. A man with-out sight wasn't much of a threat. Laing swam in syrupy darkness, fear and anger raging within. He'd let himself fall for Frank's serrated morality. Savakis had weaseled his way inside—loosening Laing's guard for that crucial instant. But in the end, he was Company, first and last. Like Dillon. Now, Frank was good-copping him with half-hearted protests.

"Andrew, this has to stop. He's here to help," Frank said in exasperation.

"No." Dillon responded to Frank, but was speaking softly in Ryan's ear.

Dillon's icy crackle resonated through Laing's darkness. Ryan tried to hold his bearings. His head swam. Desperate for breath, he tried to force his mouth open. Nothing. He struggled with greater ferocity, sucking air through his nose in high-pitched whistles. His mind reeled, body twitch-ing in convulsive flops. He reached up and dug at his face. The smooth consistency of soldered flesh made his skin crawl.

"Andrew—" Frank began again, but was immediately cut short.

"Frank, interrupt again and you'll join our friend here."

Laing sensed Frank shuffle back. He smelled Dillon looming over him, rancid flesh. He needed to get away from that smell but each breath forced the stink down. How much had the infection twisted Dillon's mind? Was he dealing with a rational man? No. This man had ripped right through his envelope.

Andrew began again, still in Ryan's ear. Ryan recoiled from Dillon's blood-moist cheek touching his own.

"You returned to take the crown. You destroyed Echelon. You want EMPYRE—and Sarah Peters was your cat's paw. I'm sure you were good once. Twisted, but good. Now you're just another piece of tech past its sell-by date. I'm going to squeeze you for everything you possibly know, twist it from you a drop at a time. When I'm finished, Sarah will come under the same . . . scrutiny."

Laing's desperation boiled, steaming off him in a vapor of helpless frustration. It left him spent. He slacked out, losing himself to the sweaty helplessness.

All the confusion, anger, and reckless emotion he had quashed for so long surged back to the surface. The encroaching city, Frank's betrayal, Dillon's mania, the relentless drive to find Sarah—it was all too much. Laing recoiled from the onslaught.

Within the turmoil, he forced himself to calm. There had to be a way out, a way through. If he could just find it.

He needed time, a plan. He needed to keep Dillon from further incapacitating him. Attack might buy such time, or the illusion of surrender. He tried to speak, forcing his voice out through his nose in muffled grunts.

"Good," Andrew said, "very good."

A thin line of pain lit up Ryan's darkness. A razor, cold sharp, cut his lips free. Ryan gasped, blood filling his mouth. Then the tickle of the drones—cauterizing.

Laing gulped at air. Finally, he founds the lungs to speak. "Echelon was something special—something worth killing for—something worth destroying."

"And now it's EMPYRE's turn? Why do you so want chaos? You used Sarah to burn it to the ground."

"Burn what?" Ryan spat, globs of drone-laced blood spewing over Dillon. "What would Sarah have killed for?"

"Good. We can agree that Sarah is a murderer. As to what EMPYRE did—we rectified your mistake. We used chaos to generate order. But you couldn't handle that, could you? You revel in pain, suffering, turmoil."

Laing tried to make sense of Dillon's ravings. "I didn't know about EMPYRE until Frank found me. I was out, done. You pulled me back by involving Sarah Peters."

The stink of Dillon's proximity ebbed.

"You're really not connected to her," Andrew croaked.

"I'm not playing her, no. I just want to find her before she gets hurt."

"I wouldn't have thought you a romantic."

At this, Frank interjected. "This bullshit has gone on long enough. I'd have told you if Laing was running a double game."

"You're right, Frank. Apologies." Dillon's voice rose an octave. "Adams!"

Laing heard scurrying feet, the shuffle of a subservient approaching.

"I want Laing hacked. If he knows something—fine. If not, work the drones. Pull every piece of code in him. Maybe there's some vestige of the Echelon system in there. At the very least, I want the drones. Pull them, reverse engineer them."

"It won't work," Ryan said.

"Won't matter to you one way or the other," Dillon replied, then turned back to the med-tech. "Wipe him."

The man drew a pistol-like instrument from his coat.

"We're going to fry the wires, Laing. Then, when your body's nothing more than warm meat, we'll hack our way into your memories."

"Andrew! This is unacceptable. I may not like this fucker—but I need him to do my job. If I had any idea . . ."

Laing shrank from the argument. Dillon would break him down piece by piece. That he wouldn't find anything of use would only drive the dying man harder. The pain wracking him inspired cruelty. There would be no end to it.

But to get free, Ryan needed vision. He considered ripping his eyelids open, letting the drones heal the wreckage. But blood still pooled in his mouth. Thrashed eyelids might take time to heal, and he had none.

An idea gripped Laing. Long shot at best, but a plan was a plan. He sank into the flow. Once meshed in, he sent out a crawler. And it pulled— every still of 80 South Street, every vid, every security feed catching a piece of the building. He hacked them all, drew them in.

Real-time images of his surroundings blitzed him, a jumbled, chaotic scramble of input. With Dillon and Frank still arguing, he sank further, coding a run. The pure mass of data bombarded him. He found it hard to hold focus. No choice.

He felt out the code within him and pushed. With excruciating languor, the data began to coalesce. Each image, each vid hyperlinked to the next, forming a lattice of interlocking data blocks that, taken together, rezzed into a seamless whole. The new vision revolved on an axis, moving in time with his thoughts, offering a full 360-degree view.

He started wide, taking in the whole building, then narrowed down on the penthouse, the patio, the beings on it. He caught the scene from outside, from a thousand different eyes, none of which were his.

The vision was nauseating but it held strong.

Ryan Laing could see.

14

His perception went fractal, a cross-cut mosaic compounded thousands of times over. It took time to adjust—a commodity Laing had in short supply. He saw Frank and Dillon looming over him. Their attentions locked, neither felt the eye upon them, the many eyes.

"Authorization?" Dillon said incredulously. "The buck stops here, Savakis. And my patience wears thin. I need what's inside this man. And I will take it."

Movement pulled the two. Ryan Laing stood.

Eyes sewn shut, he looked at one, then the other. In a single onslaught, he ingested their image in full 360. The view warped and mangled Laing's sense of reality. He struggled to retain the integrity of his new perception.

"What the . . ." Frank's anger faded to shock.

Dillon reacted more quickly. He slapped at the holo remote on his bed. His security detail rushed the patio. Clad in soft gel armor, the five mercs moved with feline grace. They surrounded him, pulling hard metal.

"*No!*" Dillon screamed. "Alive. I need him alive."

No expression from the mercs. They holstered and closed in, a synchronized dance with Laing at the center. Ryan watched, fascinated by the panoramic view.

The merc directly behind him attacked. Laing duck-turned in the instant before impact, whipping the man over his head. The man flew over the plexi railing in a high arc. But before the fall took him out beyond rescue, the safety protocol in his gel suit engaged. His hands went magnetic and he slapped back into the building's flank. Though physically blocked by the building itself, Laing saw the merc lock on to the metal lattice linking the penthouse to the outside support. The man began clambering back up to rejoin the fight.

Image flip. The four other mercs pounced. Laing spun, trying to maintain his freedom. He found an exposed larynx and knifed at it with a straight finger jab. The attack allowed one of the other mercs to land a slamming front kick into his side. Ryan's lungs released in a single whoop, chopped short by the brittle crack of ribs. Pain ripped through him, drawing tears that had no exit.

From the wing, Dillon latched a med. He dug into the man's coat and retrieved a tranq gun.

"Clark!" he shouted. "Hold him!"

The mercs surged. Laing saw it coming—the inevitability of it—the image of his impending destruction from a thousand angles. His arms pulled wide, his body exposed. Dillon's arm came down, his hand steady in spite of the pain. Finger pressure, the dull *phoot* of projectile fire.

In that millisecond, as the dart traveled down the muzzle, Frank Savakis made his move.

His hand shot out—an unconscious act. Frank couldn't let Laing become a meat sack to be harvested. A fragile sense of trust had risen between the two, and Frank would not betray it. Not yet, anyway.

He slapped the gun, altering its firing line by millimeters. The projectile slung past Laing, hitting the merc behind him in the neck.

The next moment slowed to a crawl.

Frank looked directly into the face of the man with no eyes—and could have sworn that Laing looked back. *Impossible. Totally fuckin' impossible.* But the connection ran true. The hard set of Laing's mouth eased.

Behind Ryan, the merc's knees gave out. He whipped Laing backward as he fell.

"You son of a—" Dillon didn't finish the sentence before firing again. This time, the dart launched true. Ryan flew backward, toppling over the patio's plexi rail and flipping into open space.

It was done.

Ryan arched back, torquing his body with all the force he could muster. He felt the projectile groove a fissure into his cheek. In that suspended instant, he hungered for the slow fade of consciousness. He found no such release.

From a security camera on a building across the street he locked on the dart—which continued its path behind him. The projectile's tip had missed him, a single millimeter of clearance offering him respite.

A respite that would be very short-lived. He flipped out and back, toppling over the railing and snapping into free fall. Acceleration spun him wildly, but he managed to force a hold on his multiangled perception.

With only one chance, he jerked a hand out, snagging the helmet of the fallen merc and ripping the man off the building. Ryan held the man as the fall whipped them around and over. Laing bucked, arching hard, trying to slow their descent.

They tumbled down, locked together. Ground neared in a mesmerizing blur. Hard impact with the building's outer support sent the two cartwheeling. Laing forced them into a spin that flung the merc's arms out wide. A grating, smacking scratch as the merc's gloves slapped, then slid down the support. Electromags engaged, magnetizing the merc to the support.

Laing held tight to the man's helmet, hearing the snap of his neck over the grinding slide. The dead man's hands, still locked on the structure, continued to slow their descent. In a final act, Laing pulled hard on the merc, launching himself inward. He tumbled onto the roof of the building's ground-floor atrium. From that relative safety, he watched the merc slow to a grinding stop and hang still, head lolling to the side.

Laing allowed himself a breath, then two. Dull shock crept up his system. He couldn't hold the simulacrum much longer. It began to shear. For a moment he lost cohesion and his view went fractal.

Just a little longer. Just a little.

The thought fled with a sharp cracking sound running under him. The plexi roof he perched on gave way. Ryan fell several meters and slammed into the upper level of the atrium's shopping mall. Smashing into the faux stone floor, Laing lost himself to a barrage of pain. The mosaic view toppled into black. How easy to just let go and sleep.

Then a tingle—a thought of Sarah.

He pulled himself up, forcing vision. It came, if grudgingly. Around him, thousands stared up, having heard his impact with the plexi and then watched his fall in startled disbelief. Laing found himself in the jittery image of a flow-cam held by a tourist. Using that as a center, Ryan layered images, finding a reality he could negotiate.

He grasped a piece of the shattered plexi, pocketing it as he rose on shaky legs and gazed at the tourist. The man's face paled further on seeing Laing and the smooth flesh where his eyes should have been.

"Welcome to New York," Laing said, staggering away.

Doubt hit Sarah hard on entering the 80 South Street atrium. This was a huge risk—and not just to her. If she went hot again, the people here didn't stand a chance.

She sank back into the middle of Black's crew. After stashing the mix gear, he had demanded they escort her to her destination. The black-clad punks got wary looks from the mall patrons. Sarah watched them for any hint of recognition. All she got were scared eyes, quickly averted. No one wanted them here, but no one was willing to raise a stink about it. In this day and age, it was better to lay low, keep out of the way.

"You sure dis da place?" Black asked.

"Yeah. I got biz with a boss man upstairs," she said as she made her way over to a private elevator bank.

"You want us to hang?"

"Nah—go work your gig. I'll meet up—" Sarah stopped short. From the elevator, a stream of armored mercs pushed into the atrium. Guns raised, they scanned, desperate for target lock. Sarah ducked low.

"Fuck!" she said.

Black watched the mercs disperse into the atrium. He made a quick sign to his crew, who continued straight toward the mercs while he pulled Sarah into an alcove.

"Dis heat on you?" he asked.

"I . . . I think so," she stammered.

Suddenly all her plans were dust. She'd been spotted and it was over. Over Black's shoulder, she saw his crew tangle up with the mercs, slowing their progress.

"I'm sorry," she said.

Black watched his crew heckle the mercs and grinned. He turned back to Sarah. "Sorry, hell. This beats rockin' Harlem any day." His eyes gleamed.

"I gotta get away," Sarah said. All thoughts of confrontation had vanished. A lead curtain had fallen on her plans. Maybe she could come up with something new. More likely, this was the beginning of a life on the run.

"How far away?" Black asked.

"Those guys want me dead. They got reach."

Black grinned, showing off his decayed tooth stumps. He took her by the arm and led her away from the mercs.

"You mix?" he asked.

"Huh?"

"You heard me."

"Uh—yeah—a little."

"Good. I take you to a place. Hole up real good there. These boss-man trackers never find you."

He pushed her forward. She kept her head low and moved quickly, trying to keep the fear from overwhelming her. She didn't notice the man making his way to the main exit, also using Black's crew as a distraction.

Ryan Laing slipped out onto the New York streets. Sarah never saw him.

Andrew Dillon had watched Laing fall in silence. When he turned on Savakis, the anger was gone—the rage so dominant seconds ago—now a barely remembered burst of energy. The transformation dragged Frank away from his own precipice. Before him, Dillon withered.

"He was my last chance."

"I'm . . ."

Dillon raised his bloodshot eyes, cutting into Savakis's words. "Don't you apologize. Just leave."

Frank approached the plexi and gazed down at the gap of gray space to the cracked atrium roof.

"What now?" he asked.

"Now they're both in the box. I'll rattle it until they come up for air."

"I mean for you," Frank said.

The cool urbane removal cultivated over so many years of privilege fell away, layers peeling from a rotting onion. Frank watched Dillon's vulnerability rise to the surface. In spite of himself, the sight tugged at him.

In an instant it was gone. Andrew Dillon's shell reengaged. He dismissed Frank's question as the jabbering of a lesser.

"I'm going to do my job. I'll see this through."

"Big-boy rules, huh?"

Dillon's mouth split into a grin, expelling a series of crackling, moist pops. It took a beat for Frank to realize it was laughter. "That's right. Laing gets a sanction order to match Peters's. And we go public on Peters."

"You going to issue a terrorist alert? Let the blogs know what really happened at Langley?"

Dillon nodded. "We'll get her one way or another. A data rat with her face on every blog—she won't last long."

"I don't like others cleaning our mess. It can get . . . complicated."

Dillon wheeled in a slow circle. "I think we're beyond complicated."

A merc broke the mood, bursting onto the patio in a swirl of nervous action. "Sir," he said. "Laing has escaped the pavilion. Some kids stalled my men on exiting the elevators. We're attempting to track."

"Well, get to it!" Dillon's impatience rose, energizing him.

The merc stood still, hesitating.

"There's something else," the man said. "You asked to be informed of any large-scale terrorist activity."

Andrew went cold. He swallowed hard. "Yes," he said.

The merc stepped closer, breathing through his mouth to thwart the stench. He handed Dillon a soft panel display.

"Outbreak in Australia. Looks bad."

Dillon grabbed the roll, unfolded it, and stared at the coverage. He looked up pale.

"What is it?" Frank asked.

"It's . . ." Dillon trailed off, unable to force the words out.

Frank stepped closer as Dillon contracted in on himself like a deflating balloon. Frank thought he caught a word before Dillon sank into unconsciousness. He thought he heard Sarah Peters's name.

15

Laing sprinted through black rain. He tried to keep his face hidden, slumping his head down into his chest. Even still, a path cleared before him. A commotion at the pavilion had allowed him to escape, but any sense of freedom was illusory. Dillon's men couldn't be far behind.

From 80 South Street he headed west, weaving through Manhattan's dark maze. Over him, scrapers loomed, cutting the light. What little didn't refract off the towers filtered down and hazed the streets in eternal twilight. Rain gave a staccato beat to the half-light.

Ryan stumbled down Water Street, lost in the mosaic of his perception. Even as his body healed from the fight and the fall, his mind fought to hold the sim. Couldn't last much longer. He shifted through the peds. Their quick snapping gait, their down-directed eyes, pushed in on him. The zone felt alien, uniquely uncomfortable.

Laing stumbled into a lithe form that jerked away. "Hey buddy, you looking for a . . ." her voice faded into the rain as she took him in. ". . . date," she managed to sputter, more from rote memory than interest.

From a thousand angles, he saw the shock and horror in the face before him. He watched in fascination, farther and farther from his own body. The mosaic blossomed, encompassing not just space, but time as well. Laing saw the woman not just as she was, but as she had been. He followed the line of her past—captured on cameras and surveillance systems through the city and backed up in the flow. Her timeline reversed before his eyes. He saw her stumble from a high-end apartment building. He saw the john she had entered with crushing into her in his scraper's maintenance area. Ryan pulled farther back, seeing her being watched by security men on their closed circuit—who were themselves watched by an AI maintenance node that monitored the scraper.

From this single woman, Laing spiraled out, unable to siphon the flow. He couldn't stop gulping it down. The mass of data pounded into him, engulfing him. Link on link until the entire city rose around him in a tidal flow of interaction. He couldn't pull from the sim, couldn't find himself. His breath caught. All focus yielded to the linkage.

His environment resolved under a new perception, not of flesh and steel, building and street, but of information flow. Human differed not at all from machine—all were merely conduits for data flow.

He stumbled in the face of it.

Jennifer Litvak just wanted to go home. The rain leached through her piece-of-shit outer, soaking her brand-new dress. Droplets slid down the back of her neck, over her clavicle and down her side. Add to that the dull burn from a particularly energetic client and she was in no mood. No fuckin' mood.

The man before her blurred in the monotone gray of street-level jostle. She'd thought he might be on the hunt. But no—just a wet ped looking for a quick feel. And those eyes were fucked up. As least she thought they were—couldn't quite rez them in low light. Next time she'd spend the extra and use the sub. Peds were just too freaky.

She tried to get free of the hulking figure but the man stumbled closer. He looked like a fish flopping out its last moments of life before the sushi guy sliced it into hand rolls.

He wobbled, a top losing its spin. She sidestepped to let him fall—and noticed the shoes. Nice. Black—possibly real leather. Too nice for a ped. Then his weight crushed into her. She reeled under the mass, trying to shove him off. His hand latched on to her wrist.

"Jesus!"

"Help me," he whispered.

She tried for the wallet in his back pocket. Why not, right? The man shoved her groping hand away. "I'll pay," he said in a throaty croak.

The man found his balance, using her shoulders to pull himself straight. She looked up into his face. As she did, sunlight sliced a gap in the clouds, piercing the matrix of buildings and blasting the street into high contrast. The peds coming at her took a communal stagger under the glare and ducked their heads further.

The man held still. Hard light rezzed out his face and she saw. No eyes at all.

"Holy shit!" Jennifer cried, starting to thrash in his grip.

The man let go and she stumbled back, falling under him. In the hard glare, the man held steady, blocking her from the ped swarm.

"Please," he said again.

Something in the tenor of the voice cut through her shock. "You blind?" she sputtered.

He nodded.

"Fuck you doin' on the street? You'll get crushed out here." She pulled herself back up, regaining her edge.

The man shrank into himself, shielding from the light. Mercifully, the sun faded and the street fell back to muddy gray.

"Come on, man." She grabbed his lapel and he stumbled behind her. "I could do with some good karma right now. And I want cash. Don't take credit from peds. Especially fucked-up blind ones."

"Yeah," he sputtered.

"This way. I'll take you to the sub."

"Thank . . . thank you."

She dragged him behind her. The man tripped a couple times, but didn't really seem blind. Or maybe he seemed sporadically blind. Every now and then, she could have sworn that he sidestepped an oncoming ped, or maneuvered around a pothole.

They reached the Wall Street sub station and Jennifer pulled the man down into the dark.

"Which line you need?" she asked.

The man didn't respond. His head twitched like a rat locking on the smell of cheese. He pulled away from her and weaved down a corridor. She chased after him. "Hey, shitbag, pay up!"

The man broke into a loping run and she put on the speed, rolling an ankle in her heels. She yelped but pushed on.

No good deed goes unpunished, she thought. *Blind or not, I'm juicing the fucker.*

She pulled a sone-stick from her jacket, slipped her thumb under the safety cover and armed the device. It was supposed to fire a shaped sonic pulse that would down a rhino, but she had never actually used the thing. Now seemed as good a time as any to give it a try.

Sone-stick in hand, she ran hard. Turning the corner, she found the man standing stock-still before a showcase of vid gear. Blue light bathed him, flickering images playing on the smooth screen of his face.

She approached slowly. Blogcasts flickered on a thousand screens through the plexi. But that wasn't what he stared at. Instead, he seemed entranced by his own vid shot. A slick little lipstick cam caught those passing by, outputting its feed to a low-rez monitor.

The man stepped forward, looking closer.

"Lotta good that's going to do ya," Jennifer said, stifling a laugh.

The man looked around, swinging his head in slow arcs. She followed his roving, sightless gaze. By the time she returned to him, he had pulled a jagged piece of plexi from his jacket. He drew it to his face and cut.

Jennifer forgot about the money, about the rain, about the burn in her ankle. The image before her filled her world. And the blood. So much blood.

Laing spliced into the lipstick cam's feed and took in his own image through the plexi. He felt himself sliding into irretrievable clutter.

Need to do it now.

He pulled the plexi from his pocket. Through tidal surges of data, he homed in on his own image, concentrating on that single feed. Laing brought the jagged edge to his eye and cut. Sharp, searing pain. He didn't hesitate. He switched hands and drew the edge across his other eye.

"Oh my God!" he heard the woman sputter next to him.

He stood completely still, canceling out the mosaic, severing each leg of the web, cracking each delicate tendril, one by one. Blood poured down his face. And the soft itching tingle of the drones. They swarmed to the wounds, held on the rims of his lids and worked inward.

Sight returned, first in a blur of red and movement. The pain faded to a dull, healing itch, and his vision rezzed in. It took effort to regain his own perception, to give up that of the city as a whole.

Returning fully, Laing stared into the flash blur of the blogcasts playing before him. **Crisis in Sydney, Australia**—the banner whipped from one blog to the next. **Terrorist act. Bioterrorism.**

The woman next to him stumbled back. He turned on her and noticed something falling from her hand. The next instant shattered in a sonic pump that blasted out the plexi before him and blew Laing backward. He sprawled out, ears ringing, nausea washing over him.

He looked up to see that the woman had not moved a muscle.

Jennifer had watched the operation with dull shock. The swift incisions. Then, ragged eyelids flapping over blood-wet eyes. She had seen shit—been around. But this kicked her way off center. Her jaw dropped in confused disgust.

Then it got worse. Gray slipped from the man's eyes. It pooled on his cheeks, moving with oiled fluidity. It covered his face, then retreated into his mouth, nose, ears, or simply dripped off him and went inert on the white floor.

Jennifer looked back at the face. Perfect. Eyes a dull blue-gray—wolf eyes—staring at the blogs as if nothing had happened. The man turned those eyes on her, and she flinched. Everything in her lurched. Her hand twitched.

It wasn't until the plexi blew out that she realized she'd dropped the sone-stick. It tumbled end over end, hitting the floor and discharging at max. The sonic punch boomed through the display window, blowing the man back on his ass.

Now, she stood over him, numb with shock. The man gazed up at her. Finally, he reached into his pocket and removed a cash chip. He held it out for her.

Jennifer turned and ran.

16

Sarah Peters woke to flickering color running up her arms. Reds and greens, softened by her skin tone, danced over her fingers, her thighs, the slight paunch of her stomach. In sleep, the glowing flux was impossible to control. Even in the barrio's damp stink, she had to drape herself in thick, itchy covers to sleep without arousing attention.

Consciousness pushed the dreams away, stilling her epidermal light show. With it, the panic returned, the stiff, gulping desire to hide forever that she had lived with since Matt Black had dropped her here.

She wanted nothing more than to go back to sleep. In sleep, it all went away and she lived without hesitation. Memories whipped over her, snippets of the woman she used to be.

All gone. She remembered strength, the tingle of tenacity, but it lay crushed under disappointment and—now—terror. She lay back in her cot. Just a few more minutes. One more shot of sleep and she would wake up refreshed, ready.

A bang on the door. Her entire room—all two square meters of cheap prefab—shook with the impact.

The voice blasted out any remnants of sleep. "Wake the fuck up! Shift kick in five."

"Yeah, yeah. I'm there," Sarah hollered back.

She could hear husky breathing on the other side of the door.

"You need help getting ready?"

Sarah snorted. "Keep dreaming, Carl." She listened to him shuffle off, grumbling. In a jerk of motivation she flung herself off the bed, splashed dirty water from a pitcher into a bowl and wiped herself clean of the night sweats.

Then, shimmering nude, she stood before the mirror. The now-familiar itch tingled through her side. She turned profile, checking to see if it showed. It didn't. Sarah ran her fingers down from the curve of her breast to the swell in her side, just above her hip. She found it and dug. Fingers slipped into flesh, working into the hawkeye's pocket. She grasped and pulled it free, her skin protesting with an elastic pop.

Fully charged, it hummed softly, ready for action. She reinserted it. Wouldn't be needed tonight. The hawkeye slithered within her, sending a raw shiver up her spine. It settled and she began her transformation.

Accessing pigment protocols, she jacked her overall tone to deep brown, almost black. The shift transformed her. She went from standard Anglo to exotic indefinite. She added a swatch of red across her eyes, the new style in the sonic blast scene. She took her lips to a puke-dull green. Turning this way and that, she decided that the new style suited her poorly. The green lips got all funky with her eyes. •

She slipped into tight grubby jeans and mosh boots. From the plyboard table, she snagged her flap, a torso-size piece of heat-stimmed fabric. She positioned it on her chest, the warmth of her skin making it hold fast to her body. A crisp white, the flap hard-contrasted with her new skin tone. It left her arms and back totally bare.

Sarah got to the door before she remembered. She drew up her right forearm and pocked it with pigment just below the elbow. Heroin was the drug of choice around here. Retro thing. The track marks helped her blend.

Transformation complete, Sarah stood at the door, breathed heavily and settled her face into drugged dispassion. She shoved on rusted hinges and stepped into the barrio.

Fuel-slick heat engulfed her. Steam vents blanketed the barrio in warm fog. The addition of jet fuel brought the experience right to the edge of unbearable. The quake of an airplane launch chipped at the grimy matrix surrounding her.

Home sweet home, Sarah thought.

She stepped onto the narrow passageway that hung out over cluttered space. It creaked under her weight. The barrio under the Davin Colten International Airport had grown in orgiastic spurts, uncontrolled. It rose up the flank of the elevated airport. An awning of webbing loomed overhead, blocking falling refuse. Below her, shipping containers, rusted steel girders, and prefab cubes perched on their neighbors in a delicate balance all the way down to the ground, one hundred meters below. The only order here was that of force and practicality. Force—you had to fight to keep your spot. Practicality—that spot had to remain standing.

Opened a decade earlier, the airport had kicked off Trenton's urban revitalization. The raised port stood at city center, marking transportation as the centerpiece of Trenton's new image. The idea was inspired. Trenton grew into a model for urban industrialization. Manufacturing boomed in the massive scrapers ringing the port, the fruits of which were then shipped out to points across the globe. Trenton thrived, the demand for labor quickly outstripping local supply.

The Brazilian War took care of the supply issue. A bloody civil war in the wake of Echelon's collapse had ravaged Brazil and generated a new population of refugees. Waves of immigrants made their way to Trenton, where work was plentiful. The influx maxed out the city's infrastructure. And thus the barrio was born. It grew over the years, snaking up the port's flank. Trenton needed the labor and so left the barrio to its own devices. It was a no-man's-land—a place where murder was a nightly occurrence. A place where Sarah could lie low.

She shuffled past the crowds, ducking into Father's Office. A blast bar, clinging to the top level of the barrio, Father's Office stank of stale beer and wet smoke. Sarah entered and allowed her eyes to adjust to the light.

Carl waved her over to the bar. His well-deep voice reverberated through his bulk. "You're late," Carl said, his breath hitting her in dank waves. "I gave you this gig as a favor to Black. Plenty of other mixers waiting in line."

"Place is empty, Carl," Sarah replied.

"Well, I'm paying you to change that!"

That wasn't quite true. Carl had offered Sarah a job in exchange for board. Any tips she made, they'd split. Sarah had been in no position to argue. From Manhattan, she and Black had taken their time, shifting transpo often, lying low. Here, she could lie very low. Before he left, Black had let her in on a couple bolt-holes he'd used over the years. In a place like this, it was good to know how to get out fast and quiet.

"Give it a rest," she said to Carl, "I'm on it." Sarah let a glazed, twitchy impatience pervade her features. Carl harrumphed and stalked down the bar, pushing drinks on his few patrons. Sarah turned on her heels, traversing the dank floor and danker customers to the jock socket. Another plane launch jangled the bar.

She initiated the socket, rezzing in the scratch board, track grabber, and light synch. Sarah liked the work. She'd learned to mix in another life, before Echelon found her. Truth was, she'd first noticed her own talent for pattern recog at the jock socket. In an infinity of samples, tracks, and beats she found that she could lock into that perfect line and create music from the mesh.

Now, she started with a gentle rhythm, a rolling funk tempo that hit at the very tail of the beat. Then she layered. Thrusting her hands into the holo, she weaved a synthesized, throaty woodwind over the beat. Rich waves of light pulsated around her, trapped by the music's flow. Then she pulled an antique vocal and layered it in, pushing and slowing the singer's velvet croon with a subtle flick of the wrist.

The vocal haunted its way through the beat and overlay, sifting into the bar. The sound and light show transformed the dive—made it mysterious, a place for cool biz and slow sex. From the bar, Sarah caught Carl's approving nod.

She folded layers of light and sound, sinking into them, losing herself to the work. Her hands danced in the holo, conducting the blast. She felt eyes on her—people crowding in to listen and watch. She closed her eyes and pushed on.

The creation tranced her out, allowed her to forget. Hours flickered by as she worked the blast, steadily amping the beat. The bar filled, people came and went, evening passed into night. She stayed with the same vocal throughout, pushing deeper. Over time, a serrated anger rose in the music, edging out the ambience.

The bar melded into her show, emotion shifting to her whim. Slowly, she began to poke at that raw nerve within her. She shifted tracks, the resonant vocals replaced by an acid-scratched voice raging against black solitude. The music rose in pitch and went dissonant.

She worked at it, needling the cavity, excavating emotion and slamming it up through the socket. Her teeth gritted down. Hard beat rose to clashing blasts. Tables pushed to the side. Neo Punks slammed to the music, fueled by the anger. The rumble of takeoff—even the av gas—augmented the beat and pushed the bar to frenzy.

Sarah purged, blowing all her pent-up emotion into the music. Then, when she was empty, bare to the world, a wash of insecurity flushed her. She opened her eyes, reintegrating. Deep breaths forced out the last of the release. She shook free, set the socket to repeat and headed for the bar.

Carl stood ready with a warm draft. "Nice. That vibe will tear this place apart. Any damage comes out of your take."

"Whatever, Carl." She grabbed the beer from his long fingers.

Raising the glass to her lips, she saw it. Fear slipped up her spine, rising ice cold and inexorable.

"Oh no . . ."

Carl swiveled, tracking her gaze. Along a piece of wall behind the bar, a vid-screen rolled through an unending stream of flesh, action, and sports. On screen now was a cut-in vid of bodies wracked and bleeding—thousands of bodies.

"Oh, that. The feeds won't let up on it—been running like all day. Tempted to turn the damn thing off. That kinda shit don't sell booze."

Sarah ignored him, watching the words run along the bottom. Fifteen hundred dead. Terrorist action. Some kind of virus burst.

The report scanned over the bodies. Sarah couldn't pull away. The carnage looked so much like Langley. The images stopped her cold, her blood turning icy. She grabbed Carl's arm.

"The fuck?!" Carl yelped.

"Where?" Sarah managed.

"You're riding the dragon too goddamn hard—"

"Where is that?" she asked again, pointing to the feed.

"Australia!" Carl said. "The gov down there's blaming some terrorist group out of Indonesia."

She let go of him, eyes glazing over.

"Fucking psycho," he added as he scurried away. The feed pushed in tight on a young boy, lips curled as he went into convulsions and finally died, eyes wide open. She tried to understand, to glean some truth from the info clutter. As part of her work for EMPYRE, Sarah had analyzed the ramifications of a terrorist attack in Australia, both for the region and for the United States. She had concluded that it would whip the region into a tailspin, generating large-scale conflict that would not serve America's interests. But the bioagent was too much of a coincidence. Someone had destroyed EMPYRE and was now using her reports for a very different end.

And the death toll mounted.

She gazed through the image burst. Amid all the death, through her own fear, she tried to figure a path through the events of the past days. But nothing made sense.

"Fucking bitch." Carl's vitriol dredged Sarah from her thoughts.

She focused back in and was immediately struck by an icy wash of nausea. The vid-feed had flipped to a static shot. On screen, a high-rez image of Sarah Peters. The haircut and lack of worry lines revealed that it had been captured several years ago.

"Just drop her here," a bald man at the bar said, his words liquor slurred. "One night in the barrio, and we'd fuckin' solve the problem."

Carl grunted to the patron before catching Sarah's rapt gaze. He held on her for a moment. Sarah turned to him, sure that he had figured it out. He seemed to hover over the link between the image onscreen and the dirty punk before him. Then he pushed it away, dragging a long pull off his own beer.

"They're calling her the new Jackal," the bald man continued. "A killer for hire. Saying she set up the assassination of that religious dude in China, then fucked up a bunch of people at the CIA. Now she's getting the blame for this shit." He waved a finger at the screen, which had flipped back to the carnage in Australia.

"Busy girl," Sarah said, trying to keep her tone light.

The patron slurred on. "I mean, what kinda cash you make for that shit?"

"Probably enough to settle your fuckin' tab, Will," Carl said.

The man laughed. "Then I better have another."

Carl just rolled his eyes and turned away. He accessed the vid-feed, scrolling through sites. "Fuck this. Gotta be a ball game on somewhere."

Sarah hunkered over her beer. She tried to fathom the shit storm whipping around her. How would these people react if they knew the most wanted person in the world was sitting next to them? Wasn't hard to figure. She wanted to shrink into herself, to disappear completely.

The music pounded down on her—hard, scathing vocals layered over a crushing beat.

NEW YORK CITY

Andrew Dillon scanned the blogs, the dull throb of betrayal pulsing through him. This was his scheme, his game, but someone had stolen the playbook and turned it on its head.

"It's confirmed, sir," the med-tech said. "Australian virus matches that triggered in Langley."

"Exactly?"

"It's a slight skew. Slower burnout. Adjusted to cancel the work-around that saved your life."

"You're saying it's more virulent?"

"More or less. No one survived contact. But, it also allowed those infected to live longer. So the retrovirus spread farther."

Andrew turned back to the feed.

"Anything else, sir?"

Dillon didn't bother replying. He tried to concentrate through the pain. In the past hours, the proximity of his own death had settled heavy. He tried to care about the rest—about the world, about his legacy. EMPYRE was his. Had been since its inception. He had kept the group together when their shadowy founder had vanished. He was the one who had held Phoenix to the fire. And he had found the data rat.

Sarah Peters boiled through his fevered thoughts. In the space of weeks, she had ruined it all, and the United States would pay the price. Now she had flipped his play, triggering hot conflict in Asia. But to what end?

Peters had nailed the Australia gambit. The incident had kicked off precisely the event stream she had predicted. In the space of hours, Australia's already shaky market crashed. The hawks in its government found their rallying cry. They were already demanding retribution, and Dillon had good intel that plans had been drawn up for a surgical strike on Indonesian targets. Dillon was also certain that such attacks would fail. Australian special forces would die on Indonesian soil and the entire region would ignite. Combined with the Sino-Indian hostilities, the region would plunge into a hot war. While low-level conflict bolstered American interests, massive destabilization would be a disaster for everyone.

Peters had run the numbers. Now, what the hell was she doing flipping play? She was responsible for Australia. She was responsible for his death. For EMPYRE's death. At this point, he found it hard to care about the why. He wanted revenge. He'd kill her as she had killed him. As she had killed his dream.

"Adams!" Dillon croaked. "I want all the stops pulled on the Sarah Peters contract. Everything we've got. Put a price on her head that none of our contractors will refuse."

Silence.

"Adams?!" Andrew yelled.

Still nothing.

Dillon pulled from the flow link and wheeled around. He pushed out of his bedroom and into what—only weeks ago—had been the living room. Machines hummed away, his DNA slowly rotating in holo. But no people.

"Goddamn it," he muttered, frustration mounting. Dillon pushed from room to room, finding only silence. Finally, he wheeled out onto the patio.

At first, he thought it was an illusion, some glitch in his fading perception. The pool, still calm, was also deep red. He knew it was real when Adams's corpse floated to the surface.

"Your anger is misplaced." The voice had a velvet richness to it, as if slow-dipped in old world charm.

Dillon did not turn immediately. He gazed down at the bodies, trying to wrap his mind around what had just happened. The ramifications of it were too horrible to fathom. His legacy was truly dead.

Finally, he turned, hoping against hope that he was wrong.

"Phoenix." The word slipped from Dillon's mouth in limp defeat.

"Phoenix is no more. The pyre from which I rose is long dead. Call me by my real name. Alfred Krueger."

"She's not your man," Alfred Krueger said with soft assurance.

He sat in a patio chair, legs crossed, arms flopped over a knee with an air of genteel confidence. His hawk-thin frame coiled within a perfectly tailored gray Savile Row suit, dark loafers, shined to high polish, a rich blue shirt, no tie. There was a damp chill in the air with the approaching night. Not a twinge of discomfort marred Krueger's perfection.

Behind him, Zachary Taylor loomed, ghost quiet.

Dillon wobbled between Krueger and the pool of blood. He could not bring himself to look at Taylor.

"You?" he asked with the desperation of the condemned.

"I thought we should chat without interruption."

"No!" Fury rose in Dillon. He lunged forward, hurling himself and the mag bed at Krueger. Krueger didn't move—didn't even flinch.

Taylor did the moving for him. He spun around the thin man and grabbed Dillon's arm, whipping him up and off the suspensor. It veered wildly, slamming into the railing. Dillon shrieked from the pain of contact as Taylor wrenched down on his arm. Unable to support his own weight, Dillon's legs buckled. His shoulder ripped free from the socket. Taylor held him for an instant longer. Then he let the man fall. Dillon crumpled at Krueger's feet.

Krueger gazed down with fish cold eyes. He uncrossed his legs and lifted Dillon's head with his foot. Dillon had no resistance left, and no more energy for pain. He gazed up at Krueger, ready to die.

Krueger leaned over, inhaling Andrew's putrid scent. He did not recoil. The hint of a smile curved his upper lip.

"How long did you think I'd be EMPYRE's whipping boy?"

Dillon continued to stare. Tears welled.

Krueger laughed. "You didn't think, did you? I fit into your little scheme. I gave EMPYRE teeth."

"You killed . . ." Dillon couldn't finish.

"Years of doing your dirty work, and it never occurred to you and your planners that I was playing you? I'm almost insulted."

"You need us."

"Maybe once. Maybe when you brought me in and I was licking my wounds. As you can see, I'm feeling better."

"No," Dillon sputtered in a final desperate rejection. "We made you. EMPYRE did. You're nothing without EMPYRE. Just a fugitive with no future, nowhere to run."

"Wrong. You are nothing without me, Dillon. You think EMPYRE used me? This was my training ground. EMPYRE was practice for the real battle."

He threw a disinterested nod at Taylor, reanimating the man. The assassin approached Dillon with measured precision.

Andrew looked up to see his own death in the man's chilled eyes. He tried to fear it. Something—anything—to pull him from the truth. All his life, all his work, brought to nothing.

He scuttled back, his papery skin rubbing into the gritted tile, leaving spattered tracks. Taylor advanced with a killer's grace. Emotion severed from action. Hollow.

Dillon's life did not pass before his eyes. Not the achievements, at least; only a still shot of that day in Prague all those years ago. Even as Taylor stooped, Andrew saw the pivot point in his life. That moment ran quick reps through his mind's eye. Had he chosen differently on that bridge, had he acted instead of gamed . . . The thought trailed into oblivion. Taylor's smooth hands felt almost soothing as they wrapped around his neck.

"I'm sorry for the past days," Krueger said. "You should have died quickly—with the rest. You deserved that much for everything EMPYRE taught me." Krueger leaned forward, eye to eye with Dillon. His voice edged dark. "Still, I can't help but thrill to see you like this. Dying with the knowledge that I outplayed you."

Andrew Dillon looked—and knew.

"Sarah . . ." Dillon sputtered out. His papery skin ripped under Taylor's grip, drenching Dillon's neck in blood.

"Peters?" Krueger scoffed. "She has become my weapon—as I was yours."

"How?" Dillon managed. Even with death looming close, he had to know.

Krueger waited a long beat, gazing down at Dillon's final moments. Finally, he shot Taylor another look and he immediately eased his hold on Dillon's neck.

"I hacked Peters during her last augment," Krueger said. "Made her an asymptomatic carrier for my retrovirus. She slipped right through your scanners because the pathogen lay dormant within her own DNA until I triggered it. Once triggered, she started shedding virus. As you know, it's a particularly nasty creation. Phase one is a rapid onset, weaponized Ebola. Slows down the infected party, allowing time for the virus to spread before the real weapon deploys. Then, the patient's own cells begin producing a strychnine-like compound—an alkaloid that disrupts neurotransmission. Once that's in system, death is certain. The body goes into convulsions, then asphyxiates. Immediate rigor mortis sets in." Krueger leaned back, reveling in his creation.

"I survived," Dillon whispered.

Krueger's smile turned down in annoyance. "Yes. The gene work you had to offset your rheumatoid arthritis inhibited the second phase of my retrovirus. I fixed that glitch."

"And now Sarah is expendable?"

"Now, Peters is serving a much larger purpose. She dances so well to my tune. As I once did to yours."

Andrew coughed hard, forcing words through his compressed windpipe. "You picked wrong. She'll see the pattern."

"You're done, Andrew. Game over."

Dillon began to laugh, a manic high-toned bark, grating into the night. "Sarah will outplay you."

Krueger leaned back and smiled, the muscles in his cheeks knotting into hard fury.

"Really?"

"Laing will find her—and they'll turn their sights on you."

The smile froze on Krueger's face. "I'm counting on it."

He stepped forward, delicately positioning his foot on Dillon's neck. Dillon had no strength left to struggle. Krueger began to push, forcing Dillon down. Andrew splayed, neck bending over the side of the pool.

As the back of his head touched the water, Dillon tensed. His eyes never left Krueger's. The last of his will seeped into the ink-red water and he relaxed.

The snap of Dillon's neck reverberated through the water and rose into the night. The man went limp.

Alfred Krueger held still, savoring his victory.

"It's done," Taylor said softly.

Krueger pinioned Taylor under his cold stare. Taylor's eyes lowered immediately. In a moment, the fury vanished and Kreuger's glassed removal returned. He nudged Dillon with his foot. The corpse slipped into the pool, snake smooth.

"EMPYRE is gone," Kreuger said. "Dillon is gone. *It* has only just begun." He watched with satisfaction as Dillon's corpse sank into the black.

Only when it had been completely subsumed did Krueger return his attention to Taylor. "Trigger Peters for an extended virus shed. Time to draw in the big fish."

Taylor nodded.

Krueger turned from the pool, the click-squish of his footsteps breaking the silence. He left a single track of blood on the white tile.

17

Laing slumped into the plastic contour of the subway bench. He'd been riding the rails, trying to figure out his next move. Slowly, the bone in his ribs had spidered back to whole. His mouth and eyelids still burned but had regained their previous form. The vision shift took longer to manage. He found it hard to recalibrate to a single pair of eyes. He felt confined in his own flesh.

Ryan shook off the feeling. He needed to hone down. Go offensive. Needed to find Sarah before she went too deep. Slinging subway, he felt helpless. How was he supposed to outmaneuver an entire infrastructure on the hunt for one woman?

He slumped farther into the hard seat and shifted into the flow. Right now, he could only watch, wait, and hope Sarah popped up on his field.

MANUFACTURING DISTRICT. TRENTON. NEW JERSEY

For Sarah, there was no warning. One moment she sat at the bar, drinking her beer. The next, a jacked release, like an orgasm without the sex. Pure expulsion. Her face flushed hot. At first, she thought something had been slipped into her beer. Carl was known for adding psychedelics to his liquor.

But no. She quickly realized what it was and knew what would come next. Nothing she could do. Like the interminable moment after jumping off a cliff and before hitting the ground.

Then it began.

The virus struck in waves expanding around her. An impossibly perfect man sitting next to her, knife work apparent in the smooth balance of his digi-star looks, began to sputter. He coughed out his drink—surprising himself. Sarah watched him realize that his body was shutting down.

The bar quieted. Not the normal ebb and flow of social interaction—this quiet was thick doom.

The man looked up at her, his face pocking into a ghoulish mask. He caught his reflection in the bar's mirrored surface. The bloodcurdling scream that followed sent the patrons into wild hysteria. Those closest to the exit bolted. The resulting stampede created a bottleneck of sweaty death.

Some escaped to spread the plague. Most didn't.

. . . . .

The future didn't exist. Not for them. Not anymore. Sarah Peters had wiped it from them. Spreading from her like a flash fire, death burned through the barrio. With equal speed, word of the plague hurled the community into chaos.

Sarah did not move. She stood in Father's Office, looking down the barrel of Carl's twitching gun.

"Carl, please," she whispered.

"I knew it was you. I fuckin' knew it!"

Most of the other patrons were dead, eyes wide open, bodies locked in rigid spasm. Those who still lived had withered to a pulpy gore, their cries filling the tight space. Carl propped himself on the bar, eyes blood wet. He had been on break when it began, returning to bloody carnage with Sarah at center stage.

Now, he tried to hold focus. "You're not sick," he huffed out.

"Carl—" Sarah started.

Carl cut her off. "It's her!" he yelled to those outside the bar—to anyone who would listen. "From the blogs. It's Sarah . . ." Carl's voice trailed off as he tried to pull her last name from his fevered mind.

"Peters," Sarah said, tears streaking her face.

Carl nodded slowly. He looked down at Will, the man's bald head now blistered, his eyes open in a death stare. "Will got his wish. Sarah Peters—terrorist fuck—in the barrio." He nudged the man with his foot. "Lot of good it did him."

Outside the bar, Sarah could hear the slow rise of voices—a mob forming. She couldn't bring herself to care.

Before her, Carl gripped the last strings of life with ruthless determination. Convulsions began, his neck arching back in spasm. The barrel of his ancient shotgun wobbled.

Sarah stared down the black muzzle, unable to look at anything else. Time slowed. Carl pulled back the hammer, clicking it home. His finger curled on the trigger.

This is better, she thought. *End it here.*

In her fear and longing, Sarah lost her hold on the tat. Her skin pulsed as if she had ripped the northern lights from the Arctic sky. Carl's eyes widened, the sight cutting through his haze.

Sarah longed for the shot—an end to this nightmare. It did not come.

"Who are you?" he asked, his eyes lost in the dance of color.

She shook her head. "I didn't want any of this." The words came with slow precision, dredged from her darkness. "Please." She eyed the gun.

In the bar's mirror, she caught her reflection. She turned from Carl.

"No!" Carl shouted. A plea, not a demand.

A shuffle of movement and Sarah felt Carl's hand on her cheek. She turned with the fingers' jerking pressure and gazed into the man's eyes.

"It's . . . beautiful." Though locked jaws muffled his voice to a hard grunt, the anger in it had faded.

Tears hazed her view. She watched the man die, his eyes never wavering from her own. The gun fell into Sarah's hands. She handled it instinctively, fingers curling over the grip. Carl directed the barrel to his chest, stepping into it, locking it to him.

"Please," he sputtered through clacking teeth.

She understood, but couldn't move. Wouldn't. Her fingers went numb. She dropped her head, tears streaming.

Carl forced a shaking hand to her chin, pulling her back to his gaze. They faced each other, separated by the length of the gun.

"It's beautiful," he said softly.

The words tunneled into Sarah, dislodging that part of herself locked in darkness. She gazed into the man's eyes, an ember of connection breaking through the fog of her tears.

Carl could no longer speak. Before her, he began to asphyxiate, unable to draw air. He simply nodded. A request she could not deny.

The hammer struck home.

Sarah did not remember squeezing the trigger. The quiet moment burst into sound and gore. Buckshot obliterated Carl's chest, blowing him back into the bar. He crumpled at its base, eyes glassed.

Sarah stumbled backward, bile rising. She hacked it out, her throat burning. The weapon was heavy in her hand. She pitched it to the ground, unable to pull her gaze from Carl's mangled form.

The moist curl of fingers on her ankle tripped her. She fell hard, coming face to face with a woman about her height, her weight. Sarah stared into the face. The woman looked at her and then beyond, into nothing. Coagulating blood puffed from her nose to the rhythm of her breathing.

Sarah scuttled away, unable to contain her cry. She pulled herself up and bolted for the door, slipping on the blood. She ripped the entrance open to new horror.

The virus had spread. Along the catwalk, ragged men and women advanced on her. Their eyes gleamed with desperate determination. They had clubs, knives, anything they could get their hands on.

"That's her," one of them gurgled.

They pushed in.

18

The Wall's surveillance center was the loosest secret in Manhattan. Ringing the island, the Wall held the waters at bay. It also watched those within.

Everyone knew the eyes were there. That the watcher surrounded them, unseen yet pervasive. At first, there had been an uproar: intrusion on privacy, overreaching governmental power. But with each successive threat, those protests had withered. If only the government had seen a bit more—known a tad more. Every disaster was one that could have been averted.

And so, the Wall continued to watch. And it watched well. Since full implementation, terrorist attacks had gone to zero. There were simply easier targets in the world.

But with that security, the pendulum began to swing in the other direction. The Wall's gaze pushed into the city's demeanor—a reverse panopticon. New Yorkers operated under the raw nerve of being watched. It set the city on edge.

In one of the Wall's many control rooms, Frank stalked back and forth, unable to hold still. He had come here to find Laing. So far, he wasn't having any luck.

"He's not in the city," a dull-faced tech said through chomps on her Danish.

Frank stood over her, watching the woman manipulate the eye. "He is. You just can't track him."

"Sir, we can track everyone."

Frank just laughed. He turned from the techie and gazed into the city. Seaside, the Wall was a smooth slab of self-sealing, algae-sustained biocrete. The inward face was another story. It glistened, flickering translucent and pocked with antennas and dishes. Most of these were inoperative—just for show. Frank stared out through the filmed plexi. Across the river, Manhattan looked like a silver dream: ethereal scrapers, impossibly close together.

Something drew him to 80 South Street. An inconsistency. A red flicker within the structure. He didn't have long to ponder it. The penthouse puffed, then blasted out in white heat. Before him, 80 South Street lit up like a candle.

Boom.

The concussive force of the blast tipped him back into his chair. Cries of surprise filled the room. The watchers had front-row seats on this one.

"Ah, fuck no," was all Frank could manage.

He leaped to his feet and put his hand to the plexi, watching in horror. The penthouse did not burn—the explosion had simply demolished it. Debris rained down on the twelve other cubes that made up the building.

"It's going to hold," one of the techs said with more hope than assurance.

It didn't.

Two wide supports and a central core held the building together. The penthouse's absence set the building into a slow wobble. It teetered, torquing hard. Then one of the cubes fell. It smacked into the one below it, and the building toppled like a series of dominoes.

In seconds, there was only smoldering rubble.

Around Frank, stunned silence broke into pandemonium. The techs beat into their flow decks, setting a perimeter and pushing the first responders to the scene. Frank watched, trying to work out the past seconds.

The techs buzzed around him. Frank grabbed the closest one. "The fuck's happening over there?!"

"We're efforting that now, sir."

"Was the blast internal, a missile? What?"

The row of tech-men latched themselves into the flow, pulling feed. In spite of the insanity surrounding them, they sat frozen.

"Oh shit!" one cried.

"Oh shit, what?" Frank whirled on him, ripping off the man's visor.

The man blinked away the flow shift.

"Come on, man! It's one of our own in there!"

"No—it's not that. I'm picking up a tag—full pattern match. Ten for ten."

"Spit it the fuck out."

"We got viral contamination."

"The Australia thing?"

"No, sir, it's in our backyard. Trenton is red hot."

"Son of a bitch!"

"Dispersal pattern matches Langley's. It's Peters."

"Do we have confirmation on that?"

"Sir, the pattern match—"

Frank cut him off. "What did I fuckin' ask?!"

The tech swallowed, then turned into the flow. After a moment, he replied with smug I-told-you-so assurance. "We have confirmation. Reports on scene. Peters is there."

Frank was too preoccupied to notice the man's tone. He grabbed his jacket and bolted for the exit.

"Sir!" the female tech shouted after him. "Do you want to continue the Ryan Laing search?"

"Don't bother. You won't find him."

She looked at him like he'd lost his mind. "Of course we will."

"You just get help to those people down there. Figure out who blew up that fuckin' building. I know where Laing's headed."

MANUFACTURING DISTRICT, TRENTON, NEW JERSEY

Zachary Taylor waited. His specialty.

His thoughts didn't track with those of others. They weren't normal. He could remember the way he used to think, to worry. Now, he floated over the sea of life, dipping into it only as directed. He sat in the back of Father's Office, sipping at skunked beer. Around him, Sarah Peters's carnage offered an infernal ambience. The stink of bile filled Taylor's nostrils but did not alter the steady rhythm of his breathing.

He had tracked Sarah after weaponizing her. Knowing what to look for, he had managed to slip into the barrio before the CDC and Department of Homeland Security threw up their net.

Taylor had entered on street level, just before the real carnage began. Shanty shops peppered the lower floors of the vertical maze, selling everything from ramen to subderm memory caches. An energetic bustle surrounded him, people buying and selling, children scampering through the tight passages and up the swaying ladders.

Taylor worked his way up, sifting through the maze of barrio life. On the lower levels, the airport traffic came across as little more than a rhythmic grumble, a far-off storm. But as he ascended, the thunder loomed ever closer. The scaffolding shook with each takeoff. He entered the Keep. In the Keep, darker desires drove commerce. Quaking under the jet wash, the Keep offered satisfaction. Meth-tipped psychedelics, sexual perversions, the lure of oblivion.

Taylor slipped through the dealers, pushers, and pros. His Armani singled him out from the shabby grunge of those around him. Eyes followed him. His battle tension rose. Hardly breaking his gait, Taylor smashed his right palm into the face of a burly man who had decided only an instant before to hassle him. All Taylor had needed was the subtle clench of the man's cheek to know. He attacked before provocation was even a full thought in the man's mind.

The man dropped to his knees, stunned. Gouts of blood burst from his pulverized nose.

"Excuse me," Taylor whispered, stepping around the man.

After that, eyes no longer tracked his progress. The aura of violence clung to him. Street sense kept one alive in the Keep. He was given a wide berth. As he ascended, Taylor sensed a rising tension. There was action on the levels above. There was fear in the air. Lots of traffic heading down in a hurry.

Then, the hacking cough of a man drowning in his own bile. A smile broke the plane of Taylor's face. He followed the sound. Working his way up a series of ladders quivering to the rhythm of the port, he pushed into a fast-expanding hot zone. Before him, men and women sprawled at the door of a dilapidated bar. He approached, unhurried.

A man slumped in the passageway, hacking out his last breaths. Taylor stooped to look at him. He stared into the man's eyes, lifting his chin with a slender hand. The man's face had blistered black. Taylor heard the distinctive crackle in the man's lungs.

"Please . . ." the man spewed.

Taylor held his gaze. After a beat, his hand dropped from the chin to the man's neck. He found the soft thump of the carotid and pressed. The man shivered, jerked once and died. A last expulsion of air frothed over his lips.

"You're welcome," Taylor said.

Taylor entered the bar to silence. Sarah had already fled. Just as well. She wasn't the target.

Now, Taylor sat in a corner seat, having pushed the corpse of a young man to the floor. He wrapped his hands around the man's drink, sipped lightly, and waited.

MANUFACTURING DISTRICT, TRENTON, NEW JERSEY

Ryan ghosted into the middle of a firefight.

The barrio lay under heavy quarantine. Feds in hazmat gear enforced the quarantine with maximum force. From ground level, the port looked like an aircraft carrier on steroids. Its thick block form rose over Laing in a jet of black steel. He got as close as he could to the barrio, which rose up the port's flank. The ragged park that extended out under the barrio now swarmed with cops and civs. Pandemonium pulsed through the crowd, mostly residents of the barrio refused access to their homes and families.

Within the quarantine line, civs clustered, sick and terrified. The virus had spread fast. Men, women, and children fell where they stood, writhing. Herd panic pushed those with any strength left to stampede. As they approached the quarantine line, a squat, multibarreled cannon set on a heavy tripod swung their way.

Laing recognized the weapon system—a Metal Storm cannon. Within the barrels were thousands of stacked rounds. The propellant behind each projectile was fired electronically, giving the Metal Storm a rate of fire exceeding two million rounds per minute. Push the button and out burped a wall of death.

With infected civs closing, the perimeter guards fired. The barrels of the cannon chattered for an instant, ejecting hundreds of thousands of rounds. They shredded the stampeding people, sending the few survivors into a frantic retreat. The civs fighting to enter the barrio immediately fell back in shock and fear. Soon the anger rose.

Ryan retreated into the throngs. Punching through the quarantine was too risky. He had to find another way. He circled the field and cut over to the massive factory buildings that ringed the airport.

Sprinting through the streets, he tried to fathom Sarah's actions. Was she really responsible for this? What would he find on getting to her? And, if she was too far gone, what would he do? The questions boiled in him. He ran out the energy, putting on a burst of speed. He turned the final corner onto Front Street.

The shift was immediate, from rough industrial to slick commercial. A two-hundred-meter-tall woman hung over the bustle. Her succulent, if holographic, lips flittered over a carton of Coke, pulling sips as if it were ambrosia. The entire wall of the port exploded in color and lights, ads and entertainment, an orgiastic symphony of consumerism. The far side of the street was jammed with stores, bars, and restaurants, all catering to the suits. It hardly seemed possible that the barrio lay on the port's far side. That it was now a killing zone seemed only to amp this population's drive to consume.

A woman laden with holo-encrusted shopping bags burst out of a high-end shoe store, crashing into Laing. The impact sent her purchases flying. She screeched, the intrusion pulling her from the input daze everyone seemed to be operating under. The woman didn't acknowledge Ryan beyond picking up the bags scattered around him.

Ryan didn't move for a moment, the sense of unreality pervading him. The crush of glossy input insulated the street from the horrors beyond. It was an active feed, flow-tranced, consumer-driven denial that ran near total.

Laing shook free of it and pushed back into a run—realizing that he was now covered in perfume. The thick scent wrapped him, clouding out even the hamburger onslaught the six-story McDonald's pumped out.

Absolutely perfect, Laing thought as he cut into the port's south entrance. Inside, the bubble of opulence only hardened. Laing gazed down the terminal at the sharply dressed passengers all queued up in clean lines. A soft hum of efficiency pervaded the place. So discordant with the chaos and death just a wall away.

MANUFACTURING DISTRICT, TRENTON, NEW JERSEY

Savakis reached the park under the barrio as a tense, heartsick calm took hold in the throng. He pushed through the slag of civs. Before them, a cordon of feds marked a black swath between the living and the dead.

As Savakis stepped forward, an overeager G-man flipped into tough-guy mode. "Back off, now!"

"Take it easy, kid," Frank said, and continued to walk.

The G-man clicked to active fire, hands twitching with fear.

"You don't want to aerate me, kid. Scan my code."

"Wha . . . What?" the G-man sputtered. Shell shock flashed through his features.

"My code. I'm Company, you idiot!" Traumatized or not, Frank didn't have time for this shit.

He stepped forward as the kid checked his arm display. A scan of Frank popped up.

"Sorry, sir," the kid said to Frank's back.

Frank barged into the mass of armored men, guns, and slick fear. He found the control tent. Before it, a squat, thick man gruffed out orders.

"You in charge?" Frank asked.

The man's great bulk shifted, his heavy eyes turning to Frank. A dogged street cunning showed through the man's exhaustion.

"Name's Flip," the man said. "Trenton PD. Feds are here too, but they're suddenly not so interested in helming this mess."

"I'll bet they aren't." Frank said, extending his hand. "Frank Savakis. CIA." Flip grabbed it and shook hard.

A cop pulled Flip's attention. As he dealt with the man, Frank looked out on the carnage before him. A thick soup of gore blanketed the hundred meters to the barrio's base.

"Fuck me," Frank whispered.

"Yeah," Flip responded.

"What happened here?"

"The residents tried to break quarantine. G-men were here with area denial weaponry." Flip motioned to the Metal Storm cannon.

"And they just opened up?" Frank asked, staring at the weapon.

Flip nodded to the carnage before them. "All of a sudden, I'm in charge. It's now my mess."

Frank added his own gruff chuckle to Flip's. "Well, unless you got a problem with the CIA working domestic, I'll help you clean."

"About time," Flip said. He beckoned Frank into the control tent. Frank looked up into the eight haphazard stories of barrio suspended over them.

He had a pretty good idea of what was going on in there.

Laing pushed through the clean, pressed passengers, each pretending to be the only sentient being in the room. That calm isolation cracked as Ryan sprinted through the main atrium. Nine stories above, hulking planes fought their way into the sky.

The scent of anxiety wafted through the air, competing with Ryan's perfume. That tension, and the beefed-up police presence, were the only hints of the crisis occurring on the other side of the airport wall.

Laing bolted up the vert, pushing past the travelers as he reached gate level. By now, people had begun to stare. In hindsight, blowing through the scan station might have been a mistake.

The electronic immobilization devices shocked him repeatedly, frying the perfume stink into something akin to roasted lilac. Beyond that, the shock did little to Laing's system. He shouted something about national security to the police—but it didn't take. Six cops bolted after him, chasing him down the terminal.

Laing could incapacitate the men, but that would take time—a resource he had in short supply. Instead, he put on a burst of speed, cutting hard right as they opened up with gel frags.

He sliced into the boarding zone for a flight to Santa Barbara, California.

"Wait!" the woman at the counter shouted as Laing smashed through the alarmed door. "Plane's not here yet!"

Ryan sprinted hard, the cops on his ass. He rounded the corner, knowing that the next moments weren't going to be fun. Frags pounded into the wall over his head. No time to ponder.

With no plane, the end of the boarding ramp hung suspended ten meters off the tarmac. Ryan put on an extra burst of speed. He hit the passageway's end like a long jumper arcing out and up, legs churning.

Jacked to high, he landed in a smooth forward roll, dissipating the impact through his right arm and down the diagonal of his back. One of the cops, unable to siphon off his momentum, wavered at the gate's end, teetering on the edge in a jerking dance. Another cop grabbed him, yanking him to safety.

The distraction gave Laing a few meters before the cops could fire their frags. The gel slugs hit Laing's back in pocking splats. Their force was enough to knock most out cold. Laing stumbled hard but managed to keep his feet under him. The shots continued to plaster him, but their power lessened as he got farther from their source. Finally, he got out of range. He'd done it. One step closer to Sarah.

Now, all he had to do was cross a live runway.

The voice boomed through the evening air, overwhelming all else. "Sarah Peters, vacate the premises immediately. Failure to do so will result in further casualties. We cannot lift quarantine until you are apprehended." Bullhorned up at the barrio, the harsh male voice ran the lines over and over.

Frank burst into the control tent, fuming. He approached Flip, who was standing over a bank of cops manning the monitoring gear.

"Fuckin' feds!" Frank spat. "The idiots think their message blast will flush Peters out."

"It's a possibility," Flip replied without much heart.

"Yeah, right. That message paints a big old bull's-eye on her chest. Those poor fuckers in quarantine will hunt her with everything they got. It's their only chance."

"Guessing that's the scenario the feds are hoping for," Flip replied. "Let the civs do their dirty work." He turned back to the row of projections before him. "Pull up the scan," he said to one of the cops. "Look here," he said to Frank, pointing into the holo. "IR shows hot flares closing in on a single individual."

"Peters."

"Most likely," Flip said.

"Looks like an old-fashioned posse. Picking up a good deal of weaponry. Even if the target is healthy, she can't hold 'em all off."

Frank watched the holo. Finally, he looked up at Flip. "I'm going in."

Flip looked at Frank like he'd just lost his mind. "You gotta be nuts."

"I need Peters alive."

"Sir, you'll be exposed to the virus."

"You telling me there's no hazmat team here?"

"No, of course not. It's just—"

"Got no time for this," Frank said. "Get me a suit, and get me in there."

Flip just shrugged and showed him the way. "It's your funeral, brother."

Over the next minutes, Frank began to think Flip might have been right. He stood in the hazmat team's trailer, butt naked, a plexi mask over his face. Soft Seal sprayed down from every angle, matting him. A tingling shrinkage as it firmed over his body. In another minute, Flip entered with a jumpsuit.

"Still up for it?"

Frank just grabbed the suit, forced his still tacky body into it and exited. He grabbed a large-bore shotgun from one of the feds as he trotted through their front lines. Passing the hastily erected bioshield caused his small muscles to spasm. The shield set up an irradiated field around the barrio.

Frank lurched his way past, electricity arcing off him in a blue haze. Then he was through—and into the dead zone.

Wayne Pierson ran on empty. Eyes blurred, he'd been going full-tilt for the last five hours straight. With the exponential increase in air traffic leaving Trenton, he'd been forced to call in all his controllers. Even the processors handling the airport's integration into the skynet ran well over capacity. Two processing plants had already buckled under the data load.

"Sir!" One of Pierson's less-skilled controllers was waving from the far corner of the air traffic control spire. The spire vaulted high over the passenger terminal, a slender spike rising up out of Trenton's pollution haze. Its clear line of sight had struck Pierson as an antiquated precaution. Air traffic controllers, on the average day, did little more than monitor the smooth flow of launches and landings that the computers operated. This was not an average day. Today, that sight line was all important.

"What is it, Rob?" Pierson shuffled over.

Rob, a sloppy lifer not quite incompetent enough to fire, didn't bother responding. He just brushed at the holo before him. The code line and three-dimensional rep of the airspace surrounding Trenton slow faded into a flurry of snow. Dead crash.

Normally, Pierson ran ice cold. He loved the active, geometric precision of flight control. From his days running jets off aircraft carriers to this, he would clock in and conduct the symphonic ebb and flow of planes with cool perfection. Now, staring into the snow, he felt an unfamiliar adrenaline spike kick at his chest.

Looking down the row, each controller's holo crashed in succession. Only the distance feeds—those from the national skynet tracking the flow of planes down the eastern seaboard—remained intact.

Wayne gulped, allowing himself a single moment of indecision. Then he locked it down and forced calm. "We go old school. Visual control, boot up the radar."

"What?!" Rob sputtered.

Wayne pushed on. "Inform the pilots to flip to manual."

"They're not going to like it," another controller grumbled.

"Then they can stay right where they are and we'll dance 'em out once the crush dies down."

Silence for a beat.

"Well, get on it!"

The room erupted in a staccato mash of controllers informing pilots. Fortunately, all the flights were outbound. With the disturbance in the barrio, the suits wanted their product off the ground. Couldn't have their shipments quarantined. That fucked up the bottom line.

Pierson wiped his eyes, trying to keep up with the exodus. For the first time in years, he stepped to the arced plexi that bubbled the spire and watched the action below.

Planes were stacked all the way back to the hangars, eight or nine deep. He'd be here all night. They all would. Still gazing into the mayhem, he toggled his link and updated skynet. Their reaction was only slightly brighter than that of his controllers. But what was he supposed to do, shut down the airport? That would be a career killer.

Slightly zoned, trying to capture a full picture in the maze of planes below, he almost missed it. Just a speck, moving fast. It staggered slightly. In a jolt, Pierson realized that nothing mechanical moved like that.

"Oh, Jesus," he muttered, unable to fully process what he was seeing. He whirled. "Rob!"

Rob was deep into manual operation and didn't notice the intrusion.

"Rob!"

"What?" He looked up, eyes dazed.

"Runway three."

"Yeah?"

"There's someone on it."

"Well, yeah. On three, we got the Air West flight to Paris, stacked behind the express shot to Caracas."

"No—there's . . ." Pierson almost couldn't bring himself to say it. He blinked, hoping it was just exhaustion, or nerves. No luck. "There's *someone* on the runway."

Laing ran in the wake of giants. Hulking planes surrounded him. The world he had plunged into operated on a different scale. He felt like a rat crossing a city street.

Laing bolted under a candy-red Airbus. The gear loomed over him, tires a full meter over his head growling past in a crunch of weight and force. Laing misjudged the time he needed to clear the plane. He pushed harder, every muscle in his body screaming. No use.

He tried to double back—but it was too late. The plane's jet-wash lofted Ryan into the air, flipped him over and spat him backward. He slammed onto the tarmac. Rolling softened the blow, but he felt like he'd been hit with a meat cleaver. A barrage of meat cleavers.

Laing held flat for a moment, struggling to draw air, trying to see a way through.

Wayne Pierson watched the runner loft up into the air and slam to the tarmac. No movement after that. The lump stayed flat.

"Okay," he said with his first exhale in some time. "It's done. Hold traffic on runway three long enough to get a med cart out there." He turned to Rob. "Just long enough."

Rob began the transmission. But before he could finish, Wayne held up his hand, his face pressed into the plexi.

"Emergency shutdown. Hold all traffic. Cut power to all mass drivers, *now!*"

Within the raucous hubbub of verbal transmissions, there was a shift-click into emergency. Rob's nerved, tinny voice pierced through. "Shutdown in process. But we have three sleds charged. Too late to power them down."

Wayne scanned back and forth between the runway's two ends. As there were no incoming flights, he had been snapping planes out both ways. He'd gotten some shit over the added fuel cost of launching with the wind. Pierson had made it clear that the suits could eat the cost or return their planes to hangar. None had pulled their flights.

Now, on each end, three planes dropped into sleds. The port's location required its planes to lift off more quickly than their internal engines were capable of. Thus, planes were catapulted into the sky via induction drives. The planes rolled onto giant aluminum sleds, which were then shot forward via electromags. These catapults slung the huge planes into the air, getting them up to speed in time to clear the scrapers ringing the port.

"Emergency shutdown!" Wayne repeated.

"No go—sleds are already moving. We stop now and the planes will dunk right into the scrapers."

Pierson watched the acceleration blur of the first two planes. Time slowed. He hung over the scene, unable to stop the grisly action about to play out before him.

The man began to run.

. . . . .

Laing wrenched himself off the tarmac. Around him, a pitched whine gained force. He felt the power potential building to release. Ryan stood at one side of the first of three live runways. Looking in either direction, he could just make out the planes' hulking silhouettes. All were beginning to accelerate.

The tingling crackle maxed. Laing tried to pull back but the magnet's force dragged him into the runway. The sled, accelerating in a coil of electromagnets, would suck him in and crunch him flat.

Laing turned into the oncoming plane, running hard to gain a slight angle. The pull increased, threatening to drag him into an engine—or worse. His legs felt like iron, his lungs bursting. He ran harder.

The next moment pushed out to infinity. The sled passed in front of him, moving so quickly that even the jet-wash didn't reach him. The trailing edge of the magnetic field dragged him along. It sucked him forward, and at a slight angle due to his run. Laing let it take him, abandoning himself to the magnetic whirlwind.

The timing had to be perfect. One misstep and it was done. The field's force launched Laing through the second runway before releasing him. He got to his feet and stumbled forward, making it across the third runway even as he heard the slicing acceleration of the sled flashing behind him.

He reached the tarmac's far edge. Under him—the barrio and Sarah. He was so close. Just a little farther. Stretched out before him, a rigid carbon-fiber net jutted into the night, protecting the barrio from tarmac clutter. He pushed out to the net's edge. Peeking down, he saw that it overhung the barrio by at least ten meters.

Behind Laing, the final sled maxed power. It approached with a piercing screech. Then there was only the buzz of electricity. Laing had no time for fear.

He took a couple of steps back, jacking the drones within him. This needed balls-on timing. The sled approached too quickly to track. Instead, Laing closed his eyes and worked the flow.

In the data rush, locking on the sled wasn't easy. Finally, he found the signature and latched on to the approaching field. As it hit, Laing coiled and launched, arcing out into the night. He extended, arms wide in a full swan dive. The power of the passing magnet arrested his outward velocity, drawing him back in a whip roll. He flipped under the carbon net, now falling toward the top spires of the barrio in a thrashing tumble.

Impact.

. . . . .

The flash of speed stopped short as Laing slammed into the barrio. The dull crack of his sternum breaking was all that welcomed him. Ryan felt bone grinding on bone. Pain lanced him, a shock-ache that would not subside. Then, it all vanished. He felt only a moist drip below his hips. The speared tip of a plastic rebar beam had impaled him.

Through the haze, Laing's head flopped down and he got a look at the barrio extending below him. Each level had grown over the last in haphazard spurts of need. The topmost section, which Laing had crashed into, remained a mishmash of plastic scaffolding and cannibalized building supplies. Those who would live so close to the mag-drives were the worst off. It showed.

In slow, soupy time, his sternum stitched together. Still, he couldn't move his legs. The urge to lean back, to sleep, washed over him.

No, he thought.

The pain in him, the need to find Sarah, Frank's betrayal, all of it distilled into a binary choice—black or white. Move or die.

Laing wrapped his arms around the rebar jutting from his side. He pulled. With each centimeter of freedom, he felt the beam tug on shards of his flesh.

Move!

He snagged an overhanging cross joint and pulled. The rebar came free with a sickening pop. He dropped to the walkway, gritting through the searing bite of his pain. Eyes rolled back. Gray seeped over him, belched from his wounds, then receded.

It didn't take long for his foot to begin twitching.

Sarah knew she had to die.

With each breath she exhaled, others fell to the virus. She staggered through the barrio, Typhoid Mary reborn. She knew what had to be done—but every part of her being drove her to live. The dilemma ripped at her, rending her capacity for rational thought. Sarah tried to stay isolated. She sank into shadows, curled back as people passed. It didn't matter. Everyone would fall to the agony.

Knees locked to her chest, she tried to right herself—to find some shred of self under her shame and horror. She pulled the hawkeye from her side. It came free, inflated and whirred to life. Surprised that anything—even mechanical—could live within her, she held it for an instant, savoring its tug before letting it rise from her hand. The hawkeye buzzed up to the ceiling. It turned on its axis, gazing down at her.

She saw herself through its eye. Revulsion rose up through her. She couldn't turn away. Her hair lay matted to a face she could no longer abide. Her body rank and disgusting. She pigment-shifted, blacking her skin to match the shadow. Better. Still horrible. She wanted to disappear completely—to mesh out and fade into the night.

Some far-off rational kernel of her mind knew that the virus she carried had been placed in her. Yet—it seemed so perfectly suited to her being. She was the prime vector, a shell filled with black death.

Self-hate gripped her. It spiraled from the blackness, wrapped around her, and extended out to swallow the whole damn world. She groped for a point of reference, something to rein in the loathing.

To escape the pain, she pushed out of herself, rising up into that ethereal plane where there was only pattern. Here she was free. Everything ran clean—cause and effect. The quantum flux of her life fell away.

She analyzed the web that her past days had generated. The assassination, the CIA, the Australian biological. All linked to her. Was it random? Hard to believe. And why use her as a scapegoat? She wasn't field rated. Sooner or later, she'd be caught. There were others who could stay alive much longer than she. People like Laing.

The thought of Ryan sent a jolt through her system. She hated that she remained so tied to him. She hated . . .

Oh, God.

In that moment, the pattern emerged. Clarity settled over the past weeks. Under the force of her realization, Sarah staggered to her feet. She needed to get away—far away.

She wasn't the scapegoat. She was the bait.

19

Sarah emerged from seclusion. She moved down a passageway canti-levered out over open air. The stink of fuel and flesh rot floated through the barrio's persistent humidity. The fluorescent glare washing the area contrasted her out, moved past, then came back to hold on her—a fact she realized too late.

From the shadows, dull eyes took her in. Her strong step set her apart. All around her, men and women propped themselves up, fighting death. She moved through them, trying not to disturb the scene.

"You!" The croaking hack of a sweat-drenched woman caught up to Sarah.

The woman grabbed her with blistered hands. Peters retched, ripping at the woman to get away, but she would not release.

"You're killing us," the woman cried.

"It's—it's not me." Even to Sarah, the words sounded ridiculous. The woman broke into a wet laugh that elevated to a hack. Still, she would not yield.

"She's here!" The shriek crashed through the night.

Around them, above and below, eyes poked from shanty hovels. Even in the crush of the woman's embrace, Sarah felt their presence. Snapshots from the hawkeye filled out the scene.

Sarah struggled, but could not break from the woman's death grip.

Then her back lit up in pain. The hawkeye homed in on a blood-slicked man, knife held high, prepping for another strike. He slashed down, the blade parting flesh at the nape of her neck. Then it hit her sub-derm carbon matrix and kicked out. The blade drew a slim line of blood down her back, but could not cut deeper.

Sarah hardened. These people were already dead. Nothing she could do about that. And she had to get away—fast. The man raised his knife for a third strike, shifting for a downward stab. Sarah waited for the blade to fall. When it came, she twisted hard, flipping the woman on the axis of her left leg. The knife plunged into the space between her shoulder and neck. A geyser of blood erupted from the wound, showering all three. The woman wailed with carnal ferocity as she dropped to the ground.

The knife lodged in the woman's neck, pulling the man over. As he bent, Sarah shouldered him, sending him flailing over the railing's edge. He spun out, flipping over and over in silent shock on the long fall down.

Sarah watched him all the way to the ground.

She pushed it away. No time. The commotion had drawn attention from below. A spot hit her dead on, lighting her up. She turned and it was like staring into the eye of the sun. In confusion, she lost her footing and tumbled down a makeshift ladder. The fall saved her life.

The space where she had been evaporated in an explosive haze. Metal Storm projectiles ripped through the barrio, upsetting its delicate structural balance. The levels over Sarah began to buckle.

She crabbed backward, getting to her feet and racing clear just as a great mass of the structure teetered and broke away. She ran hard, pushing deeper into the barrio—away from that light and the Metal Storm cannon tracking it. Doing so backed her into those whose only escape lay in her death. The hawkeye couldn't find access through the barrio's maze. She was on her own.

Sarah darted through interlocked gangways, but a posse formed up behind her. Each one sick, near dead, had nothing to lose. And each one knew it.

From the darkness, a man lunged down at her, hurling himself off a ladder and out over open space. Sarah shrieked involuntarily as the man smashed into her. The force of the blow sent them sprawling. Sarah scrambled to her feet and moved, even as the man rose to follow, his blistered skin making him look like a molting snake.

Sarah slid down a ladder, ripping it free behind her to slow her pursuers. She pushed on, dodging the dead-weight flop of a man hitting the floor by mere centimeters. As she ran, Sarah ripped at her white top, tearing it away. No time for the jeans—but their grubbiness offered solid camo. As she ran, her bare chest morphed and merged with the colors of the background. She faded into it.

With her tat spot matching the scene behind her, Sarah raced toward the outer gangway. Better to risk a shot from below than get cornered. She ran hard, gunning for a direct staircase that led to street level and the sewer entrance Black had showed on first entering the barrio. Her bolt-hole.

Behind her the pounding stampede of her pursuers. The tat worked well enough from a distance, but up close it wouldn't accomplish much. The posse gained on her, pushing at her heels.

Sarah didn't make the stairs.

At first, Laing saw only confusion. He gazed down, through the mesh of girders, corrugated metal, and detritus to a crush of people. Then a flashing blur before them caught his eye. Well, not quite his eye, but that other sense that Laing had no name for. Radiation waved off the apparition. Ryan focused on it through the chaos. It was some kind of epidermal camouflage that blended with the environment. Hacking the code source, Ryan was able to draw the figure from the background.

Sarah Peters resolved before him. He choked down a laugh. She was alive!

"Sarah!" Laing shouted, giddy excitement cracking his shell.

The rhythmic din above ebbed momentarily, allowing his voice to carry. Sarah Peters turned up to face him. For a moment, their eyes locked. Peters eyed him with animal indifference. The look made Ryan shiver. He fell headlong into her fight-or-flight drive. The moment broke.

Sarah tripped.

That single moment of distraction was all it took. Sarah fell, her chin smacking into a protruding rebar beam. While the carbon tat blocked puncture, it did little to deaden the force of impact. She shook the webs from her vision and scrambled to her feet. Too late. The mob fell on her.

They ripped into her, gouging at her belly and legs, shouting down at the feds below.

"We've got her!"

"It's over!" another wailed in ecstatic relief.

"You can let us go!"

"Get us help!"

A hand grabbed Sarah's hair and slammed her head back into the gangway. She managed to stay conscious through the beating.

Light exploded through the flail of arms and legs over her. Like a weapon, it blasted out her vision. She pushed through her pain and fear, rezzing into the hawkeye. Through it, she saw a man, deranged and frothing, rear back to bite her leg. She kicked out and heard the snap-crunch of his jaws clicking together as her heel impacted his chin.

Sarah scrambled, desperate. She knew what was coming.

"No!" she shouted. "They'll kill you all!"

"Shut up, bitch," a man grunted, lips hovering over her own as his fist pounded into her ribs.

The hawkeye zoomed wide. Below, in the mass of feds, she saw the Metal Storm cannon bear down. Barrel on barrel stacked together. She saw the operator hesitate. Then, an order was barked and his eyes glassed into those of a man whose actions were no longer his to decide. His finger twitched, then curled into the trigger.

Rounds shredded the gangway. The sheer number of projectiles ripped the posse from her in a pulpy mist. Sarah rolled away from the gun's line of fire, the gangway slick with blood. No screams—everyone was too busy dying. Then the storm found her.

Rounds smashed into her side, flipping her into the air like a leaf in a tornado. The splatter-pop of projectiles smacking flesh. Consciousness fled under the bone-crushing power. Her carbon tat held, but the bones underneath cracked under the force of the onslaught.

She faded into the searing crush, unable to scream.

"Hold fire!" Frank shouted into his com-link. "I repeat, hold your fire!"

Two levels below the carnage, Frank watched the cannon's projectiles decimate the rickety structure, chewing through flesh, bone, and barrio to ping off the siding of the port itself.

After a sickening beat, the firing stopped. "Stupid, motherfucking gun jockeys!" Frank hissed into the link. "One of your own is up here. Wouldn't care so much if it wasn't me!"

A grinding pause, then Flip clicked on. "Sorry, Frank. It's dicey down here. We're getting pushed by massing civs." Flip's cool pulled Frank from his rage.

"Okay. Just keep 'em in check. I'm getting close. Going to try to retrieve the target. If I can pick her free of the meat-patty up there."

The sterile gel made movement awkward. He felt vacu-sealed and distanced from reality—like he was watching a vid of some poor fucker plunging into the dead zone, or playing Death Troop. He controlled his movement but couldn't feel the plastic railing under his hand.

He stepped over a dead woman, bone rigid, her back arched in a convulsion held firm by rigor mortis. He reached a set of spiral stairs cannibalized from some far-gone ship. The spiral pushed him out over open space.

He turned his sights up, peering through the dust cloud sent up by the projectiles. At first, he thought it was merely an illusion, some combo of acrophobia and revulsion.

It wasn't. A massive section of the Keep had begun to teeter.

Laing's screams were lost in the firestorm pounding the section below him. When the bombardment ended, he knew Sarah was dead. No way she could have survived that. At the thought, a piece of him gave way. He gazed down into the graying dust, lost in the whirlwind.

Movement. A slow crawl.

Was it an illusion—his mind chewing reality into something he could digest?

He looked harder, cutting through the haze. Cloaked in gore, a delicate hand stretched out. A head rose, eyes vacant and glazed. A swirling flush of color disguised the face. Then it settled into a profile he recognized. She was alive.

Laing jumped to his feet, steadying himself through the wave of relief gushing through him. Despite her departure, her betrayal, their link seemed unbreakable. The knowledge gave him no joy. She had left him, damn it! And yet, he cared for her, needed her. There was love, somewhere deep in his abyss, but anger drove him forward. Anger that she had conquered him so completely, that, no matter how he tried to wall himself from the world, her life meant everything.

The structure under him lurched. Ryan lashed out, catching a support girder. The grinding shear of construction grade plastic filled the night. Clinging to the girder, Laing watched the entire section under him sway, then begin to break free of the airport wall. One by one, the adhesive seals locking the barrio's supports to the port wall popped.

The thirty meters of latticework Laing had just climbed down began to sway. The scaffolding pulled from the wall, caught a wind current and sheared clean. Whole sections of the Keep began to fall. Laing dodged to his right as a massive aluminum girder snapped and fell. The teetering upper zones pulled on the outer stanchions of the section below.

The section he was on. That Sarah was on.

"No," he whispered. Not quite a prayer. Maybe a wish.

The structure broke loose from its moorings, swaying out, then rebounding in a dance that couldn't last. Ryan craned his neck in time to see Sarah, still groggy and disoriented, begin to roll toward the barrio's edge. She thrashed, unable to abate her momentum.

Laing scanned wildly. He had seconds. Running up from Sarah's level, an ancient piece of scaffolding bent out—a thin vertical pole, ending just meters below him. And about five meters out into the black night.

No time to think—Laing lunged, arcing high. The rush of wind knocked him off-line, twisting him slightly. He was going to miss. Too jacked on adrenaline for fear, he whipped an arm back with all his force. His hand found the support, fingers wrapping it in a death lock.

Acceleration canceled in a jarring instant. Laing just managed to match hands before the stanchion bent away from the structure like a vaulter's pole, sending him out past horizontal. He got his feet around it, praying that it would hold his weight. A seal popped, bowing the stanchion further. Laing held. A suspended instant as his future balanced on the strength of a single piece of cannibalized scaffolding. The bet went his way. The stanchion torqued to full, then pulled back.

Laing came up to vertical, then wrapped his forearm around the pole and slid down it like a fireman. Friction ripped away his shirt sleeve, then the flesh of his forearm. He ignored the pain. Below him, Sarah continued her slow fall as the structure itself pulled away from the port.

A gutting despair ripped through him. He wasn't going to make it in time.

Sarah's vision snapped back to true. She wished it hadn't. She slid on the canted floor, accelerating toward the edge and the death fall beyond. Reaching out, she grasped for anything to cut the momentum. One hand found a raised piece of wooden flooring. She snagged it, finger joints popping with the strain. She had a moment of relief. Then the board gave way. Acceleration reengaged as Sarah stared at the loose board in her hands with dull shock.

Not possible. Not like this.

The barrio's edge flashed by. Her thighs and stomach hit the railing hard. She tried for a grip, but momentum ripped her fingers from the girder and she fell free.

There was only space—open and silent.

It was over.

Laing zeroed in on his target over the burn of his forearms on the support beam. Sarah's flail stuttered for an instant. She had caught on something before ripping free and hitting free fall.

It'll be enough. Has to be enough.

Still sliding down the pole, Laing pushed out with his arms, extending into space while wrapping his legs tighter around his only connection to solid matter. He reached wide, locking on Sarah's flailing hand, focusing down until it was his whole world. Getting to that hand filled his entire existence.

Arching his back with a violent whip, he breached the space between them. Hand slapped hand. He gripped down, connection sliding from palm to fingers, to tips. He refused to release, clenching with everything in him.

Sarah's added weight slammed him into the pole. It also accelerated their descent. No way he could stop them, not with just his legs.

Pressure. Sharp and deep on his thigh. The pole had drawn closer to the main structure, the gap V-ing in as they neared its epoxy seal with the level below. Laing gritted down, gripped tighter.

The abrupt halt slammed him into the barrio's metal-webbed exterior. The impact exploded through him; he could feel his back popping, his knee hyperextending. Then, silence—dead calm. Only the hulking gasps of breath pushing through clamped teeth.

Upside down, Laing's right boot had wedged between the pole and its epoxy seal. His left leg hung free. He dropped his head, looking down past his hand to Sarah. She hung below him, slack, head lolling. Laing threw his left arm down to meet his right, sharing the load of her weight. His foot sank deeper into the groove, locking down.

"Sarah!" He pushed the word out, trying not to look past her into the gaping maw below them.

"Sarah! Please . . ." He closed his eyes, muscles straining. He couldn't hold much longer.

Vertigo spun his perception. The structure continued to sway, wobbling out, adding to his burden, then crashing back to vertical. As he looked up, he gripped, even as his fingers began to straighten. He couldn't stop their slow release.

Sarah's reprieve would be short-lived.

Then—a clench on his numbing fingers. Sarah lurched, shaking free of oblivion. Her eyes snapped open. Taking in the dark space below her, she jerked reflexively, trying for safety, finding none and beginning to panic.

"Sarah! Don't move. I can't hold you!"

Through her daze, Sarah looked up. She caught Laing's eyes as her world resolved.

"Ryan?" A hoarse whisper sliced the space between them.

"I need your other hand, Sarah."

She gazed up at him in dull confusion.

"Now, Sarah!" he grunted.

She raised her hand, found his and locked in.

Laing breathed straight relief. "That's good, Sarah. That's good."

She gazed up at him, her features triggering an emotional release in him, if only for an instant. Pain, stress, and fear—gone. Her face entranced him, held him prisoner.

"It's going to be okay," he whispered.

For a moment, he really believed it. Maybe she did too. Then her face locked into another expression he knew all too well—one that had no place for him.

"No," she said. "Let me go."

The skin over her cheeks pulsed psychedelic color. Through drone-jacked perception, Laing watched in horror. She began to struggle in his grasp.

"Sarah?!"

"Let me go, Ryan. Before it's too late."

She lashed out with greater ferocity.

"I won't," he growled through clenched teeth.

Then something in him lurched. His heart fluttered high and tight in his chest. His skin. It went to paper, ripping at the wrist, spilling blood down his hands and compromising his grip. He looked down in shock.

Sarah saw. Her tears tracked through the grime on her cheeks. He had spent too long being invulnerable. He couldn't fathom the shift.

"It's me, Ryan."

The words cut into him. Only then did he realize what was happening. The retrovirus surged through him. Energy drained from his fingers as the drones went after the pathogen rocking his system.

"I don't understand," Ryan gurgled, gray blood spilling from his lips, drenching Sarah.

"They used me. I'm sorry. Sorry for everything."

He gazed down through a haze of red, unable to focus anymore. He had nothing left. The structure arced out with the buffeting wind. The pressure on his hands maxed. Blood-greased, his grip on Sarah slipped. They began to arc back into the wall.

She rezzed clear for an instant. Her eyes sparked fear. Not for herself. For him. She was not looking at him, but straight ahead—into the barrio. Grim determination set her lips.

She wriggled free of his grasp.

The yell caught in his throat. He saw her flail, smack against the scaffolding, spin on an exposed piece of rebar and smash into a gangplank. Sarah disappeared from sight as the structure snapped back to straight vertical, groaning and creaking with the effort.

Laing let it all go. Black tears fell into the gap. No one could live through that kind of impact. Sarah was gone. For a moment, the world stood still. He hung in space, utterly alone.

"Ryan." The voice broke through his fever-churned grief.

Standing on the gangway just below him was a whip-thin man with dark hair and sharp blue eyes. Laing's focus slid over the man, who leaned on the railing in a feline melt.

"Who . . ." Ryan couldn't finish.

Inside his boot, the skin on his ankle ripped. Blood trickled down his leg, loosening the wedge. Laing groped for purchase and found none. His foot popped from the boot and he slipped free.

Before the fall could even begin, the man reached out, grabbed Laing's dangling arm and whipped Ryan over his back in a smooth arc. Laing landed on the gangway with barely a thump, so smooth was the man's action.

Laing wheezed, trying to find his bearings. His vision swam. The stranger loomed above, expressionless.

"Who are you?" Ryan forced out in a wheeze. His lungs felt brittle. They crackled with every breath. No air. He couldn't find enough air.

The man stooped down, hunkering over Ryan.

"I wondered if you had anything beyond the drones in you." His words ran crisp, each syllable enunciated with cold precision.

Ryan rolled away from the man, lurching up to one knee.

The man chuckled. "I wondered if you would put up a fight."

Laing coughed blood. Within, he sensed the drones working, fighting the pathogen. Dully, he realized that something powerful enough to do this much damage would have to be coded to his genome specifically.

"But it looks like you're done, friend. Without the drones, you're just a man—and a weak one at that."

The man pulled a syringe from his jacket and loomed over Laing.

"Who—" Ryan sputtered.

"I am Zachary Taylor," the man said with slow deliberation, as if trying to convince himself.

Then he plunged the needle down.

Ryan reeled in the pathogen's grip. The drones, battling the virus, had pulled from his consciousness, throwing Ryan's awareness into free fall. Without drone enhancement, his perception fuzzed. Laing skidded over delirium, trying to focus. The man before him: he was a threat. Through his crash, Laing couldn't come up with more.

He sensed the man's proximity and raised bloodshot eyes to see the syringe coming down. Seeing the aggression in those eyes, Ryan somehow found his will. He arched up, catching the syringe just before it pierced his shoulder. The man's eyes widened for a single instant—then settled back to impassivity.

Instead of attempting to force the syringe down, he whipped right, spinning free of Laing's grip in a fluid twist. He came at Ryan again, this time in a low, arcing slice to the sternum. Ryan shifted, blocking with his arm behind the bulk of his body. He grabbed for the syringe, but snagged only air.

Laing panted, still on his knees. The man was too fast. A thin smile spread over his face like a fungus. Then he struck.

Feinting left, the man threw Laing off balance and left him totally exposed. He punched forward in a straight shot to Laing's chest, syringe ready to fire. Laing bowed his head. Finished.

The flash-bang of gunfire lit the night. Laing's attacker was launched backward, his shoulder a pulp of blood and chewed flesh. The man's face registered pure surprise.

"Don't. Fuckin'. Move." Frank Savakis stepped from the shadows behind Ryan, moving for a clean shot at the attacker.

Laing registered the change in his circumstances through a gauze of pain.

"You look like shit," Frank said to Ryan, the mask fuzzing his words.

"Good timing," Laing replied.

Before Ryan could center himself, the structure lurched. Laing toppled. Behind him, the attacker staggered as well, crashing into the railing.

Frank surged past Ryan, locked on the stranger. "Hold right there!"

The man's surprise melted into an easy grin. He threw out his good arm and flipped over the railing's edge. Frank fired, then approached the edge, gazing out over the barrel of his gun.

The man was gone.

20

They hunkered down on the lowest level of the structure. Frank had supported Laing all the way down, a royal bitch. Above them, the groan-crack of structural plastic shearing grew thunderous. They had seen no trace of the attacker who had nearly taken Laing's life.

Frank pulled his com-link up. "Flip, I want you to apprehend—repeat, *apprehend*—anyone attempting to flee."

"Not a hell of a lot of action on that front. No one coming out. The virus burns fast."

Frank looked over at Laing. "I'm coming out. With a survivor."

A long pause over the trans. "I have orders to terminate anyone infected."

Laing lay before him, blistered and panting. "He's not infected. Can't explain it. Just get a detox unit ready."

Another long pause. "Yes, sir. Unit ready for two. I'd suggest you move it. Barrio's losing structural integrity."

"No shit."

Frank dropped the link and huddled over Laing. The building swayed around them. "Laing, you hear me?"

Laing lifted his head, groggy and far off.

"You need to pull out of this ASAP. Can the drones kill this thing?"

Laing's head wobbled. Frank couldn't tell if it was in the affirmative. He pulled Laing close, the man's breath fogging his face plate. "I got no time here. This fucker's coming down, Laing. I pull you out looking like this, and we'll be mowed down. The feds won't risk transmission."

A low whine hummed over Frank's words, building to a high-pitched wail. Then another pop. The building lurched, torquing around them.

Frank played his last card. He didn't want to see Laing die. "Didn't see Sarah on the descent."

"She's dead," Laing croaked. "Has to be."

"The fuck you know? We should have seen her body—and she's got some serious augments."

Laing shook his head, eyes closed.

Frank pulled Laing close, locking eyes with him. "She might have gotten out."

The words finally registered, air to a drowning man. Ryan's eyes snapped to alert. With slow determination, he got to his feet.

War raged in him. Laing's body cried for surrender, while the drones fought to correct the destruction wrought by the pathogen. Cell by cell, the virus drilled down. He wanted to sleep—to melt away. Let the battle go and just fucking die. Didn't matter. None of it mattered.

Frank's words broke through the fever and found purchase.

"Alive?" he said in a mucus-thick croak.

"That's right. No sign of her or the attacker. So either he grabbed her, or she made it out under her own power."

Laing shook his head. He'd seen her fall.

"You that sure?"

Ryan looked up. Could he do that? Let it go? Die without really knowing?

With effort, he straightened up. With each breath his mind hardened, his will honed to a knife edge. He pushed the drones, forcing a cosmetic reconstruction. The war still raged within, but the outer shell would look clean enough.

Frank watched the transformation with a mixture of awe and horror. The blisters burst gray, then receded into pink flesh. The eyes swam, then turned clear. The pallor flushed out.

Above them, the wail grew deafening. The building torqued to fracture. This was it. Laing stood to his full height.

"Good enough," Frank said. He threw Laing's arm over his shoulder and muscled though the detritus raining down on them.

They ran, bursting free of the barrio and out into open air. Behind them, the structure warped and began a slow crumple. Stanchions bowed and compression popped, sending man-sized splinters hurtling down. Frank didn't bother to dodge, leaving their path to fate.

In a final expulsion of energy, the barrio slammed down. A great plume of dust rose with the resounding impact.

Frank and Laing reached the front line of feds as the cloud hit them.

"Hold your fire!" Flip yelled.

Frank and Laing crashed through the troops, who were watching the implosion in awe.

Frank grabbed Flip by the collar. "Lob the hot shot!"

"But—"

"Just do it!"

Flip punched at his arm console and behind them a small mortar round launched high. It landed in the center of the destruction and ignited white hot. In that flash instant, the barrio's remnants melted. The ball of flame overtook even the expanding dust cloud. It halted just meters from the feds, then receded on itself.

Frank felt the air pulled from his lungs and gasped for oxygen. The hot shot used it all. In another instant, the flame was gone. Air flushed into the void. He could breathe.

Frank got a single look at the smoldering wreck before he and Laing were thrown into the glare-white detox chamber. His ears popped as the seal locked. Steam-heated bioagents flooded the chamber. Frank pulled his suit off and flopped to the ground.

He felt the corrosive agents burn into him and breathed deeply. Ryan's shoulder brushed his own.

"Thank you," Laing said.

Sarah slouched into the microbus's passenger seat, unable to look the driver in the eye. She flicked the atmo controls to recirculate internal air. Hopefully that would contain the pathogen, but there was no helping her companion. His fate was sealed. She locked her guilt, her anguish, down and concentrated on the road ahead. As she stared out, her crazed escape from the barrio blurred with the passing scenery.

Images of the fall cycled through her thoughts. Pulling free of Ryan's grip—the flashing panic in his eyes as she fell. Crashing hard into the barrio. Only the searing pain of her already-broken ribs had kept her conscious. She remembered scrambling to her feet, knowing she had to get as far from Ryan as possible.

Pitching down the barrio's latticework of stairways, she reached the bolt-hole that Black had told her about, a long-forgotten entrance to the sewer system that snaked under the port.

It was just high enough for her to squat, and she rolled up her jeans and hunch-walked a thousand meters in that tube, its stink and slopping rot suffusing her. She had vomited everything in her stomach, down to yellow bile, by the time she pushed up a manhole cover and emerged into the night.

Once out, she melted into the shadows of the nearest alley. Using water from a puddle, Sarah washed off as much of the sewage as possible. The reek faded to manageable. Squatting over the puddle, Sarah checked her murky reflection. She dropped the camouflage and returned to her normal coloring, holding pigment over her bare chest to make it appear that she was wearing a skintight tee.

After her makeshift ablutions, she wandered through the dead streets, stewing in dull shock. She hit Canton Street. At the far end, prostitutes swarmed the slow-moving cars. Sarah turned away—afraid of further contamination.

Then the Bento microbus had pulled up, the driver's eyes roaming her body with nervous interest. In that moment, she had wanted to run, to save this man from the killer within her. But he might be her only means of escape. Did she have the right to decide his fate? Her pause, the quizzical look in her eye, the swath of dark just covering her breasts—it had entranced the man. He dropped his window and it was over.

Now the Bento cruised, deadlocked on the speed limit. A boxy chunk of plastic and steel with a shit-poor hydro-cell motor, the Bento microbus had become the transportation of choice for two very different sets of clientele. Suburbanites loved them for the interior space that shift-molded to the varying needs of a family: from a flow-jack for homework, to compartments for the kids' netball gear, to a cordoned-off, ventilated space for the family dog. Bentos blanketed the burbs, a must-have in any gated hood.

The other group favoring Bentos were hackers. In the back of a Bento, a hacker could chill, have a burrito, and slam through a little coding—all while tooling down the road.

This man is no hacker, Sarah thought. *Better that way.* While the flow-port would be flashier in a data rat's Bento, a soccer mom's car was less likely to be tagged.

"Like your bus," Sarah said.

"Uh—yeah. I have a Harley—a real rocket. Just thought this would be better for . . ." The man stalled out.

"A quick fuck?" Sarah finished, her vitriol evident. She needed to hate this man—to not care that her escape meant his death.

The man's jaws slapped shut, his cheeks going red.

"You single?" Sarah asked, hoping against hope.

The man lifted his chin. "How does that matter?"

Sarah smiled weakly, eyes still averted. "It doesn't, I guess. Sorry." She tried to get into the act. This man was her ticket out. "Just want to know what you need. Is there something special the wife won't . . . indulge in?"

"No—it's not like that," he replied, his voice hesitant. "Shit, maybe it is. I don't know. I don't do this—pick up . . . women. It's not me."

The man's fusillade hammered into Sarah. She couldn't bring herself to respond, so he machine-gunned on. "It's just, well, I have the wife, the kids, the mortgage that's kicking my ass, and then—on top of that, the world's, like, crashing down around me. No place is safe! Not anymore. I mean, terrorism—here? In Trenton? I just know we're headed for war. We gotta be, right? It's all such"—the man looked over to Sarah, who hadn't moved a muscle—"shit," he finished, embarrassed by his tirade. "Listen, I'm sorry. You want to run for the hills, don't you? Maybe I should just let you off."

"Why don't you lie down—in the back there," Sarah said.

The man hesitated, unsure of himself.

"It's okay," she said. "I understand."

"I just want some peace." he said. "To forget it all. . . ."

For a moment, Sarah thought she'd lose it as her distaste for the man crumbled. Then cold ice returned. No going back now. The decision had been made and she would see this through.

"Go on," she said, motioning to the back.

He nodded, set the Bento on auto, and scrambled into the rear. He reset the seating configuration so he could recline, then jerked free of his clothes in a quick, self-conscious fit. Sarah watched the first signs of the virus emerge on his chest and face. Through the euphoric expectation pulsing through him, he hadn't registered what was happening—yet. His skin grew taut and pale.

"What?" he asked on seeing her hesitate. "You backing out? I have money."

Sarah got into the back and drew close, wrapping around him. The man gasped, fingers crawling over her, finding that she was topless. He looked down in confusion. He wanted to ask, then let it all go as she drew him closer—crushing into him, rocking him to the street hum.

His breath grew husky, then labored. A fit of coughing tore through him, making the hair on Sarah's neck bristle. The pathogen took hold and worked through him.

"What's happening to me?" he managed, drawing away. His eyes pocked red and began to bleed.

Sarah just shook her head and hugged him closer.

Then the convulsions began. She felt his muscles jump, hating herself, and the world that forced her to this. He jerked free of her grip, his head smashing into the Bento's molding, eyes wide in shock and pain.

She watched to the very end, her body petrified under the horror's crush. There was a long quiet between them, the man suffocating under the clenched lock of his sternum. The fight in his eyes faded to blank. She watched him for what could have been seconds and what seemed like years—maybe a lifetime.

It was the sewer smell, the faint wisp of it still on her skin, that kicked her to action. She ransacked the microbus, finding the washing machine in the back—a popular option on burb Bentos. Throw in Johnny's dirty jersey and out came a pressed shirt that would pass muster with the pickiest soccer mom.

In it, Sarah found a selection of workout clothes. Must be the daughter's. She squirmed into the shirt. It was small, but the fabric quickly adjusted to her dimensions. She ditched her trashed jeans for a pair of yoga pants.

Sarah slid back into the front seat, trying to ignore the corpse as she crawled over. She found the jackpoint and goggled into the flow's clean data streams. She accessed the Bento's drive control and mapped out a meandering route that would take her far from the city.

Finally, she jumped to coverage of the barrio. The vid played and replayed through the blogs. In it, the barrio wavered, then ripped free of the port wall.

She couldn't watch the rest.

21

Dave Madda was not well.

Sure, he'd started life strong—pulled out of the gate running fast. Words like *whiz kid, prodigy,* and *genius* had followed him from an early age. Madda wasn't sure if he deserved such praise, or if it gradually came to define him. Either way, he believed the hype, and for years swam deep in his own bullshit.

Growing up, Madda had only wanted to be a hacker. Every bone in his body itched to sling through the flow, to be its master and direct its stream. In the backwater bars of San Francisco's Tenderloin, he learned the craft from anyone willing to teach him. He learned too well.

No one cut code like he did. He had a knack for it. While larger patterns eluded him, Madda was all about the details—the basics. He could spot the single flaw in a billion lines of code. Still in his teens, he was running hard hacks on corporate targets. It was on such a run that his life changed.

Madda was never one to let the letter of the law affect his wallet. He loved the fight too much. To get the work, you needed the tech. To get the tech, you needed the dough. To get the dough—you needed to take any damn job that came your way.

A small software concern had contacted Madda. They had developed a new chip. It doubled processing power, replacing silicon with carbon nanotubes. The company was poised to make billions. Only one glitch. Word had spread that Josh Simpson out of University of Melbourne had developed a processor concept that would amp power by an order of magnitude.

Madda had jumped at the gig. The run was a cakewalk. Academic firewalls were inherently porous. Stemmed from some long-held belief that information should flow freely. Madda knew better.

He used his standard interface—a simple physical endeavor that simmed the complex hack he had coded. In uncoded white space, Madda drew his saber. The firewall appeared as a host of faceless opponents.

He lunged at the first, triggering his run. Each move within the simulation translated to raw code flying between Madda and the target computer. In the flow, perception was the key to any battle. To truly see the enemy was to know his flaws. This firewall had six layers. Thus, six opponents.

None of the systems interacted; shit-poor coding as far as Madda was concerned. Thus, each opponent stood numb until the one before it fell. The battle was brief.

In a matter of minutes, Madda was surfing over Simpson's data field. He was about to launch a virus that would subtly tweak the research, thrusting Simpson down a dead-end path and leaving Madda's client free to bring its product to market, when a twitch in the sim stopped him cold.

Dave pushed into the coding.

Couldn't be right, he thought.

Smothered in the base structures, another virus sprouted and infected the data field. A subtle, beautiful web, spindling through the flow. He had seen no evidence of a previous incursion, but someone else was there— someone with very serious skills.

Then Madda felt an eye on him—*the* eye. He backtracked very quietly, leaving no flow wake. The next day, Echelon knocked on his door and made him an offer he couldn't refuse.

Using their far superior incursion software, Echelon had hit Simpson just minutes before Madda's run. They had done so for reasons too subtle for Madda to glean. Something about maintaining a steady flow of progress so as not to upset the status quo.

They explained it to him. While it all sounded cool, Madda didn't really care about the reasoning behind Echelon. Sure, he had some vestige of morality, deep down in the black. But with the tech Echelon offered him, Madda was willing to bend. So, at age nineteen, he left San Francisco, disappeared from society's grid, and began his work for Echelon.

For years, his work for the organization satisfied him. He punched through the cutting edge, awash in the flood of toys Echelon offered. But, ever so slowly, the novelty wore off. His lab in the abandoned subways of Los Angeles went from an altar to a tomb. His tomb.

Ryan Laing had released him from that living death to help destroy Echelon. And then he was truly free. With a world full of opportunity, Dave had decided on a life of hedonism.

In the space of months, Madda pushed several products to market that made him Gates rich. It hadn't been much of a challenge—all were products he had developed under the Echelon aegis.

The money had led to trappings. Indulgences. Women. Luxury. He dated actresses and models, reveling in his new playboy status. But the cravings could not be sated. No matter what he had, there was always something beyond his reach. Slowly, that unfulfilled need pulled him to a darker world.

Obsessive compulsion pushed his friends away. Sycophants and suck-ups remained. He grew more and more reclusive: unable to trust anyone, wanting only to push into the flow, wishing he could go back to his life within Echelon's comfortable grasp. He sucked at freedom.

Then the Burners found him. They offered another way. The offer wasn't pushed, just floated out there in a manner he found impossible to ignore. They caught him at the tail end of a three-day flow stretch. His mind ached, his body cried out for movement, but he couldn't bring himself to return to the flesh.

Then it popped through his node. A straw man, massive, hundreds of meters tall. The edifice stood alone in a vast, dry-cracked desert. It burst into flames, red ripping through the night in rich bursts. It didn't burn down but remained alight, a phoenix locked in the act of becoming. After the image faded, Madda had hunted for its source. Wasn't hard to find.

The process was slow. Consultants came to visit him. They took over his finances, easing him out of the hated interactions that drained him. They allowed him space. Then his health took a turn. Clarity ebbed and flowed. He existed in a mental limbo as his physical being withered.

Few accepted his choice to go with the Burners. His friends and colleagues warned him, cautioned him—they said they just wanted him to be free. He shivered at the very word. Fuck freedom.

That's when the consultants collected him. They took him home. To Burning Man.

Burning Man had begun centuries ago in the desert outside Black Rock City, Nevada. And there it had grown. Now, it spread for hundreds of kilometers over the dry, caked plane. Those that entered the Burning Man didn't leave.

Here, in the grip of his consultants, Madda found peace. He went internal, hollowing into his own solitude. He signed over all his assets. In return, he lived under their umbrella, utterly incommunicado. It suited him. He festered in neurotic solitude, unable and unwilling to separate flow from flesh, truth from lie.

That was before that unfulfilled need rose up and found him. Before Sarah Peters pushed back into his life.

Sarah had to disappear. If she couldn't control the game, she needed to pull free. Pushing out onto the throughway, heading west, the Bento hummed under her.

On leaving Trenton, she had hacked the Bento free from its previous owner, who was now buried off a lonely road outside Melcroft, Pennsylvania. With all identifiers altered, the car wouldn't be pegged as stolen. It gave her time.

Now, lost to the blur, she tried to make sense of what was going on around her. The terrorist acts. The pathogen. Only one answer. Whoever was behind this knew EMPYRE from the inside out. But what was the endgame of all this killing?

Clearly, Ryan Laing was integral to the plan. Sarah had been made the scapegoat—forced to run a gauntlet that would surely finish her. All to flush Laing out. Her lips thinned. She thought about the man who had held her in his grip, suspended over the barrio. Should she have stayed with him in his self-enforced isolation? Maybe. Now she had forced him to come back to a world he hated. And she knew he wouldn't rest until he found her. So she needed to disappear—to ghost out. Then she could turn the tables and hunt her hunter. But to disappear, she had to disable the virus. Until then, a trail of death would follow her.

Sarah pulled her gaze from the humming road. She jacked back in and tunneled into the flow. It had been a while, but she knew a man who could help. Whether he *would* was another matter. He had been a friend once, and a good one. At this point, she wasn't sure if there was anything left of him to salvage.

Sarah punched the defenses arrayed around Dave Madda with the subtlety of a rhino charge. No time for a clean hack. She needed him—and quick.

To her, Burning Man was just another cult that had suckered in one more believer. Watching Madda slip, Sarah had tried to purge him of their bullshit, but it was too late. By the time she pushed through the clique of consultants, Madda had disappeared.

Weeks later, he had reemerged on the blogs, bleary-eyed, saying that he had given his life over to Burning Man. He had chosen to live behind the makeshift city's electronic barrier. What more could she do? That he'd been brainwashed, or worse, was obvious, but she had her own problems. She grew to hate Madda, as she hated Laing. Another person who had abandoned her.

She couldn't seem to hold on to anyone. Ryan. Madda. Her family. They all ran from her. So why not remake herself? One cell at a time if she had to. Each time the knife jockeys cut, a piece of her fell away and she was glad of it. Maybe she would become someone who could be loved. Or someone strong enough not to care.

Now, her need pushed her to action. On her own, on the run, she needed Madda. She couldn't run forever. With the pathogen in her, she would leave a trail that Ryan would certainly follow. And she couldn't allow that.

So she crashed Madda's system. From the Bento, slinging west at speed limit, she charged Burning Man's firewall. Breaching the system and getting to the world's wealthiest recluse was no easy matter, especially with the Bento's hardware. She craved the challenge. It occupied her, and allowed her to forget.

Sarah prided herself on running clean hacks. She left no trace, slipping through the flow like a ghost. But not now. She didn't have the time or the hardware to run silent. Instead, she submerged her hack in a mountain of code.

Looming over Burning Man's flow representation, she set the avalanche free, allowing the virus she had created to build steam and power, rolling faster, harder. By the time it hit the first firewall, it was unstoppable. Defenses couldn't restrain this much coding. The virus surged through the target's infrastructure, leaving chaos in its wake.

Sarah smashed into it with vindictive glee. If those she needed wanted to barricade themselves from her, she would destroy their carefully created defenses. The avalanche rolled through Burning Man's network. This kind of hack was rarely attempted as it tagged the culprit and destroyed the system data it blew through. It was a suicide run.

From the ruins of Burning Man's system, hunter-killers tunneled out, tracking her. She ignored them, punching farther, locating Dave Madda's flow point. In a last burst of raw destruction she pushed through. Voicelock blinked, then held strong. She spoke into her mic.

"Madda."

A withered voice bounced back to her. "Sarah? No. Oh, no. You can't be here. They'll be angry." Madda's voice halted and surged like that of a tired child.

"Dave, I crashed the system. They'll be very angry."

Petulance rose in the voice. "Why would you do that? Leave me alone! They said you'd come. They said you'd all try . . ." He trailed off, then renewed with a frenetic vigor. "Everyone needs to leave me alone!"

"Jesus Christ, Dave. I would have let you rot in that coffin, but *I* need you. And you *will* help me."

"Everyone needs me." The voice ran shrill and tinny. "I give up."

"Not today. Today, I can't run solo. So I'm forcing the issue."

"You can't . . ."

Sarah lost the link as the Burners' hunt-kill 'ware smashed through the walls she'd erected. She didn't have much time.

"Listen, Madda," she said. "I'm coming to you. Do you know what that means?"

A muffled noise.

"No?" She triggered the second slide. Another data torrent ripped through the target system. But this one was directed at Dave only.

She hoped it wouldn't kill him.

The rush of vid-captured events blasted over Madda. He struggled to hold amid the whirlwind of swirling input. He saw Sarah's run through Dubai, the mayhem at Langley. Then Trenton hit him—a steamroller of information patched together from a thousand blogs and news clips. The sheer mass of it threatened to push him catatonic. He didn't want it. Didn't want any of it. He wanted only to play his games. The world could get along without him. And that included Sarah Peters.

"Monster . . ." It was all he could say.

"No. Dave, it's me. You know me."

"You've killed thousands. I want no part of it!"

"No! Yes. Those people died, Madda. But—it has to end. I need you to fix me."

"Me?"

The edge in her voice dropped away. "I don't trust anyone else."

"Sarah, no." Madda just couldn't. "Not now. Too tired. Way too tired."

"Dave, I know. But I have to finish this thing. And you don't get a choice."

"I'll—"

"Listen to me, Dave. I'm coming to you. Do you know what that means? The pathogen in me will decimate everything in its wake. Maybe you'll survive within Burning Man's shield. Maybe it will bust through. Either way—every pilgrim at your gates will die."

"You are a monster."

"I guess I am." The voice trailed into silence. Something in it, in the desperation, the truth, the raw need, kicked at Madda. From that deep well, his feelings for Sarah, his need for her, took hold of him once again.

"I'll be ready," he said.

22

Ryan Laing dreamed. He wandered through transient fantasies, unable to latch on to reality and not really wanting to. Fever sapped him, rising in hot sweats and ebbing to chills that shook him to the core.

His wandering mind settled on a single scene, familiar but unwelcome. He clung to knobbed granite, climbing high over the California desert. The sharp tang of warm rock infused him. He slammed a fist into a vertical fissure, savoring the rock's bite. His feet splayed out wide, climbing slippers grasping protrusions in the sheer face.

Looking up, he saw the climb's familiar progression. Each step, each lunge, each hand placement. He'd done it many times before. Laing relaxed into the sharp edged routine. The jagged granite spikes of California's Joshua Tree National Park rose above him. His refuge.

Then the scene wavered, a furnace shimmer blasting the air. A single ripple and it reset. Only now, Ryan knew he was dreaming. And he knew what came next.

He craned his neck to see the shot. This time, he could stop it. This time, he would not fall. On a ridge across the valley, he saw the gun's barrel. Exposed, out of control, he scrambled with mad abandon—trying to evade the inevitable.

When the shot came, it was almost a relief. Expectation shattered in the crumble of rock and a long fall to the valley floor. Impact.

The pain, the confusion, the soft anger of finality. Ryan remembered it all and experienced it again. He closed his eyes to the sun's glare. In darkness, he savored these last moments.

He opened his eyes. A figure stood over him. A sun-tipped silhouette, cool dark on seared heat. It stooped, lifting him from the red caked dirt with no effort. The pain in Ryan ceased.

He looked up at the figure. Before him, the man rippled, then settled. Brown hair, touched with gray. Deep brown eyes over lined cheeks. A smile that made life feel manageable. Christopher Turing.

Laing knew this wasn't real. In reality, Turing had revived Ryan from the fall by injecting him with the drones. In reality, Ryan had been forced to kill Turing as Echelon crumbled.

Ryan shook himself. He craned back, looking to the place where the assassin had been.

"Did you kill me?" He stumbled over the words, unable to pull from the waking dream.

"No, Ryan." Turing's lips moved out of synch with the voice, as if the transmission hadn't quite locked true.

"Then what . . ."

Turing's hand gripped Ryan's shoulder. With the touch, a pulse of relief swept though Laing. "I missed you." The words felt trite and small, like a goldfish trying to describe the ocean.

As he stared at Turing, the past years crisped and flaked away. For a moment, Ryan glimpsed the man he used to be. The man who knew that life was controlled. That no matter what, Christopher Turing, and Echelon, would be there for him.

Turing smiled as if nothing had happened—as if Ryan had not killed him to end Echelon's tyranny. He smiled with the love of a father looking down at his son.

A heat ripple. The cliffs over Ryan shivered. His vision fuzzed to an image of Turing, lying dead.

"No," Ryan whispered. Joshua Tree and Turing's smiling face snapped back.

Then, the long fall through the flow as Echelon died. And after . . . Flickering images of Sarah leaving him. Of chaos ripping the world apart.

The images overpowered Joshua Tree's granite spires and Turing's gentle gaze.

"No, no!" Ryan screamed. Turing's grip on his shoulder evanesced with the decaying scene.

Ryan reached out for Turing. His hand slipped through the apparition. Turing's image blasted out. Joshua Tree vanished.

Now there was only darkness, the ink black that ran through Ryan's life since he'd lost Turing. Through the few good times, and the more plentiful bad ones since Turing's death, Ryan's experience of life had faded to monochrome. Without the man who had been more to Ryan than his own father, life was less. The darkness of loss hung over everything.

Ryan reached into the void, needing to pull the dream back to him.

"*No!*" he screamed into the black.

Cold permeated him. Then the images returned. Turing's death kicked into the following years and kaleidoscoped over the last days. Finally, the present expanded around Ryan, covering the darkness but not vanquishing it.

"No!" His scream expanded, lost to infinity.

BALTIMORE-WASHINGTON CORRIDOR

Hands on Ryan's shoulders. Shaking him.

"No! No! No!" Ryan's screams reverberated off the walls of a small room, his own voice lurching him back to reality.

Frank Savakis stood over him. "Fuck, Laing. Shut up. You'll wake the neighbors."

Laing whipped an arm out, shoving Frank's hands from him. "What . . ."

Frank stepped back, rubbing his wrist. "You got issues enough to finance a team of psychs."

Laing sat up, regaining composure. Amid the brown clutter of Frank's apartment, he flashed back to the peace he'd had just a moment ago. He scratched the vision of Turing from his eyes, rubbing them to bloodshot.

"Sorry," Laing said, voice hoarse. "Bad dream."

"If I dreamed that bad, I'd give up sleep on principle." Frank kicked aside the detritus of dirty clothes littering his floor to get to the kitchen. "You want food? Coffee?"

Laing rose, the effort drawing a wheeze that crescendoed into a coughing fit.

"Still sick, huh?"

"Yeah," Laing grunted.

The dark funk of Frank's stack apartment pushed in on Ryan. He needed air. Quick. He lurched across the narrow room to dust-brown drapes and ripped them open. A corrugated wall greeted him.

"Fuckin' stacks," he sputtered.

Frank just laughed. "Not on for exterior view till seven." Frank shoved a cup of coffee into Laing's hand. "Work on this," he said.

Laing took the coffee, pacing the room in slow circles as he drank. Each time he passed the window, looking dead into the side of another stack apartment, he grimaced.

Finally, Frank had enough. "The fuck?! You live in a fucking tent—in Antarctica!"

"Why live in the stacks? The CIA has to pay better than this."

Frank gazed at the surroundings as if surprised by Laing's criticism. "Comfortable here," he said. "Feels homey."

Slammed up against the Port of Baltimore's Seagirt Marine Terminal, the stacks were an urban development concept gone, to Ryan's mind, horribly wrong. A framework of steel rose five hundred meters into the sky. Within it, mobile housing units—stacks—nestled like eggs in a carton. Tens of thousands—one slotted against the other—each moving to the exterior and then turning back, allowing each a glimpse of the Baltimore-Washington Corridor for a few hours per day.

Laing shivered, thinking about how many housing pods stood between him and daylight. "This feels homey?"

"That's right. I grew up here. Actually in a box format. This here," Frank said, waving his arm with regal nonchalance, "is about twice the size."

"Double wide, huh," Ryan said, to which Frank laughed.

Laing continued his lap. On a shelf, lightly dusted, stood a framed vid shot. It showed a man standing on a dock, a massive hauler looming behind him.

"This your dad?"

Frank grunted in the affirmative. "He was a longshoreman. Automation would of ended his career eventually. A malfunctioning load winch sped up the process."

Laing turned to Frank, who stared back with hard eyes. The man wasn't the type to break down on bringing up a dead parent.

"Sorry," Ryan said.

Frank just went back to his breakfast, a freeze packed ham and egg plate. He snapped the edge of the package, the chemical sizzle warming his food.

"Long way from here to Langley," Laing continued.

"Something those Ivy League fucks never let me forget. That's all right, though. They got pedigree. I got talent." He spit out the last word like a pit. "I stay here to hold on to my roots. Too easy to get lost in all the shit, you know."

"My parents were ranchers." Laing couldn't bring himself to say the rest. That his parents had also been pushed into uselessness by the hand of global commerce. That their sad lives had also been cut short.

"I know," Frank said, not looking up from his steaming meal.

Laing nodded and continued his pacing as he worked on the coffee. "Even your coffee smells like foot."

"Well, aren't you the fuckin' critic," Frank replied, shoveling a load of egg into his mouth. "Ma always said that fish and guests begin to stink after three days."

Laing pulled away from his coffee, swiveling to Frank in shock. "I been out that long?"

"Near to it."

Laing vaguely remembered getting here. After detox, they'd emerged into a gray silence. Flash burns arced up the wall of Trenton's port, the barrio's shadow embossed into the carbon steel. At the base, only a swell of ash. Nothing else remained. Frank had taken him home. Then a marathon of fever and dream.

Didn't make sense that the drones couldn't kill off this pathogen. He felt their roving swarm through his body, a swirling battle on the cellular level. Were it not for the drones, his body would have killed itself by now. They were the only thing keeping his cells from self-destructing.

For now, the battle seemed to have reached an equilibrium. He felt like shit, but he could operate. A thought occurred to him. He jumped to the counter. Frank sat over his food, sawing on the ham steak with supreme concentration. Laing grabbed the knife from him.

"Hey!" Frank sputtered.

Laing ignored him. He opened his palm and pressed the knife down, sliding it over the length of his hand. He pulled the knife away and stared in shock. He closed his hand into a fist.

Frank grabbed his wrist. Laing couldn't bring himself to move.

"The fuck you doing?!" Frank demanded.

Finally, Laing opened his hand. His palm was covered in blood.

Blood spilled from the wound and flowed over Ryan's palm. Drones clustered in the blood like patches of oil, but not enough to suture the wound.

Laing showed it to Frank. He walked to the sink, ran his palm under the water and wrapped it in a towel, which quickly streaked red.

"How's that possible?" Frank asked.

"Whatever's in me is so severe that the drones can't do more than keep me alive."

"What would do that?"

"Only something targeted at me specifically."

Ryan watched that settle over Frank.

"But it's not spreading. We're sharing the same air, and I'm fine."

"Like I said—I'm fighting this thing. Hard to describe what the drones are doing, but I can shift the virus just enough to disrupt transmission. Takes everything I've got, though."

"So the virus serves a double purpose," Frank said. "It puts the mother of all bull's-eyes on Sarah Peters's head. Anywhere she goes, at any time, the virus can kick up and she's suddenly surrounded by corpses."

"Add to that, she becomes the perfect scapegoat for bioattacks around the world—like Australia."

"Some coldhearted shit. And then, this pathogen in Sarah hits you, hurts you—but doesn't quite knock you off."

"You complaining?" Ryan asked.

"Just saying . . ." Frank paused, digging a clean knife from the drawer and reengaging the ham. "Someone wants you vulnerable—and they knew you'd hunt Sarah to the ends of the earth."

"We're—" Laing stopped himself. That wasn't right. "*I'm* being played."

"*We're* playing catch-up here."

"And we're no closer to the truth."

Frank grinned, bits of egg pocking his smile. "Not quite right. Check this out."

Frank flicked at the remote and the plexi window went opaque. Then it rezzed into a screen. A still image of the Trenton disaster came up.

"While you were getting your beauty sleep, I've been working."

"You find Sarah?"

"No. She either slipped away or got incinerated."

"She's not dead." Ryan tried for conviction, but it came out as a weak plea.

"Yeah . . . okay." Frank stumbled over his words, uncomfortable with Ryan's display.

Ryan reined in his emotions, locking back into cold analysis. "Any more virus blooms?"

"No! Will you get your mind out of that babe's pants and listen to me?"

Laing turned, anger flushing out his pallor. Frank plowed on before he could get another word in.

"I'm not so interested in Peters. She's known. I'm interested in the other guy. Tall, thin, brown hair—beat the shit out of you—ring any bells?"

Frank flicked at the screen; the image wavered, then slid backward. The barrio rebuilt itself. In reverse time, Laing watched Sarah seemingly launch up into his hands, then saw his climb up the stanchion. Time slowed, then froze.

"Am I missing something?" Laing asked.

"Guy was pretty good at staying off vid. None of the fed links caught him."

"So—"

"So the fucker didn't count on my wire. Probably didn't count on my buckshot pounding into his shoulder either."

Frank flipped the feed.

On screen, a fast-motion blur tracked Frank's working up the barrio and toward the commotion. Then the fight, fast and brutal. Finally, an arm rose, and the shotgun discharged.

Frank slowed to frame-by-frame.

The screen went white from the single shot. Just as the flash faded and the buckshot found target, Frank froze the playback.

"Son of a bitch," Laing said.

On screen was a frame of the assailant, shoulder blown back with the impact of Frank's shot. Surprise wiped through the clean features of his perfectly rezzed face.

"Yup."

Laing turned away from the man and looked to Frank.

"Well, you get an ID?"

"Wasn't easy. This fucker gets more knife work than a porn queen. Cheeks shaved, nose sharpened, then later plumped. Eye color shifts—the works."

Laing gave Frank a look, pushing him to get on with it.

"All right, all right," Frank said. "I see you're not gonna praise my stellar fucking work. Short answer, yes. I mapped the guy's mug, morphed the features to account for surgical variants, then did a long scan on our archives. Took all night. But we got him in Lhasa on the day the Dalai Lama got snuffed."

"But that was an EMPYRE job."

"Also tagged him in Dubai and then in New York just hours before Dillon's place blew."

"Jesus."

"Yeah. He makes the rounds pretty good—for a dead guy."

"Come again?" Laing asked.

Frank flipped to another screen load. It showed a man of similar proportions, this time dressed in fatigues.

"He was one of ours. Name's Zachary—"

"Taylor," Ryan cut in.

"Yeah," Frank responded. "How do you know that?"

"He . . . he told me," Ryan said. "I just remembered."

"Well, that would have been a nice piece of information to pass on," Frank huffed.

"Sorry. Slipped my mind while I was trying so hard not to get dead."

"Yeah, well, I guess that's fair." Frank pulled up a shot of a hovercraft, flipped and burning. A bloody corpse floated next to the hulk.

"That's Taylor—dead. Doesn't look like him now, after all the knife work. But I've analyzed these images six ways to Sunday—bone structure, body proportion—and that's him."

Something about the shot pricked Laing's curiosity. He approached the screen and looked at it for some time.

"That hovercraft looks . . . It's not a military vehicle."

"Nope. That's a United Nations transport. It pulled Taylor from the Crimea. He was on his way to The Hague for trial."

"Son of a bitch."

"Taylor had been on active duty for three years straight. Deep in it. He finally went bat shit—blew up a school bus that he claimed held arms."

"Did it?"

"Oh, yeah—big-time. It also held thirty-seven kids." Frank flipped back to the head shot and stared into Taylor's dark eyes. "Fucker was going to fry."

"So, what happened?"

"The Crimean Tartars weren't exactly thrilled with seeing him shipped off to a cushy UN facility. Had their hearts set on some eye-for-an-eye style justice. So they hit the craft. Stink over that forced the UN to leave the combat zone. Neither side held back after that. The region was decimated in a matter of weeks. In the end, worked out pretty well for the good guys."

"And who's that?"

"That's us. That's the USA." The look in Frank's eyes told Laing not to prod further on that subject. The man was a believer. "With the UN out of the picture, the Crimean push for independence faltered and we were able to install a more cooperative government in Ukraine."

"And now—years later—here he is. Living. Breathing. And always in the wrong place at the right time."

"He's the key. The link between Sarah, you, EMPYRE, and . . ." Frank paused.

"And?" Laing raised his eyes. Frank kept his lowered. "Come on, man. Too late for secrets."

"And Phoenix." Seeing Laing's confusion, Frank continued. "EMPYRE farmed out their dirty work. They made the call and Phoenix went into action."

"Jesus. If just once the people doing the scheming then did the killing . . ." Ryan let the words tail into silence.

"Hey, I don't love it either. Nearly pissed my career away tracking Phoenix. That said, can't very well have American fingerprints all over the kinda jobs EMPYRE was pulling. EMPYRE had to stay clean. Phoenix solved their problems."

"You're saying Taylor is Phoenix?"

"Maybe. Or part of it."

"So EMPYRE's pit bull goes off leash and kills its master."

"I'd think you'd appreciate the move."

"How's that?"

"You were the pit bull that ended Echelon. Looks like these conspiracies gotta be more careful crafting their killers."

Ryan didn't take the bait. "So why does Phoenix want me?"

"The fuck do I know? Don't really care. I'm more interested in inflicting a little Old Testament retribution."

The hard edge in Savakis's tone pulled Ryan from his own musings. The blood-deep drive for revenge was evident. "That's all you care about, isn't it?" Ryan asked.

"They were my team. My people."

"EMPYRE would have killed you in an instant if it served their purpose."

"Oh, give it a fuckin' rest. You think you're the only guy who sees big picture? I mean, shit, we all get used and abused. That's the job. If you didn't like it, you would never have gotten as far as you did. So—you can trust me or not, like me or not, but here's the deal—you're a big fat, fuckin' target. You've got someone after you that knows you better than you know yourself. You want that person. I want that person. Doesn't fuckin' matter why—our goals run the same path. And you're not Superman anymore."

The slow burn in Ryan faded. It had been a long time since someone had pushed him this hard. But Frank was right, Laing needed help.

"Okay," Ryan said in quiet surrender.

"Okay. Then we go after Taylor."

The floor shifted. Laing could just sense the slow-motion kick as Frank's stack began to move. Laing took the remote from Frank and flipped over the images, nose to nose with Taylor. Finally, he flicked the screen to transparent.

The mechanical claw gripped the stack, pulling it free of the dark. Light broke over Ryan in a slow plane as the stack moved to the outside of the building.

"You're going after Taylor," Ryan said. "If I'm really the mark, you'll be better off going solo."

"You like my place that much, huh? Just want to hang here?"

"I'm going for Sarah."

"But—she could be anywhere. Or, she could be dead."

"I have to know one way or the other. If she's alive, there aren't many places for Typhoid Mary to hide. I got an idea where she'd head."

Laing turned from the view to see Frank appraising him. He held the man's eye for a long second. "I *have* to know," Ryan repeated, his need suffusing the words.

Slowly, Frank's cold stare eased and he nodded. He picked over his plate and shoved a fork's worth into his mouth. "You want breakfast before we go?" he asked through a mush of eggs.

23

Stress consumed Sarah. She couldn't last much longer like this. The pursuit, the knowledge that the killer within her would strike again, exhausted her. Maybe with the Burners she'd be safe—for a while. More than anything, she needed rest.

For now, the pathogen had gone dormant. Or she thought it had. The churning itch within her had ebbed and her lungs weren't thick with fluid. She felt hijacked, like a vector for someone else's will. She'd be triggered again, and the map would light up with death. More regret—as if that word could even approach the waves of shame and revulsion rolling through her. The optimism that used to reside at her core was lost. Nothing would ever be the same. Guilt threatened to overwhelm her. As the death toll mounted, she felt herself retreat from the human race. At some point, it would be too much to bear.

She pushed into Nevada's desert. The small town of Black Rock clung to oblivion's edge, a final outpost of civilization. After this, it was sand, grit, sun, and Burning Man. Somewhere between a cult and occult, Burning Man had become a pock on the map—a place one didn't venture. Sarah shook off her trepidation. She needed the man inside.

From the mirage of whisping sand, Burning Man materialized. It sprawled larger than she had expected. The pulse barrier around it gave the ramshackle city a netherworldly shimmer—as if anything were possible within its walls. A ragged chaos of buildings—some utilitarian, others fantastical—spread over the plain. And, in the center—the burning man itself. A giant, looming deity, always blazing, never quenched.

Burning Man had begun in the twentieth as a wild, rugged, psychedelic experiment. For one week each year, the desert was transformed into a piece of communal art. No money changed hands; all trade was done by barter. Wild structures flashed into existence, flights of fancy realized, if only for a moment. The celebration ended with the burning of a massive effigy, thousands watching it ash out. Over the years, Burning Man drew a following, became an institution, and expanded into a year-round event. Its participants began to stay, to hold, to create a structure that firmed into something approaching religion.

From the ashes of the burning man, a new structure was created: a figure that would not burn down, that would last through time. In that moment, Burning Man shifted on its axis, becoming more and less than had been imagined.

Now—for those who believed—who wanted to believe—it promised something fresh in a sea of disappointment and fear. To Sarah's mind, it was all a hoax. But it was a grand hoax. That Madda had committed to it so fully surprised Sarah. Still, everyone deserved peace.

Approaching the camp, the road deteriorated into rubble, then finally petered out. She abandoned the Bento in a massive junkyard. Pilgrims brought nothing to Burning Man. Their slag became parts and pieces for the camp to ingest. Around her, Burners tore through the junkyard, hunting for raw material.

Before her, a line wove to the gate. The line of people snaked into the desert, a tail of life running up into City Center. She formed up and waited. Finally, Sarah reached the barrier.

"Empty out," the guard said. He wore tattered shorts, sheared by wind and sand. His bare chest was caked red with grit.

"What?" she said, craning over the man's shoulder.

"Money, credit—" the man said in a bored monotone.

"You want my cash?" Sarah asked. She didn't have much, and wasn't thrilled with the prospect of relinquishing it.

"You won't need it here."

"But I won't be here forever." Sarah's annoyance rose. Vaguely, she wondered if the virus was triggered by an amp in her emotional activity. She hoped not.

The man smiled at her, a long, flat grin under low-slung eyelids. The look of a man who knew better. *No one leaves Burning Man. Why would you?*

When it became obvious that the man wasn't going to let her pass, she pulled her credit and cash chips, placing them in the bowl the man held before him.

"Thank you for your contribution."

Sarah started to pass, but the man pulled her short.

"No vid equipment here either."

"What the hell . . ." Sarah started to pull from the man's grip, but he held on, iron strong.

The man slipped his hand free of Sarah's shoulder and dug into her side, causing her broken ribs to shoot hot pain. He reached up under her T and pressed harder, gritty fingers slipping into her flesh.

Sarah struggled like a wet cat. It did no good. With a dull pop, the man pulled the hawkeye from its holster. Holding it in his hands, he let her go. Sarah, startled by the attack, pulled away from him, crab walking back as he held the hawkeye aloft. To sense the hawkeye required serious tech. Someone in here wasn't fucking around.

"What happens at Burning Man, stays at Burning Man," he said with a wry smile.

No way Sarah was letting that piece go. The man leered down at her with calm piousness, as a woman who deserved pity and a strong arm because she did not yet see the way.

From the ground, Sarah arched, torquing her left leg around her right and rocketing it up at the man. It struck his hand, snapping his wrist. The hawkeye, freed from the man's grasp, launched into the sky.

The man staggered back, crumpling around his flopping wrist, a primal wail escaping into the desert. By the time Sarah got to her feet, a small cadre of heavily armed mercs had burst from what looked like—and clearly wasn't—an ancient lean-to. The smooth precision of their movements again took Sarah by surprise. They surrounded her, taz sticks drawn.

Around them, the other pilgrims cleared away. Sarah began to raise her hands—very slowly. She got the feeling these guys were looking for a fight. From the hawkeye, she saw the merc behind her lift his taz.

The soft flush of tech-maxed adrenaline suffused her. She fell into it, swimming in the clarity of heightened vision. Her body whipped sideways just as the taz fired. The shot pounded into the merc in front of her, lighting up his soft-coat armor with current.

Sarah continued her arc, grabbing the merc's taz hand and whipping him around. While there was no piercing his armor, the man within had tolerances like any other. His shoulder popped from its socket. She wrenched him in front of her, using him as a shield.

In unison, the mercs fired on their own man. The force of impact blew them both backward. In the air, her thigh lit up. A taz shot had smacked into the meat of her leg. It didn't penetrate the tat, but its force did damage to her thigh. She fell to the earth in a hard thump.

Mercs surrounded her. She lashed out with her good leg, hitting a merc's knee with hard crushing force. The knee popped back and the man toppled, screaming. She twisted to her good foot and stood. For a moment, she thought she had them.

Then a taz stick clicked at her head. Tat or not, if the merc fired, it was over. She froze in that moment, suspended, quietly hoping he'd pull the trigger and let her rest.

"Do not fire." The voice was slow, as if pulled to action from long hibernation.

"Do not fire," the man repeated.

The voice had a startling effect on the mercs. All but the man holding the taz to her head pulled away and surrounded its owner in a protective shield.

"Sir," one said. "Please go back into the city."

The man parted the sea of mercs with a shrug of his hand. He hobbled into the clear, allowing Sarah to see him for the first time. Slack flesh hung off his cheeks, pallor highlighting red, twitching eyes. His mouth worked on words that would not form. His body looked beaten, junked long ago and then reluctantly kicked back into service. One arm hung limp at his side.

"Oh my God," Sarah said.

"Hello, Sarah," Dave Madda replied.

24

Frank Savakis was all for dirty tricks. He just didn't like being on their sharp end. He prided himself on always knowing more. More than his allies. More than his enemies. In pursuit of that information, he was relentless. Morality had a place—maybe in raising a kid, or tipping your waitress. But out in the cold, it held a man back, made him weaker. For some, the ability to push that ethical envelope and get the job done came from faith—in a god, a religion, a life after. For Frank, it was allegiance to country.

He was the real deal—a self-made man. With no silver spoon, he'd thumped his way through the docks, got himself through college, and was ready to repay the country that had offered him such opportunity. His father had demanded no less.

And life in the service had been all he'd wanted. Frank knew his breed was in demand. He liked being the weapon, unsheathed only when the battle got ugly. It satisfied the street fighter in him.

But that kind of service hadn't been enough to get him far in the CIA. The planners, the fuckin' cake eaters, still ran everything. And he would never break into that circle. There was too much wharf rat in him. And he wouldn't bend. Not for them. That such trivial shit mattered only goaded him to further action.

It was that stubborn streak that kept Frank going, even though his rise within the CIA had stalled years ago. So what he couldn't get by upping his position, Frank found by lurking in the trenches. No one knew more techs, assistants, and low men in the Company. That he didn't bullshit them or feed them a line drew these people to him. And he was loyal—to the point of self-destruction.

Frank operated with a single mindset, whether in the field or behind Langley's high walls. There were good guys, bad guys, and what you were willing to do. Everything else was a circle jerk. Politics plagued the CIA. Fuckin' ivy choked the place.

Years ago, returning to Langley after a stint in Cairo, Frank had found that one of his best sources had been dragged into one of the many political skirmishes that characterized life within the Central Intelligence Agency. One of the ivies had decided that Hannah Beck needed to go.

A career executive assistant, Beck did her job with smooth precision. She worked hard, then went home to wife and kid. Frank knew the family. He'd eaten at their home, met Hannah's wife, Jacqueline, a plump homemaker.

Somewhere between forty and fifty, Beck had a slick beauty, a presence she couldn't hide under her conservative garb. Her boss, a fuckin' cake eater first rate, had requested more "assistance" from Hannah than she was willing to offer.

Rebuffed, he'd begun the slow process of firing the careerist. He gave her assignments at which she could only fail. He made life uncomfortable—forced her to work more than she was willing. Retribution, pure and simple.

It had taken some coaxing to get the truth from Hannah, but no one was better equipped to do so than Frank. On getting the picture, he took action. While the CIA fostered an air of informality, busting up the chain of command was not done lightly. Frank went at his target with a sledgehammer. He dug into the guy, found all the little indiscretions of a man who played life like a game. But there were no second lives with Frank.

Armed and ready for battle, he had barged into the man's office, a tablet under his arm. Before the man could call security, Frank slapped the tablet on the desk. It only took a glance to see that Frank had dug up enough affairs, oversights, and indiscretions to end the man's career, reputation, and marriage.

"You leave, or that tablet goes wide." The man was gone two weeks later—off to a corporate gig that probably paid twice his CIA salary. Hannah got transferred to a new boss within the Company—a different cake eater. But this one was higher up the ladder and rising fast. Hannah rode Andrew Dillon's star right to the top. After that, Frank's rep went platinum.

Now, at the shit end of the whip, Frank needed info. Hannah owed him. They met at a tea joint outside her burb. He found the place easily enough. The old chapel stood out in the landscape of uniform prefab. Over the stained glass, holos pumped signage in mixed fonts: Church of Skaten. Inside the vaulted space, Frank could make out dozens of skateboarders lofting off the vert ramps that covered the area once reserved for pews. A small sign led Frank into the church's basement.

The scent of exotic teas wafted through the low-slung space. In the dim light, it took a little time to find Hannah. She sat by herself in a far corner, sipping her tea under the glow of actual candles. Each table got one, jammed into the head of a wine bottle. Wax spilled down the sides.

She sat with her back to the entrance, knowing Frank would want full sight lines. "You gotta be shitting me," Frank said, sitting heavily. "There's a diner down the street. I'll buy you some real food."

Hannah looked up, her dark eyes twinkling. "Time you broadened yourself. I'll buy you a cup of chai. You might like it."

"This some kind of dyke chic I'm not in on?" He gave the musty environs another quick glance. "Think I'm immune."

Beck snorted. That Frank was equally gruff with everyone allowed him leeway she would never grant another. "Jimmy's upstairs, skating. Mostly parents down here, waiting for their kids to tire themselves out. Didn't realize you were interested in switching teams. If you'd only told me, I'd have made arrangements."

"Hey, dykes I get. We got similar interests."

"Maybe. But you'd look shitty in a dress."

It was Frank's turn to laugh. "How you been, Hannah?"

Hannah's face shaded, her grin faltering. "It's been tough. I'm on a real shithole's desk. After Andrew . . ." She let the sentence trail off.

"This one after your body too?"

"Not quite. She's just a bitch. And a straight one at that."

"The horror." Frank took another slow look around the room.

"Spit it out, Frank. You want something. What is it?"

"EMPYRE." Frank let the word hang in the air.

Hannah gazed at him over the candle's flicker. She remained silent.

"Before you clam, I know what EMPYRE did—I have full access on Andrew's feed. And you know Dillon recruited me to the project."

"So what do you want from me?"

"I want to know its nuts and bolts. It was all off book."

"That's an understatement. Dillon didn't share, Frank. And I didn't ask. Seemed like something I'd be better off not knowing."

"Too fucking right. The casualties are stacking up. Someone's cleaning it all up—erasing it from existence."

"And you want me to stick my neck out for the next chop?"

"Yes." Bullshitting someone like Beck wouldn't work. Frank needed real help. He didn't have to say that she owed him. People like Hannah and Frank didn't forget their debts.

She gazed off, looking above Frank, up to the ceiling. He knew she was thinking about her kid, her wife, everything she had worked for.

"What do you want?" she asked, turning back to him with grim-faced determination. "Specifically."

Frank nodded. That was all the thanks she'd get. She didn't require more. "There's someone I think was involved with EMPYRE. Someone who should be dead."

"Frank, I don't know—"

"I know you don't. But there's a trail somewhere. Maybe not on Andrew's feed. But somewhere in the Company. We both know money doesn't move at Langley without heaven and earth shifting to get it by."

"Tell me about it."

"So hunt around. I'd do it myself, but that would raise a lot of flags. Give me a scent and I'll run it down."

Hannah shook her head. "There was a stink to EMPYRE, Frank. I don't know what they had in mind, but it stank." She started laughing softly. "I knew they'd offer you a place. And I knew you'd say yes. Maybe the whole thing stank of you."

"Couldn't have smelled worse than that dirt soup you're sipping on."

Hannah ignored him, holding a midline stare. "I don't know what they had running. But it was black."

"Hannah—"

"That kind of shit sticks to you. I know you're not a lily, Frank, but I don't want to see you . . ." She couldn't finish.

"Hannah, I'm in too deep to walk away."

At that, she pulled her gaze back to Frank. "We both know that's not in you anyway."

"Whatever EMPYRE was doing, someone's mopping it up. That someone killed Andrew."

"And you want your pound of flesh."

"You're damn right."

She nodded. "Give me a name."

"I'm sure it's an alias behind a legend—and so on. The man died years ago."

"Frank, give me the fucking name and let me get out of here. I've got PTA tonight."

"Name's Zachary Taylor."

Hannah stood to leave. "I don't know the name, but, like you said, someone does."

"Thank you."

She hesitated before turning away. Tentatively, she placed a hand on his shoulder. She didn't have to say it. The look in her eyes was enough. A cold shiver ran through Frank. Hannah was saying good-bye.

It didn't take long. Hannah knew everyone. And she understood the idiosyncrasies of the Company. Even outliers like EMPYRE couldn't hide from the bureaucratic masher that chewed through every aspect of the CIA. Behind all the cloak and dagger, all the tech and espionage, there was payroll, requisition reports, logs filed and lost to the data soup sloshing through the mainframe. In the end, the Company was government. If you knew where to hunt, nothing was truly off book.

Frank got the call a day later. It came from a public flow port, and had neither tag nor subject. Frank knew just who it was.

"Zachary Taylor is a ghost."

"No shit," Frank shot back.

"I got nothing on him. He's never been paid by the CIA."

"Son of a bitch," Frank muttered to himself. Then he heard a soft chuckle over the link.

"That's the bad news, isn't it?" Frank asked.

"Couldn't leave you empty handed. Zachary may have ghosted out, but his genes haven't."

"Run that by me again," Frank said.

"Taylor's corpse was matched after the accident. How he was ID'd."

"That I know."

"So I ran that code and found a match."

"You found him?" Frank betrayed his shock.

"Not quite," Hannah Beck replied.

25

"Un-fuckin'-believable," Frank muttered to himself, staring at the sculpture. He didn't get it, a fact that made him the odd man out. The tour guide and the rest of the group seemed to think it was the next coming. Before Frank, slender, metallic arachnid limbs laced together to form a stylized Viking longship. Bug legs arced out like oars along the sides of a curved hull that rose to tridents on each end. The skeletal sculpture rose like a ghostly apparition from Faxaflói Bay.

"This, as I'm sure you are all aware, is *The Sun Voyager,* or *Sólfar,* by Jón Gunnar Árnason," the tour guide said. "This creative triumph has been preserved through the years, as it marks both Iceland's past and its push to the future." The tour guide continued his drivel while Frank's travel companions marveled at the thing.

Frank gazed at it in the dying light of a polar winter. It flickered over a circular base, skeleton white, both ominous and fragile.

After a hard day of travel, Savakis found himself mired in heavy night. Reykjavík lay low to the frozen earth. None of the buildings rose higher than a few stories. It was like no city Frank had seen. The moment he had set foot here, he was ready to bolt. The country was too perfect, too clean, and too goddamned quaint.

I'll bet they shit white here, he thought.

Frank turned from the sculpture and bent into the biting wind. He had entered Iceland on a tourist visa. Not many of those this time of year, but he wanted the flexibility that an official visit by an American intelligence officer wouldn't offer. With Iceland's hard restrictions on immigration, an attempt to shutter out the violence ripping across the globe, Frank had been forced to sign on to a government-chaperoned sightseeing tour.

A hand fell on his shoulder. "Sir, can I help you?" The guide had left his flock to catch up with Frank.

"Oh, no," Frank said, steering his voice and appearance toward frailty. "Just getting chilled. Think I'll go back to the hotel and thaw out."

The guide looked flummoxed, not sure what to do.

"Don't worry, I know the road back," Frank said through a shiver—which didn't need forcing.

"Okay, sir. If you wouldn't mind, check in with the front desk—so I know you arrived safely."

"Of course. Very kind of you," Frank said, shuffling off.

Iceland's restrictions weren't quite draconian. He had just enough leash to do what was necessary. As Frank left the guide's sight, he straightened up, stretching out his gait. If he didn't check in, the guide would alert the authorities and that was a headache Frank didn't need. He didn't have much time.

Get the job done, and get the fuck out, he thought.

Frank worked his way through the hibernating streets. It looked as if winter had sapped the city's lifeblood. He pushed through, reaching the base of Hallgrímskirkja. The tallest building on the entire island, the church arched up from a thick base to a needle-sharp point. Its hexagonal columns hinted at cooling lava. The small house he was seeking hunkered beneath the chapel's black shadow, only slightly denser than the twilight blanketing the city.

While travel was restricted, Iceland had an open code policy. Since the twentieth, every newborn's DNA had been coded. The genes of each and every man, woman, and child on the island nation were open to public consumption. That information had become grist for research around the world. It also led Frank to Zachary Taylor's son.

Hannah had run Taylor's genetic code for a possible trace. She'd found a match in the Icelandic database. Taylor had a child. And while the database didn't link genomes to names, it hadn't been hard for Hannah to do so. There was no record of Company payouts to Taylor, but Beck had found irregularities in his family's income.

The CIA hadn't paid them, but someone had.

Frank padded up to the house, placing his palm to the door. The low chirp signaling an unknown visitor at the door reverberated through the black air. Frank was struck by the odd consistencies that had spread over the world. Even here, in Iceland, far from the docks, that soft ring was the same as the one at his own door. Slowly, differences were melting into a sea of consumerism and comfort. Wouldn't be long before it all looked the same. If Frank had any say in the matter, it would all look American.

He palmed the door lock again. Inside, the house pulled from hibernation and roused itself. With the low drone of a vid wall going live, voices splintered the chill. Frank stamped his feet, trying to keep the blood flowing. He hated the cold—hated being bundled up and restricted by heavy clothing. He had been tempted to pick up a new bioware suit, but that kind of tech was too expensive for his low-budget tourist cover. Plus, few Icelanders wore them. They seemed to crave the cold.

A whole country of masochists, Frank thought.

He hit the door a third time. It shifted from translucent up to transparent. Before him, through the wall of plexi, stood a young boy. Tall, thin for his age. Striking, dark eyes and a ridgeline nose.

"*Halló?*" the boy said.

"English?" Frank responded.

A hand slipped from the shadows and wrapped around the boy's shoulder, drawing its owner into the light. A striking beauty, blond hair and glacier-blue eyes, she was Iceland personified. Her features fused with those of the land around her, one running into the next, inseparable. The quiet depth in that face betrayed a fissure, like the crevasses creasing Iceland's glaciers. For a moment, Frank didn't want to open that wound further. For a moment, he couldn't bear the thought.

"Can I help you?" the woman asked, her voice soft but penetrating, cool wind over ice.

Frank shook himself free of her aura. "I'd like to ask you a couple questions."

The woman brushed away his request. "I'm sorry, we—"

Frank cut her off before she could black the door. "Var, it's important."

"You know my name," she said, a trickle of surprise running though her chilled speech.

"It concerns this young man," Frank said.

Her blue eyes locked on Frank's.

The boy noticed her reaction. "I'm the man of the house," he said. "You can talk to me." The pride in his voice was impossible to miss. The woman patted him on the shoulder and smiled.

Frank stooped to look the boy in the eye. "Of course you are." Then he looked up to the woman. "It's about Zachary Taylor."

At the name, the woman's smile faded. She turned to the boy. "Arles, go to your room."

The boy began to protest, then saw the look in his mother's eyes. He turned and shuffled up the stairs. About to leave Frank's sight line, he turned and glared. Frank felt the threat loud and clear. *Don't hurt my mother.* Frank nodded to him.

"My kinda kid," he said.

"I'll make coffee," Var said, releasing the security system.

Var glided into the milk-white living area, placing a tray before Frank.

"This isn't necessary," Frank said. "Really." In spite of himself, Frank had an irresistible urge to still the flurry of emotions in her blue eyes.

He caught Arles's face peeking around the stairwell. When he turned, the boy shot back, hiding in the shadows. Var saw as well.

"Like I said, my kinda kid."

"Thank you, Mister . . . ?" She stopped—waiting for an introduction.

Frank preferred to keep her on the defensive. "He looks like his father."

Var fell into a temperfoam bucket chair like an ice block shearing into the ocean. She crossed her legs and tucked her arms under her, losing her cold removal in the chair's comfort. Her eyes swam, blue refracting with budding tears.

"I wondered how long it would take," she said. "Before you all came calling."

"I'm calling."

"You knew him?"

Frank didn't answer.

Var forged on. "You're a blogger, aren't you? Please—don't run this story. Arles doesn't need to know that his father was a butcher. This is a small city—a small country. We'd be hounded."

"I'm not a blogger, Var."

Deflected from her concerns, she locked back on Frank. "You did know him, didn't you?"

"I do know him. Zachary Taylor is alive."

Var's eyes swam, the cut deepening within her. Frank saw pain. He didn't see surprise. "But you know that, don't you?"

"I—"

"I saw him two nights ago. He tried to kill me."

"No," The word ran flat—an attempt to negate the man before her.

"He didn't die in that hovercraft, Var."

She turned from him and stared into the thickening night. "I wish he had."

Frank pulled a roll screen from his coat pocket and flopped it onto the table between them. Touching the screen, he kicked it to life and ran through the terrorist actions linked to EMPYRE. People wracked by the pathogen. Explosions. Assassinations.

Frank sat back, letting the horrors play out on Var's coffee table. "You and me both," he said.

She watched the screen, unable to pull away. Her words tumbled out. "He was just a fling, you know. Just a boy I knew—but I can't believe he'd do this—any of it." Memories flooded Var. What was and could have been, it all flowed into the present, accented by the carnage playing out before her. "He was good to me. Loved me, maybe . . ." She trailed off.

"What happened?"

"He lost himself over there. He stopped linking with me, going deeper and deeper into the fight. He reupped without telling me. And then—"

"The school bus," Frank prompted.

"He's not a bad man. At least he wasn't."

"I need to understand, Var."

"He wanted so badly to fix it all, to pull it back together. He was so passionate. I didn't want him to go. But there was no stopping him." She looked up at Frank. "I can't help you understand him. I know what he was. What he *is*—"

"That's a mystery to both of us."

She sipped her coffee. "I see some of him in Arles. The boy has passion. He's strong. He gets in fights. And he's fragile. He doesn't sleep the night."

"You've seen him," Frank said. "Taylor."

"No. I came home after the pregnancy. I stopped waiting for him long ago."

Frank took the vid roll from the table, pocketing it. "The money, Var."

"Who are you?" The woman's hard gaze melted under her fear.

"Doesn't matter," Frank said.

"I didn't think it was him. You have to believe that."

"Doesn't matter what I believe. Let me tell you what I'll do. I'm going to bring the media right to your door. WAR CRIMINAL HAS LOVE CHILD will be splashed across every blog. Should play well. Nice and juicy."

Var slumped further. "Please."

"Where are you getting the money?" Frank pressed.

"It's sent to me. Started a year ago."

"Bullshit. I'd have tracked a transfer."

"No. It's actually sent to me."

"You get hard cash? Like, in the mail?"

"I know. It's ridiculous. Who uses mail anymore? But I started getting packages. Each one held a toy—for Arles I guess. I threw the first one away. When the second came, I accidentally broke it—trying to figure out who it was from. It was filled with bond chips."

"So you cashed them and told no one?"

"Listen, I have bills. I want the best for my son."

"Well, I hope you still do—'cause you're both in a world of hurt right now."

"I don't know anything else," she said, descending into reluctant sobs. "That's the truth. I didn't let Arles have any of the toys. I threw them all away—burnt everything."

"Pardon me, but that sounds guilty as hell."

Her eyes welled, but she said nothing.

"All right. We play it the hard way. Tomorrow, you'll be knee-deep in bloggers."

She just shook her head, wisps of blond hair falling like ash over her eyes, sticking to her face through the tears.

Frank stood, frustration mixing with guilt. He'd traveled here for nothing. This woman knew jack—absolutely useless. Just the same, maybe he could draw Taylor out by harassing the man's family. Long shot—but what the hell else did he have to do? Dirty tricks.

He made for the door, opened it and pushed into the wall of night. The cold hit like a ton of bricks. He stutter-stepped, knocking into something behind him.

Frank wheeled to find Arles staring up at him. Dressed in a T-shirt and jeans, he didn't shiver or even seem to notice the cold.

"You want him, don't you?" the boy asked.

Frank looked into the boy's eyes, deciding to play it straight. "He's done bad things. Hurt people. He'll do it again."

Arles nodded. "Mom didn't think I knew. But I saw the packages. The toys. I knew."

"Of course. You're the man of the house."

Arles didn't see the humor in the comment. "You're going to hurt us, aren't you? You're going to hurt Mom?"

"Yes."

The boy nodded again.

"What makes you different from him?"

Frank's eyes hardened at the question. He stooped to look the boy straight in the eye. "I'm the good guy."

The boy held his gaze, then looked back into his house at his mother, still hunkered in the chair, immobile. Finally, he pulled a scrap of plaz wrap from his back pocket. It was worn, handled. Maybe the boy had slept with it under his pillow.

"She thought I didn't know," he said. Then he turned and ran back into the house, slamming the door behind him.

Frank looked at the scrap. It held a stamp and—much more important—a postmark.

Through his scope, the image of a boy closing the door on an overstuffed man wavered, then held firm. Zachary Taylor pulled away from the sight, shaking off the vertigo. That's what he had decided to attribute the feeling to.

A sense of déjà vu washed over him. The image, flicking through the sight's optic enhancement, tracked that which he'd had only hours ago. Then, in a quiet burb outside Langley, Virginia, Taylor had sighted in on another young boy, skating over the perfect blacktop of a perfect street in a perfect neighborhood.

A woman had walked from the house, calling the boy in for dinner. Taylor sat perched in an unoccupied house down the street. He watched the woman as she watched her child. Another woman wrapped herself around his target. Together they called to the boy, who pretended not to hear. Taylor locked in, homing in on the arcana of assassination. Wind direction, trajectory, projectile speed.

He worked through slow breaths. In. Out. In. Out. Hold—and a slow exhale. Firing was an afterthought. In his mind, she was already dead. He savored the snap instant after trigger pull and before the hit—when his will hung poised in the air.

Impact. No more painful than a fly's landing.

The projectile, designed to be mistaken for an insect, shed its outer layer under the woman's swat. The remaining nanothin device burrowed into the woman's carotid artery. She didn't feel it. She couldn't. Even as she hollered to her boy and leaned into the woman behind her, death began its slow progress.

The device ascended up through the carotid canal and into the woman's brain. It lodged in the anterior communicating artery. From there, it took only seconds.

Once lodged, the needle point ballooned, rupturing the artery. The aneurysm was massive—devastating. Blood flooded her brain. The woman's face went slack. She crumpled onto the doormat, sputtering, vomiting. The convulsions began.

Taylor turned his sight, watching the boy kick around on his board, alarmed by his mother's scream. He scrambled up the porch steps, sliding down beside the woman. She tried to speak. Opening her mouth— yellow-green froth foamed out.

Hannah Beck was dead.

Now, Taylor shivered into the chill, wiping away the memory. This was a different time, a different place—and a different boy. Through the Reykjavík night, Taylor watched this other boy walk to his mother, fold his arms around her angular form. They leaned into each other. Through his mic, he heard the boy telling his mother it would be okay. The man was gone. He wouldn't be back.

It seemed fitting that the first time Zachary Taylor laid eyes on his son, it was looking down the barrel of a gun.

He swiveled the gun around, finding Frank Savakis. From Taylor's vantage atop the chapel, Reykjavík spread out before him. House on house flowing into the bay. He homed in on the CIA man, watched him place the plaz scrap in his pocket. The man now had the one piece of Taylor that had gotten through to his son. Zachary's finger curled around the trigger. Firing would be so easy. The need pulsed through him, sending a pang through the shoulder wound the man in his sights had caused. Just a little pressure. All it would take.

Then his com-link buzzed.

"Don't do it." The voice ran flat.

Taylor's finger pressure wavered. "Target is in my sights."

"He is not the target," Alfred Krueger replied. "You know that."

"Yes." Taylor forced the word through a clenched jaw.

"Does Savakis have the information?"

"He . . . he does."

"Good." A long pause. Then, the voice filtered back in. "Normally, this transgression would call for your retirement. But, considering the circumstances, you've facilitated an optimal scenario."

Taylor tried to clear his mind. He had started sending the packages in a moment of doubt. He felt better sending them. The memory of life, real life, pumped through him each time he put a package in the mail. That boy was the only proof that he had lived. The life of one boy, and the death of thousands. Zachary Taylor's legacy. He wasn't sure when Krueger had discovered the packages. They were the only transgressions Taylor had ever committed against the man who had pulled him from confusion.

"Taylor."

"Yes, sir?"

"Now that Savakis has the information, you will stop sending the money."

Taylor didn't breathe. Rage cycled up and, with equal ferocity, discipline slammed down. He allowed Savakis to slip from his sights. He turned back to the little house that could have been his—in another life. The boy and his mother talked in the living room, their affection obvious, even through the rifle's sight.

"Yes, sir," he said.

He pulled the gun off target and began breaking it down. Once that was accomplished, he clambered down from the chapel's turret, walked through the pews and out into the night. He passed the plastic sealed monument to Leif Eriksson that stood before the church, a gift from the United States centuries ago, and faded into the night. He would never see his son again.

Zachary Taylor did not look back.

26

Junked airplane fuselages lay stacked one on the other like pickup sticks. Rusted, paint chipped, dull gray, the haphazard mass of them pocked Burning Man, a hulking heap rising into the dust-brown air.

Dave Madda called it home.

Sarah had stopped cold on first seeing the edifice. Madda held her forearm, balancing on rickety legs.

"Come on," he croaked.

"Jesus, Dave."

Madda squinted up at the mass, as if noticing it for the first time. "You don't like it? Designed it myself."

"I'd say it's the perfect lair for a mad recluse."

Madda chuckled at that. "I thought so too. Gotta keep up my image."

Then he led her inside. The soft cast on her leg bore her weight. The opiate embedded in the cast's shell provided her an airy distance. Getting closer, Sarah saw the joints and solders, the hatches and passageways that linked the fuselages together. A sense of order fell on her as she gazed up at it. Under all the chaos, a symmetry reigned.

"You see it, don't you?" Madda asked.

"I'm not sure what I see, Dave."

"You see order underlying the form."

"Maybe."

"Each cylinder rests on its neighbors, like dominoes mid-fall. The whole thing wraps a central support—like the keystone in an arch."

"Where is it—the center, I mean?"

Madda wheeled on Sarah. "Why do you want to know?" His words skittered over twitchy paranoia. "You want to break it down, don't you? You do—I know it—you want to break me down."

"Dave, come on," she said, trying to calm him. "I don't want to hurt you. Of course I don't. We're friends."

"Friends. Right," Madda said with slow precision, as if trying to solidify the memory. "It's the air. The space. Too much of it. Let's get back inside. Then I'll be better."

With that, Madda led Sarah into his inner sanctum.

. . . . .

Laing hung in space, slender icicles dripping from the tips of his cram-pons. A biting wind turned him on the axis of his rope, knocking him against the rock face. Ice rose up one arm and melted into his jacket. He struggled to see through a veil of frost. Below him, a gray cliff fell into nothing. Above, rock melded seamlessly into sky.

The primal, unrelenting fear of the dream swept over Ryan. No fight-ing it. He opened his mouth, desperate for air, cracking through the black, brittle skin of a frostbitten face. He flailed at the cliff with frozen limbs, unable to find purchase. His arms and legs felt like brittle husks. Ascent was impossible. He could only hang.

The dream did not blow apart. It did not shatter in the face of his will to wake up. Instead it lingered, lead heavy. Only grudgingly did it give way to reality.

From his vertical nightmare, Ryan sank back into the blurred fade of desert rushing past. In the space of waking, he hunted for some resonance—something he could cling to as real. The world moved too quickly for him to grasp. Now—with the pathogen raging in him, with the drones silent—he felt alone for the first time in years. The relief he'd ex-pected did not come. He felt dismembered. And tired—like he'd never been before. Tired of fighting in a way he didn't think possible. Maybe it was age—his slow fade.

Laing pushed away the bleakness. He sat up, force-locking himself into reality. He kicked out of auto drive, taking control of the car. An e-mag, it ran on the current flowing under the major highways, a smooth, fast ride. He exited the interstate, and warning lights buzzed. He was about to go off-grid.

Lanes dwindled from ten, to six, to four, and finally trailed into a rut-ted two-laner. The current died, cutting off the e-mag's drive power. It slowed, bleeding momentum until it came to a rolling stop amid a flat stretch pocked with the detritus of modernity.

Ahead lay Burning Man.

27

"No!" Sarah cried, adamant, shaking her head. "That can't happen."

Madda had escorted her into his central workstation. The fuselage was filled with next-gen hardware. High tech gadgetry rose from the clutter like new life. Giant vid screens ran the fuselage's length, colors molding and fusing in an algorithmic dance.

"Sarah, there's just too much. I can't separate the virus's genome from the gene work done to facilitate augment integration. It's all mixed up in your DNA. You really want freedom? Ditch the augments."

Sarah just shook her head. She couldn't let it go. This was her. The augments encrusting her, armoring her—without them she'd stand bare to the world. And that she could not accept. Not again.

"Can't happen. There's too much going on out there. I need my skills."

Madda pulled from his flow-port, swiveling to give her a watery stare. Sarah shuddered. The man before her was so different—so fragile. His madness gripped her.

Madda looked away in embarrassment. "They're not your skills, Sarah. They're skills you bought—augmented perception, jacked fight/flight, armored body shell—all for sale on the open market."

Sarah tried not to let her desperation show. "So—amp me higher. Jack me up a little more and maybe I'll be able to expel the pathogen."

Madda responded with moist laughter. He swiveled back on his chair, spinning around in the dank confines. Sarah sat under a sensory array he had cobbled together from a sea of tech. Lensed sensors stared down at her, rotating slowly. She held still under the mechanical gaze, her anxiety rising.

Dave drew close, his rank breath making Sarah gag. A skeletal hand ran the length of her leg. It wasn't sexual—just cold analysis of data points. Sarah had shed her clothing, and now lay before him in a ratty bathrobe. It was open, allowing the mech eyes to do their work. Madda's hand slithered over her, then thrust inside, pulling the hawkeye from her flesh in a clean jerk.

"Jacking you up won't do a thing." He held the hawkeye before him, examining it even as its perception of him fed Sarah.

"There's too much going on," Sarah replied.

The laugh again. "You can't expect me to buy that," he said with derisive condescension. "Look around you. I put myself here. I built this. Do you think it's any different than what you've done to yourself?"

"Dave—"

Madda cut her off. "It's not." He waved his arms over his head, his skin loose over shriveled triceps. "I've got my shell. You've got yours. Difference is, I stayed in mine. You took yours out into the wide world. And guess what—it cracked. Now you can ditch it, or let the ocean flow right in."

Sarah looked into his eyes for a long beat. Then she pulled herself off the table. With a smooth flick, she snagged the hawkeye from the air. One side of her robe flapped open as she holstered the device.

"It was good seeing you, Dave."

"You're not really going to go?" Madda said, incredulous. "You're someone else's fucking toy! A killing machine on remote control. How many more will die because of you?"

The words hammered at Sarah. She refused them access. She couldn't let her tech go. She'd find someone else. She'd go recluse. Anything.

"Good-bye, Madda."

"Wait," he said, grabbing her arm as she hobbled past him. His head bowed in acquiescence. "Okay. Okay, there is one option. But it's a long shot—untested, probably lethal. I . . ." He tried to restrain his emotions. "It's not an option I want you to take."

Sarah nodded, sitting back on the examining table.

"You're crazier than me, Sarah. That's saying something."

At that, Sarah smiled. Madda's sallow face broke into a grin of its own.

So much had happened since they'd destroyed Echelon. "Look at us," Sarah said. "We're not cut out for the world we created."

Madda stared at her for a long second. In that look, Sarah caught a glimpse of the man Dave had once been. And something else. Something deeper.

Madda turned away, dousing his embarrassment in cynicism. "Well, that probably won't be an issue for you much longer. Not with what I'm shooting into you."

He swiveled back to his flow-port. On the vid-screen, a massive image of a ship rocketing through black space came up.

"Ummm, I'm thinking that's overkill," Sarah said.

Madda continued typing, running through stacks of inventory. Finally, he found what he was looking for.

"That's the *Urizen Explorer.* It annihilates antimatter for propulsion. What that porker uses to push through space, I'm going to put into you."

. . . . .

Where else would Sarah go? There was no quarter for her—not anywhere official. If she was alive, Laing felt sure she'd seek out Madda. He only hoped the man was capable of helping her. Protecting her.

Laing walked to the barrier—just another neo-Burner, ready to sacrifice for the promise of release. He did not offer a name and no one asked. The cold sweat of fever blanketed him. He felt so weak without the drones. The red-laced desperation in his eyes was familiar to the gatekeepers. They understood weakness. They stripped him of his meager worldly possessions and let him through.

Laing walked into the sprawling city of Burning Man. Before him, the massive effigy flamed hot red. He studied the people around him, living in bizarre domiciles rising into the fading desert light. They moved with a cool, dazed contentment—people who had given up the need to struggle. Something in Ryan revolted at the sight. He put his head down and trudged on.

Close to the sprawl's center stood a spindling crystalline form made of airplane fuselages. Laing saw Madda's hand in the architecture. He'd be there. And Sarah.

Laing approached and palmed the hatch, feeling like he was stepping under a scorpion's tail. It refused him, setting off slow-burn countermeasures. They weren't fucking around here. Laing stood firm, even as sonic blasts, just out of human range, set his teeth on edge. He calmed himself, drawing what remained of the drone amp. Immediately, he felt the pathogen take him. Each moment the drones didn't fight it, he got weaker. Falling to his knees, Ryan pushed into the coding, cracking the security system. Madda might be a great hacker, but no one lived with code like Ryan. He slapped his hand to the hatch. This time it opened.

Laing released the drones and staggered to his feet. The halls ran narrow and skewed. Lit soft, each fuselage melted into the next. Laing pushed forward, stumbling over technological detritus left to its slow decay. Bots twitched around him, Laing's movement triggering remnant coding.

The windows had all been blackened. This was no fortress; it was a crypt. Soon, Ryan lost his bearings. He climbed and descended at random, trusting instinct to lead him.

A woman's scream broke the tomb-still air.

28

—*Sarah. Sarah, I'm here.* Ryan pushed his thoughts into her, forcing the drones to action.

For years, Laing lived with Sarah in his mind. Every moment of every day, a core-deep link. He had grown used to the intrusion, grown to need it, even to love it. But Sarah had severed that connection, ripping their link free. Its loss had nearly destroyed him.

—*Sarah. Please.*

No response. Now, staring down at Sarah's prone form, he felt like an interloper, barging in where he didn't belong. To force the link felt like this—it felt like rape.

Laing pulled back from his focus and turned to Madda. The man stood canted, his stance matching his psyche in a twisted symmetry.

"She knew the risks," Madda said. "Wouldn't let me pull her tech."

Laing's cold eyes burned into Madda. In that gaze, Madda's fear bloomed—a quick-twitch tick flickering through him. "But maybe she was right," he said. "Yeah—I mean those augments run deep into her biological systems. She's so meshed in, I'm not sure I could have clean-pulled the woman from the add-ons."

Laing turned back to Sarah. "She's not responding to our link."

"Could take some time. Restarting your connection isn't like goggling in. I don't know what kind of code your drones have been spinning over the last years. And then interfacing your shit with her new shit is, well—it's a gamble."

"And radiating her wasn't?" Laing spat back.

Madda looked away. He purposefully ignored the antiproton gun lying beside Sarah's pale form. "Listen, I didn't want any part of this. I didn't want to make these decisions. Not again. Not anymore. But she pushed!" Madda took a breath, easing out the hyperventilation gripping him.

"Radiating her—as you call it—was the only option," Dave continued. "The retrovirus she's carrying is totally slick. It's spliced into her own DNA at a bunch of different points. I couldn't be sure that I found 'em all."

"So you nuked her."

"Jesus, Ryan." Madda broke into an extended twitch session, as if his body refused to operate under the stresses that now bore down on him.

"To find all the code would have taken time—too much time for Sarah. So I destroyed the trigger."

"You operated on her?"

"Well, I didn't cut her or anything. No knife work. I used this." Madda whirled, tapping the screen of his flow-port. The antiproton gun came to life. It buzzed and whirred, panning across the room on smooth actuators. "With this sucker, I blew the trigger that initiated virus shed. Her on-switch."

"Madda, if you're telling me—"

"No, no. It's not an explosion like you'd think. This sucker fires antiprotons. You know, like antimatter?"

Laing's blank glare pushed Madda deeper into the tech. He seemed glad to lose himself in the explanation. "They don't like each other. A matter/antimatter collision is serious. Any interaction and you're talking—boom! Just a microgram of antimatter will send a spaceship to Mars in less than four months."

"You're not making me feel better."

"This gun—it accelerates antiprotons to very specific speeds." The servos hummed, the gun's long barrel turning on Laing. "Here, I'll show you." Madda smacked the trigger button before Ryan could stop him.

Laing advanced on Madda. "You crazy—"

"No. No!" Madda stammered, backing away. "If it's going fast enough, the antiprotons punch right through you. Won't leave a scratch."

Laing stopped himself, hunting for a wound. He found nothing.

"By honing the speed, you control where the matter-antimatter collision takes place. Allows precision surgery."

"So you blasted the remote that kicked her cells into making the pathogen?"

"Right. Far as I can tell, I succeeded. She's permanently deactivated. The retrovirus is still part of her genome, but the trigger that makes her into a walking weapon is gone. Total success."

"So why does she look like a lobotomized rat?"

"Well, the trigger wasn't just a frickin' transmitter sitting in her frickin' head. It was a bioengineered masterpiece, wrapped around her brain stem." Madda held up the gun. "This sucker may be precision, but that doesn't change the fact that I annihilated matter in her head. There's going to be fallout from that. Some serious scrambling."

"How much?"

"The fuck should I know? Stop asking me questions and link back in. Find her. And find her fast."

Ryan read a desperation in Dave's voice that he hadn't expected. Was there something between him and Sarah? Ryan pushed the thought away, realizing he'd been stalling, grilling Madda to cover his trepidation.

He lifted Sarah's hand, taking it in his own. It was fish cold. He gripped her, hating what he was about to do—and longing for it in a way that terrified him. He picked up a rusted piece of metal from the sea of junk filling the room.

Laing breathed deep, opened his hand and placed the shard in his palm. He gripped back down on Sarah's hand. The metal cut into them, spilling blood from their palms. Drones welled and flushed the wound, migrating into Sarah and, for a time, making her part of him. The blood link filled Ryan.

He gripped harder.

29

Sarah Peters floated through a soft haze. Isolation intoxicated her. The static silence of it—like an ear buzz after a night at the bar. For so long she had forced down a constant bombardment of data. At first, she had wanted to understand Laing. To see the world as he did. She had longed for his abilities, to share a view of the world beyond human capabilities. And she got a taste of it. After the first round of knife work, perception cracked, admitting such magnificent light. It stunned her, broadened her, locked her into a course she could hardly imagine. But it brought her no closer to Laing.

When they parted, her need didn't ebb. Instead, it built, fueled by that new lack within her. She filled the space inside with tech. Sarah shaped her perception like a sculptor, trimming it from her own clay, finding a new form that suited her better. Each round dulled out the pain, allowing her to sink deeper into a world so brilliant, so intense, that she need never look within. She pushed her pain down, blanketing it in a constant data burst.

But the release was fleeting, the flurry of input fading to vague transparency. Then it was back to Dubai for another hit. The cycle became the person. She lost herself in the drive to cloud her pain.

And now there was stillness. Something in her had lost the need to run. She floated, kicked out beyond perception, beyond her pain and self-loathing.

Then the voice. Not a voice really. A communication, a transmission, resonating within her. Recog swept her, piercing the stillness with razor-perfect cruelty. The link flooded her, drove her to the spot she had feared for so long. Hate swelled in her. For the one who had driven her here.

—*Sarah. Please. You need to come out of this.*

Ryan fucking Laing.

Laing accessed the full power of his drones to bolster the link with Sarah. His body withered under the loss. With fewer drones to fight it, the sickness surged, slow death working through him. Relentless. He ignored it, pushing deeper into Sarah, allowing his emotions to link with hers.

Her cold silence engulfed him.

—*Sarah—please.*

No reply. Only the dawn rays of her presence coursing over him. Familiar, filling out his need. Then her hate engulfed him, the raw loathing of the weakness he had created in her. And the loss. Ryan sank into it, the pain of it flushing him. He continued to hold.

—*Sarah.*

He reached for her. Not in a way that could be translated, but on a core level as one animal to another. It was beyond words, under them. Naked. Nothing held back—the pure whole of him asking for her, defenseless.

She raged back, cold fury and soft need. The space between them barbed, pricking him like an appendage that had lost circulation. The link blossomed. Pain ran into pleasure. Sarah writhed, lashing out at him. He took it, accepting her pain—trying to take it away. It sapped him. Her supply ran endless, welling with each gulp he took. Laing foundered under it. He couldn't continue.

He couldn't fix her.

So he stopped. Laing flashed reflective. He rejected her pain—refused to take it in. He couldn't make her whole.

—*I'm sorry.* The words tumbled from his mind, scattered in the wave of emotion flashing over him.

The act stilled Sarah. Laing felt relief flooding her. She didn't want to be repaired. Not by him. She loathed him for trying. In her, he felt a sea shift. The crushing swell eased to rough chop, desire churning through the hate, welling up in her.

In this place, she drew him close. No raw sensation of flesh slapping flesh, but an emotional tug and release. She pulled Ryan into her desire, pushing into him with all of her. Roles reversed, grew malleable and shifted with their combined ebb and flow. Ryan fell into her need—her animal desire meshing with his own until he couldn't separate his emotions from hers. When release came, it hit them both, slow pulsing female, hard smashing male.

The ripping impact of it sucked Sarah from her solitude, forcing her toward consciousness. She sensed him wrapped around her, her own being enveloping him.

Her eyes snapped open.

—*Sarah.*

"Sarah." The thought and the word came out together, meshed in the flood of release.

He stood over her, hands clasped. The drone flood had faded to a trickle. Laing's face had gone sheet white. He wheezed slow, crackling breaths. He let go of her hand, but she continued to hold on, gripping hard.

Sarah's green eyes bored into Laing's. She pushed him out, consciously, cruelly, removing herself from him by force of will. And still she gripped him, forcing the shard deep, making Ryan bleed.

She rose out of the reclining chair. With each moment, her strength increased. She held Laing's gaze in a seared burst of remembrance. Re-initialized, her body tat flooded color, an aurora rippling over flesh, flickering with the emotions running through her. Ryan's degeneration continued, his pallor contrasting with Sarah's multicolored brilliance.

—*Ryan.* Emotion burst within her. The memory of love, the gratification of need, and the anger.

She released her grip. As if that was all that had kept him standing, Laing crumpled to the floor, hacking. Sarah stood over him, boiling color, restraining nothing.

From the corner, Dave Madda watched. Eyes wide, mouth open. "Ummm, did I miss something?"

30

It's hard to unknow a man.

To have Laing before her—to see him munch down a turkey sandwich, wash his hands, gaze at Madda's junk piles with that bemused, crinkled lower lip—all of it sucked her right back in. The ember she had doused for the last years reignited. Their shoulders rubbed over the cutting table in Madda's kitchen and all she wanted to do was to throw her arms around him. But the high faded fast. He couldn't hold her gaze. His weakness drove her to hate him. Then the cycle started anew.

"Sarah, you're running clean. The virus's trigger has been destroyed." Madda's clipped words broke the tension. He stood at what used to be an emergency hatch that was now linked to an up-canted fuselage leading to his workstation. Dave held a flow-screen in his hand. He walked over, somehow able to navigate the flotsam on the floor without taking his eyes off the data.

"Everything feels smooth."

"Yeah—well, I do nice work."

Sarah smiled. She waved a hand before her, triggering the cam protocols. Pigment shifted, shade-linked to her surroundings. Her arm faded into the fuselage's monotone. Madda stood fascinated. She caught Laing from the corner of her eye, his expression unreadable. She turned away.

"Best money could buy," she said.

Madda laughed. Not a comfortable laugh, but it cracked the ice.

"And whose money was that?" Laing asked, his tone sharp.

"Does it matter?" Sarah shot back.

"You know, I think it does."

"Fuck you, Laing."

"After everything we did. After Echelon—you went right back to the tit. So, yeah, I think it matters. I'd like to know what you did for EMPYRE— and why." Ryan spat each word.

Sarah covered the ground between them flash fast and slapped Laing across the jaw. Ryan spun with the force of the blow, crashing to the floor in a hulk.

Sarah raged hot. Before she could get to Laing again, Madda had jumped between them.

"Wow!" Madda's eyes glassed with fear.

The look broke Sarah's rage. She peered over Madda's shoulder and down to Laing. He brought a hand to his mouth, feeling the trickle of blood. His eyes locked on hers.

"I'd like to know how many died to get you the best money could buy," he said.

The words cut her anger, but it was his vulnerability that expelled it. Sarah pulled the hand that hit him into her chest. She had hurt him. She had thought him indestructible—armored so hard and deep that nothing could break through. But now . . . She had struck him. She had hurt him.

For how long had she longed for this moment? Here it was—and it brought no satisfaction. The spark driving her faded. She stepped back, gaining distance from Madda.

He caught her look. "You're jacked tight, Sarah. You're stronger than Laing."

Sarah took another step back. The dull pound of realization flooded her. Had her motivation over the past years been merely to get to this place—this confrontation? And how much of her was left to close it out?

Madda mistook her look for confusion and blathered on, keeping himself between the two. "The matter annihilation got your transmitter, Sarah. You're back in business. But Laing's going to take more time. The pathogen you produced affected him on a genetic level. For most, that's instant death."

Madda turned to Laing, still on the floor. "Your drones will hold the line—but they can only do so much."

He turned back to Sarah. "There's good news, though. I got the flow-link between you two locked back in. Should be five by five now. So you've got that . . ."

Sarah pushed off the curved wall of the fuselage. As she came at him, Madda began to realize how unwanted that link might now be. "I mean— You don't have to use it or anything." Sarah sidestepped Madda and he breathed a sigh of relief.

Sarah stooped down over Laing.

"Guess I'm back in your head," she said.

"We could continue to ignore each other."

"Yeah, that worked well." Sarah's lips cracked in the slightest smile. "Maybe I can't ignore you—no matter how much I try."

Ryan nodded. His eyes told the rest: the depth of his feeling, and the naked need to reengage.

Sarah's hand shot forward, snap quick. Laing did not flinch. She caught a drop of red-gray blood that had fallen from Ryan's chin. They held that moment.

—*I'm sorry.* Her words seeped through him.

—*Don't be. I've been impenetrable for so long . . . I needed someone to kick my ass a bit.*

Sarah smiled, raising her hand in a mock punch.

—*No argument there.*

Sarah lowered her hand, stroking his face.

—*Then maybe this is all okay, Ryan. Maybe we have a shot to make it right.*

Laing smiled. He pulled Sarah close. She fell into his chest, into the fevered heat of his body. It felt good. Right. She sank into it. The walls in her buckled and fell away. Tears rolled down her cheeks. She didn't care.

31

"You shitting me with this?" Frank Savakis had no patience for the freak sitting before him. So the twitchy fucker was rich. The fuck difference did that make to him?

"You're not into the design?" Madda asked.

"I'm not into dragging my ass through the desert."

Frank peered out through the black-tinted plexi and into Burning Man. Makeshift structures poked up from the dirt in a cantilevered maze. He shook his head. "You make the fuckers out there look sane."

"We're all here for a reason," Dave said defensively.

"I'll bet."

"This is a place of freedom. A place where you can—"

"Spare me, all right?" Frank shot back. "I'm not drinking your Kool-Aid. You wanna sit out here and howl at the moon, go right ahead. Just get Laing and I'll be on my way."

"There's unchecked anger in you that the Burners could really—"

Frank's look stilled Madda's train of thought. "Laing. Right. I'd give him the time. Man's fucked up."

Frank shrugged and sank back into the chair opposite Dave. Silence sat with them. It was an awkward threesome.

"You built this, huh?"

"Yup. Before Sarah came, I hadn't left it in three years."

"I'm shocked," Frank said, deadpan.

More silence. Madda squirmed. "You so ready to get back out there?"

"Case Laing didn't mention it, there's shit that needs doing."

Madda's turn to laugh. "There's always shit. We go up, we slide back. We slaughter each other, we make reparations. We muddle."

"That why you're here? Sick of the muddle?"

"Maybe."

"I don't sit well. Life ain't great. In fact, it's shit out there. Always has been. But, you know what—I work better in the shit."

"See, I work better surrounded by it." Madda waved his hand at their environs, drawing a reluctant laugh from Frank.

Ryan Laing entered slowly, struggling through his grogginess. He wore jeans, faded and ripped. His chest heaved, breath thumping through him in a rapid wheeze.

"You look like death," Frank said.

Ryan made his way to the coffeepot, picking through the selection of mugs for the least dirty specimen.

"This is an improvement," he sputtered back.

Ryan poured himself a cup and turned to Madda "Richest man in . . . well . . . the area, and you can't offer me a clean mug?"

"Cleaning staff is unpredictable around here."

Ryan grunted, hunkering over his coffee. Something pulled him from his stupor. After a moment, Sarah Peters entered the room. Hair slicked back and eyes bright, she radiated fast-twitch action. Laing's lips flipped to a grin—as if in response to an interchange Frank wasn't party to.

"Last time I saw you, you looked markedly worse." Frank stood, extending a hand. "Frank Savakis."

"Sarah." She shook his hand. "Guessing you're here to tell us the vacation's over."

"Back to work."

"You find Taylor?" Ryan asked.

Frank waffled. "I found a lead. Got solid intel that he's in *The City*."

"Oh, God." Sarah's face had gone white. "EMPYRE lives."

The shut-in stink of Madda's cramped labyrinth was getting to Ryan, edging him out. With liquid filling his lungs, he couldn't seem to draw in enough of the lead-heavy air.

Sarah's words pulled him from his slow-burn panic, infusing him with a quick shot of adrenaline. "What are you talking about?" he asked.

Sarah looked away. "*The City* is a node—a focal point in world affairs. Its variable location makes it a multinational mecca. The UN may be in New York, but most serious issues are dealt with in *The City*. A disruption there would affect the balance of power in a dozen countries."

"But *The City* is impregnable," Madda replied. "No goods enter or leave. They take the shirt right off your back."

"I pulled some time there a couple years ago, working an Iraqi businessman I was trying to turn," Frank said. "At customs, they strip you fuckin' naked. No baggage, no personal items of any kind. Took forever. I was just glad they didn't do a cavity search."

"Oh, they did. They scan you six ways to Sunday," Madda said.

"So, with all that security in place, I'm thinking Taylor uses *The City* as a safe house—a place where your average assassin terrorist fuck can go to relax."

Sarah shook her head. "I don't think so."

"We talking woman's intuition here, or you got something to tell us?" Frank pushed.

Sarah looked up at him. "So far, every target I analyzed for EMPYRE in the past six months has been hit."

Frank looked away. "Son of a bitch!"

"*The City*'s on that list."

PART 3

32

Heat wicked from Laing's body; he couldn't seem to retain it. Cold felt different with the drones unable to zero out the pits and peaks of experience. The wind lashed him, bringing with it mingled scents of forest and ocean. A dull wash of anxiety rose in him, the smells kicking off a cascade of memories.

Laing took a deep breath, the snap shift of scene jarring him more than he wanted to admit. Hobart was a long way from Burning Man. And to be here with Sarah was stifling. The halting dance that he and Sarah now waltzed was so different from the easy confidence they had shared the last time they'd stood in this place.

Ryan watched her from the corner of his eye. She gazed out at the cargo ships filling Hobart's Macquarie Wharf. But she wasn't really looking either. He knew she was also scanning their mutual past, hung up in its thick cloud.

"Of all the places . . ." she said.

Laing laughed. "Three years."

Sarah turned to him.

"That's how long it takes for *The City* to circle the globe," he continued. "In all that time, with all those ports—we catch up with it here."

The City had just passed through the Bass Strait and now sucked onto the Tasmanian coast like a giant leech. So massive it couldn't enter the port itself, the ship churned slowly down the coast. Through the cargo ships before them, Ryan and Sarah could just make out *The City*'s gleaming white bulk on the horizon.

"It's different now," Sarah said.

"You can say that again," Laing replied, gazing down at the teeming throngs below. With *The City*'s arrival, Hobart buzzed in an orgiastic frenzy of commerce. What started as a trickle of tourists hitting Hobart had turned into a deluge.

"Growing up, we had a terrible mosquito problem one summer," Laing said. "I remember a cow dying from the bites, the mosquitoes totally blacking her out. Feels like that here." *The City*'s hundred thousand occupants thronged Hobart, shifting the town's balance. Laing could feel the carrying capacity of the fragile island canting hard. *The City* did this everywhere it went. There was profit in its arrival. And it took about three years to recover.

Sarah stared down at the masses, then to Ryan. "I didn't mean the place. Well, maybe I did."

"You mean us in this place."

Sarah nodded.

"I know. I miss it."

Sarah shook her head, looking off. "I don't."

Now it was Ryan's turn to stare.

"Ryan, I was miserable. You were miserable."

"But we had a chance—I so wanted to be happy. To have some peace."

"Peace? Jesus, Laing. You know anyone at peace? You see it anywhere? It's a figment! The truth doesn't include peace."

"Sarah—"

"Can you be here—truly—with me and know that you're never getting out of the storm? It's going to keep coming, Ryan, right up to the day you die."

Ryan wanted to speak. He wanted to say he loved her, that he could be with her through anything. But that would be a lie—and she would know it.

Frank broke the tension, which he pretended not to notice. "We're on the next ferry," he said.

Laing was glad for the distraction. Work pushed out the larger picture. Like that first move in rock climbing, his wider world dropped to background static and he focused on what was to come.

"You link to the Sec Op?" he asked.

Frank grimaced, his annoyance obvious. "The CIA rep has officially informed *The City* of a credible terrorist threat."

"And?" Sarah asked.

"And *The City*'s Security Operations assures us that the threat will be processed."

"What does that mean?" Laing asked.

"It means they could give a fuck about our intel. They're that sure of their precautions."

"Well, when we get onboard, we can explain it out," Sarah said.

Frank shook his head. "Sec Op has denied an official visit. Pretty much figured they would. No foreign intelligence in *The City*. No exceptions. We go in as civs."

Sarah's annoyance grew to match Savakis's. "Well, can they tell us if Taylor is aboard?"

Frank shook his head. "Full anonymity for all *City* residents. You get aboard and there's no surveillance, no names."

"This is a nightmare."

"As far as catching Taylor? Yup. But it does make getting *you* onboard a lot easier," Frank said to Sarah.

"Well, the CIA put me in this mess. You could damn well get me out. Pull the heat off me. Tell your cohorts to stop hunting me."

"Like I said before—that's no problem. Just come back to Langley, submit to a month or two of debriefing, and you'll go clear."

Sarah looked away, back out to the ship.

"Right then," Frank continued. "I'll keep the fact that you're not a deranged terrorist to myself, and you can continue with us."

"Even with *The City*'s flaunted anonymity, I'd do some pigmenting. Your face has seen a lot of blog time," Ryan said.

"They're really going to let me in? I mean they could DNA-check me."

"No," Frank replied. "They start with that and half the people on board would jump ship. *The City* banks on border control and cash."

"But that won't stop every threat," Ryan said.

Frank turned and looked out at the white mass pocking the smooth line of the horizon.

"Hear ya there," Frank said. "I get a real *Titanic* vibe off that fucker."

The hydro churned ocean, hurtling them out toward the monolith. They stood on the open deck with hundreds of other travelers. There was no baggage in sight. And the clothing—Ryan couldn't help but laugh. In the menagerie surrounding him, each outfit was more outrageous than the next.

Sarah giggled into his ear. "That's my favorite." She pointed to a man decked out in an ancient suit.

"Is that naugahyde?" Ryan asked.

"Very possible."

"You're overlooking the teacup." Frank pointed to a woman at the stern, teetering in a plaz-molded blooming skirt.

"Good God, you're right," Sarah said. "I stand corrected. Though you don't look too shabby yourself."

Frank smoothed out the crinkles of his Hawaiian shirt, then did a little jump-kick in his matching jams.

"The high-tops set off your eyes," Laing said.

The kicker on Frank's look was a pair of fuzzy laced shoes in dull mauve. "Hey, these were all the rage back in high school."

Sarah patted him on the arm. "For the girls, Frank."

Because no personal items were permitted in *The City*, anything an immigrant arrived with would be incinerated at customs. As such, a tradition had sprouted among those visiting *The City*. There were operators who did nothing more than follow the ship, set up their shops on the docks, and sell costumes to tourists. Of course, not everyone entered in such garb, but Ryan, Sarah, and Frank were tourists, and they needed to blend.

Frank stood back, taking Ryan and Sarah in. "You two shouldn't be talking."

Sarah wore a pair of rat-gnawed jeans. On top, she sported a T-shirt that was more hole than fabric, the front of which sported the slogan NORM'S TITS.

Laing wore a matching wife beater. His shirt read NORM.

Sarah did a tight spin, showing off. "Well, I think it's divine!"

"Me too, darling!" an older lady shot in, wearing what appeared to be a dress made of doilies.

"Thank you!" Sarah replied.

"It really is horrible," the woman gushed. "I love it!"

Sarah fell into conversation with the woman. Laing stared off, watching Tasmania fade into the distance. The battle within him had reached an uneasy stalemate. With effort, he was keeping the virus at bay, but his ability to utilize the drones remained severely limited. His body was shutting down, if slowly. He stifled a cough, an act that brought tears to his eyes.

Sarah wrapped an arm around him, putting her chin on his shoulder. Laing didn't turn.

"I always wanted to come back," he said, scanning the coastline. "To try again. With you."

"I promised myself, I'd never go back."

She drew him away from the churned wake and the island fading into the distance. Turning, Laing got his first close look at *The City*.

It was one thing to check it in the flow—or even see it on the horizon. But to stare up at the edged prow vaulting into the sky was an awesome experience. The chatter on deck faded, everyone entranced by the sight.

The ferry approached the front of the monolith. *The City*'s prow was a single sharp line rising five hundred meters into the air. Built on a mass of carbon steel cells welded together, *The City* had no hull to speak of. It looked more like a barge supporting a scraper on steroids.

The ship's flank extended for several kilometers, rising in levels of white plexi and clean deck. Laing could just make out the specks of people ambling along the open walkways that ringed each level. Green foliage and the occasional splash of flowers cut the white continuity. Far above, Laing saw airplanes cranking into the sky, launched off the rooftop airport.

After running the ship's length, the ferry reached *The City*'s port, located in the rear of the structure. The port had two channels, with a central promenade where residents watched approaching ships. On either side of the canals, walls rose high, brilliant white and canted forward, generating a sense of movement. One canal was for private yachts, VIP guests, and the like. The other was far more crowded, with ferries packed one behind the other, loading and offloading an unending stream of humanity.

Ryan turned to Sarah.

—*It's time.*

Sarah nodded. She pulled the hawkeye and hurled it overboard. It might pass the screening, but they couldn't take the chance. The hawkeye inflated, hovered for a moment, then vaulted into the sky.

Laing tracked its ascent, then turned back to the ship. Electromags fired, drawing the ferry to hard lock. Passengers shuffled onto the ship in lockstep. Before Ryan, lines of gaudily dressed tourists crowded into the customs center. The splashy clash of colors contrasted with the crystalline cleanliness surrounding them.

As Ryan stepped from the boat, he sensed the deep push of *The City*'s propulsion. Powered by over one hundred separate engines, *The City* pumped out just enough thrust to keep the ship on course—a massive feat. The prop sat far under sea level. There was no sound of engines, no wake to be seen. There was only a sense of power—strong and pervasive. A will to push that was unstoppable.

"You feel it?" Laing asked.

"The engines? Yeah," Sarah replied.

They took their place in the crush of people.

"I feel like a lamb heading for the slaughter," Frank muttered.

"Bahahaaha," Sarah said.

Frank turned to Ryan with a smile. "Norm, handle your tits, please. They're out of control."

Sarah looked down to see that her outfit was quickly becoming X-rated. She blushed, adjusting herself.

"This sucker's first for the burn pile."

"Not a moment too soon," Ryan said, starting a laugh that evolved into a coughing hack.

They entered a vast room, lines of people extending out before them. A smooth, sterilized female voice hummed over the general hubbub.

"Welcome to *The City*. Please follow the lines to the first available customs locker," it said. "No personal items are allowed in *The City*. On clearing customs, you will find all the goods and services you may require. Enjoy your stay." A brief pause, then, "Welcome to *The City . . .*"

Fluorescent lines arced before each guest. Foot pressure triggered the touch-sensitive biocrete flooring. Each immigrant, on hitting the customs mall, got his or her own track leading to a locker. Ryan's arced off, away from Sarah and Frank. He shuffled along with it, stifling a vague panic. Something in the sterility, the smooth flow of people, the offload of all that was personal, jangled him.

He reached his locker and stepped inside. With a pneumatic hiss, the door shut behind him. From the customs mall's vast openness, the locker confined him in vertical white.

The voice spoke: "Please remove all personal material. Failure to do so will result in immediate expulsion from *The City*."

Laing took some pleasure in ripping off the T-shirt. Once he was naked, a drawer slid from the wall. Laing placed his clothes inside and the drawer hissed shut. He could just hear the hot crackle of their incineration.

"Thank you," the voice said.

From the ceiling, a small cylinder dropped. It resembled a showerhead. The sight heightened Ryan's discomfort. He breathed through the anxiety, experience conditioning his reactions.

The cylinder pulsed. Through drone-laced perception, Laing saw the room around him color with a hot shot of radiation.

"Forgive the discomfort," the voice soothed. "Biocide complete."

Another drawer slid from the wall. It contained a new set of clothes. He shuffled into them—very ready to get free of the box.

"With our compliments, please find a custom-tailored set of *City*-sanctioned apparel. Please consider these our gift to you." The voice dropped a measure, growing conspiratorial. "They'll make a great souvenir of your time in *The City*."

"Okay," Laing said.

"Your ticket has been read and processed. We hope you've enjoyed your customs experience."

"Umm, I have." Laing wasn't quite sure if the voice was responsive, but didn't want to risk a lack of cordiality. In his experience, customs officials weren't to be fucked with. He didn't see why the machine should be any different.

"Proceed to the receiving area."

At that, Laing breathed a sigh of relief—which grew bigger as the floor lowered slowly, taking him down a level and releasing him from the white coffin. He stepped into a sprawling atrium. Formal gardens spread out before him. Throughout, people mingled. He found Sarah bending over a blood-red rose, taking in its scent.

"Welcome to *The City*," he said.

She smiled, stood, and kissed him softly on the cheek. "Let's find Taylor and get the hell out of here."

"Amen to that," Frank said, sidling up next to them. "Place gives me the creeps."

33

Commodities were few in *The City*. Security mandated restricted intake. There were some trinkets for the tourists. Beyond that, *The City* traded in a single product: information. The entire population dressed in uniform, one person fading into the next. Here, you were who you said you were. All that was required for such freedom was money. With a full *City*-sanctioned credit chip, every tycoon and crook, dealer and diplomat was welcome to ply his trade.

Ryan and Sarah checked into their room, a standard tourist cabin, with Frank next door. With nothing to unpack, no toiletries to deal with, both stood in awkward silence. Sarah opened the sliding doors to a rush of ocean breeze.

From the room, Ryan watched her. The thin fabric of the uniform hugged her form, drawing out the clean curve of her neck. His eyes flowed with the whipping wind, catching the rise of her breasts, the smooth curve of her hip.

He stepped outside, sliding into her heat. He nuzzled Sarah's neck and she leaned back into him. The pressure of her on him, the rub of her ass, the sigh he barely caught in the passing air—it cut through his fever and pain.

She turned into him, her facial pigment shocking him out of the moment.

"Let it go," he said.

Sarah looked confused for an instant. He ran a finger over her cheek. She pushed the tat, reshading her features. Light and shadow shifted. Ryan looked at her for a long time, locking her in his gaze.

"What is it?" she asked.

"It's not right," he replied. "Not how it was."

"I'm not . . . I'm not doing anything now."

"I know. It's the tech."

"What does that mean?" Sarah asked, suddenly self-conscious.

"It changes you, Sarah. Becomes part of you. You are different."

"There's an old expression about a pot criticizing the kettle," Sarah said, crossing her arms.

"I say it because I know. I just hope you like what you've become."

Sarah pulled away from the balcony and walked to the mirror in their small cabin. She studied her face, trying to remember.

She caught Laing's reflection behind her.

"Do . . ." she hesitated. Then hard determination washed her face. "Do you like it? What I've become?"

Sarah held still, bottling her tension. Laing locked her in the reflection. Then he stepped forward, wrapping her in his arms. He didn't say anything. He didn't have to.

Sarah relaxed into his embrace. She reached behind her, taking him in her hand, rubbing into him with slow, deliberate strokes.

Ryan ran his hands up under the gossamer fabric of her shirt, cupping her breasts, drawing a sigh from deep within her. He pushed closer, grinding into her. The move forced Sarah's arms to the sink. She pushed back, urgent.

Ryan stepped away, aching with the loss of contact. He pulled her shirt over her head, mesmerized by the tumble of hair down her shoulders. The smooth curve of her back transfixed him—wide shoulders into a slender waist and out again to her hips.

He removed her pants, revealing the twin indentations of muscle at the base of her back. The sight, the feel of her drove his need. Ryan dealt with his own clothing in a series of tugging rips. It was disposable.

He pushed close, flesh on flesh. She reached back and guided him. He sank, gasping with the sensation. Then slow thrusts, each building on the last. Harder. Faster. She arched back, driving him deeper.

In the mirror's reflection, Ryan watched emotion and carnal need play over her flesh in waves of color. The writhing, twining colors danced on her skin, pulsing as they fucked.

Shudders ran through her. No sound, but a cascading light show over straining muscles. And the clench-release of climax. He followed her.

Eyes tight shut, Sarah kept Laing close even as he slipped from her.

And even then, when it was all over, Ryan couldn't pull his gaze from her.

—*Feels like old times,* Ryan thought.

    —I still don't see why I'm sitting back when you're the one who's fucked up.

    —You're the only one who can hack The City.

    —Flattery, huh? I didn't know you were capable.

Sarah's quip brought a smile to Laing's face. Walking next to him along *The City*'s port-side outer causeway, Frank watched Ryan's expression shift and grimaced.

"Cut that, man. Whisper sweet nothings on your own fuckin' time."

"Sorry," Ryan said. He walked on in silence. The cold tingle of action infused him with energy—something in short supply with the virus coursing through him. Having Sarah in his mind, at his back. Having a mission. It rang true. In its embrace, he could forget the past years. Life was simple. Find Zachary Taylor.

—*All right, Sarah.*

—*Hold. I'm initiating the run.*

Back to data rat status. Sarah wasn't a fan of the shift. She'd pulled her time. And she knew Ryan was just trying to protect her. Stupid move; she was healthy—far more of a match for Taylor than Ryan was without the drones and sick as a dog. Jacked up and well fucked, she felt so good—so focused! Sarah was ready to take on the world. The crushing helplessness of the past weeks, the past years, had evaporated. Confidence surged in her, clear and sharp, driving her forward. It wasn't Ryan. But maybe his presence had forced her to push the darkness away. She felt alive for the first time in years.

Through the hawkeye circling high above *The City*, she focused in on Laing, walking along the outdoor causeway. Something reassuring in watching that gait, long and deliberate, with Frank's choppy, thrusting steps cutting the tempo.

She flipped into the flow.

The City ran on a bubbled radiation transmission system. Outside the bubble, hacking its mainframe was nearly impossible. With Echelon, she might have had a shot, but those days were long gone. Now, she'd have to do it dirty.

She'd follow the shit. Literally.

The City was a zero-emission system. Were it not, a pool of solid waste would track the behemoth as it traversed the globe. Bad economic policy. With clean waters, *The City* could take on aquatic meat and produce without the expense of decontamination. Dealing with all the waste was thus a major issue. Each toilet on the ship included an incinerator. After each . . . deposit . . . the incinerator reduced the product to ash and gas. The gas was then vented, while the ash was used on the agricultural levels.

The procedure required serious processing power to coordinate. Within the transmission bubble, it didn't take much to hack into the waste management system. Then it was just a matter of following the shit to its source.

Once she was inside *The City*'s mainframe, the real challenge began. Plugged into flow space, Sarah rezzed into the central processing system. The true artistry of her hacks lay in their interface. In any system worth a hack, there was far too much information to process as raw code. So the hacker engineered an interface. Despite all the advances, all the power computers held, they still needed to process data in a linear fashion. A human could go tangential. And that's why hackers still had the upper hand. Gut instinct was the last human trait to fall. The key to hacking was finding an interface that allowed the hacker's gut instinct free rein.

Sarah dredged her free running interface from her flow-point. She used different interfaces for different operations. Free running was perfect for *The City.*

Before her, the central processing codes shifted to her will, settling into a format she could fathom. It took the form of a city. Not *The City*— just *a* city. Each building represented a processing node, each car and bus a packet of information being transferred. Even as the shift locked into place, she began her run.

Free running had come into vogue late in the twentieth, an extreme sport rising from the ghettos of Europe and sweeping the globe. Cities became playgrounds for those hunting freedom.

All the walls and barriers that separated and stratified became obstacles for free runners. The best could traverse a city by hurtling from rooftop to rooftop using a mix of gymnastics and climbing techniques. Those off their game suffered the consequences. There was no room for error. One had to commit totally. It was the perfect interface for a hack.

Sarah began her run. Each step had to be light and fast. Holding in any one spot would alert the system's security protocols. In her interface, that meant she'd glue-stick to the spot, and the city itself would consume her.

She hopped from the intrusion window into the world she had created. It landed her in a ratty apartment building. Her foot hit worn carpeting and she immediately felt the pull. The system was sensitive. Very sensitive. She'd have to move quickly.

Reality adjustment held her for a crucial instant. The door before her slammed shut. There was no breaking through it. Sarah pumped her knees, unsticking herself and gaining some speed. Just before the door, she flung herself up and sideways, slamming a foot into the wall and pushing up and off. The force of her move flung her headlong through the ventilation window over the door. She flew through, got a snap peek at the ground before curling hard and throwing her right arm into an arc. When she hit, the force of the impact rolled her back to her feet.

She gained speed down the hallway. Triggered by her landing, a hunt-kill avatar resolved and closed in on her. In the interface, the avatar took the form of a rabid dog. An instant before its jaws sank into her thigh, Sarah lunged up, grabbing what looked like an electrical conduit, and pulled high. The avatar glanced off the wall and crashed out. No time to stop. Sarah monkey-manned off the conduit and around the hallway's corner.

She hit the hall's end, crashing through the window and grabbing the fire escape, holding fast as the force pulled her back to the wall. She vaulted up the escape, reaching the roof as several more avatars rezzed before her.

One dove at her just as she gained a standing position at the roof's edge. Before she had time to think it out, Sarah arced back, lunging off the roof. The dog flew over her chest, so close she could have smelled its breath—if it were real. Sarah continued her arc, backflipping to land on the stairwell.

The impact smashed her knees into her chest. Sarah dispersed the force, snap-rolling back and smacking her arms out wide. Before the material could grip her, she popped back up and made for the roof.

Another avatar appeared behind her. Sarah pumped. She'd need two huge jumps to reach *The City*'s central processing plant. Reaching the building's corner, she hit the wall and pushed hard, legs bicycling in the air. She got a single flash of space below her, hundreds of meters to a hard paved street. The building before her loomed, closer and closer. She hit the roof with slamming force, leaning forward to offset the momentum. She rolled hard and pulled out to a run.

The central plant loomed before her. One more jump—but it had to be dead on. No room for error.

Legs churning, she pushed off with all her force, vaulting high into the air. Dogs followed her, forcing Sarah to go for a straight-line dive. If she missed, it would be over.

She locked in on the black fissure at the roof's center. Her target. She dove, headfirst, laid out flat, and snuck through with no room to spare. Dogs smashed into the space she left behind—the security protocols unable to enter the core.

Sarah took a moment to breathe, thrilling at her victory.

Secured within the plant, she killed the interface. Here it was 1, 0, and nothing else. She scanned *The City*'s heart, hunting data. After the visceral rush of the incursion, the dead mass of data before her felt anticlimactic. It didn't take long to find what she needed.

—*Laing. The credit chip that Taylor paid shipping with—it's just been used. Mezzanine deck. A snack bar called La Cocina.*

—*On it.*

34

Expectation jump-started Laing's haggard body, charging him for action. He pushed through the mingling throng on the mezzanine deck and knew he was close.

A swatch of green amidst *The City's* white, this was the ship's main park. Designed as an amalgam of the great parks around the world, it had a shrunk-in-the-dryer, Disney reality to it. People laughed and mingled, hunkered over espresso and chessboards. The park sprawled.

Ryan and Frank ambled with the rest, trying to blend with the general air of levity while feeling anything but light.

"Too many people," Frank muttered. "This whole place—"

"Like living in a sterilized dream," Ryan finished.

"That about covers it. Though most of my dreams involve more tail than I've seen here."

"Nice," Laing snorted, shaking his head. He'd grown used to Frank's crass edge. It had been a long time since Laing had anything like a friend. Madda maybe, years ago. The notion startled Laing. He defined himself as separate, other. The tug and pull of his life had forced it. Not many who could understand him, or would want to.

In spite of himself, Ryan found that he craved the bond. The driving urgency that was his life needed a foundation. Sarah had been that, and maybe would be again, but she was too close. She had bored so deep into him that his internal life included her. Frank was different. He was someone to spend time with. To work with. A man he respected—maybe even trusted. With Savakis, he could just walk.

They strolled along the wide sanded path, nodding to their fellow residents, eyes hunting for their target.

"Long way from the stacks," Laing said.

Frank shrugged. "People are people. Same bullshit everywhere, on the docks, in this," he waved his arm over the scene, "this nuthouse."

"Does feel like an asylum with all these uniforms."

"Yeah—got the uniforms, got the clean, futuristic thing going on. It's all crap. People are people. They sweat, they fuck, they kill. This just covers the stench in clean sheets."

"I thought *I* was cynical."

"Fuck—I'm not cynical. I'm a realist. I'm all about sweatin' and fuckin'."

"And killing?"

"I do what I have to. No pleasure there. But I'll tell you now, I'd rather go down with a garrote around my neck in some dark alley than piss out my life here."

"Never married?"

Frank laughed. "Almost. Once. Didn't play out. The fuckin' I got wasn't worth the fuckin' I got."

Laing smiled, eyes continuing to scan. "We've done a full circuit here."

Frank nodded. "Looks like a bust."

Even as Frank spoke, white terror electrified Ryan.

—*Ryan* . . .

Sarah's flow-link snuffed in a blaze of static.

Sarah almost made it.

Deep-probing the central plant, lost in a world of information, she shouldn't have heard the dull scratch of her cabin lock flipping back. Her augments saved her life.

Low-amp sound waves washed the room, slipped through the reduction static of the flow goggles and entered her ear as the slightest flicker of input. It tickled her—a tiny piece of reality that didn't fit. Adrenaline pushed to max. She ripped off the goggles, not bothering to end the flow-link, and dove off her chair.

Sarah felt the cold swipe of fingers just touching the back of her neck and flashing over her collarbone. Had she stayed in the chair, the blow would have struck the side of her neck, impacted the vagus nerve or, worse, her carotid artery. Unconsciousness would have been the best possible outcome.

But the attacker hadn't counted on detection. Sarah continued her roll, pulling her legs tight, the force of which flipped her up to her feet.

She gulped air, fighting for stability. Flow shift took time to zero out. Part of her mind remained in *The City*'s infrastructure. She shook it off, flushing the flow from her perception as she backed against the wall, putting as much distance as she could between her and the attacker.

Focusing in, she got her first look at the man.

"Hello, Sarah." The voice was soft—cold frost on the wind.

Zachary Taylor.

He circled her—a shark regarding its kill.

Peters had nullified his advantage of surprise. He made up for the loss by communicating the expectation of pain. He had seen it before, so many times. Something in him coveted that response: the involuntary bulging of the eyes, the scratch of dry lips closing, the rise and fall of the throat as the terror was swallowed down.

Sarah's fear was particularly appealing. He allowed it to fester, the urge building within him. The expectation of contact drove him to frenzy, the softness of her skin as he pressed in on her, dominated her. He took a step forward. The room was tight. She had nowhere to go. He circled, a snake toying with its meal. It was better when they knew what was coming.

Then, a shift. He watched, fascinated. She saw what he was doing, saw how important it was—how necessary—that she be terrified, and that he inspire it. But even as he zeroed in, her eyes hard-focused, glassy fear vanishing. Her lips clamped shut. Her hands curled into fists.

Before he could process the transformation, Sarah Peters attacked. Not the desperate flailing that Taylor was used to. Her fist flashed out, poised and deadly: a fast strike at his Adam's apple. Through his surprise, Taylor lowered his chin just enough to protect the larynx. Sarah's blow landed hard, punctuated by the crack of his teeth smashing together.

He stumbled, crashing into the bunk. His chin burned. He spit a shard of tooth from his mouth, looking up at the woman before him—a different animal from seconds earlier.

Sarah sported the slightest smile—terror bleached white. In its place there was only grim determination. The defilement he'd so wanted wouldn't be had here. She would fall defiant.

So be it, he thought.

Sarah lunged forward, whipping a leg over her head and bringing it down in a heel strike. Taylor rolled off the bed, the blow bouncing off the mattress.

They circled each other in the small space. Taylor watched her move, the easy flow of limber muscles. The novelty of a fair fight excited him. Usually, his targets didn't see it coming. But here, under *The City*'s bubble, Taylor's standard implements of death were unavailable. It would be hand to hand.

She watched him with cold analysis, as he did her. As she moved, he pinpointed the single moment in her gait when she was off balance, exposed. He knew her augment specs better than anyone. She flashed out—a side-hand strike to the side of his head that was actually a cover for a sharp kick at his forward knee. Taylor stepped into both blows, spinning around her before she could adjust. They continued their circle.

"You can't beat me," she said.

"That belief is your greatest weakness," he replied in little more than a whisper. He didn't want his voice to muffle any misstep she took.

"I'm teched to the gills. Neurochem—knife work. The best—"

"I know. I watched Judson cut into you."

"It was you in Dubai," Sarah said, her voice cracking under the realization. "You killed Jud."

Taylor's thin lips curled into a smile. "I had a hand in it."

Sarah's eyes widened for an instant. "Then you know," she said. "I'm stronger than you. Faster."

"Most likely."

She attacked again, this time a flicker-fast series of punches and chops. He zoned into them, phasing his moves to hers, parrying only.

"How—" Sarah sputtered.

"You jacked your speed, your power. Maybe even some training after all the augments—a quick intro on how to access your new abilities. Not sufficient."

He threw a straight jab, snapping it off at the last moment, gaining more information from her parry.

"I have no tech. No augments. I have focus. I have dedication. I *am* a killer. You just play at it."

Taylor watched the knowledge infuse her. Her eyes fluttered for a single moment, her mind elsewhere, maybe a prayer to her god, maybe something else.

It was the instant he had been waiting for.

The single moment was all he needed. He struck out, not with a flurry of blows, but a single open palm strike to her chest. His work had been done in the analysis, in the circling. He required only one punch.

The link died, Ryan's own name ringing through the rush of static.

Then, nothing.

Frank steadied Ryan, pulling him off the main path. They found themselves at a fountain shaded by oak trees. At the far end, a cascade of water dribbled down a wall of carved figures, each struggling over the other to reach heaven. Wrought-iron chairs ringed the dark pool. The place stood vacant, save for a thin man seated with his back to them.

"Laing!" Frank said, urgency tinting his voice. "What's the matter?"

Ryan's surprise triggered a rapid, staggering breath that devolved quickly into a coughing fit. He forced the cough back, gulping down the urge and grabbing Frank's arm.

"We have to get back to Sarah!" Ryan said.

"What?" Frank was ready to argue. Then he saw the look in Ryan's eyes. "Yeah. Okay."

"Sit down, gentlemen."

Ryan and Frank both turned toward the intrusion. Confusion sprinkled over Frank's standard annoyance. Laing knew that face.

"Impossible." It was all he could say before another coughing fit ripped his breath away.

The man stood, watching Laing with fish dead eyes. Then he turned to Frank. "While Mr. Laing is indisposed, let me introduce myself." He extended his hand. "I'm Alfred Krueger."

35

Alfred Krueger sat facing Ryan and Frank. He gazed into the pool's dark reflections, idly rolling a credit chip over his knuckles. It tumbled from one to the next in a mesmerizing slide, disappearing behind his pinky only to reappear at the top of his hand to start its journey again.

"You're dead," Ryan said, confusion saturating his voice.

"Yes. Well . . ."

Frank turned to Ryan. "You know this guy?"

Krueger flicked the chip at Frank, who caught it in midair.

"The credit chip you were hunting for."

Frank stared at it, then chucked it into the pool. "I don't like being fucked with."

"Then we're in the same boat."

"Sarah." Ryan forced the word out, stifling his cough.

"She's okay, Mr. Laing. Zachary Taylor has seen to her."

"If you—" The threat felt ridiculous coming off Laing's tongue. He stopped it in midstream.

Krueger nodded. "Good. You understand."

"What's going on here, Laing?" Frank asked, clearly annoyed at being the odd man out.

"Oh, he's as much in the dark as you, Frank. I run Taylor, and others like him."

"You're Phoenix," Frank said, incredulous.

Krueger smiled. "For a time—yes. I'm many things. Have been many things. A biologist. A weapons manufacturer. I am also what EMPYRE made me."

The glazed shock in Savakis's eyes drew a chuckle from Krueger.

"No. It's not possible," Ryan said with desperate assurance.

Krueger blew past Ryan's statement, eyes on Frank. "EMPYRE dragged me from the ashes and offered a new life. I had certain—talents—that EMPYRE capitalized on. It's one thing to plan a murder. Quite another to have the will and capability to follow through. I had—have—that will. And I found others like me. Men who understood that the world needs taming. I wiped them down and rebuilt them."

"Men like Taylor," Frank said.

"When I saw feed on his action in the Crimea—"

"Where he blew up a busload of kids," Frank shot in.

"And a cache of chemical weapons that could have wiped a city, yes. I watched that feed and saw Zachary's cold-honed will. I gave him an alternative to life behind bars. The attack on the hovercraft was a set piece that both served EMPYRE's political ends and allowed Zachary a new life."

"And you were behind the action in Tibet?" Frank asked.

Krueger nodded. "The assassination of the Dalai Lama and many more." He laughed as if reliving a fond memory. "My last act for EMPYRE's grand plan of targeted destabilization. Have to love Andrew Dillon's ability to suck the blood from even the harshest act. Shame he had to die." Krueger turned and stared at Laing before continuing. "But every child must, someday, surpass his parent."

Laing felt locked in an infinite loop, unable to find a route through the quagmire before him.

Krueger pushed on. "Family, Mr. Laing. Nothing more important. Wouldn't you agree? A legacy, passing from parent to child, running back into history. I had that. Until you took it from me."

"Murder and genocide isn't the best family legacy," Laing shot back.

"A legacy of power! The Krueger family made and sold arms for generations. We didn't make war. We *were* war! But, like all things, it couldn't last. Echelon destroyed what had taken centuries to build."

Ryan's eyes went wide.

"Didn't think I knew?" He turned to Frank. "Christopher Turing and his mighty Echelon hunted me down. You hunted me down."

"For supplying the chemical agent used in the Memphis attack," Ryan growled.

It was Frank's turn for surprise. "That killed thousands!"

Krueger shook his head as if addressing petulant children. "People die."

"I should have killed you," Ryan said.

"You should have. But Christopher Turing forbade it, didn't he?"

Ryan stared in disbelief. "How do you know this?"

"You turned me over to Turing yourself. I'll bet he told you that I didn't survive interrogation."

Confusion ebbed under a growing sense of betrayal. Ryan locked it down.

"Trying to figure out how I ended up under EMPYRE's thumb?" Krueger asked, enjoying himself. "Can't tell you myself. Turing spiked my memory. I remember nothing of that time. One moment, I was safe and secure in my ancestral home, the next I was in EMPYRE's hands. They knew everything—knew what I had done. And they held it over me. I could either help them, or submit to a trial that would destroy both me and my family name."

"So this is revenge?" Frank asked. "All this?"

Krueger did not turn to Frank, but held his eyes on Ryan as he continued. "Took some time to figure out what had happened to me. I'll admit, it's been a pleasure to watch you squirm, Laing. But all this—weaponizing Sarah, drawing you out—has been part of a larger plan."

"To cut EMPYRE's hold on you," Ryan said.

"Well, yes. But that was just the opening salvo. EMPYRE's goals were too small. I'm branching out. And you're going to help me."

"Not likely," Ryan replied.

"I want what was taken from me," Krueger said. "What Turing stole."

"Your memory?"

"Yes, Ryan. Turing took something fundamental from me. I want it back. Yes, he left me with my childhood, my past, even the knowledge necessary to work for EMPYRE. But he took something, Ryan. Something my whole life was driving toward. Something I need to fulfill my destiny."

A dead silence filled the space between them. Then Ryan lurched forward. He grabbed Krueger by the throat, relishing the act of killing this man.

The moment didn't last.

Krueger's hand pulled free of his pocket. It gripped a *City*-approved com device already on call.

Frank saw it first. "Ryan," he said.

But it was too late. Laing was far gone—rage, fueled on helplessness, driving him. He drew Krueger close, boring down on the smaller man, ready to kill.

Krueger managed to bring the com-link up to his mouth and rasp, "Send." That was all it took.

In seconds, the announcement began. The female voice piped into the gardens, cutting the moment. "Attention residents. Threat level has been elevated to Severe. Sarah Peters, wanted terrorist, has entered *The City*. She has hacked our system infrastructure with plans . . ."

The voice trailed into static. Replacing it were images. From every wall panel, every monitor, every flow node, images of the devastation in Trenton and Australia cycled through.

The City erupted in terror.

36

The blurred rush of images flashing over the vid walls pulled Laing from his rage. He released Krueger, who fell back, sputtering softly, eyes burning with fury.

He recovered quickly. "Evoking terror," Krueger said. "Something I've had a great deal of time to perfect."

"What more could you want from her?"

"From Sarah? Please, Mr. Laing. I don't want anything from her. She's just a vector—a weapon which I used to destroy EMPYRE and weaken you. Now, she's a lever to get what I want."

Frank stepped forward. "Where is she, Krueger?"

"Right now, Taylor is escorting her to my yacht. Trust me, you want them to reach that ship. *The City* is about to self-destruct."

"Please," Frank scoffed. "An imagined threat isn't going to titanic *The City*."

Krueger raised an eyebrow.

Through concussion-hazed vision, she saw Taylor goggled in at the flow-port. She struggled against the restraints he had wrapped on her. They didn't budge.

Sarah's run had plugged this flow-port into *The City*'s heart. Taylor knew it—had counted on it. He pushed in and ran vid shots of the bio-attacks. Then he began a system shutdown, first hitting the cabins, then extending the lockout into the communal areas. Lights blanked out, the soft hum of vibrancy ground to a halt.

Finally, their cabin went to black. He dropped the goggles and turned to Sarah. "Time to go."

—*Ryan, I'm sorry.*

Her thought chilled Laing's rage. She was still alive.

—*Sarah! Where are you?*

—*Taylor has me. He's shut down the core systems.*

—*I know. Listen, I'm coming. Just hold tight.*

Laing turned on Krueger. "Take us to her."

"Gladly," he replied.

The garden had faded to a musty black. Lights extinguished and the

216 > JOSH CONVISER

faux sky went neutral, revealing that the garden's ceiling was in fact quite low—just higher than the tallest trees. A feeling of claustrophobia settled over the place.

Already, the anxiety sparked by Taylor's vid storm had risen to a boil. Now, with the power grid offline, panic flashed through *The City's* population. They were trapped at sea with an invisible killer.

Laing pushed Krueger through the crowd.

"You see, Laing, if the threat is real enough, you don't need the act to spark the response. *The City* is about to tear itself apart."

Bursting into *The City's* central thoroughfare, Laing pulled up short. It was bedlam.

"And we shall be as a city upon a hill," Krueger quoted, softly chuckling.

Frank wheeled, sucker-punching him in the gut. Krueger crumpled. Laing glared at Frank.

"What? Fucker deserved it."

Laing hauled Krueger back to standing.

"Terminal 6, berth 456," Krueger sputtered.

Before them, the masses thronged, spilling into the thoroughfare. Ryan dragged Krueger into the mosh.

"You feel it, Ryan?" Krueger shouted over the din. "The tension? The fear?"

Far ahead of them, black-armored shock troops flooded the thoroughfare, forming a sharp V and pushing forward.

The City's voice rose: "Do not panic. *City* military has been called out to maintain order."

"The key, Ryan, is to know your enemy. *The City* doesn't have a police force. Never needed it. What it does have is a highly effective military. *The City* moves through dangerous waters. Those troops don't know crowd control. They only know how to kill." As Krueger spoke, civs, pushed from behind, piled down on the wedge of shock troops.

The press grew stronger, catching Ryan, Frank, and Krueger in its crush.

"Those troops will ignite the terror I generated," Krueger said.

Frank turned on him. "Will you shut the fuck—" He didn't finish. A single gunshot rose over the mob frenzy. Then a scream.

"Oh, shit," Laing said.

"Shit is right," Frank replied.

The sounds sparked the mob. Fear turned to riot.

In slow-motion synchronicity, the shock troops drew down.

"Bloodbath," Krueger whispered.

The surrounded troops opened up, splashing red over the residents' uniforms. Civs on the front line fell in fleshy waves, unable to stop the stampede.

"Come on," Laing shouted, trying to hold back his cough.

They pushed through a side street. Around them, panic spread like a flash fire. When steam ducts scattered throughout *The City* hissed open, blanketing everything in fog, the riot went nova.

Laing led them out into the open air. Men, women, children crowded the outer causeway. The mass push forced more and more over the railing. Already, Laing could make out the staccato splashes of bodies hitting ocean fifty meters below.

Laing and Frank fought their way down the causeway, punching through panicked residents.

—*Ryan, The City's done.*

—*I know, Sarah.*

Ryan, Frank, and Krueger reached the ship's stern. Residents ebbed and flowed in waves of terror and desperation.

"We're never getting down there," Frank screamed over the chaos.

"Maintenance ladder—far side," Krueger broke in.

They scrambled over, and sure enough, a maintenance ladder ran down to Terminal 6.

"I should kill you now," Frank fumed.

Krueger laughed. He hopped onto the ladder and began the descent. Frank followed, Laing bringing up the rear. From his vantage point, Ryan watched the havoc spread. There was no disaster, natural or otherwise, that could sink *The City*. As such, life rafts were never a consideration. With no means of escape, civs flung themselves into the water like lemmings, fleeing an imagined bioattack, and the very real shock troops. Already, corpses flecked the ocean around the ship.

The three reached the deck only to find a phalanx of shock troops guarding the terminal. Their stand was fruitless—a dam about to burst. Troops splintered off, picked away by the massing throng. The rioters broke through the line, charging into the marina, swarming the yachts, desperate.

Behind the wave, Krueger led Frank and Ryan into the marina. At berth 456, a wall of bodies blocked access to a sleek yacht. Cresting the bloody crush, Laing watched Taylor calmly firing on anyone who got too close, killing with cold precision.

He held Sarah before him on the yacht's aft deck. Seeing Ryan, Taylor pushed closer to her. Ryan could just see his taunting smile through the curtain of Sarah's hair.

Laing charged.

Taylor only smiled larger. He holstered the gun and pulled something else from his jacket, something black and sharp.

Sarah flushed on seeing Ryan. Taylor's psychopathic killing spree had numbed her to zero. Ryan pulled her back from grim oblivion. He charged at her. She forgot her restraints, pushing hard to reach him.

Taylor held her fast.

Then, cool ice pervaded her. She saw it for an instant. A needle, long and sharp, attached to a palm-sized device. Taylor slammed the device down. The needle punctured the lens of her eye and entered her pupil.

Laing stopped short, Frank jamming up behind him. Ryan watched the needle slide in, smooth and languid. Then the contraption at the needle's end sprouted pincers that bore down into Sarah's eye socket, holding it fast to her face.

Sarah shuddered for an instant, then stood stock-still.

Krueger shifted past Ryan and Frank, hopping aboard. "Echelon took my memories, I'm taking hers. The eyes are a pathway to the brain—a window into the mind. As you can see, I'm interested in the view."

"Motherfucker," Frank said with cold fury.

"Listen very carefully," Krueger said. "I want what Echelon took from me. What Turing took. For every moment I don't have it, Sarah loses a slice of her past. The spike I have inserted will slowly wipe her memory, taking it down to zero if you don't move fast."

Krueger grabbed a digi-palette that served as the yacht's control module and kicked the craft into an emergency egress. At the bow and stern, the pincer cables gripping the berth retracted into the ship. As its engines churned, Laing could only watch Sarah slip away. The mayhem around him faded to nothing. He focused on Sarah. A single tear of blood slipped free of the spike.

Behind her, Taylor grinned cold.

37

A force-induced quiet hung over *The City*, thick and claustrophobic. It hadn't taken long for *The City*'s tech-men to regain system control and reinstate order. A new voice issued calm pronouncements that the past moments had been nothing more than a hoax. There was no pathogen. Sarah Peters was not onboard. Residents were free to return to their business.

But the damage was done. *The City*'s impregnability had been challenged and the exodus continued unabated. Ferries rocketed from their slot ports. The floating bodies oil-slicking the water around *The City* had been pushed aside to allow passage.

Residents fled en masse and the world reverberated from their flight. *The City* had been an anonymous zone where the world's powers could meet in clandestine security. No longer. High-level negotiations between the United States and Canada being held on-ship broke down, sending the peace accords into a tailspin. Word got out that Israel and Egypt had been working on a trade pact and violence surged through the two countries. As *The City* floundered, world politics stutter-stepped.

Ryan and Frank walked down empty causeways. The echo of their steps rose through dead air. What had been a bustle of people and commerce just hours ago was now a graveyard. Ryan hazed into the click-step of his feet, not quite ready to acknowledge the silence.

"You knew," Frank said. "You knew about Krueger and still dumped that psycho on EMPYRE."

Ryan shook his head. "No." It was all he could say.

"Well, someone did."

Ryan's mind reeled. All those years ago, Turing had assured him that Krueger was taken care of—and now the man was back from the dead.

"You took this guy down, right?"

A long moment elapsed before Ryan processed Frank's question. "Yeah."

"And what happened? How did he end up in EMPYRE? Why didn't you just off him?"

"I wanted to," Ryan said absently. "They wouldn't let me."

"They?"

Laing didn't respond. He churned back through his memory. It wasn't *they.* It was *he.* Ryan had run down Krueger for Turing. And he had turned the man over to Turing himself.

Frustrated, Frank continued. "Why did Echelon bother with this guy at all? Was it just Memphis?"

Ryan jumped to reply, pulling away from a thought line he really didn't want to go down. "There's no one like Krueger."

"The fuck is this guy?"

"The Krueger family? You haven't heard of them?"

"I don't do history, all right?"

"Kruegers have been around since early in the twentieth. German. They supplied arms to their country through both world wars. Imagine a country of that size whose weapons industry lay in the hands of a single family. They *were* Germany."

"And they didn't get knocked off their pedestal after the wars?"

"They got a hand slap. To truly gut them would have broken the German industrial infrastructure. The Krueger empire survived. It teetered through the years, expanding and contracting as it entered new industries. But—"

"Nothing's more secure than making weapons."

Ryan nodded. "Echelon cut into them. We engineered a hostile takeover, flushing the family with so much cash that we hoped apathy would set in. It almost worked."

"And Alfred?"

"He's a genius, Frank—and determined to supply the world with Krueger weaponry."

"But you said you cut out their industrial legs."

"Krueger saw that the new battle zone wasn't on the field, but *here.*" Laing tapped his chest. "Inside."

"Biologicals," Frank said with the slightest hesitation, as if uttering the word forced its reality.

"He designed pathogens, weaponized viruses, and he supplied them to a widening range of . . . customers. Echelon caught most of them."

"Most."

"Okay, we missed Memphis. But Memphis wasn't the reason we went after Krueger. If it was just that, we would have fed his location to the UN and let them haul him in."

"Krueger had something worse in his arsenal?"

"We thought so. Or Turing did."

"Right. Turing—the genius who spiked Krueger and handed him over to EMPYRE."

"No," Ryan said, adamant. "There must be something more. Something we're missing."

Frank shrugged.

Krueger's cold patience sent a shiver through Laing. How long had he sat in the background, waiting to reap his revenge on Laing and the world?

"I should have killed him," Ryan said softly.

Frank laughed. "Well, now's your chance."

"He was perfect for EMPYRE. Almost too perfect. A man who understood death—and terror. An organization that fostered such action. It's like EMPYRE was built to house Krueger."

"My dad used to say, don't wrestle with a pig. You both get dirty and the pig likes it."

"Looks like EMPYRE took the wrong pig into its pen."

They entered Ryan's cabin. Vestiges of Sarah's fight with Taylor lay strewn across the room. Laing felt the violence of their confrontation with each step through the wreckage. Guilt ripped into him. He had let her down—again. His chest spasmed at the thought. He fought through it, carving out breath after breath. Maybe it was the virus. Maybe something else.

Sarah fought hard. Once she was free of *The City*'s bubble, the hawkeye sighted in on her. From above, she saw the yacht, herself, and the hideous thing protruding from her eye. As it neared, Taylor plucked the hawkeye from the air—a move she didn't think possible. He drilled the hawkeye back into the holster in her side, his fingers lingering within her for a bloodcurdling moment. The violation ran to max.

Sarah reeled back, hands dragging over the memory spike in her eye. She began to pull it free, her good eye tearing up with the pain.

"I wouldn't do that if I were you." Krueger's words came out soft and cruel. He was relishing this. "Pull the spike and your entire memory will be fried. It's part of you now."

Taylor hauled her back up to standing. Sarah thrashed against him. Krueger pushed closer, grabbing Sarah's hand, drawing it up to his own eye. Under the skin of his eyebrow, she felt protrusions.

"A similar device was once screwed into my own eye."

The yacht crested an ocean swell, knocking at the trio's balance. Sarah used the moment to drive her fingers into Krueger's eye socket. Despite the pain and the terror running through her, jacked reactions did their work. She managed a slice with her fingernail before Taylor pulled her away.

Krueger spun back, stung by the rush of pain. He drew a hand to his eye and it came away bloody. Krueger looked up, composure evaporating. He slapped Sarah across the jaw, a fleshy pop punctuating the moment. Her cheek retained the bloody imprint of his strike.

"Laing stole my life's work!" he railed. "You couldn't understand."

"So this is revenge? All this? Destroying EMPYRE, setting me up, drawing Ryan into the open to—what, kill him?"

"Oh, it's revenge. And it's more, Sarah—so much more. EMPYRE had the right idea. But they thought too small. The used me as a bullet, when I, in fact, should be the one wielding the gun."

"So you'll become EMPYRE—using terror and chaos to fuel your own ends."

"Is that so wrong? You saw the power of it—you pulled data on most of the recent jobs. You know just how powerful terror can be."

"What are you going to do?"

"I'm going to finish what you started, Sarah. You and Ryan. You brought Echelon down. You pushed the world into a new era. But you couldn't handle the ramifications. Evolution is messy. It's struggle. It's death. It's violence. And out of it, we grow."

"So all of this is for the greater good?"

"Can you deny it? You were part of EMPYRE, Sarah."

Sarah looked down, the weight of the spike pulling at her eye. "Something I'll be happy to forget."

Krueger laughed. "Small-minded. You. Laing. EMPYRE."

Sarah shook her head. "No matter how you push, you're just a small fish in a big pond. You might become a gun—but just one of many."

"Depends on the size of the gun. Echelon wiped me for a reason. What did I have in my head that was so very dangerous?"

Krueger leaned back against the railing, ocean running under him in whitewash. "I think I know, Sarah. I see pieces of it in dreams. And Laing will get it for me."

"No."

"Oh, he will. I'm not going to disrupt your link. You'll be able to burrow into his head and give him running detail on your slow fade. It will tear him apart."

Krueger nodded to Taylor. He pushed Sarah into the ship and down to a cabin devoid of furniture. Its dull black seemed to eat the light from the hall. Taylor shoved her in. She wheeled on him, defiant.

"I see it. You're thinking you can suffer through the loss in silence." Krueger slid close to Sarah, just out of arm's reach. "But you won't. It's not about strength. It's more primal than that. You'll link to him. And he'll return what's mine."

With that, Krueger stepped back and Taylor slammed the hatch shut. It vacuum-locked with a pneumatic hiss, leaving Sarah in total darkness.

Krueger was right. She didn't last long.

In the darkness, she stumbled, then squatted down on her haunches, trying to remain calm. She pulled the hawkeye from its holster and lofted it. She could just make out its muffled impacts with the cabin's insulated walls. It saw nothing.

The hawkeye plunked to the floor. Sarah splayed out, scratching for it. She fumbled over it and holstered the thing.

Then, with measured deliberation, she studied the spike plugged into her mind. Loss welled in her—the smooth trickle of water over rock. Sarah forced herself into memory, pushing deep into her past, even as the images faded. Waves of regret engulfed her.

She couldn't know what parts of her life were being chewed through. Couldn't know what she had forgotten. She only had a widening sense of solitude. It grew in her, squatting in the space her memories left behind.

In black isolation, she fought against a need to link to Ryan. He had to stay away from her. Whatever Krueger wanted, he could never get. But the pain threatened to overwhelm her—as if she were grieving her own slow death.

If only I had been stronger, she thought. *If only I had gone under—just one more time.* The comfortable mantra revolved through her mind.

No. The word reverberated through her. *Not like this.* She would not end like this, locked into the binge-purge cycle she had succumbed to for so long. One more time would have done nothing. All her tech, all her augments, and she was still Sarah Peters. Nothing changed that.

Now, she turned from the cycle and did what she had feared for so long. She turned in and looked at herself, under all the tech, beneath the shell of armor she had constructed. The reality stung. The shape of her degradation. How could love have done this to her? How could it have weakened her so?

As she stared into her fading picture show, rage surged up in her. For Ryan. For the man who had put her here.

—*Goddamn you, Ryan.* She couldn't help herself.

—*Sarah. Are you okay?*

—*No. I'm not. I've got a fucking needle in my eye sucking my life away.*

—*I will get you out of there.*

—*Ryan, just stay away. Krueger's got your number.*

—*I'll get him what he wants.*

—*Oh, please. We both know where that will lead.*

—*I don't care.*

—*You know what—don't bother. I'm sick of being the lure. I'm sick of being fucking sick. I'm sick of you, Laing.*

—*Sarah . . .*

She cut right through him.

—*There are some things—some people—I'd rather forget.*

38

Sarah's hate sliced through Laing. He tried to tell himself it was frustration, or desperation. But the justification wouldn't hold. Something in her was better off not knowing him. Laing coughed, the staccato hacks pulling him from his ruminations. Recovering slowly, he gazed out the skim jet's window to the Pacific Ocean flashing below him.

Through the trip, Laing had fallen into Sarah's slow loss. He found it difficult to engage in the world around him with her thoughts flowing through his head.

"Regret's comin' off you in buckets," Frank said, relaxing into the soft leather of his seat. "Have a beer. We got full bar on this thing."

Laing pulled back from his musings, focusing on Savakis. His boxy frame looked out of place within the jet's elegance. He bulged from the seat, his bulk discordant with its elegant lines.

"I should have stayed away," Ryan said.

"Oh, come on. There's no resisting my charm. Oh—you meant Sarah?"

Laing looked through him, unable to connect with the humor.

"Christ!" Frank said, bucking back in the chair. "You got angst, man."

"Sarah's losing her mind. Krueger's after something so bad that Turing spiked him. And I'm right at the center."

"It's not angst. You got doubt."

"So far, I've been played."

"Like a bigmouth bass. We both have."

"So a little doubt's in order." Laing paused, hating to admit weakness. But at that moment, the gut-wrench so gripped him that he couldn't continue without expelling it. "I don't think I can do this. Not anymore."

"The fuck you can't!" Frank shot back. "You got the game. Own it, or it *will* own you."

Laing laughed, sliding deep into his seat. He envied Frank's black-white world. Ryan closed his eyes, letting Frank drop away. After a time, even Sarah's thoughts faded. And just as sleep crept in, he felt it. That place in him where Christopher Turing wasn't dead—where the past years hadn't happened and he had peace.

They clocked the kilometers, tracking over rough ocean. Nearing land, the skim jet banked into the sky, churning air to reach altitude. Laing looked down on the city of Los Angeles, a place he had once called home. He couldn't find a piece of himself that cared.

The jet lanced west, into the desert. Madda had been reluctant when Laing contacted him. At least until Ryan related Sarah's present position.

After that, there had been a long pause, soft static snowing the line. "Better come get me," he had said.

Now, they approached Burning Man. High overhead, Laing could make out the effigy's unending blaze. Buildings spread from it, amoeba-like, into the desert. The jet went into slow descent. As it did, people began to emerge from the buildings, breaking into the heat-dried air. At ten meters, the jet shut down its engines and went to electromags, coming in on a pillow of magnetic resistance.

Landing, Frank and Laing hit the stairs. Even as the heat enveloped them, both sensed a rising panic running through the Burners.

"Keep us hot," Frank said to the pilot.

He received a deep chirp from the cockpit. None of the CIA jets used human pilots. Mechy piloting gear didn't require security clearance.

They descended and were quickly surrounded by a mass of Burners. The hot stink of body odor rose from the group. Glazed eyes followed their moves, not hostile, but certainly not comforting.

"The great unwashed," Frank said to Laing under his breath.

"Smells that way," Laing said, drawing a soft chuckle from Frank. "Come on."

They pushed through the crowd and entered Madda's fuselage labyrinth. Trampling through hall after hall, they heard sounds and movement ahead.

Reaching Madda's inner sanctum, they found six Burners hovering over a twitchy Madda. Hands placed on him, they appeared deep in meditation—all save Dave, who shot up as Frank and Laing entered.

"Hi, there!" His voice was high-pitched and nerve-raw. Madda snaked his way through the pile of hands.

"What's this? A final lovefest?" Frank asked.

"Ahh, funny. No, they were just—"

"We're helping our friend," one of the men said as he rose. His face was grooved, hard lined like desert rock. A matted gray beard hung from his chin.

"I'm sure," Laing said.

The old man turned from Laing and Frank, pushing them from his consciousness. His eyes burned into Madda, forcing his presence on the frail man.

"It's not time for you, David. Leaving here would be a mistake."

"A mistake," Madda repeated, eyes wavering, unable to hold on the old man's. "Maybe you're right, Allan." He turned uneasily to Laing, eyes teary with fear and confusion.

"Madda, we don't have time for this," Ryan said.

"There's time, here. Always time to help our friends."

"Fuck me," Frank said to himself, then flipped on Ryan. "We need this fruit loop? Really?"

"Yes," Ryan replied.

Frank grunted and wheeled on Allan. He slammed the old man into the curved wall and held him there for a long moment. The man didn't fight back.

"Listen, Allan," Frank spat.

One of the Burners, a thick man in ragged pants and no shirt, stepped forward. Frank dropped him with a boxer's uppercut to the jaw, dirty and effective.

"Allan Simon," the man replied, his smooth tone unchanged by the shift in his circumstances.

"Listen, Allan Simon, I can see why you want this twitch bucket sticking around. I get it. He's your meal ticket."

"It's not like that," Madda stammered.

Neither Allan nor Frank paid any attention to Madda. Frank pushed closer to the old man. "It's exactly like that, isn't it? You been sapping this guy for a good long while. Well, gravy train's comin' to the station. You'll have to manage this shit pile without him."

The man's face radiated contentment, never slipping. He raised a hand to Frank's neck, fingers flexing down with light pressure, a move of assurance. Frank slammed him again, but the man's nirvana calm didn't budge.

"That's not our way, friend. Through the journey of his life, David has come to himself in a dark wood."

As he spoke the lines, Madda began to recite with him, the mantra resonating through the tight room. The other Burners picked it up.

In unison: "How hard to tell the nature of that forest—savage, dense, harsh, the very thought of it renews the fear."

Madda's voice trailed off, stuttering to a close, even as Frank's began. Savakis didn't know the words, but mumbled with the tone, his resolve slackening.

"How we came there, we cannot tell. We were full of sleep when we forsook the one true way."

The words rang familiar to Laing, memory stilling him. He'd read them in an ancient poem about Hell and Heaven.

Madda shook out, reviving even as Frank fell. A Burner stepped forward to place his hands back on Dave. Dave, seeing the move, struggled to a workbench and grabbed a syringe. He tried for Laing, who watched the scene in dull confusion, clouded by his own fog of sickness.

The Burner that Frank had punched grabbed Madda's leg, toppling him. The man pulled at Dave's pant leg, revealing skin and slapping his hand to it. Laing began to realize what was happening as Dave's eyes slid back to placid. But just before nirvana closed in on Dave, he raised the syringe and slammed it into Ryan's boot. It pierced flesh, punching into the small bones, and releasing its contents.

The mantra rose back. "Let us wake, rise through the fire and find the path again."

Ryan fell. Madda's injection coursed through him. He felt its pulsing rush through his body. A ringing grew in his ears, like the reverb of fast-cooling metal. He coughed, dredging something green and horrible from his lungs. It lay before him, festering on the dirty floor.

And something in him flipped. Renewed. A charge he hadn't felt since . . .The drones pushed into his mind, resurging to max capacity.

Madda engineered a cure for the virus! With the realization, the tingle of augmented awareness flushed Ryan.

Laing felt hands on him, and the pulsing mantra.

The hands!

A cold rush seeped into him from the contact, the slow-push psychedelic holding his mind for an instant, bending him to the Burners' will. He shook through it, drones attacking the drug with vigor. Killing it.

Laing rose. He jammed a shoulder up and through the lock Allan had on Frank, breaking the contact. Frank stumbled back. Laing lifted Madda from the floor and away from the Burners' hands. Now he could see what they were holding: subderm drug packs with compression shot injectors. They continued to paw each other, feeding the nirvanic bliss.

Seeing he had lost, the old man broke into an enraged yell. He flew at Ryan, slamming into him, clawing him, biting him with all the force he could muster. Laing felt the man's teeth sink into the meat of his neck. He allowed it to happen. Then he held the man to him, letting drone-soaked blood flow into the man's mouth, choking him.

With the drone connection, he felt the man's rage, and the fear creeping over his bliss. Laing recalled a line from that old poem. He forced the words into the man's mind.

—*Through me, into the city of woe; through me, a message of pain; through me, the passage for lost souls. Abandon all hope, you who enter here.*

Laing pushed in on the old man, who had stilled with the onslaught.

His legs fell from Ryan's hips. He pulled away, mouth dripping gray. He watched the bite on Laing's neck fade to soft pink flesh, then looked up at Laing in confused terror.

Ryan pulled Frank and Madda out of the room. Several of the Burners pushed to follow.

The old man stilled them.

"Lll . . ." he couldn't seem to find the word. "Let them go."

39

Back in the skim jet, Ryan slumped into his seat. Whatever Madda had given him continued its course, stilling the retrovirus. Laing drank as much water as he could stomach. He hadn't eaten in days. But with each moment, he felt better. Stronger.

Opposite him, Frank and Madda continued to bicker.

"You knew they were drugging you?" Frank rubbed at his head, still working to clear the cobwebs.

"Well, yeah." Madda couldn't seem to find his balance. He wobbled with the turbulence.

"And you just let them do it? For a smart guy—"

"Listen—Frank, is it? I'm in no mood right now. You want my help? Shut up and listen." Madda twitched with the effort, putting a hand over his eye to shield his view out of the skim jet.

"Madda, will this wear off?" Ryan asked.

"No. I found enough of the retrovirus's genome that I could engineer my own splice virus to corrupt its code. You're pathogen free. Back to fighting form."

"What'd I tell ya? It's gonna work out." Frank grinned at Laing.

Ryan smiled back. Then, he pushed close to Madda. "We need to talk about Krueger."

"No."

"Madda—"

"We need to talk about Christopher Turing."

The name stung Ryan. He pushed through. "Madda, what was in Krueger's head?"

"Like you said—that's something between Turing and Krueger."

"You don't know?"

"Well, I know what Krueger was into. He'd been tracked for a long time before you retrieved him. Turing was obsessed with the guy from a long way back, but I'm not sure why. I mean, Krueger was an academic from an old family. Sure, that family developed weapons, and Krueger designed his share of biologicals, but it was nothing Echelon couldn't handle. Then there was Memphis."

"And I hauled him in."

"But not for that. I mean, we could have just turned him over. Turing spiked him for something else."

Madda held silent. Finally, Frank lost patience. "What?!"

"I really don't know," Dave replied. "He had big-time skills working biological coding. Smart. Very, very smart. Scary smart. There's the average bear, then there's—"

"Madda." Laing caught him before Dave spiraled out.

"Right, sorry. He got deep in, man. Had some scary knack with biological patterns. His work at the Center for Advanced Studies dealt with computational equivalence."

Madda got blank stares from his companions. "Right," he continued. "That's the idea that simple rules, applied over many iterations, can lead to vast complexity. So, if you can capture those rules, you can extrapolate larger patterns. Means Krueger was trying to uncover the core patterns upon which life is based."

"So what?" Laing asked.

"So, if he got deep enough, Krueger could have generated a means of upsetting those patterns."

"Upsetting patterns?" Frank asked.

Madda gave him an exasperated look. "He figured out how to kill people real good. That simple enough for you?"

"But he can do that now. Sarah's virus proves that. So what did Turing spike?" Laing asked.

Madda shrugged.

"In your time at Echelon, did that happen often?" Ryan asked. "Turing hoarding a data pull?"

"Only this once."

"So, to distill all this down—we're fucked. We don't know shit," Frank said.

"Well, I do have a theory," Madda said, the old smile rising.

"Okay, spill," Frank said.

"*Kryptos.*"

Laing cocked his head. Frank went red with frustration.

"We're going to Langley," Madda continued.

"That's the one place we know Krueger's not!" Frank steamed.

"Wrong," Madda replied.

The skim jet headed east, swooping low over open ground, then rising with the burbs to gain max altitude over the cities.

"How long you been at the CIA? And you never noticed it?" Madda had repositioned himself as far from Frank as possible.

Frank turned to Laing. "Your genius better start making sense. I'm way beyond a mood for twenty questions."

"Madda," Laing urged.

"*Kryptos,* man!" Madda exclaimed. "The sculpture! Designed by James Sanborn in the twentieth? It sits plunk in the middle of Langley."

"Oh, shit," Laing blurted. "The cryptology sculpture. Turing had a holo of it in his office. He was obsessed with cracking the code within it."

"You're talking about the stone and metal thing with all the letters?" Frank asked.

"Yes," Madda replied with scorn. He called up an image of the sculpture on the vid screen.

"So what?" Frank shot back. "So Turing liked the sculpture? The fuck difference does that make?"

"He didn't just *like* it. I found something while you were getting to me. Did a deep run on Turing's activity during the Krueger affair."

"And?" Laing asked.

"And, through a series of shells that would house all the clams in the sea, Turing made a generous contribution to the United States government. Specifically, to the restoration of *Kryptos.*"

"No shit," Frank said.

"No shit," Madda replied.

40

Darkness had become the constant. For hours, days maybe, Krueger had kept Sarah in the rad-blocked cabin. The black had eaten through her, isolation as damaging as the spike itself.

Finally, the eternity had ended. Blinding white glare pierced the darkness. The stimulus had been too much. She remembered Taylor's hands on her, street sounds, exotic smells. Then she was shoved down a ladder and into insulated silence.

Descending, her vision cleared to the point where she could see stone columns disappearing into black water. Taylor pulled her along, down a softly lit hall to a door. He opened it and she clued to the rad-blocking film on its interior.

Panic shot through her—drawing her back to reality.

"No!" she raged, desperate to stay in the light. She threw her arms out, bridging the door. But Taylor was too strong. He pushed and she fell.

Before her head hit the floor, the door slammed shut. The darkness was total. For a time she had the pain of her head wound to keep her company. Then it faded and there was nothing.

CENTRAL INTELLIGENCE AGENCY, LANGLEY, VIRGINIA

The atrium bustled with activity. Vaulting walls arched to a translucent ceiling from which diffused light filtered down. All construction within the CIA was done with rad-blocking biocrete. The material rippled and flowed, luminescing tracks on the floor and walls that led employees to their assigned locations. A side effect of the navigation system was that few felt comfortable loitering. The blipping dot that indicated a standing employee was easily noticed.

As a result, employees raced through the atrium without taking notice of the statue that occupied center stage. Its aged tarnish stood in stark contrast to the slick biocrete and hypermod space.

Ryan regarded the serpentine curved copper screen emerging scroll-like from a trunk of petrified wood. Rising well over his head, the plate held four sections of encrypted text punched into the tarnished metal.

"It used to be outside," Madda said.

Ryan, Madda, and Frank stood under the statue, the only people lingering in the cavernous atrium. Around them, employees whipped by, few making eye contact. Security eyed them with suspicion. It had taken all the chits Frank had saved up to get Laing and Madda into the building.

Madda reached forward, touching the punched metal. "It's amazing."

"Turing loved it," Ryan said. Wisps of comfortable memory filled him. So many times, Ryan had sat within Turing's flow-constructed office, this statue rotating in the corner. Turing had never mentioned it, but every so often, Ryan would notice his eyes floating to it, lingering on it.

"Okay—so let's get to it," Frank said, breaking the spell. "We break the code here and the statue'll spit out whatever Turing spiked from Krueger, right?"

"Uhh, no." Madda shot Frank a look that brought the larger man's blood to a boil. Laing stepped between them.

Madda continued unfazed, "*Kryptos* was erected in 1990. That's a tad before even Turing."

"So he hid some sort of cache in the sculpture while restoring it."

"And slipped it into the CIA's security bubble? Seems unlikely. They'd have scanned this six ways to Sunday before letting it back in the building."

"Then what the fuck are we doing here?"

"If I knew, I'd have told you."

Madda began a slow tour of the sculpture. "The sculptor used a combination of systems to encrypt this thing," he said, pointing to the metal scroll. "Basically, it's a Vigenère cipher—a substitution system using multiple alphabets. It's a real bitch—"

Frank cut in, "I don't give a shit, Madda. We got some time pressure here. What does the thing say?"

Madda pulled himself back to reality as Ryan continued to circle the sculpture.

"Okay," Dave said. "First three sections were hacked a long time ago. First one reads:

Between subtle shading and the absence of light lies the nuance of iqlusion."

Madda fumbled over the last word. "It's a misspelling within the cipher," he explained.

"And you know all this by heart?"

"Sure. *Kryptos* is a huge deal. Though I am paraphrasing a bit." He turned back to *Kryptos.* "Anyway—second section was debated for a while, but the sculptor himself finally settled it to:

It was totally invisible hows that possible? They used the earths magnetic field x the information was gathered and transmitted undergruund to an unknown location x does langley know about this? They should its buried out there somewhere x who knows the exact location? Only ww this was his last message x thirty eight degrees fifty seven minutes six point five seconds north seventy seven degrees eight minutes forty four seconds west x layer two."

"The fuck does that mean?" Frank's annoyance was in no way diminishing Madda's excitement.

"Search me," Madda replied.

"Who's 'ww'?"

"Think it's William Webster. He was the CIA director when *Kryptos* went up. The location's a bust. Nothing there."

Frank paced, trying to focus. "This is a jerk-off," he mumbled.

Laing listened to them bicker. Madda's staccato rambling fell away as he focused on the letters punched into the metal plate. His drones began to tingle. They were pattern matchers. They had linked to the patterns within him—his genetic code. They spoke to him as he spoke to himself. Augmented internal dialogue. And now as he gazed at the cipher, they tingled with pattern recognition but couldn't seem to pull resolution.

"This thing's complicated," Laing said, lost in it.

"Tell me about it. It's badass, to have stumped everyone for so long. Last section that's been deciphered is a rip on some dude's journal, where he talked about breaking into the tomb of Tutankhamen. That's King Tut," Madda said, looking at Frank. "Kinda cool. Reads,

Slowly desperately slowly the remains of passage debris that encumbered the lower part of the doorway was removed with trembling hands I made a tiny breach in the upper left hand corner and then . . ."

Madda's words faded as Laing pushed into the cipher. The drones buzzed within him. Then the expansion began. His mind's eye widened to take in the breadth of the world—the same fractal perception he had experienced in New York. Data swamped him. Then he focused down, locked into crypto-flow, and it began to rez clean.

Ryan spoke the words as they popped from the cipher. It took him a moment to realize that he was speaking in time with Madda.

"Widening the hole a little I inserted the candle and peered in the hot air escaping from the chamber caused the flame to flicker but presently details of the room within emerged from the mist . . ."

Madda broke off, looking at Ryan with a mixture of shock and awe. "You cracked it? That fast?"

"It's not me. Well, I guess it is. I just see the pattern."

"Holy crap, that's cool. You get the last bit?"

"It's harder," Laing replied.

"Well, yeah," Madda scoffed. "Everything else was deciphered long ago. Those first three passages are themselves a key to unlocking the fourth. Shit—you coulda just pulled them off the flow."

"Right," Frank shot in. "I'm sure his priority is impressing you."

"Will you two kill it for a sec?" Ryan broke in.

They did, both turning on him, waiting.

Something in the cipher picked at Ryan. He was missing something crucial. "Is this it? Is there more to the sculpture?"

"Ummm, yeah. There used to be a pool of water curving under the copper plate. Didn't survive the renovations."

Ryan looked back to the statue. He pushed back in. With the drones, he sifted into the cipher, ingesting it. His mind spun. He saw not just the sculpture, but all the information on it that floated through the flow. He saw the sculpture as it had been, with the pool beneath. Suddenly a pattern click. *The pool!* Something about it was drawing him. Finally, Ryan realized that it was the waves themselves. The water had been pumped into the pool in such a manner as to create a standing wave.

For most, decrypting the cipher would have been a rational process. For Ryan, it was a combination of logic and gut instinct. The drones used the standing wave's characteristics, plugging them into the *Kryptos* cipher. Through the cold focus, he sensed a phase shift. He needed power to rez out the transformation. To get it, the drones co-opted the CIA's system. It wasn't a hack. It was an expansion of self. In New York, Ryan had used the flow to augment his perception of the physical world. This was another step down that road. Ryan became the confluence of physical self, the drones, and the CIA system—the outside processors augmenting his own mind's capabilities.

The shift swamped him. Under the wash, the Ryan Laing standing in the atrium of the CIA shrank to a mere part of a much bigger whole. His being was no longer housed within that physical core, but spread through the CIA's data-net. He reeled under the transformation, struggling to maintain a sense of self. He needed focus—something to lock onto. The cipher! It had pushed him here, and he could use it to get back.

He used the cryptogram as a focus point. Under the brute force of his expanded perception, the cipher began to resolve. The crypto-flow came to a rest, finding perfect order. But as the cipher resolved, Ryan felt his augmented mind bottling down, processing power dwindling. He fought to retain it, but couldn't. The system crumbled around him.

Then, another jarring perception shift. Reality jammed down on Ryan, squeezing his augmented perception out. He rezzed back to Frank shaking him violently.

"Laing!" Frank shouted.

Ryan locked back into physical reality, ingesting the scene shift that had occurred while he'd been out. What had been a cool-flowing workplace was now blasting panic. Sirens wailed. People ran.

"What's happening?" Ryan asked, still blurred out from his experience.

"Breach of the CIA mainframe. Full hack. The system shut down in response."

Laing looked at Frank, finally pulling back into himself. "I think that was me."

"What?"

"I needed more processing power to crack the code. It just happened."

"Just happened? Cracking the CIA's mainframe doesn't 'just happen.' You pulled the whole system offline." Frank looked down on Ryan with fear in his eyes.

"I . . ." Ryan couldn't understand what he'd done, let alone explain it. "I'm changing. It started in New York. This is new to me."

"You're fucking changing? Into what—a goddamned butterfly? You crashed the CIA," Frank said with slow deliberation, as if trying to believe it himself. "No one should have that kind of power."

Ryan held Frank's gaze but couldn't respond. He had nothing to say.

Before he could digest the full ramifications of his new ability, Madda pushed past Frank. "You got it, didn't you?" Dave blurted. "You cracked the cipher. Not even a fucking hacker and you got it. No fucking justice."

Ryan nodded. "The answer's not here. There's more to *Kryptos* than this."

"Come on," Frank said, grabbing Laing's arm. "Let's finish this before you decimate anything else."

Madda struggled through the rush of people to keep up with the two. They skirted the main exit, sliding down a side hall that fed into the building's infrastructure. Cleaner bots hustled on servos through the low-ceilinged passageway.

"What's this?" Ryan asked.

"Side exit. No one knows this building like me," Frank shot back.

They burst through the exit, hitting the spongy sod surrounding the structure. The door slid back into the wall, disappearing with a pneumatic hiss.

Laing didn't slow. He extended his senses, integrating sat imagery, and even the CIA's own surveillance. He pushed into a soft thatch of trees at the building's far end.

"This used to be the main entrance to the New Headquarters Building," Laing said. It was now derelict, long abandoned. "Come on, this way." He pushed into the oaks.

"Stop!" Frank shouted with cold authority.

Laing did, Madda crashing into his back.

Frank caught up with Ryan. "This is the fucking CIA, dumbass. You don't just run into the fucking woods. There's shit in there you don't want to know about."

"There's also another piece of the sculpture."

"What are you talking about?" Madda stammered.

"The sculptor placed slabs around the buildings. Most are decoys—large granite slabs with copper sandwiched in them, all junked up with Morse code. But there's one other. It's subtle—nothing flashy. It's the solve!"

Laing pushed on. Frank grabbed his arm. "That's death on a stick. No-access zone. I need to kill the security to get us in there."

"And how long will that take?"

"After you just hacked in? It might take some time."

"Forget it. Sarah doesn't have time for that." Ryan pushed forward. After a step or two, he realized Madda was following.

"I'm coming," Dave said. "You're about to solve the unsolvable. I *am* coming."

Ryan looked over to Frank, who grabbed Madda and reeled him back. "You gotta find some perspective, man," Frank said.

Ryan stepped forward, pushing on alone. Immediately, the slow-tick hover of stimuli bombarded him. He tried to block the hunt-kill surveillance system that ran through the CIA's grounds, but it operated on an isolated system that would take Laing too long to crack.

Laing pushed forward, breaking the radiation corridor. Bots rose from the soft earth and began to swarm. Ant small, they worked on a system of rules modeled after schooling fish.

Ryan tried to fool their acquisition protocols by ghosting images of himself into the woods. But the bots got better at seeing through the digital ruse. They went after Ryan's decoys but, each time, they learned a little more, abandoning the attack more quickly. He didn't have much time.

Laing reached the slab outlined in the cipher. He pulled moss and dirt from it, revealing the aged imprint of a compass chiseled into the smooth granite. The bots centered on him, pushing to target.

Laing scratched away the remainder of the grit. Amid his launch of countermeasures, he tried to hold the *Kryptos* cipher in his mind. He cycled through the solutions, coming back to Howard Carter's journal entry on finding the tomb of King Tut. Ryan ran it again, trying to concentrate with the bot swarm closing in.

Slowly desperately slowly the remains of passage debris that encumbered the lower part of the doorway was removed . . .

The swarm reached him, pushing through his remaining decoys. They bore into him, a sensation rising from dull itch to hot pain. The bots piranhaed his leg. A thousand bee stings—and then worse. They injected something that slowed him down. The drones fought the effects, but he couldn't last long. He swiped at the bots, clearing them, knowing they'd be back.

Ryan tried again to focus, pushing back into the solutions.

With trembling hands I made a tiny breach in the upper left hand corner . . .

If each clue built on others, maybe the solve lay in mimicking Carter himself. It was worth a shot. Aligning himself with the compass, he searched the slab's upper left-hand corner. Nothing. It was as smooth as the rest of the slab. Panic rose. The swarm pushed in, chewing his legs, injecting venom.

Desperate, Ryan slammed a palm into the corner of the slab. It cracked.

He did it again, excitement growing. The chunk swivel-popped free. This wasn't a natural fissure; it was definitely man-made. He hunted for something in the new space—but found only rock. He had no time for a goose chase. Not now. Desperation overwhelmed him, the fight against the bots' venom all-consuming.

He couldn't concentrate. Not anymore. He needed help.

—*Sarah* . . .

There was only the trickle of loss, splashing her like Chinese water torture. Sarah swam through an all-pervading darkness. Then, a word. Her name, slamming into her consciousness through the drone link.

—*Ryan?*

She pushed the thought through slow-spun static. Memory fade consumed her. Anger had melted into a suffocating depression. Laing cut into that haze.

—*I need help.*

—*Ryan, I can't. I've got nothing left.*

—*Sarah . . . please.*

—*Just let it go. I'm not worth it.*

In darkness, she pulled into herself, the crush of her knees into her chest as far from her as Ryan himself.

But Laing pushed. He always pushed. He loaded the *Kryptos* data in a single spew that sent Sarah reeling. She tried to grasp it—finding that she was starving for stimulation.

She knew about the sculpture. All hackers did. One of the very few mysteries remaining. Something in her pulled out of black depression. The simple drive to solve the puzzle filled her.

—*The compass, Ryan. North isn't north, right?*

It took Ryan some time to decipher her question.

—*You're right. Points southwest.*

—*Okay. I . . .* She trailed into a wash, the drain overwhelming.

—*Sarah!*

—*Yes. Okay. You said you got there using the standing waves in the pool. So maybe this uses a similar physical constant—a secret within the physical world.*

—*Sarah, I need clarity here. I'm getting eaten alive. Literally.*

—*The slab itself. I think it's magnetized. Removing the piece changed its field strength.*

—*Jesus, you're right. Magnetic shift. I can read it with the drones.*

—*Okay, take the compass needle as straight north, then adjust by the magnetic shift of the slab. That's your north. The last code is . . . It's . . . Oh, God, Ryan. I can't hold it.*

—*Sarah, please.*

—*The fourth part of the cipher—it's a distance. With your new north, use it.*

Silence. It sank through her, radiating into a black cosmos. Desire floated through that darkness, the raw needs that wouldn't die with her memories. But they evaporated so quickly, lost to the ebb, like sand pulled into the ocean by a receding wave.

—*I found it, Sarah. I'm coming for you.*

A wave of excitement shot through her, but that too quickly faded to black.

· · · · ·

Ryan stumbled from the forest, bots latched to him, boring deep. His face was raw fire, arms and legs dead. He pushed—his entire effort going into a single step, then another, and another.

He gazed through haze-puffed eyes at the blur of Frank and Madda before him.

Each step was torture, each a world in itself. And suddenly, he was free. Beyond the bots' cordon, the swarm released. Laing stumbled through soft grass. Madda and Frank caught up to him.

"Christ, Ryan. That's some ghoulish shit." Dave couldn't tear himself from Laing's face. That look, combined with the inner slither of drone work, told Ryan that the bots had done serious damage. Pain radiated through him in electric arcs.

"Good news is, you're gonna live," Frank said. "Bad news is—you're gonna live."

Ryan toppled into Madda's arms. From his hand fell a tarnished copper disk.

41

Dreams pulsed through him. A swirling barrage of images. Slowly, the mass condensed around him, contracted like a black hole crushing space. So much information, compacted to a single form.

It was full-view perception. The push and pull of human interaction flowed through Ryan. The vision ran wide, pushing larger and larger.

He saw not just the world, but the patterns underlying it. He saw how they fit together to make a larger image. And he saw that they could be broken.

The entirety of human knowledge flooded him. And still he drew more. Constantly sucking, an unending desire, all information distilling into a pattern he could almost resolve.

It was too much. Ryan reeled. Terror welled in him. He shook, bucked against it, and finally—broke free.

Ryan woke up screaming.

THE *MERCY*, HOSPITAL AIRSHIP

"Laing," Frank said. "You have to calm down. You're okay."

Ryan tried to orient himself—to still his breathing and regain a lock on reality. The dream continued to haunt him. If that's what it had been. He wasn't sure. He was awake eyes open. And yet the dream continued to play before him.

"Madda," Frank said. "Turn off the monitor."

"Oh, right. Sorry," Dave said.

The vid wall before Ryan hazed to black, then reformatted to show his vitals. Across the wall, a green line blipped to the rhythm of his heart. From that, Laing pulled out to see the room. Standard hospital setup. With Dave and Frank standing over him, Laing guessed he was the patient.

"Sorry about that," Frank said. "Med-techs insisted you wear a neuro-monitor. You had some big spikes they were worried about."

"Those are some wild dreams you got," Madda said. As Laing turned on him, he quickly added. "Sorry—we shouldn't have looked."

"Where . . . ?" Ryan sputtered, his mouth cotton dry.

Frank offered him a glass of water, which he sucked down. "You're on the *Mercy*. Hospital airship."

The *Mercy* was part of a new breed of flying machines, an ungainly cross between a blimp and an airplane. Its massive lozenge-shaped bulk was propelled by a single tail propeller. The ship's semirigid frame allowed it to lift and carry a payload far exceeding any other airborne vehicle. The size of a football field, the *Mercy* could handle large-scale medical issues while maintaining absolute quarantine.

"Hospital ship?" Ryan stammered.

"You were fucked up, Laing. No better way of getting you off Company grounds. *Mercy*'s been hovering over the CIA since the bioattack. We put you on a medevac. Got you admitted up here to a private, sealed suite. All med data stays in this room."

"How long?"

"You've been out for an hour," Madda replied.

"And the disk?"

"It's nothing," Frank said.

"Ah, fuck," Ryan said, exhausted desperation flooding him.

"Just an old trinket."

Madda pulled the disk from his pocket. "It's a cipher disk," he said. "Two concentric circles, one over the other with an alphabet ringing each. It was one of the first cryptology machines."

Ryan stared at it. The copper was tarnished and dirty. On the disk, only one letter was embossed, repeating over and over: Ω.

"But all the letters are the same," Ryan said in confusion.

"Like I said, worthless." Frank's irritation was obvious.

"No," Madda said. "It makes sense. It's the perfect finale to the *Kryptos* enigma. It's a cipher machine with only one letter—omega. In Greek, omega's the end—the last letter. It's everything. So this is the final key— that which deciphers everything."

"Yeah? Show me," Frank snapped.

Madda shook his head in frustration. "It doesn't really decipher everything. It's an idea—a concept to take from the sculpture. That the universe itself—just as you see it—is both ciphered and clean. Just depends on your point of view."

Frank rolled his eyes.

Ryan's frustration rose to match Frank's. Could he have risked so much, wasted so much time, for nothing? He reached out and Madda plunked the disk in his hand.

A drone tingle. Still-frame recollections of his dream flashed through his head and shot over the vid wall.

"What the fuck?" Frank said, catching the images.

"Spikes in brain activity kicked the neuro-monitor back on," Madda said, also riveted to the picture.

Ryan stared at the vid image of his own thoughts. In his hands, the disk itself was linking to his drone technology.

"It's the disk," Madda said.

"The dream must have been from Ryan's contact with it in the woods."

"There's more . . ." Ryan said. But he couldn't get anything else out before being ripped into virtual.

It held suspended before him, its two concentric disks spinning. Laing floated over it, lost in uncoded space.

Back in hard reality, Laing could just hear Madda speaking. "It's— fuckin' amazing. That code work. Masterful," Madda said.

A sense of violation whipped over Ryan. He didn't like Frank and Madda staring into his mind—or whatever this was. But before he could process the thought, the disk began to spin faster. Laing watched it, transfixed. Finally, he reached for it.

"No!" Ryan heard Madda yell. "That's sticky code. You interface and it will chew right through your system."

But it was too late. Besides, what other choice did he have?

Code punctured Ryan, burning through the drones' system. He felt them go; black settled heavily. Then, a slow resolve. Darkness morphed through gray to white. The disk was gone. In its place, a man resolved.

A ghost.

"Hello, Ryan." The voice was so familiar.

Christopher Turing stood before him.

42

Slowly, Ryan grew accustomed to the emptiness. He centered on the man before him, trying to understand what was happening. And not wanting it to end.

"I'm dead," Laing said, riding the edge of shock.

"No, Ryan. This is digital stasis. I'm a backup. The disk keyed me. Well, your bio signature on the disk keyed me. You're not dead, and I'm not real."

"Not real," Ryan said slowly. Despair threatened to overwhelm him. Then, relief. Looking into Turing's eyes, Ryan could almost believe that the last years had been a nightmare from which he was finally waking up. Ryan restrained himself from wrapping his arms around the man. He knew there was nothing to touch.

"I've missed you," Ryan said, barely able to get the words out.

Turing nodded. "That doesn't bode well for my longevity."

"You've been dead for five years."

Turing nodded again.

"I . . . killed you."

That got through Turing's smooth veneer. His mouth fell open. "You?"

"I . . ."

Turing stopped him. "Ryan—it doesn't matter. Whatever happened, I'm not that man. Whatever I did—whatever you did—it's irrelevant. I'm a figment of the past. I'm the man who would never harm you."

Ryan shook his head. "You're nothing. You're a program. Software." He needed to believe that to hold himself together.

"Walk with me," Turing said.

Before them, the no-space cracked and a scene coded into existence. Grapevines sprouted, one by one, filling the space. Laing's feet sank into rich earth. The sky shifted to a soft blue, clouds speckling in. Rolling hills cut into the horizon. Turing walked down the vineyard. Ryan followed.

"I am Christopher Turing. I am his memory. I act as he would act. I satisfy the artificial intelligence test fashioned by my namesake, Alan Turing. You cannot distinguish me from my flesh-and-blood counterpart."

Ryan slowly nodded. Turing smiled and trudged into the vines.

"It's been hard." Ryan didn't want to say anything, admit anything, but how many times had he longed for this moment? For one more second with this man?

"Coming online, I knew there was a strong probability that my corpo-real incarnation would be dead. I am sorry I couldn't be there for you in the years since my . . . death."

Ryan shook his head, the shell within him beginning to crack. "It's bet-ter. I'm not the man you knew. I feel compacted—weighed down by the decisions I've made—the havoc I've caused. And without you, there was no end. No way out." Ryan didn't want to speak the words, to admit this to anyone, especially himself, but he couldn't stop the rush of emotion.

"You want release? Absolution?"

Ryan laughed, shaking his head. "Just peace."

"Then we are in agreement. I too want peace. Echelon was built on that desire."

"Echelon is dead. It died with you."

"No, Ryan." Ryan looked up at Turing. The old man continued. "Echelon was an experiment. That you found the disk means it failed. Peace through gentle manipulation didn't work. I always knew that was a possibility. And I made contingency plans."

"What?"

The shift in Turing's tone, edged down to cold rationality, was star-tling. "Humanity is a tough nut. We humans are fighters, Ryan. We're pro-grammed to respond to the hunt, the flight, the kill. Echelon tried to deaden those extremes. Obviously, it failed."

"Turing," Ryan's relief ebbed under a surge of doubt and fear. "What are you saying?"

"Have you heard of the spadefoot toad?" Turing asked.

The question threw Ryan into confused silence. Christopher smiled. With a wave of his hand, he wiped the sim. The vineyards went to white space. Then color pixelated over the blank, finally settling into an arid desert. The roll of time commenced as Turing spoke.

"They are indigenous to the North American desert. They're very suc-cessful. The toads hibernate deep in the earth for most of their lives. Then, the rains come."

Clouds rolled in and drenched the desert, pocking it with small pools of water.

"The toads lay their eggs in these pools. The tadpoles have only days to go through their cycle and emerge fully formed. If they can't do it in time, the entire population dies."

In a pool at their feet, Laing saw a mass of tadpoles. In fast time, the land around them began to dry.

Christopher continued. "They have a rare technique to ensure their survival. Among the algae-eating tadpoles, there are a few who morph to carnivore—and more specifically to cannibal. They eat their brothers to ensure the survival of the species."

Below them, several toads emerged from the pool even as it dried. The carnivorous amphibians buried themselves as the pool's remaining tadpoles baked in the sun.

Ryan watched, confused. "Why are you telling me this?"

"I seeded humanity with a carnivore—in case Echelon's pool ran dry."

Ryan stared at the man before him. In the face he'd been longing to see for so many years, he now caught something else: something foreign, or maybe a facet he had always refused to acknowledge.

"Krueger?" Ryan cringed at the word, so wanting it not to be true and knowing it was.

"Yes."

"No." The word rose dead from Ryan's lips.

"I knew him, before."

"You what?"

"Before. Before Echelon, before I became Christopher Turing."

The ghost saw Ryan's expression and laughed. "I know. Hard to accept that I had a life before you came along."

"You're not Christopher Turing?"

"I am. I was. But I was other things before. Krueger and I weren't close. But our world was small."

"Your world?"

"Mathematics. I worked on pure math. Krueger worked at the forefront of computational biology. Sounds boring, I know. But, you see, we were both obsessed with patterns. And we were both good. Very good."

"What happened?"

Turing laughed again, waving his arm around the white space. "Life. I found Echelon. I dropped the identity I'd grown up with and chose another. I'll admit to some hubris in choosing the name. But Alan Turing was my hero, the father of computer science. My work was a derivative of his inspiration, so I became Christopher Turing."

"And Krueger?"

"He had a different path to follow." Turing gazed off into the distance. "I'd never seen a mind like his. His ability to burrow under all the clutter to find that nugget of truth was astounding. He was a genius. And he was mad."

Laing looked down at the disk, which had reappeared at their feet.

Turing continued. "We're each a product of his environment. Me. You. Krueger. Generations of death preceded him. He was his father's son."

"I know all this. The Krueger family. Memphis. That's why we brought him down."

"It's part of it. But there's more. Krueger saw the pattern underlying the biological flow. And he saw that pattern on a large scale. He saw that the world itself, all life in it, makes up a single entity. And—being his father's son—he found a virus that would corrupt that entity."

"So you spiked him."

Turing continued, lost in the recall. "He saw an image that even I couldn't fathom. I envied him for that. And I feared him."

"But you let him live?"

"I did. And not only that—I honed his cruelty to suit my purpose. I showed him how to shape the world through the terror he was so inclined to wreak."

"EMPYRE . . ." Ryan muttered the word.

"As Echelon formed you, EMPYRE rebuilt Krueger."

"But why?"

"Krueger saw the earth as a single entity. Good or bad, we humans are the driving force on this planet—the entity's brain, you could say. Just as Krueger created biological viruses to disrupt neurotransmission, so he created a new virus—this one capable of cutting the connections in that larger brain."

Ryan looked at Turing in confusion. Then horrible understanding filtered in. "The flow. Krueger created a virus to kill the flow."

Turing nodded like a proud father. "We once used computers to model organic life. Ironic that our technology has grown so complicated that it is now through biology that we understand computer systems."

"Jesus," Ryan gasped. "Cutting the flow would change everything. It would destroy the connections binding us."

"A neurotoxin to the global organism."

"But why would you want to keep that kind of doomsday device? And why keep the man who built it?"

"Because, Ryan, I knew Echelon might not succeed. There needed to be a backup plan. If humanity would not bend to my soft manipulation, it would to Krueger's hard will."

"I don't understand."

"I shaped EMPYRE, Ryan. I manipulated Andrew Dillon and the others into forming it. I pushed Krueger into their midst. EMPYRE was a training ground for Krueger—an environment that would show him the power of fear. I always knew he was willing to use terror. With EMPYRE I sharpened that will into something useful."

The words crushed Ryan. Tears welled. He couldn't stop himself. For so long, he had missed this man. And now . . . "He took Sarah. Krueger spiked her." It was all Ryan could think to say.

Turing's hard eyes softened for an instant. "Ryan, I am sorry."

"How did he know? To come after me? To use Sarah as a lever?"

Turing looked into Ryan's eyes, unable to speak.

But Laing saw the truth. "You . . . told him," Ryan said.

"I did." Turing let the words settle. "The real me created a set of conditions—Echelon's demise, world turmoil, et cetera—which, if met, triggered an info leak that would lead Krueger to you."

"You created a monster."

Turing's hard edge returned. "Some would say the same of my fostering you." He looked away, off into the distant ripple of a desert mirage. "But maybe Krueger is what we need to survive."

"The cannibal . . ." The word trailed into silence.

"People used to speak of humanity hitting a singularity—a point where technology had so changed our lives that we became unable to understand the future in terms of the past. With Echelon gone, we've hit that singularity. Yesterday gives the average man no clue about tomorrow. Nothing to count on. It's all flux. And that shift has led to the violence you see around you. People falling back to old faiths, national allegiances, anything to understand their world. They are terrified, Ryan, and they're ripping humanity apart."

"But it will calm. Technological advancement will slow. People will get used to the new reality."

Turing laughed. "Have you?"

Ryan could only look away.

"No, Ryan. There's no lag time, no pause in progress that will allow humanity to catch its breath. Our rate of acceleration has gone exponential. We have created an extended singularity that will tear us apart. Echelon kept us from this condition. Echelon is dead. I'm dead. It's Krueger's world now."

Ryan shook his head. He wanted to hate this, to push it away. But he felt the truth in Turing's words. Maybe he was right.

"I've given you the choice, Laing."

"He has Sarah," Ryan said, trying to stoke his hatred for Krueger. He couldn't let it slip.

"You can give Krueger his memory—let him become his true measure. Or you can destroy that information."

"He has Sarah!" Ryan broke down.

Turing seemed unable to fathom Ryan's emotion. "So, take that into account."

"I won't let her go. Not her too."

"Ryan. The option is yours. Give Krueger his memory, and the chaos will abate. There will be order, even if it comes at the point of a blade. Or, wipe the info and walk away."

"I don't want this decision. I didn't want it with Echelon. I don't want it now."

"I'm sorry." Turing stared into Laing's eyes, cold and calculating. Ryan shuddered.

"Why me?"

"Because you are alone. I'm not sure you even see how isolated you are. I'm not sure you can."

"I have people."

"Of course you do. Me. Sarah. Maybe others. But each of us is tied to a worldview. Maybe it's a religion. Maybe it's allegiance to a country. Maybe an ideal. You don't have that. At center, I don't think you have anything. That makes you impartial. That makes you able to change paths. Who better to arbitrate humanity's future?"

"Bullshit! I followed you like a puppy. Why do all this? Why put me through this? You could have just told me what to do. I would have done it!"

"No, I don't think you would have. You are Krueger's final test. Is he calculating enough to beat you? And you're his final arbiter. You needed to know exactly what he is capable of to make your decision. You needed to know that he is a carnivore. A cannibal."

Ryan pulled from Christopher's gaze. He shook his head. "You're not the man I had thought."

"I know that, Ryan. I'm more. And much less."

Finally, Ryan turned back. Somehow, he knew that he would never again dream of Christopher Turing. Black loss pushed deep. Turing cared for him only as he cared for a treasured piece on his chessboard. Ryan's own emotions began to wither under such cold calculation.

"I'm sorry," Turing said again.

"I am too. I'm sorry for what I did to you. And I . . . I wish I hadn't seen you like this." He picked up the disk and walked into the desert.

Turing nodded, calling after him. "To walk your own path, you have to hate me—if only a little. You and Krueger are my two creations. Light and dark. I've taken from you both. Hurt you both. But that wasn't my desire. It was necessity. You owe me nothing, Ryan. The choice is yours."

Ryan kept walking. Slowly, the desert succumbed to its digital transience. It wobbled, then bleached to white. Ryan refused to turn.

Finally, there was nothing left—only white and silence.

. . . . .

As he rezzed back to his hospital bed, reality settled slowly. From the white, shapes resolved and found clarity. The hospital room. The tang of chemical cleaner not quite covering sick sweat. Madda sitting before him, shocked.

And Frank Savakis, looming over Ryan, holding a lazknife to his temple.

43

Ryan looked up from Frank's arm to eyes that held him with forced indifference. At Ryan's temple, the lazknife flickered, searing skin.

"We saw everything, Laing," Savakis said, nodding to the vid screen.

"Frank—" Madda stammered as he reached for the laz-knife.

Frank backhanded Madda across the face, sending the smaller man sprawling. His eyes stayed on Laing. "Can't let you leave here, Ryan."

"Frank?" Seeing Turing again had pushed Ryan to his limit. He couldn't take this further betrayal. Ryan looked up at a man he'd come to trust and saw only cold determination. One by one, each person connected to him was slipping free. Within each of them was something that would not yield—ideologies, compulsions that wouldn't be held by the bonds of friendship . . . or love. With the lazknife buzzing at his temple, Laing knew he'd reached the end of the line with Frank.

"Dissolving the partnership?" Laing said, his lip curling slightly.

"This is bigger than us," Frank replied, his stone gaze unwavering.

Laing shook his head and looked out the window into the cloudscape beyond. The *Mercy*'s soft sway gave an unreality to the action around him. His head spun. He locked it down, hunting for a plan. Desperate. To end here was unacceptable. But his will wavered. There was no one left. He was on his own.

"Can't let you out of here with that virus. Can't let Krueger have it," Frank said.

"But, Sarah—" Laing managed.

"Sarah would agree with me. The United States government should have that virus. Turing knew it. He hid it in Langley, for Christ's sake."

"And you're better than Krueger?"

Frank didn't answer that question, his faith resolute. "I would die for my country, Laing. I have killed. And I will kill you if that's what it takes. Give me the disk. Give me the virus."

Laing hung his head. On the floor, Madda twitched.

"There's nowhere to go. *Mercy*'s hovering ten thousand meters in the air. Give me the virus. It will be in good hands. The right hands. And, I promise, we'll find Krueger. We'll get Sarah back."

"Bullshit."

"Your options are running down. You don't want that clicker to hit zero."

"You won't kill me," Laing replied.

Frank bent down, the soft hum of the lazknife unwavering. "I will."

"*Et tu*," Ryan whispered.

A curl of Frank's lip. Then his features locked solid. Ryan saw the resolve and knew it was unshakable. There was nothing more.

Madda phased back into consciousness. Nausea flooded him. His head felt so heavy, his cheek saliva-stuck to the hospital floor. He tried to clear the daze, to get his body back under control. Limbs responded with reluctance.

Pushing up, he caught Laing's gaze. Then he saw the lazknife at Ryan's temple and ran it back to Frank's hard-set hand. There was no waver in the man's eyes. No negotiation. In those eyes, Madda saw Sarah's lifeline fraying.

He got to his feet, still woozy, the start of a world-class headache twitching at the back of his temples. Wrapped in their own war of wills, Frank and Ryan didn't notice his movement.

The terrifying mystery of Krueger's virus touched Madda's thoughts. What clean-line perfection it must be. Seemed fitting that the flow killer, the hack to end all hacks, would come from a biologist, someone who understood a code far older than the ones and zeroes Madda dealt with. Part of him wanted to see that virus, to study it. The rest of him was too tired to learn one more goddamned thing.

Dave's reality distilled to simple cause and effect: if Frank got the virus, Sarah would veg into flatline. She would forget him. Somehow, that eventuality seemed most horrible. The possibility that she would lose him to the void wrenched Madda to action.

He knew it was ridiculous to throw his life away on a crush. But it was all ridiculous. No point to any of it, as far as he could tell. And she cared for him. Maybe not in the hard-passion, fuck-you-to-bits way she obsessed over Ryan, but there was love. Once, Sarah had tried to save him. Now, he would do the same for her.

He looked at Frank and Laing, so locked in their Caesarean moment that they didn't notice him. He was tired of being the lackey, the techman. For this single instant, he would take center stage.

He had made so few decisions in the past years. Life had taken him on a ride. No longer. He covered the space between himself and Frank snapfast, his atrophy lost to adrenaline.

His hand flew, slapping the knife from Ryan's temple. The three of them watched the weapon arc from Frank's hand and clatter onto the floor where its laz edge sputtered and died. Then all eyes turned to Madda. Ryan looked at him in shock—Frank in burning rage.

Madda lurched for the knife, scrambling over the tile to retrieve it. He got hold of it and rose to confront Savakis. He flicked the switch and the laz went hot. Madda held it before him, tip pointed at Frank. He moved forward hesitantly, unsure of what to do next.

"Put the knife down, Dave," Frank said in cold fury.

"Just back away," Madda's voice wavered, "I know how to use this."

"No."

"I was a fencer!"

Frank's lip curled at that. His voice fell to a whisper. "Give me the knife."

"I won't let you hurt her . . ." Madda realized his slip, ". . . him."

"You don't have a choice."

The words burned into Madda. He did have a choice, and he made it. Ryan shouted at him to stop, but Madda was beyond listening.

Dave lunged. At the moment the laz would have found Frank's ribs, the larger man sidestepped, coming chest to chest with Madda. Frank grabbed Madda by the collar and pulled his knee up in a crushing groin shot.

Dave's air vanished. A sick pain radiated through him as he slumped into Frank's grip. "Probably didn't learn that one on the fencing mat." Frank threw Madda to the floor and turned back to Laing.

Crumpled and deep in sweaty pain, Madda heard Frank mocking him. "Hope you didn't expect Madda to be your white knight, Laing."

Fury rose in Madda. He had been dismissed for the last time. "No further," he said to himself as he lurched to his feet and swung the knife in a wide arc. Frank's back was exposed. The knife came down and Madda readied himself for the resistance of flesh and bone.

It wasn't to be. Frank shifted away from the knife even as he grabbed Madda's hand and forced the weapon to continue its arc.

Madda's rage turned to shock. He knew it was over.

The flesh of his stomach ripped wide. Dave's hands fell to his gut, his fingers curling into hot viscera. He tried to hold himself together. Pain lanced him, then faded to exhaustion. Madda couldn't help but sink into it. He dropped to the floor, red spreading over the hospital white.

Before him, Frank's face had blanched in surprise. He had moved on instinct, only now realizing what he had done. "Son of a . . ." Frank whispered.

That was before Laing's fist ended the sentence. Laing pulled free of the bed and kicked Frank with vicious abandon. Madda watched in dull comprehension.

"Ryan," he sputtered.

The word pulled Laing from his attack. He turned and hunkered over Madda, holding his lolling head.

"Dave," Ryan said in a choking cough.

"It's . . . it's okay, Ryan."

"No."

Over him, Laing seemed to deflate, his rage ebbing to blank loss. "Really. I've been dying for so long. Easing into it. This just caps the process."

Ryan shook his head, as if trying to dislodge the image before him.

"I look that bad, huh?" Madda said with a smile.

The high-pitched buzz of Laing's monitors, which had been ripped free, pierced the quiet. Sensor patches dangled on Laing's arms.

"You've got to go. Before the techs show up."

"I won't abandon you."

Madda smiled again. "You can't save everyone, Laing." Sleep pushed in on him, soft and urgent. "But you can save her." Madda choked—gasping for air in staggered breaths. His head fell to the side—Madda couldn't hold the weight. Laing knelt closer, his own forehead touching Madda's.

"Go . . ." Madda whispered. "Save her."

The pressure of Ryan's head calmed him. His breathing eased. Then stopped. For an instant longer, Madda held on. Life's constants ceased—heartbeat, breath, the pump-rush of blood. There was only silence. In their absence, Madda's flailing thoughts, images from a lifetime, distilled to a single feeling. It subsumed the blur, wiping away his achievements and failures, his fears and friendships. From the mash of emotions that filled his life, there remained only one. Excitement. He was ready to see the other side. Above him, Ryan's image splintered. It went fractal, disintegrating into the flow of information that defined the universe. Madda wanted only to fade into that code.

44

Sarah's thoughts echoed through Ryan as he kneeled over Frank.

—*Do it, Ryan. He killed Dave. You kill him.*

Wheezing through broken ribs, Frank lay faceup. With one hand, Ryan gripped a handful of the man's shirt, and pulled Savakis's head off the floor. Ryan ground his other palm into Frank's chin, forcing the man's neck back. Weak and disoriented, Frank struggled against the force. Ryan pushed harder.

—*Sarah.*

—*In cold blood.*

The desire surged through him. He torqued Frank's neck to max. Just a little more to get the snap—and the end.

—*Do it, Ryan. Murder him.*

—*It's not murder . . . It's revenge.*

Below him, Frank's eyes watered, rivulets streaming over his temples.

—*He's helpless. He's no threat. Do it.*

Ryan looked to Madda. Dead. The image should have been enough to drive the issue. He wanted this so badly. His fingers touched Frank's lips, slick with saliva. And Laing knew he couldn't do it.

—*I can't.*

A long pause from Sarah. Ryan could almost touch her relief.

—*I know you can't, Ryan. If you could, I wouldn't love you.*

Laing eased the tension, dropping Frank back to the floor. Somewhere in Frank's dazed eyes, Laing saw recognition.

—*You love me, Sarah? Still?*

—*You need to run, Ryan. Now. Get here. Please.*

Ryan got to his feet and stumbled for the door. He felt wiped. The cycling rage and loss slowed his thoughts. And there was still so much left to do.

—*I'm coming.*

Doubt and confusion slipped away as Ryan shifted to flight. He pushed out of the hospital room and into the hall beyond. Med-techs crowded the hall, pushing for Laing's room. Ryan knocked through them. Then, rising around him, the emergency siren sounded.

Laing bolted into the central hall. Curved, transparent panels revealed the cloud cover over which the *Mercy* floated. Med-techs mingled in the massive space. Laing slowed down, tried to blend, but his in-patient garb gave him away. People turned and stared, then got out of the way as security blasted into the hall behind him.

Except for the med-techs, the *Mercy* was all mechy. No pilots, no staff, no mercs. Everything was taken care of by bots. This allowed the massive ship to deal with the worst outbreaks across the globe with minimal risk of infection spread. It was the perfect hot zone responder.

The security bots—called raptors—were top-of-the-line, cream of the DOD's crop. They ran upright on flexing carbon bands. Their trunks housed the power supply. Arms held weaponry, both lethal and non. Stacked over the trunk was the sensor package. The raptors caught full-spectrum radiation. They saw in the dark and could lock on a heat signature and track it to the ends of the earth.

Laing abandoned any attempt to blend in for raw speed. He burst through the hall, the raptors closing on him, cutting off his means of egress one by one. Brutally efficient, they ran military-grade pursuit protocols. Outthinking them was going to be a bitch.

So Laing went random. The raptors knew the ship too well for Ryan to hide. His best chance was to pull the unexpected. Instead of evading, Laing turned fast and ran straight at the raptors. They stopped cold, their pack-hunt programming not having this reaction on roster. They quickly shifted to action, but their moment of indecision was enough.

Laing crashed into the raptor before him, smashing it into the two behind it. He lashed a side kick out wide, aiming at the raptor's weak point—the rad sensor in the head zone. His heel found its mark, cracking the plexi sphere. The raptor bounced away, sightless.

One of the felled raptors regained its footing. It bounded at Laing, flex-torquing its legs to reach head height before firing a Taser dart. Ryan wheeled left, the move evading the dart, but also throwing him right into the path of the raptor's descent. The legs pounded into him, blowing Ryan back. Hitting the deck, the raptor bounced off him, aiming for another shot. Laing swiped its leg, and it fell backward, tucking into a ball to offload its momentum.

Laing kicked on the speed, sprinting down the length of the hall. The raptor sprang after him, closing the distance between them in arcing lopes. Ryan knew he was quickly running out of options.

The raptor sprang high. Glancing back, Ryan dove out of the way. *Almost* out of the way. The bot adjusted mid-flight, torquing toward its prey.

Coming down, one of its legs got caught up in Ryan's sprawled form. The uneven landing threw the raptor off-balance. It careened into one of the plexi panels that ran the length of the hall, blasting through it.

The flashing suck of decompression turned the hall to chaos. The panel broke out, sucking several techs into the air. With nothing to secure him, Laing had little choice but to follow. He managed a gulp of partially pressurized air before being ripped into free fall. Amid the rush of acceleration, he held his breath, knowing that any intake here wouldn't hold enough oxygen to keep him conscious.

Immediately, Ryan's drone sense locked on the gryphons tracking his fall. Winged bots, gryphons were deployed as a standard safety measure at any breach in the ship's hull. They swooped out of the *Mercy*.

Arching back, Laing also saw that two raptors were diving toward him in fast pursuit. He streamlined, hoping the gryphon would follow his plummet. The raptors fell with him. Wind whipped his face. His eyes teared to blindness.

A raptor closed the gap between them, shifting to fire on him. Laing shot out an arm and canted over, sending himself into a side spin. It flipped him hard over, the raptor's dart zinging by.

Then they hit cloud cover. The scene flash-shifted to white. Laing went for broke, pulling free of the dive and arching his body open just seconds before the raptors caught him. The move worked. The raptors shot past, unable to slow themselves. Their black forms flashed by.

Ryan broke through cloud cover and—just as he got a real look at the ground—a gryphon caught up with him. It latched to his back, locking tight. Then its wings shot to full length and he went from falling to gliding.

Laing spent the rest of the descent hacking the gryphon's locator tags to make sure Frank couldn't track him.

—*Sarah, I'm coming.*

She told him what he needed to know.

45

The ancient city rose before Ryan. He tried to take notice, to stay synched with the action around him, but found himself falling deeper into Sarah's link.

—*It's beautiful.*

—*I guess,* Ryan replied.

During his transit to Istanbul, Sarah's dialogue had scatter-splashed over the gamut of her life, splotches of memory hurled into the void. He had tried to keep her clear, to hold her to the memories that were important—to him at least. But she continued to slip, her mind faltering with each passing second.

Istanbul crowded in on Ryan, the hard shock of culture shift amping his isolation. Madda was gone. The cold operator in Ryan hated that he couldn't push past Madda's death, and Frank's betrayal. But the events haunted him, a dark smudge on his perception.

The raw-nerve edginess that ran through the city did nothing to settle Laing's turmoil. Fear burned through the coffee shops and markets, searing the normally energetic bustle of street life with dark foreboding. People were scared—the future in flux.

Laing pushed it away, focusing on what was to come.

The Hagia Sophia loomed before him. One more monument to a history of blood and battle. Four spires vaulted into the sky around the church's massive dome. The building had been maintained, which in itself set it apart from the rest of Istanbul. The city had no discernible plan. Modern buildings smashed against the ancient. But most structures contained both new and old, supplies ripped as needed from wherever they could be found, picked from the flea market of past and present.

The Hagia Sophia remained pristine. Mold- and pollution-eating microbes had been sprayed into the building's walls during restoration. Its dome descended to walls of soft pink.

—*I like the name.* Sarah's words floated through the ether. *The Church of the Holy Wisdom of God. Built and then burned in the fourth century. It was rebuilt and became the center of the Eastern Orthodox Church—the apex of Byzantine architecture.*

—*Why are you telling me this?*

—*I visited the Hagia Sophia as a . . . I'm not sure when.*

Ryan felt the gut pull of her memory slip. Normally, he pushed Sarah's monologues into the background when he was on mission and she got chatty. Now, he coveted every word.

—*Go on.*

—*It then became a mosque after the Ottoman conquest and Constantinople's fall. Inside the building there's a pillar with a hole in it. Mosques face Mecca, right? So, when Hagia Sophia became a mosque, it was slightly out of whack—off center. So the angel Gabriel comes down and pushes on the pillar, shifting the building into alignment.*

—*His alignment.*

—*I guess that would be a matter of perspective, Ryan.*

—*I'm starting to feel for Gabriel. Always under the thumb of someone more powerful. No matter who's in charge, he winds up being the guy shoving buildings around, killing the wicked, announcing the end of the world.*

Laing had the sudden need to see the angel's imprint on that column. Were his own actions so different? He had realigned the world in destroying Echelon. Today, no matter what happened, he would force a similar shift.

—*You're no angel. That much I remember.*

Ryan laughed. His procrastination faltered with her words.

—*True enough.*

Ryan turned from the grand entrance and got under way. He followed the directions Sarah had given him, supplied to her by Krueger. Laing wasn't thrilled about walking into such an obvious trap, but with Sarah's memory on the table, he didn't have time for recon.

He veered on a diagonal, heading for a towering scraper that lanced up into the steel-gray sky. Pushing through the street hawkers that swarmed Istanbul, Laing skirted the scraper's entrance. He cut down an alley between the scraper and a mishmash of neighboring buildings. The alley was a combination of modern biocrete and centuries-old cobblestone, a haphazard collection of past and present occupying the same space.

The corridor ran tight, the scraper's bulk blocking all but a single shaft of light into which Ryan proceeded. While the scraper's mirrored black was unsettling, it was the jumble on the other side of the street that made Ryan nervous. The pock-work buildings offered prime positions for a sniper. He had no doubt eyes were on him. Darkness closed in as he walked deeper into the scraper's shadow.

The sounds of the city faded. Here in the shadows, honest commerce could not thrive. This was a place for illicit trades—skin, amps and depressants, body mod. From doorways, quiet solicitations were whispered. Ryan pushed deeper.

"Laing." A grainy voice spilled from the black.

Ryan turned and peered into a fissure cut between two ancient buildings. Even with the drones, he couldn't see into its back depths. The stink of rot filled his nostrils. He inched down the alley, hand to the rough stone wall for guidance. He felt the eons slip away. The flow of centuries did not reach into this crevasse.

Darkness. The shuffling of his own feet. And the smell. Then, light pierced the black. It hit him dead in the face.

"You have what he wants?" the voice croaked.

"Let's get on with this."

A pause. Then the beam of light dropped and broadened. Laing could just make out a cloaked figure holding the torch. Below him, an ancient manhole cover had been pried loose. The figure motioned for Laing to approach.

Ryan stepped close, peering down into the well and seeing nothing. Confused, he looked up and into the figure's face. The image seared through him, forcing Ryan back a step. The face was all gore and bone. Cracked teeth rose to black gums, which Ryan could see clearly as there were no lips. One eye socket lay empty and bone white, the other held a dark eye. The nose had lost its cartilage. A living nightmare.

"He's waiting for you," the man said.

Ryan held still, trying to curb a vicious revulsion. It went beyond rational, lodging in the place where childhood terrors reside. He managed another look into the man's face. This time, the man caught his reaction.

"Weaponized leprosy," he said.

"Krueger did this to you?"

The man laughed in sickly, wheezing heaves. "Keeps the tourists away."

Ryan could only nod. He pulled from the grisly image and tried to focus. Had to hold focus.

—It's dark, Ryan.

—Sarah, I'm close. You have to hold out.

—Yeah. Hold out. Hold on. Just here—holding.

Ryan pushed it away. Pushed her away. He stooped to the manhole, his feet finding the rungs of a ladder. A wave of fetid warmth hit him, drawing a gag. He swallowed the nausea and dropped in.

The ghost handed him the torch and slid the manhole closed.

Laing descended into a conduit corridor. Just big enough for him to stand upright, the tunnel ran fiber optics, quantum connections, and the general clutter of linkage that webbed a city together. Bioengineered bacteria kept the tunnel clean. A sewer pipe ran down centerline.

Laing pulled schematics from the flow and visually overlaid them on reality. He found a line through the labyrinth under the city, veering from Krueger's instructions. Ryan hoped the deviation would allow him a few moments of surprise. He fell into the sim and moved forward at a quick, stooped jog.

Five hundred meters, two lefts, one right and a ladder down, Laing stopped. The soft sim hovered over his visual draw. This was the spot. He knelt, pulling a circular device from the holster strapped to his leg.

Nicknamed the Blazer, the XN-901 was a controlled incendiary device used to silently breach almost any barrier. He stuck it to the tunnel's floor. The Blazer latched firm, hooks setting to form a clean seal. Ryan could just hear the whir of combustion. The device used massive, targeted heat bursts to do its work. Ryan scuttled back.

Shift, lock, and a muffled sizzle.

The tunnel melted clean through in less than a second. As the incendiary seared through the tunnel wall, the Blazer exuded a ceramic weave behind it, killing the heat and stifling fire spread. Once it had punched though, Laing triggered the Blazer's reel. The device retracted up through the man-sized hole it had burned out. Ryan snapped it back into its holster.

He bent over the opening and looked down into another world. Another time.

Laing peered down into the gloom. Ancient columns rose from oil-black water. They pushed up to an arched ceiling, which Ryan had just punctured. He slipped through the hole, grabbing on to steel rods that interlinked the columns for added support.

He monkeyed along the bar and reached one of the columns. Its musty rock smell pervaded the space. Laing hugged it, orienting himself. Columns stretched out in both directions, melting into black. Even infrared offered him little in the way of sight. Darkness held thick.

Ryan used the diagrams locked into the drones to guess at location. His fingers, wrapped over ridges at the column's peak, began to tire. He had to move. Body hugging the column, he slid down its gritty surface, trying not to upset the chamber's silence.

He reached the column's square base and slipped into the black water. It stank of slow rot, ages of death festering under the glassy surface. Ryan pushed forward, ripples breaking the dead calm.

—You there, Ryan?

—I'm here. Krueger certainly has a sense for the dramatic.

The space radiated history—a past so potent that it eclipsed the world above. Centuries of illicit meetings and intrigues must have gone down in this subterranean space. It was like entering the castle of a long-dead kingdom.

—*I am forgetting you.*

—*I'm almost there.*

—*No, you're slipping away. It's so odd, Ryan, watching pieces of myself degrade. My past is evaporating. I focus on a memory, then it vanishes like a magic trick. All I get is a gap and this heavy feeling, like I'm drowning. Funny, huh? Here I've been trying to forget for so long. Now I get my wish and it's crushing.*

—*Tell me one.*

—*One?*

—*A memory. Tell me. I'll hold it for you.*

Ryan pushed through the waist-deep water. Around him, column on column rose into the black. Each was slightly different, as if cobbled together from a menagerie of buildings. Eras mashed together.

—*I remember a man.*

—*If you're going to tell me about your long-lost love—*

—*Shut up and listen.*

—*Yeah, okay.*

—*I remember that time we had in Tasmania—before I started hating you. Before you hated yourself.*

—*Sarah.*

—*Just fucking listen.*

Ryan held silent. He peered through the gloom. Krueger's instructions had him entering the cistern about one hundred meters ahead. Laing hoped his change of plan would shift his odds, but suspected Krueger had factored in Ryan's inability to take orders.

—*I liked having you inside me. Swaying up over the canopy, the slow sex. Your drones letting me feel what you felt, letting me be part of you for a little while. I remember that. The heat of it. Then, after you turned away, after you saw what had happened to the world, I craved that connection like an addict.*

I remember feeling so helpless under the force of that need. I hated myself for it. I hated you for revealing it. So I left. I worked. Tried to fucking save the world—and look how that turned out. And that need for you, it wouldn't let me go. I . . .

—*Tell me, Sarah.*

—*Fuck it—I'm dying, right?*

—*You're not dying.*

Sarah pushed through.

—I hated you, Ryan. Really. And still, the need. It was love. Even after all you did. All I did. The fucking love wouldn't let up. I thought, maybe if I became like you, I could be strong like you—get over you. Every time I went under the knife, I remember . . .

—What do you remember?

A long pause. Too long. Ryan felt Sarah hunting for the linkage in her mind—trying to hold her past together.

—One more time. I remember thinking, one more time and I'll be . . .

—What, Sarah?

—I remember . . .

Pushing through the darkness, Laing sensed movement. The slightest scratch. A flicker, impossibly fast, flashing over him. Sarah's narration came to a sputtering halt. A moment of quiet, so pure it cut through his pain.

—Sarah?

No reply.

Ryan peered into the gloom. There was nothing to see. Nothing to hear. Yet he knew. In the dead silence, he felt the cold chill of a presence. He knew they were waiting for him.

—Sarah?

Still nothing. He didn't have time for this. Sarah needed him now. He abandoned quiet for a splashing lope that drove him forward. From his shirt pocket, Ryan pulled a pen gun flare. He held it high, ready to fire.

Before he could pull the trigger, stiff pain shot through his hand. The flare dropped from his grip, splashing into the water.

"No need, Mr. Laing." Krueger's voice filled the black.

Light.

Adjusting, Ryan found that he was the center of attention, and staring down the barrel of Zachary Taylor's gun.

46

Ryan's eyes adjusted to the light. He leaned into the column at his side, trying to find balance under the perception shift. Krueger stood above him on a platform jutting into the water. Behind the platform, a fast-form prefab had been erected. The blocky carbon structure ran up the cistern's wall, hard-contrasting with the antiquity surrounding it.

Clinging with grip gloves to the column, Zachary Taylor hung over Ryan, gun trained for another shot. Around Taylor, stationed throughout the cistern, a phalanx of mercs stood waiting, each of them gazing down with the same fish-eyed indifference.

For a moment Ryan was distracted from the threat by the massive face cut into the base of the column next to him: the gnarled relief of a woman upside down, snakes slithering from her head and down into the black water.

"Medusa," Krueger said. "These cisterns were built out of the detritus of the civilizations that came before. The gods of the past, drowned in the name of progress."

Ryan shook his hand, his fingers tingling from Taylor's shot. Before him, Alfred Krueger stood triumphant, his eyes like cold steel.

"It's funny, Mr. Laing. How places such as this—with so much history—are built, then forgotten, rediscovered, resurrected, then lost again."

"Not really my style," Ryan said.

Krueger laughed. "It's sixth century. Built under Justinian at the height of the Byzantine Empire, it can hold some eighty thousand cubic meters of water. Probably an enlargement of a cistern built by Constantine himself. Building material was pulled from ancient pagan sites." Krueger's words echoed through the cistern, the acoustics building his tone to a rich, reverberating drum.

"Istanbul pushes on over our heads, but I like it here," Krueger continued. "Here, the past rules. Here, I never forget what was taken from me. You have what I need?" he asked.

Ryan lifted from his crouch.

"Where is she?"

Krueger pulled Sarah from the prefab's shadow. The spike clung ugly to her face. Ryan held her gaze, but saw no recognition. Her good eye held him in green reflection. Nothing more.

"It will be okay, Sarah," Laing whispered.

She nodded dully.

"I want my past back," Krueger demanded. "I want what was taken."

"You want more than that."

"Have you slotted it then? Have you seen my creation?"

"No."

Krueger laughed. "I knew you wouldn't. Pity, though. I want someone to see it—to appreciate it."

"The virus will destroy us."

"No! It will free us. You had it right, Laing. Destroying Echelon. We humans don't prosper under kind conditions. Evolution requires hardship. That's the truth. Look around. You think this would have come from peace and prosperity? Progress comes over the rubble of the weak. We need chaos."

"And you're here to supply it."

"I am—in just the right measure to both inspire and assure our survival. Fear. Terror. It's our base desires that push us to strive. I will end the long coddle. It's a big job. An important job. I could use your help."

"You're no different from Echelon."

"I am, Ryan. I see that humanity needs fear to hold it together. Manipulation only stifles. But fear inspires! Everything I've done has been to that end. EMPYRE taught me the power of fear and the judicious application of terror."

"No—it justified your psychotic needs."

Krueger pushed on unfazed, his voice tipped with conviction. "EMPYRE was my incubator. It honed my skills as Echelon did yours. And look how well I've learned. Look at what I've done to you." Krueger placed his hand on Sarah's shoulder. "I found your lever, and I pushed."

Ryan itched to throttle Krueger—to watch his life wither. Above Laing, Taylor shifted slightly, reasserting his presence.

"You and I don't need to fight," Krueger continued, his voice echoing through the cistern. "We are not so different. Both of us want to save humanity from itself."

"I only want her."

Krueger stared at Ryan, penetrating him. "You're a coward, Ryan." The words filtered through the musty air. Krueger let them settle, then continued. "I think maybe I used to be like you. Unwilling to make the hard decisions. Maybe that's why Turing created EMPYRE for me. Maybe I needed it to become the man standing before you."

"And who is that?"

"A man willing to become a monster to hold humanity together."

"You don't seem so noble to me."

"Then look more closely. I'm not a psychopath, Ryan. Each move I made, each death, has been for a reason. I will continue my wave of terrorism, priming the world for my arrival. Fear will run thick. Then, I'll reveal myself. I'll reveal the virus."

"And take the world back to the Stone Age?"

"No, Ryan. The ability to destroy a thing is the ability to control it. Without Echelon, there needs to be a control—a stop point before the brink. I'm supplying that."

"And the masses will cower under your thumb."

Krueger laughed. "Forget what you know. Look from a larger perspective. What will keep us walking this green earth? What will keep the global organism from dying?"

"Your divine presence?"

"Just look at our history," Krueger continued. "Those times when fear reigned were also the most fruitful. Take the Cold War between the USSR and the United States. Both sides built armories capable of destroying the world. And each held the other in check."

"Mutually assured destruction," Ryan said.

"That's right. Under that umbrella of fear, the world had relative peace. And it wasn't the numb, forced peace of Echelon. Human evolution ran its course. Advances came lightning fast. But always, there was the fear to hold humanity in check—to keep any one faction from pushing the envelope. Then, the USSR fell and the world tumbled into chaos."

"Not really a model for enlightenment," Ryan said.

"Isn't it?"

"Maybe humanity can take care of itself."

Krueger looked down at him with pained condescension. "Please. The mechanics of the universe don't run on optimism. Humanity has many abilities. Dealing with change isn't one of them. Without Echelon to dampen the rate of progress, the world is moving too fast for people to get comfortable. To the average man, the world is out of control—slipping ever faster into an era he can't fathom.

"Look at the two of you," Krueger continued. "Man-machine hybrids, pushing the edges of what it means to be human. That's evolution, Ryan. And it will not slow. Progress will not give humanity a breather. So all the inequities you see in the world, the haves and have-nots, the restless masses gripping ancient religions to ground them, the anger and confusion, all that will increase. There are only two options, Ryan. Stifle the evolution or impose a larger threat that brings the world together. Echelon failed at the first. As to the second, there is no larger threat than me. If this really is a global village, the ability to poison the well puts me in control."

"And you want my help with this?"

"Well, you're to blame for a lot of the pain in the world right now. It's on your shoulders. I can lighten that load. You see it, don't you? The elegance of it? Join me, Ryan. Help me like you helped Turing. Take the harder path."

Ryan shook his head.

Krueger's eyes ran cold.

"I had hoped it would be different. But in the end, you're like the rest—like EMPYRE. Small-minded."

"I won't help you sow chaos."

"Oh, you will," Krueger said, throwing a look at Sarah's spike. "One way or the other."

Sarah's past trickled out. The slow draw diminished her, bit by bit, memory by memory. The spike was pulling at random from her life. She grasped at images with ferocious intensity, but couldn't place them in order. Soon, there would be nothing.

There was a freedom in the loss. She saw fresh, without the filters of a lifetime, without the confusion. In her mind, there was only light. She was the product of her memory without the hang-ups. Two men stood before her. Both were familiar.

One had to die.

47

Ryan pulled himself from the dank water and got up onto the platform where Krueger held Sarah. He drew the disk from his pocket. Within it, Krueger's virus festered. The disk, so thin in his hand, weighed Ryan down. So much revolved around the next seconds.

He hated this and knew he wasn't the right man for the job. Yet he wouldn't be content anywhere but at the nexus. He craved that moment at the needle point of decision where the wrong move spelled disaster. The intensity spurred him, drove him. From this moment, the course of history would shift.

"Give it to me, Ryan." Krueger's voice had gone soft, almost fatherly.

The urge to plunge into Krueger's vision tugged on Laing. It was a cruel world Krueger would create—but a workable one. Not a world Ryan wanted to live in, but neither was the one he himself had triggered. Maybe Turing was right. Maybe Krueger was the last, best hope.

"Reverse the spike," Laing replied, "or I destroy this and we can all go to hell."

Krueger smiled, stretching out his hand. Laing stepped forward. Why shouldn't he do this? What was there without Sarah?

He placed the disk in Krueger's hand.

"Thank you, Ryan."

Krueger turned to Sarah and touched the pad on the spike's flank. It read his bio-signature and shut down. "I've stopped the pull."

"Reinsert her memories."

"That will happen automatically—when I'm far gone from this place. Then, and only then, her memories will return and the spike will disengage. Pull the spike before I disengage it, and her memory will be lost forever."

Ryan burned hot. "You have what you want."

"Please. I'm no fool. You're not a man who walks away. Your vision is too narrow, Ryan. You care too much about the individual. It's your flaw. And the reason you can't stand in my shoes."

"Maybe no one should," Laing growled, making the threat clear.

"You won't come after me, Ryan. Because I'll hold up my end of the bargain. It's in my best interest. If you're not with me, I want you out of the game. Sarah will come back—all of her. I grant you a small life with this woman. You can have love . . . marriage. Maybe you'll have children. And, with each passing day, the web of dependence will tighten around you. You won't risk it all just to come after me. You'll survive—like the rest."

Ryan glanced at Sarah and knew Krueger was right. He would leave the fight to others. Sarah looked at him, tears beginning to flow from her good eye. He didn't know what she remembered at this point, but he hoped she saw the love in his eyes.

"I . . . Don't do this," she said.

"Maybe I want that small life," he replied. He wouldn't let Sarah fade. That was a step he could not take, and Krueger knew it. The rage crimping Ryan's features relaxed to acceptance.

Sarah reacted to the transition. She opened her mouth to speak. Before she could, an explosion ripped through the cistern's cold peace.

Sarah's confusion ran thick. She had only vague recall of the men before her. Yet she knew them. Knew them both. One she feared. The other . . .

White light bleached her vision. An instant later, the shock wave slammed her into the prefab's hard carbon wall, as the percussion blast reverberated through the cistern. A part of her understood what was happening, but she couldn't seem to lock reality into conscious understanding.

Through her shock and fear, she registered a figure snaking down one of the columns and dropping next to the man she loathed.

"Taylor. What's happening?" Krueger's voice had upshifted an octave.

Taylor replied, quick and choppy. "Breach. Perimeter compromised. Jamming tech blocked our surveillance and countermeasures. I'm reading American signatures off the 'ware."

"Laing!" Krueger's fury blossomed—then calmed as quickly as it had arisen. "No. It doesn't matter." He turned to Laing. "Whatever you did—it doesn't matter now. You will slow them down. If we don't escape— well . . ." he motioned to Sarah.

Laing's eyes burned with rage—and acceptance. Something in that look cut into Sarah. She couldn't allow the slow death this man had embarked on. And she couldn't let Krueger escape. Assurance pushed up through her. She knew.

Another explosion. This one closer. Part of the cistern's ceiling imploded. From the gap, men in dark coveralls dropped down. The firing began.

Sarah had one chance at this. She had to act while the men were distracted. She stared at Laing, realizing that if she had her memory, she'd probably be as helpless as he was. Her connection with him was so strong. She pushed it away. The promise of her memory, of a new life, melted before her. She lost it to action and the moment.

Sarah drew her hands up to the spike. It was cold to her touch. She gripped it with both hands, feeling how firmly it had bored into her skull. With a deep breath, she twisted and pulled. Pain blasted through her cheek and eye. Her cry pierced even the gunfire chattering through the hall.

The men turned in unison. Krueger's eyes went wide in surprise. Laing leaped at her, hands outreached, trying to stop her. She torqued the spike, felt it rip free from her bone, and she pulled.

The spike came free of her eye socket with a slushy pop. Blood gushed from the wound.

A kaleidoscopic burst of images blasted through her mind. She watched transfixed. Then, darkness. Nothing.

She opened her eyes to see the man, her man, standing before her, dumb struck. She let the spike fall to the floor.

"No, *no!*" Krueger screamed.

Laing's eyes filled with pain. Something gray fell from them. His arms reached out, drawing her into him. She felt warmth there. Contentment.

Krueger's wail fell to a growl. "Kill them. Get me out of here."

The figure next to Krueger raised his weapon. Sarah didn't hesitate. She spun, getting herself between the two she hated and the one she had to protect.

When the shot came it was almost a relief. She didn't feel the impact, only the slamming force of the blast throwing her forward. The man in her arms crashed into a column and she landed on top of him. She heard splashing behind them. Men running. Sounds ebbed as pain engulfed her.

She could not breathe.

Ryan felt the blast as if he had been hit himself. It lifted him off his feet. His head hit the column with a dull thump. He slid down it and Sarah tumbled with him. Her eyes found his. Her mouth opened and closed. Nothing came out.

The sudden loss wiped Ryan clean. The life he had seen so clearly just a moment ago was now gone, obliterated. He looked into Sarah's good eye, refusing to acknowledge the pitted one. His hands slipped over her back and came away blood wet.

Above Sarah, Ryan registered movement. Mercs swarmed down, soup thick. In their black body armor and Hazmat masks, he couldn't distinguish one from the next. They landed around him, then pushed into the cistern, engaging the enemy. *Enemy:* the word rang hollow.

After the mercs, another man rappelled into the cistern. He moved with a bearish confidence that Ryan recognized. The man reached Ryan and loomed over him. He pulled off his mask.

Frank Savakis gazed down at Laing. There was no anger in the face. He stooped and Ryan flinched, drawing Sarah close to his chest.

Savakis tried to pull her off him. Ryan resisted.

"It's okay, Ryan." Savakis's words just reached him over the chattering firefight ripping through the cistern.

Something in that voice released Ryan from shock. He let Frank pull Sarah from his chest. Savakis propped her against the column. Her mouth continued to flop open and shut, like a fish sucking air.

Laing pulled himself up to his feet.

Frank stooped over Sarah, put his hand to her cheek. "Breathe," he said.

She looked at him, eyes wide, suffocating.

"Breathe," he said again.

The gunfire held for an instant. In that relative silence, Sarah gasped. Then she began pulling in huge gulps of air.

"The tat," Ryan said in dumb relief. "It held."

Frank turned back to Laing. "Krueger?" he asked.

Ryan pulled himself from Sarah and peered into the gloom. "He's there. Out there. He has the disk."

Frank nodded.

A need rose in Ryan, blood thick. An itch that would not relent. He craned his neck, peering into the darkness.

"Go on," Frank said. "I got it here." He gave Laing a nod—as close to an apology as Frank could offer. "I will take care of her," he said. "End this fuckin' thing." He pulled a Glock 60 from its holster and extended it to Ryan, butt first.

Laing nodded, taking the gun. He turned from Sarah and plunged into the firefight.

48

Thoughts of Sarah fell from his mind. There was only fight left in him. Part of him had died, and part was reborn.

He caught the radiation flicker of Taylor dragging Krueger through the water, away from the firefight. The manic ardor of Krueger's men had stalled the invasion force. Their hard-fought deaths would give Krueger time to escape.

Ryan moved faster, reaching the point he had been driving for. He pulled himself out of the water onto the flat base of a column. Behind him, gunfire lit the cistern in sporadic flashes, illuminating the columns and then blanking the ancient space to black. Time slowed to a glacial drip.

Ryan jacked his drones. Adrenaline surged through his system, muscles fired and released in expectation. He remained still, going quiet against the column, grinding into its gritted surface.

Taylor came into sight below, pushing Krueger before him. Ryan tensed for action. There was no way Taylor could have heard him, and yet the man turned as if on instinct, throwing Krueger into the water and swiveling with fluid grace. The gun appeared as if by magic, rising lightning fast in Taylor's hand. Ryan felt the weight of its black eye on him. He sprang from his perch. Too late. The gun fired, the bullet spinning Ryan in the air and sending him sprawling.

Laing splashed down, pain lancing his gut. He felt the cold lurch of water sloshing into his stomach wound. It permeated his entire body in an instant. Before Ryan could find his footing, Taylor was over him, gun held with cool assurance.

The eyes pierced Ryan. It was like staring into the eyes of a shark. No sympathy. No emotion. Fear surged through him. Drones seeped from his wound out into the water, then receded to his core. The violation ran to max. And the man before him, looming, eyes gleaming with carnal ferocity—a will to act without hesitation, without doubt.

For a moment, Ryan longed for that peace, that confidence. To climb out on oblivion's edge and push the world away.

No.

The chain wrapping him broke. He refused to take his last breaths smothered under the shield he'd spent a lifetime forging. If this was the end, he would live it raw. A tidal surge within him. He opened the gates to love and hate, fear and hope, rage and sorrow—to the full measure of emotion.

A baseline shift, like blocks locking into place and allowing a new structure to rise. The drones jacked his perception. The flow, in its entirety, coursed through him. This time, Ryan didn't back away from the deluge of data, but allowed it to sweep him up. He opened himself to the vision—his mind going porous, matching state with his body. But his sense of self did not dilute under the crush. The power of his emotions, and his acceptance of them, kept him on keel.

"Good-bye, Ryan Laing." Standing over Ryan, Taylor uttered the words from a place beyond contempt.

Taylor was right. This was the end of Ryan Laing—and the beginning of something new. Something that didn't require an icy distance to act, something that could take in the world's flow and still operate. There was action and will. There was also emotion, and perception.

Ryan surged into this new existence, charged to fracture. He saw Taylor's smile unfold, watched the man's finger curl on the trigger. Ryan relaxed into action.

His arm shot from the water with a speed far beyond his previous capabilities. He reached Taylor's gun just as the trigger was pulled. The pistol's crack and flash filled reality. The bullet accelerated down the barrel as Ryan's hand slapped the gun, altering trajectory by centimeters. It was enough. The bullet missed his heart, blasting through the meat of Laing's shoulder.

Caught off guard, Taylor didn't realize what had happened for a crucial instant. In that time, Ryan scrambled backward, getting the column between himself and his attacker.

Drawing his own weapon, Ryan threw his back into the column. Pain arced down his arm, muscle ripped from bone. It hung useless at his side. Ryan accepted the pain and listened. He heard Taylor kick into action on the opposite side of the column. Laing matched Taylor's movement. The two circled, keeping the column between them.

Ryan smoothed into the cycle, hunting for a clean shot, finger on the trigger. His consciousness fell to a sweep of action and reaction, a dance of predator and prey. His perception reached a clarity he hadn't thought possible. Movement. He caught the twitch of Taylor's cheek muscle as the man cleared the column, heard the sound of his finger pulling the trigger.

The shots came lightning fast. Bullets chipped the column, whizzed past Ryan's head, one stinging his ear. Ryan held steady.

He sensed the man lean away from the column's protection, trying for the clean shot. Amid Taylor's firestorm, Ryan pulled the trigger. One bullet. A perfect shot. Taylor's firing stopped. His hand fell, gun splashing into the water.

Taylor stood still. A trickle of blood slipped down his forehead and over his cheek. His face went slack. He crumpled as if caught in slow time.

Laing watched Zachary Taylor disappear into the black water.

"You are a hard man to kill." Krueger's voice—looming close. Too close.

Ryan spun, trying to bring his weapon around. But the dead weight of his wounded arm threw off his balance. Before he could bring his gun to bear, Krueger lashed out, punching Ryan in the stomach. The strike sent electric pain through him. Laing toppled in a gut-lurching wave of nausea. The gun fell from his hand.

Through waves of exhaustion, Laing sensed Krueger closing the distance between them. He tried to get to his feet, but before he could, Krueger reached down, fingers digging deep into Laing's shoulder wound.

Ryan screamed in pain, the sound piercing the firefight continuing behind them. Tears boiled from his eyes. Through them, Ryan could just make out Krueger's thin-line smile.

"You are good," Krueger said. "Very good. I'll give Turing credit. He created a perfect killing machine."

"As did EMPYRE," Laing managed.

Krueger only nodded. "There's no need for you to die here." With his free hand, Krueger pulled the disk from his jacket. "Help me use this."

"You don't need me." A whisper.

Krueger's lips curled. "No. But you need me." He returned the disk to his pocket.

Ryan's head wobbled. Krueger gripped down on his shredded arm. "Face the truth, Ryan. You needed Turing to give meaning to your life. You were lost without him. Now, you need me."

"You are a monster."

"I'm what the world requires."

Ryan's eyes glazed out.

"Sarah is gone," Krueger said. "There's nothing left for you, Ryan."

Ryan shook his head, as if trying to banish the reality he'd fallen into.

"No. No more." The words fell from Laing's lips. A pronouncement. Ryan began to stand.

Krueger gripped hard on his shoulder, grinding muscle and bone. "You can't stop me, Laing. It's over."

Pain drove Ryan to the edge of unconsciousness. He held the line, rising to his full height.

For the first time, fear torqued Krueger's features. He released Laing's shoulder and turned to run. Laing stumbled after him, knowing he was down to the last dregs of his energy.

Ryan lunged, snagging Krueger with his good arm. The two splashed down. Expecting the jolting impact of the cistern's floor, Laing got only a black descent. As he sunk, locked on Krueger, he realized that the floor in this section must have collapsed.

Krueger thrashed. Ryan's strength ebbed with each passing second. He gripped down with everything in him, but Krueger managed to slip free and kick for the surface. Laing, fighting to maintain consciousness, gulped black water.

Lost in the darkness, only the fight remained. He shot out a hand, snagging Krueger's ankle and dragging him down. Then pain blasted through him—Krueger's fingers scratching over his stomach, expanding the wound.

Ryan wrapped his legs around Krueger, locking them together. He ran his good hand down his leg, hunting. Ryan knew he only had seconds. After that, Krueger would inflict more damage than the drones could repair. As the pain mounted to an unbearable apex, Laing found what he'd been searching for. He pulled the Blazer from its holster.

Falling into black, he ground the device into Krueger's chest. The hooks set deep, burrowing into the man's skin. Krueger flailed, ripping at his chest. Laing wrapped his arms around Krueger's chest, pinning the man's arms.

Detonation. The heat surge flashed their underwater world to vivid clarity. The incendiary shredded Krueger's sternum. Water churned to a boil.

As his feet hit bottom, Laing's arms folded into his chest.

There was nothing left of Alfred Krueger.

49

Dripping, Laing staggered back to the platform. The drones stanched the blood flow from the bullet wounds and burns covering his body. Krueger's men were dead. The fight was over. Reaching the platform, the mercs broke ranks for him. Laing pushed past them to see Frank hunkered over Sarah. Ryan nodded to Frank's unspoken question.

"Good," Frank said. "He needed to die."

"How did you find us?" Ryan asked.

"The CIA isn't entirely useless."

Laing looked at him and laughed. "No. I guess it's not."

"The disk?" Frank asked.

"Gone," Ryan said.

"But it's still in you, right? I mean, you downloaded the virus."

Laing's eyes went cold. "I won't give it to you. Not to you. Not to anyone."

Frank bore down on him for a long moment. "It's a mistake, Ryan. No one person should have that kind of power."

"Is that why you came here? To retrieve the virus?"

Another long moment. Finally, Frank shook his head. "No . . ." His mouth stayed open, as if to say more, but nothing came out.

Laing nodded. He moved to Sarah.

"She's okay, Ryan. Broken ribs, some internal bleeding. But she'll live."

Ryan crouched, pulling a wisp of hair from the clotted blood on her cheek. She woke, her good eye slowly focusing on him. She took in her surroundings over long seconds.

Frank backed away.

Heat flushed Ryan. The pain in his stomach and shoulder flash flamed. He fell into the sensation. "Sarah . . ." he whispered. An exclamation. A prostration. He cupped her cheek in his hand, then leaned close and kissed her.

The touch of her lips was soft and welcome. He pushed closer, craving connection. Under him, Sarah did not retreat. But she did not return his kiss. He pulled away.

"Who are you?" Sarah asked.

The question iced Ryan.

She looked up at him, her fingers softly touching her lips.

Ryan shook his head. "It doesn't matter. Not anymore."

He stood, breaking contact.

Frank put a hand on Laing's shoulder, blocking further retreat. "We'll get her memory back," Frank said.

Laing shook his head.

"Then just fuckin' *be* with her, Laing," Frank said, adamant.

Ryan did not pull his gaze from Frank. He couldn't. If he looked down at Sarah now, it would be over. "No," he said, his words forced through gritted pain. "I'm not the man she loved. Not anymore. It's better for her to forget. Better for me."

Frank held his gaze for a long moment, then nodded. He put out his hand. Ryan shook it.

"I'm sorry," Frank whispered.

"Take care of her," Laing said.

Frank nodded. "What will you do?"

"Fade."

"Ryan, word will get out. Others will want what's in your head."

"I know."

They held for a final second, then Laing turned away. Frank signaled for the mercs to let him pass.

Ryan Laing dropped into the water and was soon lost to the maze.

ACKNOWLEDGMENTS

From idea to finished product, *EMPYRE* has been a whirlwind. While writing may be a solitary task, many people have worked to craft the book now in your hands—and to keep me sane in the process.

My deepest gratitude to the Del Rey clan, especially to my editor, Betsy Mitchell; David Moench, my publicist; Kim Hovey and the whole marketing gang; Michael Burke, my copy editor; David Stevenson, who designed the cover; and Evan Camfield, my production editor.

My thanks to the poor souls on whom I inflicted draft after draft: Martine, Mom, Babs, and Jud. I couldn't ask for better readers.

Thanks also to Rick Ridgeway for relating his experiences in Antarctica.

Barrie and Arlene, your friendship and advice have been a great gift. And for keeping me on an even keel through the process, my thanks to Rob, Dianne, Stew, Mariaelena, Amanda, Jeb, Steve, Erik, Allan, Dave, and Paul.

I'm indebted to my agents, Matt Williams, Sarah Self, and Simon Lipskar; none of this would have been possible without you.

And thanks to you, my reader, for taking the time to join me on this flight of fancy.

Josh Conviser grew up in Aspen, Colorado, graduated from Princeton University with a degree in anthropology, and has lived in Europe and the Far East. An avid mountaineer, he climbed in ranges around the world, including the Himalayas, before giving up the mountains for the jungles of Hollywood to pursue a career in screenwriting. He was the executive consultant on HBO's hit series *Rome* and has several films in development. His first novel, *Echelon*, was published in 2006. He lives in Santa Barbara, California, with his wife and daughter. Visit him at www.joshconviser.com.